"I'm leaving."

"Sit down, Sam. You're upset. You're not making sense."

"I'm making sense of everything," she said, trembling at his touch. This man she didn't know terrified her. She couldn't even look at him. "I don't want to talk to a . . . a criminal."

Nathan released her, his voice cold. "It's dark outside. You don't know what's out there."

"I don't know what's in *here*, either. I'll take my chances with the snakes and wild animals." She staggered through the front room and yanked the door open. In her haste, she nearly tripped down the steps.

Laughing, Nathan leaned against the doorjamb. "That's typical. The little saint is too good for the sinner."

She whirled around. "How *dare* you say that? All you've done is make fun of me and . . . and patronize me!"

"Patronize *you*?" He stomped down the steps and didn't stop until he stood toe to toe with her. "Who's patronized who? You and your little prayers, your holding me in front of the fireplace like I was a child! I'm not a boy anymore, Samantha, I'm a man! I don't need you to look after me!"

Her head ached, swirling. "No, you're doing just fine on your own," she whispered. "You're a killer, a robber, and a . . . a . . . *fornicator*. You lied to me, bringing me here to your . . . hideout . . . with other criminals. Including the one who tried to take the one thing I've been saving for my husband. I don't belong here, and I don't belong with you."

"Run, then!" He jerked his head at the road. "Run if you don't want to hear the truth."

The FUGITIVE HEART

The FUGITIVE HEART

JANE ORCUTT

WATERBROOK
PRESS
COLORADO SPRINGS

THE FUGITIVE HEART

PUBLISHED BY WATERBROOK PRESS

5446 North Academy Boulevard, Suite 200

Colorado Springs, Colorado 80918

A division of Bantam Doubleday Dell Publishing Group, Inc.

The characters and events in this book are fictional,
and any resemblance to actual persons or events
is coincidental.

Scripture quotations are from the
King James Version of the Bible and
New American Standard Bible (NASB)
© 1960, 1977 by the Lockman Foundation

ISBN 1-57856-022-5

Printed in the United States of America

1998—First Edition

1 3 5 7 9 10 8 6 4 2

*To Mary Ford James,
Jennifer Sanders, and Dianne Knowles*

ONE

Kansas
Spring 1864

The sun stung Samantha Martin's wet eyes as she fled the house for the barn's dark refuge. Everybody probably thought she was childish for bolting from the Sunday dinner table, but she didn't want her family or the Hamiltons to see her tears. She was fourteen now, too big to cry.

The stock had been turned out to graze, and she stumbled into an empty stall. Choking back sobs, she braced her arms against a weathered post and buried her face against her clean calico dress sleeves. The pungent smell of lye soap mingled with the barn's familiar odors of animal, harness leather, and hay. How could Pa talk about leaving? Didn't he know how much they needed him? How much *she* needed him?

It had only been a year since the grippe took Ma. Since then Samantha had had no mother to confide in about the embarrassing changes in her body, no mother to warn her she was growing up. Pa certainly hadn't bothered to talk to her about that. Or a great many other things, it seemed.

The barn door creaked open. Samantha muffled her sobs and wiped a sleeve across her eyes. It was probably just Caleb coming to accuse her of being a baby. All her life her older brother had teased her about one thing or another.

"Samantha?"

Her breathing slowed, and she cautiously peered around the stall. Sixteen-year-old Nathan Hamilton, her best friend and neighbor, stood in the shadows, watching her, waiting. As far back as she could remember, he and Caleb had been a big part of her life. When she was little, Samantha toddled after them, joining in their boyish games on the adjoining farms. Years went by, and the games evolved into far-flung expeditions down to the river and beyond. Caleb was disgusted at the intrusion, but Nathan urged her on: climbing the big cottonwood to the best lookout branch, tightrope-walking the fallen log across the water, racing through the wheat fields. Higher, farther, faster.

And when she'd failed or, worse yet, cried after too much of Caleb's teasing, Nathan had tended her skinned knees and comforted her bruised feelings. He'd read countless books to her and shared his dreams of becoming a doctor and seeing the world—even opening her own window on it by teaching her to read long ago. He was her champion, and she'd known since she was seven that she wanted to marry him.

Nathan opened his arms in silent invitation, and she went to him without question. Sobs welled anew and spilled out. He stroked her hair, his hand curiously strong yet gentle. "Shh. It'll be all right."

"Why didn't they tell us? Pa . . . and your pa . . . are joining the army! They're going to the war and leaving us!"

"Shh."

"They might . . . get killed!"

His arms tightened around her. "Cry it out," he whispered

against her hair. When her sobbing stilled, he said quietly, "I have something to show you."

She drew back, sniffling. "Wh-what?" He'd always known how to stop her tears.

He smiled down at her, then ran the pads of his thumbs across the wet trails on her cheeks. "Come see, Sam."

She swallowed the last of her sobs, and her stomach warmed with pleasure. *Sam.* Nathan was the only one who called her that. Trusting as always, she followed him out of the barn and around the newly growing wheat field.

She looked at him as he walked ahead of her. His gait was quick with the vigor of youth, his body strong from years of hard farm work. When had his shoulders grown so broad? All of a sudden he looked . . . different. Like a stranger, a grown man, yet somehow still the Nathan she'd always looked up to.

He led her all the way to the edge of the woods, then knelt. Bewildered, she got down on her knees beside him.

"Look." He carefully eased up a thatch of loose grass. Four tiny bunnies snuggled together in a shallow bed. Their ears were pressed flat against their bodies, and Samantha could see the quiver of their little hearts.

Awestruck, she reached to scoop one up, but Nathan stopped her. "Don't touch them. The mother will abandon them if she smells your scent."

Samantha drew back. "Why isn't she here?" she whispered.

"She's probably watching from the woods." Nathan gently replaced the grass, then smiled. "This is our secret. I'll check on them every day and make sure they're safe. Will you help me?"

She nodded, solemn. Nathan had taken care of every stray,

lame, or sick animal that crossed his path, but this was the first time he'd ever asked for her assistance.

Nathan took her hand, and she glanced up, startled. His green eyes were luminous. "When my father told me he was enlisting, I told him that I wanted to go too. But he won't let me. He says I need to stay here."

She shivered. "I'm glad. You might get hurt." She blinked back tears at the thought of Pa in the army.

"Sam, I'm tired of waiting for something interesting to happen around this dull place. I want to go out and see the world. If I have to go to war to do it . . . well, at least it's for a good cause."

Samantha swallowed hard. "I . . . I'd be sorry if you went, Nathan."

His eyes deepened. "Would you?"

"Y-yes." His gaze was doing strange things to her—her heart rang hot like a blacksmith's anvil, but her feet and hands felt as cold as the winter ice she chipped from the horse trough.

Nathan gently took both her hands. "Would you be sorry because I wasn't here to chase you and Caleb to the river any-more or because you would miss being alone with me?"

"Both," she whispered, confused. Had she revealed too much of her heart?

Nathan smiled, and her hands felt heavy and clumsy in his. Unnerved, she turned her face away, trying to sort through her tangled emotions.

For years they'd played together, laughed together, and her world had been orderly and happy. Now Ma was dead, and Pa was leaving. Even Nathan, her rock, was changing. And in the process, somehow she was changing too.

He turned her chin back with a gentle finger. "I've always cared about you, Samantha," he said softly. "I wouldn't hurt you."

She blinked back unshed tears and swallowed hard. "Then tell me why you want to leave. Why our pas want to leave."

His eyes searched hers, and she could see he was struggling for words to explain. Their fathers' imminent departure had something to do with Nathan wanting to go, too, and a greater sense of loss swelled over her. Everyone was sweeping right by her when all she wanted was for things to stay the way they were.

"Samantha . . . ," he said, then moved closer and wrapped his arms around her. Her heart hammered like the bunnies', and she rested her cheek against Nathan's shoulder. She felt his cheek, then his lips, brush against her hair. His arms tightened, and she relaxed, feeling protected. He would keep her safe.

"Nathan!"

Samantha wrenched free, inexplicably mortified at the sound of Mr. Hamilton's voice. He stood at the edge of the field yet made no move to come closer. His expression softened when he caught her eye. "Your father's looking for you, Samantha," he said. "He's concerned."

Nathan touched her hand and smiled. Her stomach twisted on itself like a clumsily knotted rope. Her face flushed warm with embarrassment, and she ran past Mr. Hamilton so quickly that her long hair streamed around her shoulders. She glanced back, and she could see Nathan still standing by the bunnies' nest, watching her.

⌐⌐

Nathan shifted on his knees in the straw covering the barn floor. He wiped the newborn lamb's nose so it could breathe, and when it exhaled with a soft bleat, he smiled sadly and wiped the rest of its small body. When the lamb was dry, he held it, still bleating pitifully, against the ache in his chest.

"The ewe died?" his father said behind him.

Nathan nodded, his throat tight. The old ewe had been his mother's favorite. Hannah Hamilton refused to slaughter any of the few sheep they raised, valuing them instead for their gentle companionship and warm wool. Nathan had tried valiantly to save Buttercup during her lambing, but the birth had been breech. The ewe had bled to death before the spindly lamb could even nurse.

Nathan felt his father's hand on his shoulder. "I know you did everything you could, son."

Nathan didn't answer. With great effort, the lamb lifted its small head, but it flopped back against Nathan's chest. He laid the newborn down in the warm box he'd prepared and waited.

Bawling, the lamb hunched up, and Jonathan critically examined its body. He eased his forefinger into the lamb's mouth, shaking his head when it refused to suck. "I don't think this one'll live. Even if his ma had made it, he's too weak. His mouth is even cold."

"I'll tube-feed it cow's milk until it's strong enough to take to one of the other ewes or a bottle."

Jonathan raised his eyebrows. "That's a lot of work, and cow's milk isn't always enough. God doesn't make mistakes; sometimes we have to let him have his way in these things."

"I've saved lives before, and I can save this one with or without God's help," Nathan said stubbornly. He knew what his father would say to that, so he rose quickly to fetch the equipment he'd need.

As he gathered the milk bucket and tube, he glanced out the open barn door and saw that night had fallen. His father lit another lamp and hung it near the sheep pen, then dragged the ewe's carcass outside. Nathan stared wistfully at the darkened sky and the stars that began to twinkle seductively. He arranged the milking stool beside the cow and pressed his cheek against her warm flank while he milked. His mother had taken over the milking years ago when his father deemed him old enough to handle more vigorous work, but Nathan secretly missed the daily chore. When he finished, the cows always stared at him with their great appreciative eyes, and he felt he had truly done them a favor.

But as much as he loved caring for the animals, he felt trapped on the farm. Sometimes he'd run past the orderly rows of corn and wheat to where the grass and sky gathered, smooth and unbroken. He'd stare longingly at the edge of the world, miles beyond, where freedom surely lay. Past the imprisoning prairie to forests and mountains, big cities and small, books and love and dreams and plans fulfilled in the life he was meant to lead.

His father had taught him everything he knew, not only about the farm, but about academics. For years he'd encouraged Nathan to consider going back East when it was time for college, and last year Nathan had decided to become a doctor.

Then Jonathan Hamilton and Robert Martin announced they were leaving to join the army.

When he finished milking, he knelt beside the lamb. It squalled piteously, and Nathan eased the tube down its throat. The lamb protested weakly, and Nathan cradled it against his body. "Come on, little one," he murmured. "You need this to live." The lamb looked up at him as if in understanding and stilled at once. "That's it, lie back. You'll make it."

Jonathan smiled faintly. "You have such a gentle touch, Nathan. Why do you want to fight a war?"

"Why do you?"

"Robert Martin and I want to see an end to slavery. We feel called to help preserve the Union."

"And I feel called to see what war's like."

"You need to keep at your studies if you want to go to college, Nathan. The war has taken enough boys."

Nathan bristled. "I feel the same about this country as you do, Father. I'd like to see justice served."

"There are other battles for justice than war. I know you want to act on the beliefs God's given you, but—"

"God didn't give me anything. *You're* the one who made me read the classics and study the philosophers. You taught me to think for myself."

"And tried to teach you love for God's Word. I thought you would see that intelligence and faith are compatible."

"I don't need a supreme being, Father. I can handle myself. *And* this lamb. You'll see."

Jonathan's eyes flickered. "Your compassion for healing comes from a gentle heart, Nathan, but you allow pride to rule you."

"I know what I can do on this farm. And now I want to know what I can do out in the world beyond it!"

"War isn't the answer to your wanderlust *or* your search for freedom. At your age, you think you're immortal, but war is death."

Nathan jerked his head at the bloody spot where the ewe had lain. "*Life* is death, Father. Isn't that what you read in

Ecclesiastes? No matter how you live your life, it all comes to the same end. Death. 'All things come alike to all . . .'?"

"You're right, son, but it also says that God will bring everyone into judgment for every secret thing we've done, whether it's good or evil. It's not a matter of what's right in our eyes but what's right in his."

"So how is it that *you* know what's right for me?" Nathan said bitterly, staring down at the lamb. Nourished for the time being, it had fallen asleep. Nathan removed the tube and gently placed the lamb in its box. Sighing, he rocked back on his heels and ran a hand through his hair. Despite his bravado, he was afraid the lamb might not make it after all.

At least arguing with his father took his mind off his fear. As far back as he could remember, they'd argued philosophy, the Bible, politics—even farming techniques. He always thought of them as merely disagreements; he never suspected that his father egged him on to force him to think. But now he realized that the spirited discussions were intended to hone his beliefs, to steer him to faith in God.

Nathan felt a hand on his arm, and he turned. His father's gray eyes were soft. "How do you feel about Samantha?"

"I'm going to marry her one day," Nathan said automatically. During the past year, she had figured into his plans by day and his dreams by night. "I love her."

"She certainly is turning into a beautiful young woman."

Embarrassed, Nathan glanced away. He'd noticed lately Samantha wasn't the rugged tomboy she'd appeared to be over the years. At times she was as elusive as a butterfly and twice as fragile. He'd hugged her thousands of times before, but today there had been something different in her touch.

He'd never before noticed how soft her hair felt, like kitten fur against his work-roughened hands. He'd wanted to loosen the ribbon at the back of her head and feel the weight of her hair in his hands, then touch her smooth cheek and reassure her everything would be all right. She evoked a strange protectiveness from his heart, a fierce desire to abandon everything for her. A gentle desire to hold her closely, shielding her from all harm. A warm desire to be all things to her.

He would go away and find his freedom. Then he would come back and make her a part of it.

Jonathan smiled gently. "The feelings you have for Samantha are perfectly natural for your age. And your mother and I have always hoped you two would eventually marry. You've grown up together, and you're good friends. That's important for a marriage."

He sighed. "But for now, I need you to stay on this farm. There's been talk of bushwhackers coming across from Missouri. Robert and I are known abolitionists, so I'm counting on you to protect your mother." He paused. "Once the mortgage is paid off, no matter what happens to me, the farm will be yours."

Nathan started to say he'd never have any use for it, but he glanced at the lamb. It shivered in its sleep, and he laid his hand over its small body. He'd forfeit his own rest tonight and settle for dozing every few hours in between lamb feedings. "Go on to bed, Father. I'll watch out for things here."

Jonathan smiled and put his arm around his son. "This lamb of yours might make it after all. I'll stay here awhile in case you need some help."

Nathan felt a smile work its way to his mouth, but a cold ache formed in his stomach. His father wouldn't be around the farm much longer to help.

Two

Too soon the day of departure came, and the weather obliged with a drenching rain to match the families' collective mood. Huddled with Nathan's mother, Hannah, Nathan, and Caleb on the porch of the Hamiltons' clapboard house, Samantha tried hard not to cry. Pa and Mr. Hamilton said good-bye, kissed each of them, then rode to Emporia to enlist.

Samantha nearly choked on the lump in her throat as tears blurred the figures fading in the gray distance. Caleb stalked off toward the woods, and Nathan stared down the road, silent, his jaw set.

Hannah Hamilton sighed, drawing Samantha against her. The downpour surrounded the porch like a curtain, but the warm maternal embrace gave Samantha a small measure of peace. "What'll we do without them?" she whispered.

Mrs. Hamilton's arms tightened, and her soft reply was filled with conviction. "We'll just have to hold on to the Lord, dear."

Nathan shot her a hard look, then headed for the barn.

That night, Samantha lay awake, unable to sleep. She worried about Pa and Mr. Hamilton, but she had the feeling something had been left undone. When the rain stopped just before dawn, she dressed swiftly and tiptoed out the door while Caleb slept.

Samantha ran, feet slipping, mud splashing her dress. When she reached the edge of the woods, she saw Nathan kneeling by the rabbits' empty nest. She stopped short, panting. "I . . . remembered we didn't check them . . . yesterday."

He raised his face, his expression grim. "The mother must not have been able to get them out in time. They drowned."

Samantha sank beside him. "Oh, Nathan."

"I should have moved them," he muttered. "I could have saved them."

"It's not your fault."

"They were my responsibility," he said bitterly. "First the ewe, now this."

She squeezed his hand, knowing nothing she said would ease his guilt. Nathan could be single-minded, especially about his animals.

Nathan drew a long, audible breath. "I don't understand why animals and people have to suffer."

"Ma once told me no one knows. She said we should just do our best to see that we don't cause the suffering."

"I don't want to kill," he said. "Not even in the war. There's things I could do that don't involve fighting, like being a courier or even a spy."

"But surely sometime you'd have to fight!"

He shook his head. "I don't want to hurt anyone."

Samantha's stomach ached, as if she'd swallowed an apple core. The thought of Nathan's leaving was more unsettling than the bunnies' death. He and Caleb were her last links to childhood and the stable life she'd once known.

The rest of the spring and well into the summer, Samantha threw herself into helping the others work the two farms. She divided her time between helping Mrs. Hamilton keep both houses in running order and helping Caleb and Nathan in the fields. Secretly she preferred the outdoor work. She gathered eggs and milked the cows while the boys tended the stock. They all rejoiced when Nathan's orphan lamb was adopted by a new mother and began to thrive.

Later in the summer they began to harvest the crops. Following behind Caleb and Nathan as they cut the golden-brown wheat with scythes, Samantha gathered the stalks into sheaves to stack and dry. Sometimes she went to bed too sore and tired to even eat dinner, but the hard work eased the ache in her heart over Pa and Mr. Hamilton.

They had just begun to thresh the wheat at the Hamiltons' when Samantha saw old Mr. Jebner plodding toward the house on the tired mule he always rode. Isaac Jebner ran the nearest post office, and he seldom showed up at someone's home unless he had bad news.

Samantha dropped the sheet she was using to winnow the kernels Nathan and Caleb had flailed loose and ran for the house. "Mrs. Hamilton!"

Hannah appeared in the doorway, and Samantha pointed silently down the road. For a moment Hannah's face went white, then the color came back to her cheeks, and she smoothed her apron. "Samantha, go find the boys," she said calmly.

"But—"

"Go," she said, more firmly than Samantha had ever heard her speak before.

Trembling, Samantha raced toward the barn. When she was just outside, she called their names, but to no avail. She could hear them inside flailing the seed heads from the sheaves and talking to each other. She moved to the doorway and called their names again. They glanced up, looking startled. Tears clogged her throat so tightly she couldn't say anything but only pointed toward the house. Immediately they dropped their flails and brushed past her.

Mrs. Hamilton's face was drawn, and she straightened as the three of them raced toward her. She was folding and unfolding a piece of paper, nodding at Mr. Jebner as he mounted the mule and headed back toward town.

"Your fathers," she said, then her chin quivered. She drew a deep breath and tried again. "Your fathers . . . are missing after the battle of Tupelo." She drew another deep breath, but the tears came anyway. "They're believed . . . dead!" Sobbing, she grabbed for Nathan, who caught and held her as his face filled with anguish.

Hot tears washed Samantha's eyes as she reached for her brother to share her grief. Caleb merely patted her arm and clenched his fists, uttering a foul curse under his breath.

Samantha pulled back, trembling with shock at his display.

Nathan glanced at Caleb and released Hannah, whose tears had finally abated. "I can't stay here, Mother," he said in a low voice.

Hannah straightened and drew a deep breath, wiping her eyes with the edge of her apron. "I forget sometimes how grown-up you are now, Nathan. You and Caleb will need . . . some time, we all need time to figure out what we're going to do now . . ." Her voice trailed off, and then she said, "We'll . . . talk tonight."

Looking relieved, Nathan and Caleb turned and headed for the woods. Aching to be held and comforted, Samantha stepped off the porch to go with them, but Hannah drew her back. "Stay with me, Samantha. The boys need to be alone."

Samantha glanced desperately at their fading figures, then back at Mrs. Hamilton. The older woman's chin was quivering again, and her eyes filled with tears. She opened her arms, and Samantha moved into her embrace, feeling as lost and scared as Nathan's newborn lamb.

The children and Hannah went to Sunday worship services as always, but the meetings seemed to hold little for the downtrodden group. Nathan and Caleb sat sullenly through the Bible readings but refused to sing along with the hymns. After several weeks, Hannah compromised the day's sanctity and told all three children they were excused after the noon meal. Freed from responsibilities, only for that one afternoon a week did they find any happiness resembling their younger days.

"Race you to the river!" Caleb hollered over his shoulder. Already well ahead, he easily outdistanced Nathan and Samantha and tagged the large cottonwood by the Osage River. He laughed as Nathan drew up second.

A distant third, Samantha panted alongside them, doubling over, glaring at Nathan's good-natured smile. "No fair . . . Caleb . . . can't have . . . a head start." She brushed back straggling blond hair and sank onto the grassy bank to catch her breath against the cottonwood.

Caleb smiled impishly. "Loser has to perform a dare."

Samantha groaned. They hadn't played this game in a long time, but she was always the loser. She had been nearly eleven before she realized Caleb and Nathan would always be stronger and faster.

"That race wasn't fair and you know it!" She started to

rise, and Nathan took her hand to help her up. He smiled tentatively. Though Samantha and Caleb still mourned their father, Nathan's grief had driven him to a melancholic silence. It was nice to see him smile again.

"The dare's my pick." Caleb twisted around, rubbing his chin. "Hmm. How about—"

"How about you hang upside down from the branch over the water?" Nathan said. "That ought to be easy enough. You used to do it all the time when we came out here regular."

"Well . . ." Samantha eyed the branch skeptically. That seemed like a long, long time ago.

Caleb crossed his arms, grinning. "That's the dare."

"All right." She pulled off her shoes and stockings. When she looked up, she saw Nathan's gaze fixed on her bared lower legs.

"Come on!"

"I'm going, Caleb." She inched her way up the trunk to the heavy branch hanging over the water, then crawled out carefully. Her knees caught in her skirt, and she paused to look down. The height didn't seem as far above the water as it had when she was younger, nor the branch as wide. Samantha held her breath and crawled as far as she dared.

"Not good enough!" Caleb yelled. "You have to hang upside down, remember?"

"I remember," she mumbled. She sat sideways on the branch and parted her knees in an unladylike stretch. She grasped the branch through her calico skirt.

Samantha took a deep breath. The scary part had always been letting go. Not climbing the tree, being over water, or crawling out on the limb, but trusting in sheer faith as she abandoned her grip on normalcy to a topsy-turvy world.

Her stomach dropped as she let go and leaned back into infinity. Blood rushed to her head, and she swung her dangling arms, laughing. She hadn't fallen. "Whee!"

A form shot from the water beside her. "Gotcha!"

Heart pounding, she shrieked with fear. Her legs lost their hold, and she tumbled headfirst into the water. Coming up sputtering, she felt strong arms grab and steady her. Her feet found a hold on a sunken branch.

Nathan stood beside her, up to his waist in water. When he saw she was all right, he laughed and shook his head, spraying her with water.

"Nathan Hamilton!" Shrieking with laughter, she turned her face, and her feet slipped. Nathan reached out and held her fast, laughing and pulling her close to help her gain her balance. His gaze settled on her face, and they both stopped laughing.

Samantha stilled, and her breath caught in her throat. Nathan's eyes were serious and searching, his closeness unnerving. Her ears pounded with her heart's beats, and she thought for a moment she might faint. The water lapped around them, but Nathan held her steady. He moved closer, his voice soft. "I have to leave."

The spell broken, she relaxed. Had he promised his mother he'd help with some chore? On a Sunday? "We just got here!"

"Nathan! Let's go swim!" Caleb yelled from the bank.

"In a minute!" Nathan turned back, his face etched with frustration. "I'm leaving soon, Samantha. It's what I have to do. But I want to marry you someday."

Samantha blinked, confused at his abruptness. She'd always dreamed of marrying Nathan, but this was too soon!

Marriage meant keeping house and raising babies . . . *Babies?* Her stomach tied in a confused knot, and she felt her cheeks redden. "Caleb's calling," she whispered.

Nathan's gaze intensified. "Will you wait for me until I come back?"

His face was close to hers, swallowing her view of everything except his eyes. Her heart pounded so hard she was sure he could hear it. "Y-yes," she whispered.

Nathan smiled gently. "Samantha . . . ," he said, then bent his head. She thought wildly, *He's going to kiss me!* and leaned toward him, trusting, closing her eyes. His nearness made her heart forget her head.

"Hey!" Caleb called from the bank. Samantha's eyes flew open. Her brother looked angry as he splashed into the water.

The sound of gunfire erupted, distant but clear, from the direction of Nathan's farm. The three froze.

Passion wiped from his face, Nathan plunged downward in the water. Without hesitation Samantha followed his lead, and together they swam the river and scrambled up the bank.

"Hurry, Samantha!" Caleb yelled as she bent to retrieve her shoes and stockings. She was still jerking them on when the boys took off, and she hobbled after them.

Running, stumbling, the three pushed through rows of ripened corn back to the Hamilton farm. Stalks slapped against Samantha's wet body, but she was too frightened to feel any pain.

Caleb threw out a hand to draw them up short. "Listen!"

The field vibrated with the thunder of riders, yelling, whipping their horses as if hell were close behind. Nathan shoved Samantha onto her stomach, face down in the dirt. He and Caleb ducked on their knees, keeping a watchful eye. A blur of ragtag butternut uniforms and pounding hooves charged past, only a few rows away, headed straight for the Martins' farm. Voices floated in the air.

"Haw! Haw! Did you see the way—?"

"Shame 'tweren't time t'—"

Samantha heard cornstalks rustling. "Nathan!" Caleb hissed. "You'll just get yourself killed!"

Nathan uttered a curse and ducked back down. But as quickly as chaos had come, silence followed. Samantha raised her head expectantly, searching to see if the riders had all truly left.

"Rebel bushwhackers," Nathan ground out, addressing Caleb. "They've been crossing the Missouri border ahead of the army, destroying Union homes. Father told me to watch for them."

"Pa told me about them too," Caleb said grimly.

Samantha coughed, the smell of dirt choking her. She pushed to her knees, unable to clear her nostrils of the acrid scent. From the way Nathan and Caleb sniffed the air, they smelled something too.

"Fire!" Caleb leaped up. He and Nathan yanked Samantha to her feet, and they pulled her through the smoky field. She could hear the crackle and sizzle of burning stalks behind them. Panic-stricken and coughing, she sucked in gulps of hot air as she clutched at a stitch in her side. Her eyes stung with smoke, and she stumbled after Nathan and Caleb as they crashed through the stalks.

The crackling roar intensified. Stumbling through the last row of stalks, she ran smack into a motionless Caleb and Nathan.

The Hamiltons' farmhouse was a fireball, flames of

19

intense heat and color spewing up against the smoky sky. The outbuildings sagged and crashed under the weight of their own vibrant blazes.

A body lay at the side of the house.

Samantha rushed forward, but Nathan pulled her back. He pressed her face tightly against his chest. "Don't look, Samantha," he said, his voice sounding strained. "Stay with Caleb."

"No! Let me go!" She fought him, elbowing and kicking, but he was stronger. He dragged her away, and only when they were far from the body did he release her.

Samantha straightened, glaring at Nathan, but the devastation—the hatred—closed her mouth in shock. Near what used to be the barn, carcasses of cows, pigs, and chickens littered the ground, surrounded by wide pools of blood.

Nathan's lamb and the other sheep lay slaughtered, their throats slit.

Samantha felt lifeless, and the world spun.

Caleb caught her and held her upright. "Nathan'll go see about his ma alone, Samantha." He peered into her eyes, and when she didn't respond, he shook her gently. "All right?"

She nodded stupidly. The heat from the lingering blaze pressed against her body, against her soul. Nathan's home. Destroyed. Her heart leaped to her throat, catching. Surely Mrs. Hamilton wasn't dead!

Bile rose, and her hand flew to her mouth. "Don't look," Caleb ordered, cursing through clenched teeth as he set her roughly on the ground. He stood over her, and his hands tightened into fists. "Just . . . don't!"

Like a discarded rag doll, Hannah Hamilton lay in a bloody, twisted heap. From a distance Nathan thought he could be a man about it, but beside her, he was a little boy again. "No!"

Trembling, he reached for her hands, then stopped. Cold anger knifed through his soul, and he inhaled sharply. He lifted the clean, well-thumbed family Bible from her grasp. Wasn't that just like God to preserve his words when the people they were supposed to save suffered brutal deaths!

Nathan rose on shaky legs. "Not a mark on this book!" He shook the Bible above his head, raising his face heavenward. "Did you think I'd be forced to choose you? You didn't save my mother, and she chose you! You didn't save my father either! You want a choice? Here's my choice!"

Screaming the foulest phrase he knew, Nathan flung the book at the burning house. His chest heaved, and he brushed angrily at the smoky tears in his eyes. He watched as the thin pages twisted to a gnarled black, and his own heart burned and twisted with rage.

A cold smile etched its way across his face. It didn't matter. He'd truly rejected God. From now on his life would be his own. He was accountable to no one.

He trudged back to Caleb and Samantha, ignoring their stricken looks. They'd probably heard his screaming, but he didn't care. He wasn't accountable to them either.

They had all seen the smoke from the direction of the Martins' farm, and they weren't surprised to find it in the same condition as the Hamiltons'. Looted, the animals systematically slaughtered. Even the privy was ablaze. Without a word, Nathan and Caleb grimly tramped the mile's distance back to the Hamiltons', and Samantha tagged behind. Her heart ached with grief and fear, but one look at her brother's hard-set jaw and the anger in Nathan's eyes, and she held the pain silently inside.

Caleb and Nathan took turns digging until dark. Samantha stood to the side, watching and trying to keep her composure. She squeezed back her tears until they lowered Mrs. Hamilton's body into the hole, then she bawled like a lost calf. Caleb stared at her in disgust, and she gulped in deep breaths, mortified. She could have at least cried quietly like her brother, or not at all, like Nathan.

Stoic throughout the burial, Nathan wore an icy mask. Samantha wanted to go to him for comfort, but he wouldn't even look at her. At least Caleb hugged her briefly and salvaged a blanket to make her a bed in a patch of unburned grass. After several reassuring murmurs, he jerked his head at Nathan, and they wandered out of earshot. She could hear their garbled language for several hours. Frightened and lonely, she wished they'd include her, but they left her alone in the dark with her silent tears and wordless prayers.

Night pressed against her, every star an accusing eye. Samantha squeezed her eyes shut, trembling. She hadn't been this scared since the nighttime thunderstorm soon after Ma died.

Pa had smiled at her and smoothed her hair. "'Under his wings shalt thou trust: his truth shall be thy shield and buckler. Thou shalt not be afraid for the terror by night.'"

Remembering, Samantha cautiously opened her eyes. "'I will be with him in trouble; I will deliver him,'" she whispered.

A bright streak trailed across the sky, then faded. Samantha drew a deep breath, relaxing. God was with her. Caleb and Nathan were with her. Her eyelids closed.

A rough hand shook her awake. She blinked with confusion at the pale dawn, then gasped when she realized someone was standing over her. She scrambled upright, then relaxed. "Caleb."

He cleared his throat. "You sleep all right?"

Samantha managed a nod. Caleb's curly hair was slicked down around his clean face, and his shirt was neatly tucked into his trousers. She glanced anxiously from him to Nathan, who stood aloof. His face was still smudged with smoke and dirt, his shirt dirty and torn.

"Nathan . . . ," she said tentatively.

He turned, and his eyes pierced hers, cold. Samantha backed away, but he grasped her hand. "We're going to an orphanage."

"Wh-what?" She stared at him and then at Caleb. "We have the farms!"

Nathan's expression never changed. "Both farms were mortgaged. The bank owns the land now. We're going to Kansas City, where the orphanage—"

"No!" She jerked away. "This is our home! Pa will come back!"

"Hush!" Caleb said fiercely then thrust a pan of water in her hands. "Clean up as best you can, then we're leaving."

Samantha's protests died at his hard look. Deflated, she knelt on the ground and splashed her face and hands.

The boys drifted away. Caleb stared vacantly at Mrs. Hamilton's grave. Nathan moved off by himself, turning his back on them. He stared at the horizon, and the wind gently lifted his hair.

Samantha moved beside him, hopeful. Nathan would know the right answer. He would figure out how they could stay. "What are we really going to do?" she murmured.

"We're going to Kansas City, Samantha," he said evenly.

Her heart pounded. "Wh-what about you and me?"

He whirled on her so suddenly she stepped back. "I can't look out for you, Samantha. Everything's changed now."

"No!" She trembled, frightened. "It can't change just because—"

"We have to go." Caleb gripped her elbow. "Nathan and I already walked over to the Fletcher farm, and they're expecting us. Someone will take us to Kansas City."

"But . . . but the farm . . . Pa . . ."

"Pa's dead, Samantha! There's nothing here for us. *Nothing!* They took everything we had or burned it! Now, come on!"

Samantha threw one last glance at Nathan, but he ignored her. Caleb held on to her elbow and set a quick pace through the prairie grass to their nearest neighbors.

Tommy Fletcher agreed to drive them to Kansas City. Samantha consoled herself with the thought that she would at least be with Caleb and Nathan. But neither spoke more than two words by day, and at night when they pulled off the road to sleep, Caleb, Nathan, and Tommy pointedly excluded her. From the other side of the campfire, Samantha occasionally overheard heated exclamations but couldn't make out any words. Frightened and lonely, she trembled on her bedroll and slept little.

By the time they reached Kansas City, she was too emotionally and physically exhausted to care about the boys' secrets. Dusk settled, and her lone weary desire was for a clean bed.

Tommy let them off at an iron gate with rusted bars. A tall, crumbling brick wall enclosed the grounds like a prison. Over the peeling door, a weather-beaten sign proclaimed the building to be the Good Shepherd's Home.

Shivering, Samantha hid behind Caleb as they entered the shadowy foyer. Last summer Nathan had read *Oliver Twist* to them, and she felt eerily as if she had stepped into the book's pages. What if the people at this orphanage wouldn't give them enough to eat? What if they treated her unkindly?

An unseen clock loudly chimed the hour, and Samantha started. An older woman with thin lips as tight as her gray bun stepped forward from the shadows. "What are you three doing here?"

"We're new, ma'am," Nathan said in a smooth voice. "Where do we go?"

The woman stared at them down her long, crooked nose. "You brought yourselves here just like that?"

"Yes, ma'am." Nathan's smile fell theatrically. "We've lost our folks. Our fathers died in the battle of Tupelo."

"And your mothers?"

Nathan nodded at Samantha and Caleb. "Theirs has been dead a long time. Mine died recently."

The woman clucked her tongue in sympathy, and her face softened. "You were brave to come by yourselves. But you boys must be at least sixteen or seventeen. You're too old—"

"Yes, ma'am, we're old." Caleb nudged Samantha forward. "But we've come a long way, and my little sister is tired."

"Of course." The woman placed her hands on Samantha's

shoulders. "I'm Mrs. Matlock, child. You understand, don't you?"

Samantha dug in her heels and clung to Caleb. "Don't let her take me! I want to stay with you!"

"Don't be silly." Caleb pried her fingers loose where they clenched his arm. "All the girls stay in one place, and all the boys in another. We'll see you tomorrow. It's late."

Mrs. Matlock looked perplexed. "But I thought you understood. We can't take—"

"It's all right, Sam. Go with the lady," Nathan said quickly, looking agreeable again.

Samantha stopped struggling and stared. His complacency was more foreboding than the separation.

"That's a good girl." Mrs. Matlock took Samantha's arm and led her up a dim stairwell. At the top, Samantha glanced back. Caleb's arms were crossed, and he nodded encouragement.

Nathan's face was drawn, and his eyes locked with hers. He stepped forward, then stopped. Samantha wanted to pull free and run to him, but he smiled crookedly at her. She smiled back, relieved. Everything would be all right.

"Here's the girls' area." Mrs. Matlock led her to a room bustling with girls ranging from toddlers to Samantha's age. Most were absorbed in a sock-puppet show.

Two rows of iron beds lined the walls. Each bed was made up so tightly it looked as if a coin could bounce off its blanket.

"That one will be yours, dear." Mrs. Matlock nodded at a bed by an open window. "Sally will be next to you. She's about your age."

Hearing her name, a puppeteer with long braids stuck her

head over the blanket. Her face was flushed, and her smile wide. "Hello!"

Samantha shrank back, shy. To her dismay, her stomach rumbled.

Mrs. Matlock smiled. "You've missed supper, child. Can I get you something from the kitchen?"

"I think I'd rather just go to bed." The sooner she went to sleep, the sooner it would be morning. She would talk to Nathan then, and they would leave this place.

She lay down with all her clothes on, except her stockings and shoes. She was so weary, she barely had time to say her prayers. She fell into a dream so real she could almost reach out and touch it. Pa had come home, and even Ma. Nathan and his parents were there too. Everyone was celebrating the reunion.

A thump on the floor startled her awake. Confused, she sat up. It was dark, and all the girls were in bed. Some were stirring from the noise, but Sally padded from bed to bed, shushing them back to sleep. She drifted to Samantha's bedside, holding a rock in one hand and paper in the other. She nodded at the open window. "This rock sailed through, pretty as you please. If your name's Samantha, this note's got your name on it."

Samantha twisted the paper to the moonlight until she could read her brother's unmistakable scrawl. *Samantha— We're going to join the army. Be a good girl and be nice. You'll be safer this way. Love, Caleb and Nathan*

She rushed to the window but could only see inky darkness. Panicking, she ran for the door and down the stairs. "Caleb! Nathan!"

Ignoring the jab of rocks against her bare feet, she ran

27

down the driveway to the closed gate. Nathan and Caleb were agilely climbing the brick wall, then they dropped down on the other side.

"Wait for me!" She tugged at the gate, but it stuck fast.

Caleb's face furrowed with anger. "You can't come with us! We're joining the army!" Caleb sounded as though he was taunting her, as if this were another game they refused to let her join. But always before, Nathan had relented.

She stretched her hand toward him, through the iron bars. "Let me come with you!"

Nathan bowed his head. "No," he mumbled. "You'll be safe here. It's for your own good."

Samantha sank to her knees, sobbing. "Don't leave me!"

Caleb softened, staring at her with a look of pity and regret. "Nathan, maybe we—"

"We agreed it was the only way to keep her safe!" Nathan's eyes snapped. He turned away and started down the street. "Come on!"

"No! Wait!" Samantha threw herself against the bars, straining. Caleb paused, uncertain.

"Samantha!" Mrs. Matlock shuffled down the driveway, lantern held high. "What in heaven's name are you doing?"

Samantha's heart pounded furiously. "Please, Caleb!"

"Nathan's right. You'll be safe here." Caleb's voice was tinged with sadness. "Take care of yourself, little sister." He spun around and took off after Nathan.

Tears streamed down Samantha's face, and she pulled at the bars. "No! Caleb! Nathan! Please come back! Don't leave me!"

She flung herself at the gate like a bird against a cage, then ran to the brick wall, her fingers clawing for a hold. Her fingers bled, and she fell back, sobbing.

Mrs. Matlock drew her into her arms. "We can't keep boys here who are old enough to make their own way. You must have known they were leaving, child."

"They didn't tell me." Dazed, Samantha cradled her hands together. Numbness spread from the bleeding fingertips to her head, heart, and feet. "They didn't tell me," she whispered.

Mrs. Matlock clucked her tongue. "Poor lamb. Come back to bed, and we'll talk about it in the morning. God always works everything together for our good."

Samantha glanced down the empty road. Bereft, she pressed her face against Mrs. Matlock's warm shoulder and cried.

THREE

Battle of Nashville
December 1864

Amid the distant roar of gunfire and bursting shells, the ambulance cart creaked its protest over rocks and wet deadfall. The predawn snow had dusted the field now littered with gray- and blue-clad bodies.

Nathan dragged his wet Union coat sleeve across his face to clear his eyes.

"Had about enough of all this adventure you came to see?" From the back of the cart, McGregor laughed. "Rubbin' your eyes won't make 'em disappear, boy. Them bodies ain't going nowhere."

Nathan didn't answer.

McGregor's gums shone in his wizened face. "I'm just joshin' with you, boy. You make a fine medic, even if you are just a kid. Maybe someday I'll take you to my purty little piece of Wyoming wilderness. Would you like that?"

"Sure I would," Nathan said. McGregor was always talking about the mountain land he'd staked out years ago. "If this war's ever over."

The old man threw back his head and laughed. "These squabbles always are, sonny. Best you be thinkin' on what you plan to do then. Let's check that stand of oaks first." McGregor pointed up ahead, then jumped from the moving cart.

Nathan tugged on the reins of the horse pulling the empty avalanche. When full, the two-wheeled, springless ambulance cart was aptly named: The wounded were often pitched against each other or even right out of the conveyance like an avalanche.

Nathan set the brake, then climbed down, grim. His nostrils burned with the residual stench of gunpowder, and he pushed his way through a smoky haze. The fighting had moved to another arena.

The rule was to aid fallen comrades first, but Nathan generally took on whoever needed the most help. He dropped to the snow beside a motionless gray form and laid a hand on the neck. Dead. They'd all be better off dead. Better than having to face the sawbones in the field hospital. A man was lucky to get out of there with all his limbs attached.

Hearing a faint moan, Nathan moved to the next body. Red stained the middle of the muddy blue coat and fanned outward. Before he even glanced at the man's face, Nathan knew it was hopeless. He pulled out a thick cloth from his bag when suddenly an arm shot out and grabbed his. "Am I hit bad?" the voice croaked.

Nathan moved his gaze to a pair of steady blue eyes. He'd heard the question more times than he could count. Some dying men wanted the truth, and some needed a lie to cling to. These eyes wanted the truth. "Yes," Nathan said flatly. "I'm sorry."

The grip on Nathan's arm weakened. The soldier laughed nervously, causing the stain to spread faster.

Nathan pressed the cloth against the man's gut. "Don't! Calm down."

The laughter turned into a barking cough, and the man struggled to catch his breath. Blood seeped through the cloth and onto Nathan's hand. He could hear other moans around him, the sounds of the faintly living. In the distance, McGregor shuffled from body to body, and Nathan figured he could spare a few more minutes. This man wasn't far from the next world, wherever it was. No one should die alone.

"You got a girl?"

The question wasn't new to Nathan. Most of the dying wanted to talk about one of two things: God or women. "I guess you could say so."

"Tell me about her."

"She was real pretty. Blond."

"Where'd you last see her?"

Nathan grimaced. He didn't like to think about Samantha. "Back in Kansas City—don't talk."

The man gasped hard, and his body spasmed. "Open my haversack," he rasped.

Nathan glanced at his bloody hand, reluctant to release the pressure on the wound. "I can't—"

"Open it!"

With his left hand, Nathan pushed the man's battered canteen aside and clumsily yanked open the overstuffed haversack. A locket and a half-written letter spilled out, followed by money. Lots of money—greenbacks as well as coins.

"Take it." The man's voice was a choking whisper now. "Send it to my family. I got a wife . . . two little girls."

Nathan's eyes widened. "Where'd you get all this?"

The man coughed, and it was a long time before he

caught his breath. "Gambling, some. Stealing from the camp, mostly. Maybe I even . . . stole from you."

"The money should be returned."

"I don't even remember who . . . it came from, kid. Give it to my wife. She'll need it. Send it to her. Please!" The man's face twisted with pain.

Nathan scooped up the coins. "All right, mister. It's going in my pockets. In my medical bag, in . . . there's not enough room for it all." Hearing the sound of gunfire, he hastily stuffed the paper bills down his shirt. It sounded as though the action was moving back this way. He needed to tend to those who could be saved before the field was overrun with fighting once again. "Listen, mister, what's your name?"

The blue eyes were fixed heavenward, glassy. The stain under the cloth had stopped spreading.

Rocking back on his heels, Nathan wearily swiped his bloody hand against his coat. He cursed under his breath and tossed the stained cloth to the side.

"Nathan!" Clutching his Spencer rifle with bayonet fixed, Caleb ran up, panting. His exhaled breath held like steam in the frosty air, but despite the cold, sweat poured down his face. Somewhere in the fight he'd lost his cap, and his eyes glowed. "We got 'em! Those Rebs'll be running for their lives. We got 'em, I tell you!"

Nathan couldn't share Caleb's enthusiasm. The outcome was always the same no matter what color the victor's uniform. "Is the fighting moving back here?"

"No, most of the boys are charging the hill where the Rebs have dug in." Caleb paused and glanced around warily. "What if one of these wounded Rebs tries to kill you? Doesn't seem fair the army won't let you medics arm yourselves."

Nathan smiled wryly, tired. "Go on, Caleb. You do the fighting for both of us."

Caleb grinned and took off again, yelling. Nathan trudged grimly onward, bypassing several motionless bodies for a group of soldiers lying just beyond the trees. McGregor's advice still rang in his ears. What *would* he do when this was over?

The regimental commander had discovered Nathan's extensive book learning and had appointed him to work with the surgeons. Nathan immediately proved himself by his proficient assistance at even the most gruesome operations. When other men retched or fainted at the sight of limbs rotted green with gangrene, Nathan calmly readied the surgeon's saw.

He grew accustomed to the grotesque patterns and deformities the spinning Minié balls and artillery shells inflicted on human flesh and bone. Even worse were the disease and filth at the field hospitals. Whether a church, barn, or tent, each makeshift hospital reeked with the fetid stench of disease, dirty linens, and filthy bodies.

Nathan stuffed down his anguish at the carnage he witnessed, emotionally removing himself. He told himself each amputation or gunshot victim was just another cow or lamb to tend, another nest of bunnies to protect.

The coins clanked in his pockets as he repeatedly knelt and tended to the wounded. His hands seemed to work by themselves. He'd grown so accustomed to the gruesome work it had become routine, and he often found himself daydreaming as he went about his business. He thought about the dying thief and realized he'd have to go back later to search the corpse for identification.

"You been over there yet?" A man jerked his bandaged head at a quiet area near a creek.

"Not yet," Nathan said, gathering his dwindling supplies. "I'll get there."

The man gripped Nathan's arm. "My buddy went down there. Go see about him!"

"Look, mister, I can't see about everybody's buddy at once. I'll go when I can!"

The man withdrew his hand. "Sorry," he said brusquely. "I think a shell got him."

Remembering Caleb, Nathan relaxed. He'd be devastated if anything happened to his boyhood friend. "I'll go there next," he said and rose.

As he neared the creek, Nathan realized he probably would have missed seeing the bodies, so few were there. An eerie stillness settled over the area; even the wind was calm. A lone gray figure sat propped against a tree, but on closer inspection, Nathan realized he was already dead. Another gray form was sprawled headfirst along the bank, also dead.

Nathan stumbled down the slippery slope to the water's edge. Shivering, he knelt beside the body of a Union soldier lying motionless and facedown. He was mired in the icy mud, both ears blown clean off, his head mangled and bloody.

Nathan's stomach lurched. Bile rose to his mouth, and he shook with a heated flush of fear. Dizzy, he slumped to the bank until the nausea passed and he'd caught his breath, his emotions once again controlled.

At least this poor fool had died on the field. Better to go quickly from a bursting shell than rot from disease. Or worse yet, live out life trapped in a useless body.

"Please . . . kill . . . me."

Nathan lifted his head. Surely he'd imagined a voice. It had been so soft.

"Please, God . . . kill . . . me."

The muffled sound came from the body. Nathan tugged it over, then froze. Except for the lower jaw, the front of the man's face had been ripped away.

The parted, cracked lips moved. "Please . . . kill . . . me."

Horrified, Nathan backed away, stumbling to the ground, slipping on a patch of ice. His hand brushed against a rock, then closed around it, tightening. He couldn't move; he couldn't think. All he could see was the living body that wasn't a person, that didn't even scream like the countless others.

"Please kill . . ."

The groaning throbbed like a migraine in Nathan's head. It was cruel to let the soldier live this way. Even if he survived the hospital, he'd be grotesquely disfigured. Nathan had to ease his suffering; he had to stop the torturous moans.

Heart pounding, he lifted the rock with both hands and brought it down swiftly on the man's skull.

Nathan was still sitting on the bank when Caleb found him, dazed and unaware of how much time had passed. When he tried to stand, he realized his feet had been submerged in the icy water, and his numbed legs buckled.

Caleb helped him up. "I hadn't seen you for so long, I thought you were dead. The fighting's over."

Confused and weak, Nathan leaned against Caleb. "I . . . I have to get a man's name," he said. "I promised."

Caleb stared. "You all right? You hit somewhere? You're talking kind of strange. McGregor was worried about you. Some of the other medics helped him cart off the wounded when he couldn't find you. You're wanted at the hospital now. I said I'd pitch in to bury the dead."

"There's three here. You'll want to take care of them."

Caleb stared again. "Sure, Nathan."

By the time they reached camp, Nathan could feel the blood rushing back to his feet and walked in on his own. He stumbled first toward his tent, unbuttoning his coat as he went. He had to change out of his uniform before he helped in the hospital. He was covered with blood.

"Money!"

Men raced toward him, and confused, Nathan stopped. They knelt around him, scooping up the loose greenbacks and whooping with delight. Jostled and elbowed, he felt the coins scatter from his pockets and heard them fall, ringing against each other into waiting hands. Someone upended his bag and shook out the rest of the coins.

"Hoo-ee! Look at it!"

"I never seed so much money in all my born days!"

"Why this'll—"

"Hold on here!"

Everyone stopped at the commanding voice of the company's burly first sergeant. Arms crossed, he stood nearly a head taller than everyone else. "What's going on here? Where'd all this come from?"

Fists clutching bills and coins, the men were silent. A few hung their heads. Nathan stood motionless.

"Well?"

Someone pointed at Nathan. "He had it! It came off him."

The sergeant eyed Nathan coldly. "Is that true?"

"Yes." Nathan lifted his chin.

"A lot of money's been turning up missing around this

camp, Hamilton." The sergeant squinted. "You must be the thief who's been taking it."

"I got it from a dying soldier. He asked me to give it to his wife. He said *he* stole it."

The crowd laughed derisively, but the sergeant waited until he had silence. "What was his name?"

"I don't know."

The crowd's mood shifted like a current stirring up muddy water. "Mighty convenient," someone muttered, and others affirmed the sentiment with vigorous nods.

The sergeant gripped Nathan's bloody arm. "Come with me, Hamilton. There's punishments for thieves in this army."

For the first time, Nathan felt real fear. "Sir, I'm needed in the hospital. I didn't take the money!"

"Yeah, sure!"

"They're never guilty when they're caught!"

The crowd pressed in closer, faces just moments before jubilant with victory and the promise of money now ugly with hate. "March him through the camp with the thief's sign on his back!"

"The sign? Put him on the platform for the day!"

The crowd bellowed its approval, but one voice rose above the rest. "Put him in the sweatbox!"

"The sweatbox!" Cheers accompanied the cry, and everyone pushed against the grim-faced sergeant and Nathan. Some tore at his clothes, whether in search of more money or to punish him, he couldn't tell. He stumbled, and instantly they were on him, pummeling and kicking.

Caleb pushed through the crowd and swung at the sergeant. The big man went down, and Caleb drew his gun as he stood over Nathan. The crowd backed away. Caleb hauled Nathan to his feet. "You all right?"

Nathan nodded, his heart pounding against his bruised ribs. He winced as he drew a deep breath, then doubled over as pain shot through his gut.

"Martin!" Face red with anger, the sergeant came up rubbing his jaw and wrenched Caleb's wrist until the gun fell from his hand. "Just for that, you'll share your criminal friend's punishment. Take them away!"

Jeering, the crowd surrounded Nathan and Caleb and dragged them toward the center of camp. Just before they were thrown in the torturous sweatbox, Nathan thought bleakly that now he wouldn't have to worry about what to do after the war. One way or another, he wasn't going to survive it.

"Nathan," Jonathan Hamilton rasped, his throat dry and thick. He shifted weakly on the dirty, narrow bed, wishing they'd put just one drop of water on his tongue. They seldom even gave him anything to eat, and when they did, it was only some sort of mush they poured down his throat until he gagged. He could feel what little strength he had slowly die. He vaguely remembered a shell bursting beside him and being thrown from his horse, but his next memory was of waking up here, wherever that was.

"Nathan," he tried to say again, for it was the only thing he could concentrate on. He could barely remember his home or his wife's face, but he remembered his son. Jonathan wanted to warn him, to reassure him that war was indeed death.

"Nathan!" He felt as though he were screaming, his head

hot with fire. He wanted to die, but he had to get home. Back to Hannah and the farm. Back to his only son. "Nathan!"

Over the delirious prisoner's bed, the Confederate doctor glanced at the orderly. "This Yank always seems to mutter the same thing. Doesn't he ever say anything else?"

The orderly shrugged. "Who knows? He's been here for months. That injury doesn't get any better, but he keeps hanging on. He'd be better off if he'd just go ahead and die. There's not enough food here to keep all the prisoners alive. Not to mention that our boys are starving at the front."

The doctor grimly checked the soldier's head wound. He was in agreement with the orderly, but he was honor-bound as a doctor to do what he could for these prisoners.

"Change his dressing and keep him comfortable," he said tersely. "Maybe God'll have mercy and take this one off our hands."

FOUR

Wyoming Territory
Fall 1865

Astride his mount, Nathan leaned forward, forearms braced against the pommel. He surveyed the clearing critically, looking for fault but finding none. McGregor had said few white men came through these mountains, north of both the Oregon Trail and the path of the oncoming railroad. The isolation alone made an ideal hideout.

"Not bad." Caleb whistled. "The only way into here is the pass. It'll be impossible to get in and out during the winter, but—"

"That's what we want," Nathan said sharply. "There's no reason to jump one step ahead of the law when all we have to do is hightail it back here and hole up every winter."

Without responding, Caleb dismounted and led his horse into the woods. Nathan watched him go, knowing Caleb still wasn't comfortable with their lifestyle.

They had endured the rest of the war without the support of their company, which was firmly convinced Nathan had been the thief and Caleb his accomplice. No one covered Caleb in battle, and even the wounded soldiers refused to speak to Nathan. When McGregor died, Nathan and Caleb lost their only friend.

They'd always passed off the old man's stories as nothing but an old-timer's idle boast of having been a trapper and mountain man like the legendary Jim Bridger. But as he lay dying in a muddy field, the victim of a ricocheting Minié ball, McGregor had given Nathan the directions to his isolated land and cabin.

"You may . . . need a home. Take it . . . boy." He'd managed a grin, then his eyes stared vacantly beyond Nathan's shoulder.

After the war Nathan and Caleb drifted aimlessly westward toward McGregor's Wind River Mountains. Jobs were scarce, and so was money. Frustrated, desperate, and starving, Nathan convinced Caleb they should hold up an army payroll wagon as revenge for the unjust punishment they'd incurred during the war. After that, it had been easy to graduate to stagecoach robberies, justifying each offense with one excuse or another.

Aspen leaves rustled overhead, branches brushing each other as though in private conversation. Closing his eyes, Nathan breathed deeply, savoring the pure air until his chest hurt. In just a few months, he'd spent a lifetime inhaling the stench of gunpowder, blood, rotting wounds . . . death. Even months after the end of the war, after months of atoning nightmares, he could never get enough clean air or quiet. He couldn't even remember a time when goodness lighted his life.

For weeks, he and Caleb worked at restoring McGregor's abandoned cabin to a livable state. By snowfall, they had stocked up on supplies and were set for the winter. In the spring, they had plans to meet up with more men and form a larger gang. Bank robberies would net them more money, and they needed the men for protection. Nathan threw himself into planning various heists, each more profitable than the last.

~

Nathan sat bolt upright in the dark, sweat beading his brow. Without opening his eyes, he lunged for the gun belt hanging around the bedpost. In two pounding heartbeats, the Colt Navy revolver was in his hand. But even before he had it cocked, he knew he was being foolish.

Palms damp, he let the gun slip from his fingers to the bed. He drew a deep breath, trembling, and scanned the room with wary eyes to confirm that he was alone.

He threw back the covers and fumbled in the dark to light the kerosene lamp by his bed. By his pocket watch he could see that it was three o'clock in the morning. Frowning, he snapped the gold case shut. Father had handed down his watch just before he left for the army, the last time Nathan had spoken to him.

He shivered in the semidarkness. He always shivered after one of the nightmares.

But this was more. He couldn't shake the feeling someone was watching him. He ran his fingers through his hair and closed his eyes. He'd heard the voice again.

Find her.

He'd heard it several times since he and Caleb had arrived at the hideout, whispered in his ear by some unseen presence just before sleep. He'd imagined it was just his guilty conscience talking, but this time he'd actually been pulled from a bad dream.

He chuckled. *Find her?* She was just a girl! And what was he supposed to do, bring her here?

One thing is needful.

Nathan angrily jammed the revolver back in its holster. His conscience was awfully loud tonight. He lay back down and laced his fingers over his stomach.

He'd never be able to sleep now.

The Good Shepherd's Home
Kansas City, Missouri
1867

"And we all fall . . . down!" Samantha plopped to the grass, pulling four giggling toddlers with her.

"Again! Again!" The small bodies hurtled against her to strengthen their persuasion.

Samantha gathered them all in her arms, inhaling the sweet scent of their hair as she let them push her all the way to the ground. "My, what a bunch of wild puppies I have here!" Laughing, she crooked her fingers and burrowed them in soft tummies.

"That tickles!" Suzanna laughed, tumbling over James and Carolyn in her exuberance.

"Careful! Watch out for Aaron." Samantha scooped the two-year-old up in her arms, out of the path of the older children. Secretly, he was her favorite, having been with her since the day they'd found him on the doorstep in a basket. Sally had wanted to call him Moses, but Samantha and Mrs. Matlock had persuaded her to settle on Aaron.

"Mama?" He tugged a fistful of Samantha's hair, turning clear blue eyes to her own.

"Mama, yes!" she whispered, pressing his head against her breast. Her heart swelled with joy. Aaron even had hair as blond as her own. She loved all the children dearly, but the little boy seemed to have dropped out of heaven just for her to love. He'd filled her anxious days while she waited for word from Nathan and Caleb. The war had been over for two years, but she stubbornly held out hope that they would return for her.

Since that awful night they'd abandoned her, Mrs. Matlock had fed her, clothed her, but most of all loved her unconditionally. Samantha and Sally had become best friends, and last year when they both turned sixteen, they agreed to stay on as teachers. Mrs. Matlock promised they would always have a home at the Good Shepherd's.

"More pway! More pway!" Aaron tugged her hair again.

"Yes, Miss 'Mantha!" Carolyn clamored. "The rosie game!"

"All right!" Samantha laughed, gently brushing off children to rise. "Let's practice counting, then we'll say the rhyming words. One . . . two . . . three . . ."

"Four's next, isn't it?" A male voice laughed.

The children giggled. Samantha whirled around, breaking her grasp. "Why, Pastor Jordan!" Her hands flew to her hair, and she frantically tried to rearrange the loosened knot. The handsome young pastor had a stylish middle-aged couple with him.

"Hello, Samantha." Frank Jordan's eyes crinkled at her distress, then he glanced at the house. "Is Mrs. Matlock home?"

"That's him, Winfield," the woman said excitedly, gesturing at the children. "That one there!"

The man followed her gaze. "He is a sturdy-looking fellow."

Samantha froze. Surely they meant James, not Aaron!

"I've brought the mail, Samantha," Frank said, withdrawing several envelopes from his coat pocket. "I know how anxiously you watch for it." He glanced at the house again, this time shyly. "Is Miss Sally here?"

Any other time she would have gently teased him about whether he intended to squire Sally for another year before he asked for her hand. Today she could barely force a smile. "I'll . . . I'll show you all indoors."

Frank looked abashed. "I'm so sorry. I haven't introduced you. Mr. and Mrs. Winfield Barrett, this is Miss Samantha Martin. Miss Martin is one of the children's teachers. Miss Martin, may I present Mr. and Mrs. Winfield Barrett."

"How lovely to meet you, my dear." Mrs. Barrett nodded, and the flowers on her pancake hat gently bobbed. She smoothed her hands against a green silk dress with black piping.

"How d'ya do?" Mr. Barrett squinted at Samantha. "Teacher, you say? You know, Charlotte, we must get a governess for the boy."

"Why, yes, Winfield, what a lovely idea." She glanced at the solemn children, who had clustered around Samantha. "They all seem to love you so."

"I love them too," Samantha whispered, gathering her skirt. "Please follow me, and I'll take you inside to Mrs. Matlock."

Frank rushed to her side, carefully avoiding the toes of the chattering children who clung to her skirt. "The Barretts are here to adopt Aaron," he whispered joyfully.

Samantha halted, and the children giggled at their sudden tumble. Her heart dropped to her toes. "Not Aaron!"

Mrs. Barrett stepped forward. "We'll be changing his name to something more suitable to the Barrett name, a family name, of course. After all, he's only a little boy. He probably doesn't even know what you call him."

"He *does* know his name!" Tears burned the back of Samantha's eyes. "And he loves it here! He loves—!"

"Samantha." Frank laid a gentle hand on her arm. "We've always prayed for families for all the children. The Barretts will give Aaron a lovely home and life. The Lord used you to shape the child's first two years, just as he used Mrs. Matlock to help you. And now we will be thankful for this unexpected blessing."

Samantha bowed her head, tears rushing forward. Could she truly thank God for taking the little boy from her? She felt so wicked, so selfish. She'd always known Aaron wouldn't stay forever, but she'd foolishly allowed herself to love him too deeply, to believe in a future that could never be.

"Let me say good-bye to him here," she whispered.

She dropped to her knees, and the other children squatted around her. "Are we going to play a game, Miss 'Mantha?"

She shook her head, tears clogging her throat. "Not now."

"Come along, children," Frank said. He herded all but Aaron away from Samantha.

Mrs. Barrett looked skeptical. "What's she—?"

"Let the other children show you their game, Mrs. Barrett, so you'll know what to play with Aaron . . . er . . . whatever you decide to call him." Frank's voice faded as he drew the others away.

Samantha turned to the smiling blond-haired boy, who presented her with a wildflower. "Mama!" he said proudly.

"Thank you, darling," she whispered, pressing the

buttercup against her breast. "Give me a hug now, then go inside with Pastor Jordan."

Arms aching, she drew the child into her embrace, breathing deeply to stem her tears. "All things work together for good," she whispered, burying her nose against the soft neck to memorize its baby scent. "All things."

With childish exuberance, Aaron pulled away to search Samantha's face. His own beamed with innocent love. "Mama pway?"

Samantha smiled sadly. "No, but Mama will *pray*. For you, Aaron. Always." She touched his smooth cheek, then turned away to stifle a sob. "Go with Jesus, baby."

She heard footsteps behind her, and Frank called Aaron to the house. A child again instead of a young lady of seventeen, she raced for the orchard to lose herself in the apple trees.

Sinking to the ground among the sickly sweet smell of fallen apples, she wrapped her arms around a solid trunk and sobbed. "Why, Lord? You know I love Aaron, and I want him to have a real family. But why does it hurt so much? If you're with me, why does it hurt at all?"

The mail slipped from her hand, and still weeping, she gathered the envelopes. She sorted through them listlessly and saw no envelope with Caleb's or Nathan's handwriting.

The flame of hope that had burned steadily for two years leaped, wavered, then died, leaving a wispy trail of smoke across her heart. Pa was dead, and Caleb and Nathan weren't coming back for her. She might as well admit the truth. For whatever reason, God had chosen to take her from her family and place her in this orphanage. Maybe for the rest of her life.

Flanked between the two sedate adults, Aaron bounded happily down the steps. Samantha watched from the orchard, swallowing and blinking back a fresh wave of tears. She stared at the buttercup, now wilted in her hand, and let it fall.

Cheyenne, Wyoming

Nathan lifted his half-full glass, groaning as someone banged out a tune on an ancient piano. The twanging competed with the whoops and shouts of the saloon's crowd. Four tables were jammed with gamblers, ruffians, and Union Pacific track-layers. Nathan could barely see through the haze of cigar smoke wafting back to the corner table he and Caleb shared.

Yawning, Nathan glanced at his pocket watch. Ten o'clock. The night was still young. He'd rather be reading, but he didn't want to fall asleep and face the nightmares.

Caleb held his glass in Nathan's direction. "To change. You're right, you've always been right, and you'll always be right."

Nathan touched his glass to Caleb's and smiled smugly. He was finally in charge of his life. "To change."

"More whiskey, mister?"

Leaning back, Nathan smiled rakishly at the girl in the low-cut dress. "Why not?" His head was beginning to swim, but he deserved the pleasurable sensation. He and Caleb both did. They'd just pulled off a successful string of robberies in Nebraska.

The saloon girl smiled, leaning down provocatively as she poured. "You look mighty pleased with yourself. You working on the railroad here?"

Nathan grinned. "Not me." He certainly didn't have to sweat for his money like those poor Irishmen laying the west-ward track for Union Pacific. Cheyenne had sprung up like a weed just to accommodate the railroad, but he and Caleb would only be sticking around long enough to indulge in a few days of pleasure. Then they'd head back up into their mountains. Winter was on its way.

Caleb leaned across the table, clearly impatient. "You in for a hand of cards over there?"

Nathan glanced at the table where a steady game had been running all evening. Of the four men remaining, only the dapper-dressed portly man seemed to be any serious competition. Nathan had become more than proficient at playing the game.

The girl leaned closer, blocking his view. "Things are kinda slow for me right now. Wouldn't you rather sit here with me?"

"Why? Are you any good at poker?" Nathan tossed back his drink.

Caleb pushed back his chair and grabbed his glass. "Do what you want, Nathan. I'll catch up with you later." He ambled toward the gaming table.

The girl smiled, triumphant, and moved a chair closer. She arranged her skirt with a flounce and leaned forward. "So what brings you to Cheyenne?"

Nathan laughed. He hated pretenses. "I suppose you want to hear everything."

"Whatever you think is important, mister."

He talked easily, pouring drinks, telling her everything she wanted to hear but nothing that revealed himself. He told her he had money, but not how he'd acquired it. He wasn't stupid enough to tell her the truth.

The farm boy who'd left Kansas to enlist might have. But then that boy would be back East studying to become a doctor, preparing to take on the world, preparing to take Samantha as his bride. Not sitting in some two-bit saloon with a full glass in front of him and a calico queen beside him.

Find her.

Nathan smothered a laugh. He hadn't heard that voice for so long, he'd figured the stealing, whiskey, and women had killed it. What made him think about Samantha now?

Find her. The voice persisted, much to Nathan's annoyance.

Even if he did succeed, she'd spit in his face. No, the sweet, innocent girl had surely grown into a sweet, lovely young woman with an upstanding husband. She didn't need Caleb or him anymore.

Chuckling out loud, Nathan tipped the bottle.

One thing is needful.

A chill shot down his spine, and he righted the bottle with a thump. "She doesn't need me!" he muttered.

"Hey, aren't you listening? I said your friend's doing well for himself over there."

The girl's voice grated on his nerves, but Nathan smiled broadly. "Sure I'm listening, sweetheart. Have another drink with me."

"I'd rather . . ." She whispered in his ear, then giggled behind her hand.

The coy schoolgirl mannerism irritated Nathan, who jerked to his feet. "Come on then," he said, grabbing her hand. Drinking wasn't the only pleasurable distraction. Forgetting about Samantha was what was needful.

"Slow down, honey. We've—"

"You're cheating!"

At the door, Nathan turned. The dapper poker player

swayed drunkenly, clutching a pointed revolver. Caleb sat across the card table, looking calm.

The other players pushed back their chairs. Nathan tensed and put his hand on the revolver strapped at his hip.

"Nobody's that lucky at cards."

Caleb's eyes narrowed. "It's skill, not luck." He rose slowly, his hands held out to put the other man at ease. If necessary, Caleb could draw his Colt Army revolver fast enough to drill a tossed tin can. Nathan had seen him do it more than once.

"That's a fine-looking Remington you got there," Caleb said evenly. "I'd hate to have to shoot it up. Not to mention your hand might accidentally get nicked. So why don't you just holster that gun, and I'll take my winnings and walk away. Nobody wants any trouble."

The gun trembled in the man's hand. He glanced around the saloon, and his face flushed with embarrassment when he noticed the large crowd watching them. He swallowed. "What about my money?"

"I won it fair and square. Now put the gun away."

The man slowly lowered the gun, and his shoulders sagged.

Nathan relaxed his own hand, relieved. The room bustled to life, the incident forgotten.

Scooping up his money, Caleb caught sight of Nathan and the girl. He grinned and bounded toward them. "So you sweet-talked her—"

The drunken man swung around. Face florid, he raised his gun.

"Caleb!" Nathan drew and leaped forward, knocking his surprised friend out of the way.

Two shots roared, and Nathan saw his own land deep in the man's fleshy gut. He crumpled with a groan.

Nathan felt his own body blow backward, and he smiled at the irony of hearing the voice again today. Where he was headed, he doubted he'd ever find Samantha.

FIVE

"There is a happy land, far far away, where saints in glory stand, bright, bright as day . . ."

Samantha mouthed the words, unable to sing with the others. Tears trailed down her cheeks and splashed the handkerchief she twisted in her lap. Though businessmen, former orphans, and adoptive parents filled nearly every parlor chair, Samantha sat alone on the back row. Up front, Frank and Sally sat close together, sharing a hymnal, expressions far too solemn for a newly married couple in love. Samantha tried to keep her eyes focused on them, but her gaze strayed to the pine box.

Mrs. Matlock. Arms crossed, eyes forever closed, the Good Shepherd's Home matron lay in a coffin surrounded by a cloud of pink and yellow roses.

Her face registered peace and calm, just as it had during her final days when the doctor said her heart was giving out. Mrs. Matlock accepted her impending death with ease, quietly arranging homes or places on the orphan train for the few remaining children. Sally and Samantha nursed her tirelessly, choking back their own tears and grief to offer her solace. As usual, it was she who comforted them.

"The Lord's ready for me," she'd said softly. "You mustn't be sorry, but joyful! Sally, you and the pastor . . . are in love. Don't delay getting . . . married because of me."

"Yes, ma'am," Sally whispered, laying her cheek against the paper-frail hand on the bed. She closed her eyes, shoulders shaking.

"And . . . Samantha."

"I'll be fine." Samantha smiled through her tears. "I'll find my way."

"You can always . . . find your way . . . if you let the shepherd guide you."

Her cloudy eyes sought Samantha's. Samantha touched Mrs. Matlock's cheek and brushed away a tear with her thumb. "Thank you for all you've done," she whispered. "Let the shepherd guide you too. Home, this time."

The hymn concluded, and Frank rose. "Friends, we are here to celebrate the transformation of one of God's children."

Samantha twisted the handkerchief around her fingers to combat her rising sorrow. Had Mrs. Matlock been changed in the twinkling of an eye when she'd died? Had her parents?

And Caleb and Nathan? Where were they? Did they lie in an unmarked grave?

She bent her head over her hands. She heard Frank's voice begin the Twenty-third Psalm, and she squeezed her eyes shut.

"The Lord is my shepherd; I shall not want . . ."

"It was a lovely service," Sally said soothingly, touching Frank's coat sleeve in a wifely gesture. She wore the same black silk, her best dress, that she'd worn to marry Frank only five days ago at Mrs. Matlock's bedside. The dying woman slipped into unconsciousness the next day and never reawakened.

"Yes, it was lovely." Distracted, Samantha bent to retrieve a solitary rose. She fingered the drooping pink petals, crushed under the feet of the pallbearers.

Frank touched her shoulder, concerned. "I'm sorry Sally and I have to leave tomorrow, Samantha, but we need to get the children to Colorado as soon as possible."

"It's all right." Samantha smiled. "I think it's wonderful you're going to adopt the last two little ones. I'll be fine here. Really."

Sally ambled around the room, stopping to rub the thin, ragged draperies between her fingers. "There's not much left to sell, is there?"

"Mrs. Matlock sold everything over the years for the children. They always came first," Samantha said. "Now the house will take care of her last debts."

Sally embraced Samantha fiercely. "Won't you come with us? There'll be so much work on the new farm. And the children—"

Samantha pulled back, smiling. "You don't need a third adult in your new life. Tommy and Maria will be just fine with you as their mama."

"But you don't even have a place to live or a position! It's good of the bank to let you stay here another week, but—"

"God will provide me a new home, Sally. And when I'm there, I'll write and let you know."

"But—"

"I won't have to resort to being a match girl, I'm sure,"

Samantha said. "There must be lots of openings for teachers or governesses!"

After a tearful farewell to Sally, Frank, and the two toddlers, Samantha returned to the empty house, optimistic despite her lingering grief.

She set out the first two days with cheer rising in her heart, only to return with gloom descending. No one needed help in any of the schools or with their children. By the third and fourth days, she even inquired in the seamstress shops, despite her lopsided stitching.

The fifth day, she didn't leave the house at all but spent the day indoors. She tried to pray, but the words weighed down her heart like lead. She was twenty years old with no family. No husband. No position. No place to live.

She drifted aimlessly from room to room, remembering Mrs. Matlock and all the children who had passed through the rundown yet cheerful home. She had held a special place in her heart for the babies. More than anything, her desire was for a real home with a husband and babies of her own.

On the sixth day, she packed her bag. She didn't know where she was headed, but it seemed God wanted her out of Kansas City. She had just adjusted the final strap when the knocker pounded against the front door.

"Oh no!" she whispered. "The bank promised a man wouldn't come around until tomorrow!" She glanced down at the bag, sighing, then settled her black hat and veil in place firmly on top of her head. She wasn't dressed in mourning clothes, but just in case she weakened and cried, she didn't want the banker to see her tears. Grabbing the bag, she descended the stairs.

The knocker pounded again, more insistent.

"Just a minute!" At the bottom of the stairs, she glanced in Mrs. Matlock's old room. She mustn't forget the one possession she would take as a reminder of this home.

The knock resounded, threatening to splinter the already decaying door. Samantha felt impatience rise, and she yanked at the doorknob. "I got here as fast as—"

A tall, muscular man filled the doorway, his hand still poised at the knocker. Samantha's cheek brushed his upraised arm, and she drew back in embarrassment. His hat was pulled down so low over his face that he probably hadn't even seen her. She tried to look at his eyes, but they were hidden in shadows. All she could see was his lower face, covered with what had to be several days' growth of beard.

"I thought this was the orphanage," he said in a gruff voice. "There used to be a sign."

"It is," she said. Did he think the bank had sent him to the wrong address? "The sign fell apart several years ago, but it's still the Good Shepherd's Home. Or at least it was."

Samantha frowned. He certainly didn't dress like a banker. He wore common brown trousers, boots, and a cotton shirt. He didn't even have a jacket or a decent hat—just that disreputable-looking brown felt, pressed western style. And a gun holstered snugly around his hips. Samantha shivered.

But his face. From what she could see, it was handsome and angular. The stranger cleared his throat, and when she looked up, he smiled slow and warm like drizzled syrup over hot cakes. Irritated, she wanted to snatch the hat from his head and study his eyes. She had the funniest feeling he was studying her from head to toe, and she was glad she'd chosen to wear the veil.

"I'm looking for someone who once lived here," he said. "Have you been here a long time?"

"You mean you're not from the bank?"

His mouth quirked. "No, ma'am, I'm not from any bank."

"Then they won't take the house till tomorrow after all." She loosened her hand from the doorknob, then glanced behind her. Straightening, she warily grasped the doorknob again. "I . . . I'd let you in, but I'm the only one . . ."

The stranger stepped closer. "Home?" he murmured.

"Y-yes."

He paused, staring at her for a long, hypnotic moment, then stepped back. Samantha weakened with relief. The man's expression lightened, and his lips curved up in an impish grin. He pushed his hat back on his head, and her heart flipped at the sight of his clear green eyes.

His face clouded, serious. "I'm looking for a girl who lived here about six years ago. She—"

"Nathan?" Samantha whispered, raising her veil.

He stepped back. "Samantha? It's you?"

"Yes. *Yes!*" She smiled and opened her arms. "It's me! How wonderful! How—"

Laughing, Nathan easily lifted her off her feet and whirled her around so fast the hat fell from her head. "Sam!"

Sam. Warm with pleasure, she gazed down at him. Their eyes locked, and a magnetism passed between them, firing a path to her stomach. Nathan lowered her slowly, then set her carefully at arm's length.

Samantha clutched the door for support. Why wouldn't he look away? "I . . . I can't ask you in," she said, gesturing inside the house by way of apology.

"Then stay out here."

Samantha accepted his hand to sit on the steps. She fluffed her skirt, gaining a few moments to collect her thoughts and slow her pounding heart.

She turned to find his eyes trained on her. How grown-up he looked, and how handsome. His parents would have been so proud.

Her eyes misted, lowering.

"Have you been all right?" he said, then added, "Are you happy? Are you married?"

"No, I'm not married. I've always lived here. The matron recently died."

"And the bank is taking the house?"

"Yes, and I'm the last one left. I don't have any place to go or even a job."

Nathan took her hand. "Caleb and I want you to live with us."

Her heart pounded. "Caleb's alive?"

"Yes, we both live—"

Samantha clasped her hands together. "Oh, thank you, Lord! Thank you! Your works are indeed marvelous!"

Nathan's eyes hardened, and his face twisted with scorn. She shrank from his gaze, the blast of contempt as stinging as a dust storm. Seeing that he had offended her, he relaxed and touched her hands in a conciliatory gesture. "We live in the foothills of the Wind River Mountains," he said softly.

Samantha breathed a silent prayer of thanks for the conversation's safer ground. "Where's that?"

"Western Wyoming Territory. It's beautiful country, though it does get mighty cold in winter."

"What do you do there?"

"We have a small . . . ranch." His gaze flickered away then

met hers, and he smiled cynically. "It's not very large, but it keeps us alive."

She crossed her arms and nodded at the holster. "Does the gun keep you alive too?"

"It has so far."

A buckboard and team rumbled past, the middle-aged, unkempt driver swearing colorfully as he sawed on the reins. "Watch out there, you—"

Samantha felt her cheeks heat. Out of the corner of her eye, she saw Nathan smile.

"—you good-for-nothing louts! I ought to—"

The driver saw Samantha, and his face reddened. He pulled harder on the reins to slow the team. He lifted his hat, raining down a shower of dirt. "Begging your pardon, Miss Martin. I didn't realize you were about."

"It's all right, Mr. Walker." She nodded with her best teacher's posture. "But in the future, I hope you'll remember to keep a wholesome tongue."

He bobbed his head vigorously. "Oh yes, ma'am!" He snapped the reins. "Gee-up there you . . . critters!"

The wagon rolled out of sight, leaving a cloud of dust. Nathan stared after it, then turned, his smile still lingering. "Does the whole town bow when they walk by?"

Samantha's face warmed. "Nobody bows to me. I'm just a teacher."

Nathan shifted closer. "A teacher of what?"

His green eyes glinted, and Samantha felt their pull, their tug at forgotten heartstrings. "A . . . a teacher of children."

His hands covered hers. "I remember when we were children," he whispered.

Samantha drew a deep breath, easing her hands from his.

The old grief knifed her heart, opening the scar she'd thought healed. "Were we children when you said you wanted to marry me, then abandoned me here?"

Nathan's face hardened. "Yes, Samantha," he said tightly. "Children. Just kids. A lot has happened since then."

Samantha's heart sank. Why had she brought it up? Did she think he'd come all this way to apologize? She thought she'd forgiven him and Caleb, but the pain was as fresh as the day they'd left. "Yes, a lot has happened," she said bitterly.

His expression relaxed. "So you'll go with me? I . . . Caleb wants you."

"Seems to me he could have come himself. It won't be very proper for us to travel together, alone."

Nathan cleared his throat. "Caleb had some business to take care of with the ranch. And as for you and me, you have my word not to . . . behave dishonorably."

Samantha swallowed. Nathan's presence brought back other memories too. "I trusted you in the past. Should I trust you again?"

"Should I help you pack, or do you want to do it yourself?" He grinned and rose to open the door.

Her face flushed with the slow heat of annoyance. How had she ever been infatuated with this cocky person? She'd been worried about him and her brother for six long years, and suddenly they deigned to let her back into their lives. He'd come all the way from Wyoming, confident she wouldn't say no! "My bag is ready," she said through clenched teeth.

He stepped through the doorway, but she brushed past him. "I'll get it."

Amused at her anger, Nathan smiled. "I'll wait here, teacher," he said, then shut the door behind her.

Samantha's steps pounded against the wood floor and echoed off the bare walls. *Forgive . . . Forgive . . .*

"How?" she seethed, raising her face heavenward. "I can't forget what he and Caleb did. Nathan hasn't even apologized!"

She climbed the stairs, her hand curving familiarly around the scarred balustrade. So many memories. The girls' room, where she had first met Sally. The big boys' room, where Charlie Alton had ruled until he went west on the orphan train. The younger boys' room, where she had tucked little Aaron into bed every night for two years.

A tear slid down her cheek. Sweet Aaron. He must be five by now. She didn't even know if he still lived in Kansas City. Did he remember her?

She descended the stairs, her heart heavy. She passed through the kitchen, remembering its warmth on winter nights, the dining room, where so many had shared meals scant in fare but rich with love.

Mrs. Matlock's room.

Samantha leaned against the doorjamb. For years Mrs. Matlock had promised to replace the sagging wallpaper, but she always found better use for the money. The air clung, cloying and stale, the closed windows still holding in the smell of death. With the furniture sold the day after Mrs. Matlock's death to pay for funeral expenses, the worn rug and draperies seemed lonely and forlorn.

Bravely gracing the dingy wall was a small, solitary picture, a simple charcoal drawing of Jesus carrying a perfect lamb. Although darkness threatened the two, bright light glowed around them like a shield. The lamb looked up with complete adoration at the Lord, whose face was lowered as though whispering reassurances.

Samantha gently touched the frame then lifted it from the wall. The now-exposed wallpaper looked clean and new. She squared her shoulders and headed for the front door and her carpetbag.

Such a light load. An extra pair of stockings and under-clothes, a nightgown, a toothbrush, her Bible, and about five dollars in coins. Nothing more.

She smiled ruefully. She'd come to the home with nothing but the clothes she'd been wearing.

Nathan leaned against a pillar, smoking a cigar. He tossed it in the dirt when he saw her and took the bag from her hands. "This is it?"

Samantha nodded, not trusting her voice. She gripped the picture to stem her tears.

Nathan stared down at her hands and smiled derisively. "Is that the old lady's?"

Samantha felt a wave of anger break upon the shore of compassion, and she reminded herself to give Nathan the same chance God gave her. She angled the picture of master and lamb to Nathan's full view and drew a deep breath. "No," she said with conviction. "The picture's mine."

Six

Nathan pocketed the two train tickets to Denver, then lifted Samantha's meager possessions. "Can you watch these for us while we eat?" he asked the agent.

"Sure thing." The white-haired man beamed, reaching out to accept the bag and drawing. "Right nice picture you got here, mister. Reminds me of when I was a little fellow."

Nathan grimaced inwardly. "Thanks," he mumbled, gripping Samantha's arm. "Come on, let's go eat."

"But Nathan—"

"Your things will be fine!" Why'd she care so much about that awful drawing anyway? He'd seen real oil paintings by master artists in museums.

"I'm not worried," she said. "But you're hurting my arm."

"Sorry." He released her, then cleared his throat. "So where's the best eating in this town?"

"I'm told the place down the street is good, though I've never eaten at a restaurant before." She lowered her voice. "And I hear it's not too expensive."

Nathan smiled inwardly. She was as innocent as he remembered. He was proud that he could show her so many new things. "You won't ever have to worry about money, Samantha. It's not a problem for me and Caleb."

"It's not?" She laughed. "That will take getting used to. It's always been a problem for me, whether on the farm or at the orphanage. But God's always met my needs."

Nathan frowned. The old lady must have filled her head with fantasy nonsense so Samantha wouldn't notice how bad off she really had it. He'd seen the dilapidated orphanage for himself. Had Samantha been blind? Surely she could have found better work elsewhere or at least a husband to take care of her. She'd been pretty as a girl, but she was downright beautiful as a young woman.

He glanced at her out of the corner of his eye. She'd left behind that awful hat and veil, and her blond hair was pulled into a demure, upswept style. Was it still as silky when it flowed down her back? It must be even softer now. Her bodice and skirt didn't do much to hide her womanly form, either.

Nathan forced himself to turn away. He didn't want a future with her. She was just a friend from his past. He was taking her to her brother for safekeeping.

"I'm not heading all the way back to Kansas City," Caleb had said when Nathan told him of his plans to get Samantha. "Even if we can find the orphanage again, she won't be there. She's twenty by now, Nathan. She's probably married."

Nathan crossed his arms. "And if she's not? How much chance does a woman have on her own? What if she's had to work in a saloon? Or a crib?"

"My sister wouldn't do that!"

"She would if she was hungry. Or homeless. Would you have thought years ago that your description would be on a 'wanted' poster?"

Caleb's face darkened. "And what happens to you if you get arrested between here and Kansas City?"

"It's a chance I'm willing to take."

"Here's the restaurant." Samantha stopped beside a picture window that read River City Café.

Nathan politely opened the door and let her pass through, then tucked her hand into the crook of his elbow. She glanced up with surprise but let him guide her through the maze of tables. Conversational hum filled the air.

Diners crowded the café, and several glanced up as Samantha and Nathan passed. He smiled broadly, as if showing off his new bride. At the only available table, he grandly pulled out her chair and then seated himself at her left.

Their eyes met, and for a moment he saw an intense sparkle, as though he had seen straight to a diamond soul. She drew a deep breath, then blinked.

Bewildered, he searched her eyes again. They were the same brilliant blue, but they were now maddeningly unfathomable. A curious magnetism coursed through him, but he mentally shook it off. How ridiculous. He wasn't a callow youth anymore.

He straightened in his chair, catching sight of a businessman at the next table. The man eyed Samantha with rapt attention, his stare open and frank.

Nathan's chest filled with anger, but he carefully held a benign expression. "Something I can do for you?" he said calmly. Coldly. Under the table, he brushed the butt of his gun in its holster. Samantha sensed the movement and looked up, startled.

A knowing smile lit the man's face. "Just admiring the scenery," he drawled, his voice low enough for only Nathan and Samantha to hear.

Nathan started to rise, but he felt a hand on his arm. "It's all right. It doesn't bother me," Samantha whispered.

He turned toward her, a myriad of bitter, violent emotions rolling through him in heated waves. She winced and drew back. "W-we can leave."

"No. We need to eat," Nathan said, angered by her timidity. Did she think he'd let this namby-pamby ogle her? Maybe she thought he couldn't protect her.

The man watched the by-play, obviously amused. Nathan's nerves went as cold as a pump handle in winter. "You owe my wife an apology, mister." He slowly drew his gun and steadied it on his thigh, hidden under the tablecloth. He aimed the barrel straight at the stranger then cocked the hammer.

The man's smile faded. His eyes widened then were hidden by his menu. "S-sorry," he muttered, "I didn't mean any harm."

Nathan uncocked the hammer and replaced the gun in his holster. He gave the cowed man one final cold stare, then glanced triumphantly at Samantha. To his surprise, she glared at him. "That wasn't necessary!" she whispered.

"He insulted you."

"Do you think I've never been stared at? You threatened his life!"

How could she be so ignorant of the world's ways? Threaten or be threatened. Kill or be killed. "I didn't hurt him."

"Did you have to lie to him too?" Her mouth quivered. "I'm not your wife!"

Calmer now, Nathan smiled. "Cheer up. Maybe he'll be on our train, and we can set him straight."

"How? Would you take him out between the cars and shoot him?"

Nathan laughed. She looked so indignant, so self-righteous. The powerful rush of victory made him heady. He had protected her; she was safe. "You read too many dime novels, Samantha. He won't bother you again."

Samantha frowned, and Nathan triumphantly turned to the approaching waiter to order.

The stranger wasn't on the train. With a sigh of relief, Samantha settled into a seat at the back of a car. Nathan dropped her bag and picture carelessly on the floor, then tossed the saddlebags he'd retrieved from the livery stable onto the seat. He sat on the far side, then opened a pouch and pulled out two books. He handed her a clean leather volume.

She lifted her eyebrows. "Do you make it a habit to read while you're traveling?"

"Whenever I can, teacher." Smiling playfully, he winked. "How else am I supposed to better myself?"

"I should think your learning days were over long ago."

His smile faded. "A love of books is the only legacy I seem to have from my father."

Samantha's heart tightened in her chest. She missed Mr. Hamilton almost as much as she missed her own father. For six years, she hadn't shared her grief with anyone—not even Sally, her closest friend.

"Go ahead." Nathan gestured at her book. "It's a long trip, and it's a good story. Written by a fellow named Dickens."

"A Tale of Two Cities?"

"It's about the French Revolution."

"Seems to me there's been enough about wars lately," she said. "Can't we talk for a while? Tell me what you and Caleb have been doing these past six years. Tell me about your ranch."

Nathan smiled patiently, as though she would be slow to understand anything he had to say. "It's a long trip, Samantha, and frankly, I'm tired. We'll have plenty of time to talk."

"But—" she began, then fell silent. Nathan had already started reading the first page of his own book. Sighing, she opened the cover and was soon immersed in the novel.

Nathan was right about the trip's length. Thank goodness he had brought the books to pass the time. The story *was* entertaining. Finally, to rest her eyes, she closed the book. Night had fallen, and she could barely make out Kansas wheat rippling in unison as the train sped past.

Would Nathan really have shot that man? Just for her honor? He had changed so much from the gentle boy she'd once known.

She closed her eyes, her worries eased by the train's rocking motion, the novelty of speed. The whistle blasted, and she smiled. So many times she had accompanied children to the train station to tell them good-bye. She'd bidden farewell to Sally, Frank, Tommy, and Maria there, too, but now it was her turn. God had answered her prayer and given her a home.

Before leaving Kansas City, she had written Sally a brief letter of explanation. Nathan had been evasive about a return address, but he finally, grudgingly, said that Samantha could probably receive a letter mailed in care of the post office at South Pass City. The mining town was close to his and Caleb's ranch.

Samantha opened her eyes, vaguely unnerved. For reassurance, she strained in the dark to catch a glimpse of the locomotive around the curves in the track ahead. Unsuccessful, she gave up. Sally would probably say her efforts were as fruitless as struggling to constantly see God.

"Faith is the evidence of things not seen," her friend would no doubt scold.

A smile tugged at Samantha's lips. Someday maybe she would have a trust as deep as Sally's. It had only been a few days since they'd seen each other, but already Samantha missed her.

"You've never been on a train before."

Nathan's voice startled her, and she turned. His book lay closed across his lap, and he'd stretched his legs out under the seat in front of them. He looked calm, relaxed. In spite of the grown-up gun, he seemed more like the childhood hero she'd always admired.

She drew a deep breath. "H-how'd you know?"

"Your eyes," he said. "They look the same as they did whenever you discovered something new. Remember when I showed you the bunnies' nest?"

She smiled. "I was so excited. You actually asked me to help you take care of them."

"They drowned anyway."

His expression hardened, as though he was sorry he'd brought up the subject. Maybe he was also sorry he'd come for her. She cleared her throat and gestured at the book he'd given her. "Your Mr. Dickens is new to me. He's a wonderful writer."

"Just wait until the end. I'll bet my Sunday hat you'll be weeping on the pages."

"Oh, don't tell me what happens!" Thankfully the conversation had taken a safer tack. "And I try not to get too sentimental. It hurts too much."

Nathan raised his eyebrows. Unwavering, his gaze fixed on hers, his soft green eyes veiled in layers of secrets, of unaccounted-for time. He owed her an explanation, but she was afraid to ask. Those secrets might be deliberately cornered and best left hidden by cobwebs of silence.

He cocked his head as though studying her. A spark caught in her heart, flickering between extinguishment and flame. She felt cornered herself, and she realized she had entrusted her life to this man she wasn't even certain she knew anymore.

"We go back a long way," she said, then hurried to cover the foolish statement. "I mean, you were always my big brother's best friend."

He smiled slowly. "And you'll always be his kid sister."

Samantha chafed at the reminder. No doubt Nathan was trying to put her in her place. "I'm a woman now. I grew up quickly while you two were playing soldiers. I don't think I would have survived without faith."

Something flickered in his expression as though she'd physically struck him. She thought for a moment that she saw raw pain in his eyes, but the veil dropped quickly back into place. "I'm glad to hear you're still on the straight and narrow. You're wrong about the soldiering though. Caleb fought, but I was just a medic. All I did was help in the field hospital and transport wounded."

"Someone must have taught you how to use a gun. You looked like you knew what you were doing back at the restaurant!"

To her surprise, he grinned. "I don't recall you being so feisty, Sam." He moved closer, his gaze intense. "Pretty, yes, but not outspoken."

Her anger dissipated. *Pretty?* She nervously licked her lips, and his gaze dropped to her mouth. She started to move away, but he gently gripped her arms. "I always wanted to know," he murmured, then bent his head.

Her heart pounded wildly, and she instinctively closed her eyes. She felt his mouth slant over hers, and she trembled. "You've never been kissed before either," she heard him say softly, then he kissed her again.

Lightheaded, she couldn't breathe, but it didn't seem to matter. She'd always wanted to know what it was like to kiss him too.

"Samantha, we have to get off this train," he said softly.

"Wh-what?" Disoriented, she felt her heart thump and was surprised to find it still beating.

"I saw a man wearing a tan hat and vest come in this car," Nathan whispered. "Open your eyes and look over my shoulder. Tell me if he's looking at us."

Puzzled, she did as he asked. At the head of the car, the man Nathan had described obliviously studied a newspaper. Several nearby passengers stared at her and Nathan, shocked at their open affection.

Mortified at her behavior, she ducked her head. "No, he's not looking," she whispered.

Nathan quickly released her, then gathered the books and saddlebags. "Let's go," he said, quietly rising.

He was already halfway through the door before she rose, bewildered, then turned back. "Wait! My bag! My picture!"

Nathan stopped, looking annoyed and impatient while she snatched up her only possessions, then took off again. She hurried to keep up, following him out between the cars and through three more to the observation platform at the end of the train.

Nathan closed the door, and Samantha clung to the

handrail of the jostling train. Dizzy, she tried not to look down at the rushing land. Her stomach lurched. Iron wheels grated against iron rails. "Isn't this dangerous?" she shouted above the din.

"You don't know just how much," Nathan said absently. He moved from side to side, leaning out and scanning the darkness. "We can't stay on this train. That man had on a sheriff's badge. The law thinks I've done something wrong."

"What, Nathan? Can't you—"

"No, I can't!"

Shocked, Samantha drew back. "I . . . I don't understand." She'd never seen anyone look so nervous. Nathan was acting as if his life were in danger.

Face tense, he gripped her shoulders. "I kissed you so he wouldn't see my face. I don't think he did, but—"

"You what?" She jerked away, humiliated. How could she have thought she meant anything to him? How could she have behaved like such a wanton fool?

"You can call me whatever you want, or slap me, but do it later. We've got to get off this train." He shoved the books in the saddlebags and slung them over one shoulder, then took the bag from her hand.

Samantha's anger shoved her embarrassment aside. "I suppose it'll automatically stop just because we want to get off?"

"No, we have to jump." He propelled her to the steps. "And we don't have much time. Someone will find us soon."

"This isn't funny, Nathan!" She clung to the rail, but he placed a firm hand on her back.

"Hold on tight to that fool picture. You're going first so I can be sure you make it."

"Make it?" He was serious!

He pried her hands from the rail. "Jump clear of the train and don't try to land on your feet," he said. "The train's slowed down at this grade, so when I say 'three,' jump."

The whistle bellowed. Terrified, Samantha jerked back. "No!" She lurched for the rail, but with her hands full, she missed. Nathan steadied her, then led her to the top step again. "One."

"Nathan, no!" She turned, but he was studying the rushing ground. Her head swam, and her stomach rolled.

"Two." He braced his hand against her back, and reading her fear, grinned rakishly. "You can do it! Where's my tomboy?"

Stunned, she felt her jaw drop. *Tomboy?* Is that how he still thought of her?

"Three! Jump clear!"

Screaming, she lunged away from his hand and instinctively curled into a ball. She hit and rolled down the gentle grassy incline, protecting the picture against her body. The train roared past into the night, and she bumped to a stop.

Samantha lay still long enough to mumble a thankful prayer, then rose slowly. Good. No broken bones. But her dress . . . She clucked her tongue as she brushed away dirt and grass. Examining the picture, she grinned. It was clean as ever.

Nathan strode back toward her, hands in pockets, whistling as though he jumped from trains every day.

She straightened, infuriated. Mrs. Matlock had taught her that a young lady—especially a Christian young lady—should never lose her temper. But Mrs. Matlock had never met Nathan Hamilton.

Samantha jammed her fists on her hips. Grass shook from

her hair and landed on her dirt-smudged dress. "Why did you make me do that? What kind of trouble are you in that—"

Nathan put two fingers on her lips and laughed. How he could be amused was beyond her, but the sound of his humor was vaguely reassuring.

"You did fine." His eyes twinkled. "I knew my tomboy was still underneath all those petticoats and ladylike manners. You always were able to keep up with me."

His words broke the last of her resistance. "I . . . I was?" she said, secretly pleased.

He nodded, his gaze intent even in the darkness.

A wolf howled in the distance. Shivering, Samantha glanced around them. The flat landscape was eerie and barren. A gust of wind soughed through the branches of a lone oak, and she edged closer to Nathan. He wrapped his arm around her shoulders, and she felt safer. Even if she was inexplicably disappointed that he saw her as no more than a hoyden. "What do we do now?" she muttered.

"We walk," he surprised her by saying—she hadn't realized she'd spoken aloud. "It's a beautiful night. The moon's full. We should come to a town before long. From there we'll travel by horseback. It'll take longer to get to Wyoming, but it's safer. Caleb and I are in the middle of some messy legal business about our ranch. I didn't want you to get involved."

She wanted to ask more, but she was too tired and irritated to listen to any long-winded legal stories. It was probably just something to do with water rights or something else she undoubtedly wouldn't be able to comprehend. Nathan and Caleb would settle any business problems they had. They were too smart to let things get out of hand.

They walked nearly a mile before either spoke. "No complaints?" Nathan finally said, teasing. "No accusations?"

She shook her head. If anything, she should apologize for her outburst, but she didn't have the strength. Surely the Lord wouldn't mind if she waited until she'd had a good night's sleep. Nathan certainly wasn't offering any apologies.

"I didn't mean anything by the kiss, Sam. It was all I could think of at the time. It won't happen again."

Samantha could hear the detachment in his voice, and she chided herself again for her foolish reaction to his kiss. She wasn't a girl still harboring a crush. He wasn't a boy anymore, either; he was a man.

She squared her shoulders. She'd gotten along without him for the past six years, and she could carry on for another sixty. "If you didn't mean anything, and you promise it won't happen again, then I forgive you," she finally said grudgingly.

They walked in silence under the wide moon, their feet crunching the budding spring grass.

SEVEN

A midnight breeze gently billowed the lace curtains at the hotel room window, and the moon washed a pale slant across Nathan's bed. He lay on his back, fists clenched at his side, struggling to forget that Samantha slept just beyond the far wall.

Tired and footsore, they had tramped for hours, each avoiding further mention of what had happened between them on the train. Once Nathan paid for their rooms, Samantha clutched her bag and picture, standing back while he unlocked her door. She glanced nervously at him, then the room, then murmured a hasty good-night. Nathan stood motionless in the hallway, watching until she firmly shut the door. Since then he hadn't been able to think of anything but her.

At last sleep overtook him, but his dreams were as fitful as consciousness. Back in battle, he ran, stooped, and lifted wounded men, moving them to the first-aid station just behind the front line. Screams issued from raw throats; men called for their mothers; the dying pleaded for help. The feel and smell of smoke and blood thickened the air and his hands as he scrambled from one downed man to another. This one could walk; this one needed a stretcher; this one was dead.

"Somebody help me!"

"It hurts! My leg!"

Nathan steadfastly avoided their eyes. He could only help one man at a time. It was like trying to fill a broken bottle with water. On and on and on . . .

Suddenly he was running through a train, chased by some unseen, dark figure. If he reached the last car, he could jump off and escape. But the train was long, and he couldn't see past the blurry, stoic faces of the passengers.

At last he threw the final door open and was poised to jump. The phantom closed the distance and laid a bony hand on his arm. Curiosity overriding fear, Nathan turned. Filmy blue material swathed the specter's face, and the skeletal hand on Nathan's arm tightened.

"Please . . . kill . . . me."

The hand pulled back its blue veil, and where its face should have been was a gaping void. A scream lodged in Nathan's throat. He elbowed the creature in the stomach and flung himself from the train, trying to remember to jump clear. He tumbled through a cold mist, over . . . over . . . over . . .

"No!" He knew he was screaming, even thrashing, but he couldn't make himself wake up. *"No!"*

He shuddered once more, then jerked upright, panting. "No!" he whispered again to dispel the last of the nightmare.

His chest heaved, and his fists clutched the sheet in two tight balls. His feet had kicked the linen from its mooring at the foot of the bed. Sweat covered his body. He threw his head back and tried to calm himself by breathing deeply, but it didn't work.

Why had he bothered to come for Samantha? He didn't need the added distraction of protecting her. She wasn't some cheap woman he could buy with money; she was a lady! A lady who believed in God and every moral stricture he imposed.

He rose from the bed and braced his elbows against the window. His breathing came slower now. Silent, the town apparently slept in peaceful, contented slumber. He wanted that peace or at least one good night's sleep. He hadn't slept for more than a few hours at a time since he was sixteen years old.

Samantha was just next door, just beyond her open window. He thought about the kiss they'd shared on the train. He'd felt her response to his kiss; she might be innocent, but she wasn't cold. And she was only an open window away. He could . . .

Nathan closed his eyes, exhaling a long breath. What was he thinking? Had he fallen so far?

He turned, but his eye caught the movement of curtains at her window. He thought he saw a white sleeve pull back, and his heart pounded. Had she heard him cry out in his sleep?

He climbed into bed and pulled the covers up over his sweat-soaked body. He cursed, rolling onto his side.

What would she do when she found out what he and Caleb really did for a living? He wasn't sure he could avoid telling her much longer. Maybe he should just get it over with, then give her money to go somewhere else.

He tensed, rebelling at the idea. He'd made a lot of mistakes, and this was the only one he could right. What he'd once abandoned, he must now protect. She was such an innocent, just like the newborn lamb or the bunnies. He couldn't let her drown in the world's cesspool. Somehow he would make her see that what he and Caleb did was acceptable, that they didn't hurt anyone.

He didn't expect to gain her blessing; her religious beliefs wouldn't allow it. He could still recite the Ten Commandments by heart, even the eighth one. But surely she would understand once she heard the entire story. All he had to do was get her to the hideout first.

Nathan sighed, his body relaxing. Somehow he'd make her see the truth.

Samantha was dressed and ready when Nathan knocked on her door to take her to breakfast. He had dark smudges under his eyes but made no mention of his apparent nightmare. She had been awake herself, rocking by the window, when she'd heard him scream. Cherished memories had intruded on her sleep. What had disturbed Nathan's?

He seated her at the dining room table, pulling out a chair and smiling as though nothing unusual had happened. She breathed a silent prayer of thanks that he apparently hadn't seen her at the window, listening and praying. She'd wanted to go to him and hold him as she used to hold the little ones when they were scared at night. But Nathan didn't need her; he was a grown man. So she'd prayed instead that he would feel the Lord's loving arms and find peace.

After they ate what he warned might be their last good meal before reaching the ranch, they crossed the dusty street to the general store. At Nathan's direction, Samantha picked out a hat, a riding skirt, and a pair of boots for the trail. She had no illusions about the trip—it would be long and hard— but she sensed God's encouragement.

Nathan gazed longingly at several leather-bound books before he paid for the supplies. A final stop at the livery stable for horses and saddles, and he received in change what he announced were his last two dollars.

She stared at the two coins in his open palm. "I thought you said money wasn't a problem."

"It's not," he said cheerfully. "Once we get to the ranch, there'll be more."

She watched him pocket the money. He was certainly cocky, considering that the success of ranching depended on the condition of the stock and the weather. She narrowed her eyes. "What do you raise at this ranch of yours?"

He grinned rakishly, pushing his hat to the back of his head. "We raise whatever will get us the most money. Say, tenderfoot, we'll have to camp out every night. Can you manage that?"

"Of course!" She wouldn't admit it even if she couldn't.

He grinned, then checked their packs one final time. "How long has it been since you last rode?"

"About six years."

Nathan shook his head, teasing. "And you used to ride like the wind. It'll come back to you, but you'll probably be sore for a few days."

"Then I guess we'd better get started." Miffed that he thought her less than up to the task, she ignored his outstretched hand and mounted by herself.

Samantha patted the carpetbag strapped to her saddle. She'd discovered that if she rearranged the bag's contents, she could just squeeze the picture inside.

Nathan gently slapped his reins, and her heart racing,

Samantha followed his lead down the street and out onto open land.

Nathan's warning proved accurate, for Samantha's body protested after only a few hours, and her legs were nearly numb. When they stopped to rest, she didn't refuse his help dismounting. By the end of the day, she could barely gather firewood while Nathan watered, fed, and hobbled the horses.

The evening meal consisted of bacon, beans, and coffee. After she cleaned the few tin dishes, Samantha eased herself gingerly onto an outspread blanket by the fire, groaning. She closed her eyes for sleep, then opened them warily.

Nathan spoke out of the darkness across the fire. "I'll sleep over here," he said. "Call out if you hear anything. I'm near enough in case anything happens."

"Like what?" she murmured, drowsy. She trusted Nathan to keep her safe.

"Like Indians or wanderers." He paused. "Or outlaws."

She rolled over. A flame crackled high in the air, momentarily illuminating Nathan's form. Propped on one elbow, he lay stretched out on his blanket, studying her. His handsome face looked so serious that she shivered. Did he think something would happen to them?

"Go to sleep, Samantha," he said in a husky voice.

Obediently closing her eyes, she sighed. Within minutes she drifted from consciousness, never knowing how long he lay awake watching her sleep.

For weeks they traveled, stopping as little as possible during the day. Nathan warned that they didn't want to get caught in a late blizzard, and he constantly scanned the sky for signs of bad weather.

To Samantha the plains stretched forever as she and Nathan headed up through Nebraska. Finally one morning she saw lumps on the horizon that by the end of the day she could see were distant mountains. Nathan smiled indulgently at her childlike excitement over the first mountains she'd ever seen and promised he would soon show them to her up close.

Then at last they were in Wyoming Territory. They kept to the North Platte River but avoided all towns. Even at night they camped well away. But if the wind was right, Samantha could sometimes hear the sounds of music and laughter as she lay on her bedroll. Nathan said the towns were too rowdy for a lady, but she longed for even an hour's companionship with fellow believers.

So intent were they on riding that she and Nathan didn't talk much during the day. But when they stopped to water the horses, or at night when they stopped to sleep, Nathan talked plenty. Mostly he asked questions about what she'd been doing the last six years. Samantha loved to talk about the orphanage—Mrs. Matlock, Sally, Frank, the children.

Nathan revealed little about what he had done during their six-year separation even though she asked numerous questions—Where had he and Caleb served in the army? What did they do afterward? How did they acquire the mysterious ranch?

Nathan would smile knowingly and answer briefly, if at all, then he would talk about some of the places he and Caleb had been—Arizona, San Francisco, even Mexico. She forgot her questions and listened, enthralled by the stories he told.

He might not be the doctor he'd always planned to be, but he had certainly seen something of the world.

Yet at times she would catch him staring into the campfire, his expression hard and strained as though he were remembering things he'd rather forget. Once she came upon him so suddenly that he drew his gun before he realized who it was. He sheepishly put the gun away, but not before she'd seen the terror in his eyes.

The weather had remained warm and dry, but one day when they were following the Sweetwater River through the Green Mountains, a spring storm suddenly caught them. Rain drove down in blinding sheets, each drop a cold pellet. Miserable, Samantha and Nathan rode for hours with their heads down. Water dripped in a cascade around their hat brims, soaking through oilskin ponchos and plastering their clothes against their bodies.

The wind effortlessly whipped the heavy rain, and lightning and thunder competed like two school bullies. For the umpteenth time, Samantha tightened the reins of her skittish mare. Her arms and legs ached, and her head pounded from the force of the rain. She had wearily raised her face, when she spotted a cabin tucked back in the pines.

She cupped her hands around her mouth and shouted with all the energy she had left. "Nathan!"

He rode closer, and she pointed, too tired to speak. He nodded and urged his horse forward.

The cabin was in good condition, but Samantha could see tattered curtains at the two windows flanking the door. Nathan tethered the horses and grabbed their saddlebags, then stepped boldly onto the rickety porch. Samantha followed timidly behind.

Nathan pushed the door, and it swung open with a loud creak. "I didn't think anyone was here," he said. "Anybody in his right mind would have met us with a shotgun."

Samantha closed the door, leaving the noise of the rain behind. The quiet and coolness of the cabin was soothing. She stood just inside, letting her eyes adjust to the darkness. Nathan found a candle and dry matches, and he inspected their place of refuge.

The small one-room dwelling held a stone fireplace, a table, a spinning wheel, and a dry sink. Made up with a Star of Bethlehem quilt, a double bed stood in one corner. Between the bed and the wall was a small cradle.

"Someone must live here," Samantha said with a smile.

Nathan ran a finger over the top of the spinning wheel, then shook off the dust. "No, they've moved on. We should be safe. I'll put up the horses in the shed and see what we can do about a fire. We may have to use the furniture."

Shivering, Samantha swallowed a protest. She'd hate to burn the cradle, but her teeth were chattering uncontrollably. She removed her drenched hat and poncho to heap beside the saddlebags Nathan had dropped by the door. They hadn't eaten all day, and her stomach growled. A quick search of the saddlebags turned up the jerky, which she laid on the table. She would wait for Nathan.

Trying to keep warm, she hugged herself and paced the cabin. Maybe she could find something small to break up for kindling.

Everything seemed to be in its place, as though the occupants might return any time. The dry sink held neatly stacked dishes, and a rocking chair was pulled up to the fireplace. A tin bathtub stood in one corner, a straw broom in another.

Samantha grabbed its handle and swept debris into the fireplace and batted cobwebs from the ceiling.

In the far corner, she saw a narrow ladder, a stairway to a loft that they'd missed in the darkness. She climbed hesitantly, almost afraid she would find someone cowering upstairs. The room was even more empty and dusty than downstairs, holding only two small, stripped beds and a badly chipped porcelain pitcher and basin.

Samantha leaned against the doorway, her heart aching with loneliness. What would it be like to have a family again? What if this were her and Nathan's cabin, these beds their children's? She could picture tucking them in at night and hearing their childish prayers. Then she and Nathan would sit by the fire until bedtime.

Smiling wistfully, she carefully descended the ladder. She had almost forgotten the warm security of her family. Ma and Pa's love had been so strong, their faith so rock-solid. When they'd first moved to Kansas, they had lived in a one-room cabin much like this one. Samantha could see now that the surroundings didn't matter as much as the love of the family it held. Maybe someday she'd have a family of her own . . . a loving husband . . . babies.

She caught sight of the cradle, and her heart thumped. What was the sense of dreaming? She wasn't married and probably never would be.

The door banged against the wall, and Samantha started as wind and rain immediately invaded the dry calm of the cabin. Nathan's arms were loaded down with wood, and he struggled to hold the door open with the toe of his boot. He breathed heavily from hurrying in the rain, and water dripped in a pool at his feet.

Samantha rushed to shut the door. She took an armload of wood and followed him to the hearth, where they dropped their loads with a clatter. Nathan ripped off his soaked hat, poncho, and gloves, then squatted to stack three large logs under the black kettle hanging in the fireplace. "I found this wood in the shed."

Samantha knelt beside him, her teeth chattering anew from the cold he'd let in. Wet, dirty, and miserable, she felt like a hound dog abandoned to the elements. What she wouldn't give for a bath and a soft bed.

"There must be some sheets and blankets here for tonight," she murmured to herself.

"Sleep sounds good, but only after I get this fire started." Nathan rearranged the wood, then added smaller branches and twigs. He struck a match and held it close to the kindling, then blew gently. When the sparks caught and spread, he rocked back on his heels. Sighing, he closed his eyes.

Samantha touched his wet sleeve. "Would you like some jerky?"

"Yes." He started to rise, but she moved her hand to his shoulder.

"Sit here. I'll get it." She brought him the food and settled beside him. Studying him covertly, she could see how truly weary he was. He chewed slowly, as though he didn't want to eat but realized he needed the sustenance. Water dripped from his hair down his face and neck, and a dirty line cut across his forehead where his hat had rested.

She pulled her knees to her chest and hugged them tight. Maybe Nathan was sorry he came for her—she'd entertained her own doubts lately.

The fire barely penetrated her wet clothing, and she squirmed in discomfort. Again she laid a hand on his arm. Caught in mid-yawn, he looked up, startled. "Can you help me with a bath?" she said. "I feel like I'm made of mud and rainwater."

He followed her gaze to the tub by the door then rubbed his hand across his two-day-old beard. She could almost hear him cover another yawn. "No, I'm sorry," she stammered. "It's too much to ask. You're already—"

"I'll do it. A bath would feel good to me too." He pushed himself up. "I'll heat the water if you'll make up our beds. You take the loft. It may be colder, but I should sleep down here in case there's trouble."

"I don't mind." She hadn't realized he'd seen the loft.

Nathan set out the tub, then filled and heated buckets and kettles of rainwater. While he worked, Samantha searched until she found sheets and blankets in a cupboard, then went upstairs to make her bed first. She came back down and whacked the dusty straw tick that would be Nathan's bed, grateful for the cabin's bounty, but curious. Why was this abandoned home so well stocked?

Tucking a pillow under her chin, she tugged on a muslin case and idly watched Nathan work. While he waited for the last kettle to heat, he removed his sodden shirt and stacked the remainder of the wood. His undershirt clung to the muscles of his arms and upper body. He flipped back a straggly lock of dark hair, which had grown collar-long since they'd left Kansas City.

Samantha blinked, transfixed. She obviously hadn't realized just how grown-up he was. They may have been together for several weeks, but this was the first time they'd been alone within four walls, the pounding rain only emphasizing their confinement.

As if sensing her gaze, he turned, and for a moment the world receded. He caught and held her glance, the pull between them so warm she felt it as though a flame leaped across the room. The homeyness of the cabin, the intimacy of his stare, stirred her body and heart. He rose, slowly, and she dropped the pillow.

"I'll get cold water to mix with the hot," she mumbled, scurrying for the bucket. She grabbed the handle, but his hands closed over hers.

"The water's not that hot, Sam," he said in a low voice. "We don't need any cold." He lifted the last kettle from its hook and let the warm water slosh into the tub. Gentle steam rose between them.

Samantha lowered her eyes, nervous. She wished now she'd been content to crawl dirty into an upstairs bed. She could feel Nathan studying her from the other side of the steam.

He leaned over and gently rubbed her arms. "You're shaking. The water will warm you."

"I . . . I'm all right." She stepped back, glancing around the room.

Nathan smiled faintly. "I'll wait outside on the porch, then bathe after you're done."

She wrapped her arms around her middle, feeling like a frightened child. Nathan gently touched her cheek. "Trust me, Samantha. I would never force you to do something you didn't want."

She loosened her arms, and Nathan smiled crookedly. "Take your time," he said as he stepped outside.

Samantha breathed a sigh of relief. With a wary eye on the door, she slipped out of her wet clothes and into the water. The warmth was an immediate tonic to her tired body, but her heart was a mass of tangled emotions. Something dark inside Nathan frightened her but at the same time attracted. He'd seen so much, knew so much, beyond the realm of her experience. She had no desire for what the world offered, but she wanted to see it through his eyes, to know what caused him such pain.

Thunder crashed, and she thought of Nathan waiting on the porch. She scrubbed quickly, feeling guilty for making him stand in the rain.

Grateful that for once she wouldn't have to sleep in her clothes, she donned her nightgown. She timidly opened the door a crack and said, "I'm finished," then closed it before she even caught a glimpse of Nathan. With shaking hands, she lit a candle and clambered up to the loft.

In near darkness, she scrambled between the cold covers. Wind gusted through the crumbled chinking and blew out the candle's meager flame. Samantha squeezed her eyes shut. "Thank you for this cabin, Lord, for its protection. Take care of us during the rest of our journey. Please help Nathan—"

The front door opened and closed. Her heart pounded, and she strained to listen. She heard him bathe, dump out the water, check the bolt on the door, and bank the fire.

Then he padded to the bottom of the ladder, and she didn't hear anything at all. Her heart thumped faster.

"Good night, Samantha," he finally said in a deep voice.

"Good night, Nathan." Sighing, she rolled over. She drew a deep, thankful breath and finished her prayer just before she fell asleep. "Please help Nathan find your way."

Blaring bugles and gunfire rose above a sea of blue and gray streaked with red. As always, Nathan clawed through the material, searching.

Then he was pushing Caleb away. "No! Look out!" He heard a roar, and red burst across his own chest. He couldn't move.

"Please . . . kill . . . me."

Guns fired and shells screamed overhead. He lay in the mud, helpless and panting, life seeping away. How long would it take McGregor to find him?

His vision blurred, and he felt himself sink. "No!" He flailed his arms, fighting the darkness, fighting the pit below him filled with moaning souls.

"Please, God . . . kill . . . me."

"No!" He bolted upright in bed, gasping for air.

Lightning cracked overhead. Across the room, firelight danced like a demon. Nathan struggled to breathe, choking, his hands at his throat. He could almost feel clawlike fingers squeezing the life from him.

"I'm . . . awake!" His burning lungs dragged in gulps of air. *"I'm awake!"*

"Nathan?" The tentative voice at the top of the ladder cut through the darkness. "Are you all right?"

Nathan turned, swallowing hard. "Yes!" he croaked. "Go back to bed!"

"But you—"

Nathan cursed under his breath and flung back the covers.

He jerked on his trousers and threw up the bar, then slammed the door behind him.

The wind and rain blew straight at the cabin. He staggered across the porch and pressed both palms flat against the drenched pine rail.

Rain washed over him, soaking his skin, seeping into his bones. If only his soul could be cleansed as easily, the nightmares washed from his heart. He would never be clean. He'd lost his innocence in the ruts of battle, in the mud, rain, decay, and blood.

He raised his face to the lightning streaking the sky, and rain beat against his face as he yelled, "What do you want from me? Why do you torment me?"

"Are you talking to God?"

Nathan whirled around, anger pounding hot inside his body. Wrapped in a quilt, Samantha stood huddled in the doorway, staring at his chest. Knowing that she'd seen his scar made him even angrier. "Go back inside! Why do you torment me too? All this talk about God and your Jesus with a stupid sheep! It's not true, Samantha!"

She stretched out her hand from the quilt, her eyes tortured. "Nathan, please let me . . ."

Nathan laughed bitterly. Who was this woman to offer him her hand? Was she also going to graciously offer him her God? He closed the distance between them in two angry strides, then grabbed her arms and pinned her close. Samantha's face went white. "I warned you to go back to bed," he hissed. "Don't you understand?"

She raised her chin, calm. "You said you would never force me to do something I didn't want."

His mouth quirked. "And do you want to?" he whispered.

He reached up and traced the delicate line of her jaw. "Do you want to be taught, teacher?"

Her eyes widened, but she didn't flinch. "This isn't you talking, Nathan," she said in a low voice. "You won't hurt me."

"No?" He pressed closer and bent his head. "What makes you so sure?" he whispered against her lips.

"Because . . . because I know you. I love you," she gasped, turning her head to avoid his kiss. "*God* knows you. *He* loves—"

Nathan silenced her with a kiss. "I'm only interested in your love, Sam," he whispered. "Show me."

He kissed her again and felt her shudder. To his surprise, she took his face in her hands and brushed back his wet hair. "Then come inside with me," she said softly.

He laughed. "You don't know what you're saying."

"Shh. Come inside." She took his hand and led him through the doorway, then walked alone to the fireplace. Holding his gaze, she knelt. The warm light glowed around her, her face luminescent. She slipped the quilt from her shoulders.

Nathan shut the door, muting the storm. His knees went weak, and he discovered he was shaking like a schoolboy. Conscience battled desire. He shouldn't let her do this. She would regret it tomorrow. *He* would regret it tomorrow. "Samantha—"

She touched the quilt she'd spread in front of the fire. "Lie here, Nathan," she whispered.

His mouth went dry. "Beside you?"

She spread one end of the quilt over her lap. "No, here.

Put your head in my lap." Her eyes glowed when he hesitated. "Trust me."

Confused, Nathan did as she suggested. He was surprised he still shook and even more surprised at the softness of the quilt. Samantha drew another one over him, and her soft hand smoothed his damp hair. He felt his eyes close, then jerked them open. "But—"

Her fingers covered his lips. "This is what you need, Nathan," she murmured. "Go to sleep. I'll stay here with you in case the nightmares come again."

Too weary to argue, Nathan closed his eyes. The crackling flames soothed his troubled mind and slowly dried his wet body. Samantha enfolded him with warmth, and the indistinguishable words she murmured over him eased him into sweet, dreamless sleep.

EIGHT

Nathan awoke, groggy, to the miserly warmth of aged embers. He shivered and, burrowing his head against the quilt, bumped the puncheon floor.

He jerked upright. Samantha was gone!

Panicked, he rose, dropping the quilt she'd covered him with the night before. His eyes scanned the early light of the room for a clue to when she'd left. Surely she wouldn't have gone out in the rainy night alone!

He yanked open her carpetbag, then sighed with relief. The picture was still there. She must have gone back upstairs during the night.

He added logs to the grate and rubbed his arms until the invigorated flames chased away the morning's chill. With a brief glance at the loft, he stepped into his boots.

The rain had stopped, leaving behind a cold that braced his upper body as he stepped from the cabin. He breathed deeply, automatically scanning the horizon for the presence of danger. Not finding any, he trod carefully through the mud to see how the horses had weathered the storm.

They raised their heads and nickered at him in greeting. He rubbed their noses and addressed them affectionately, then spread some hay and made sure they had water. Hardly aware of the cold anymore, he leaned against the shed's weathered gray boards.

On the trip to Kansas City, he'd convinced himself he couldn't love Samantha, that she would only be Caleb's sister. But that had been before he'd actually laid eyes on her, before she'd opened the door at the orphans' home. Before last night.

He'd all but attacked her, yet she'd taken him inside and held him like a child. Watched over him. Said she loved him.

Nathan ran a hand through his hair. She'd be better off this morning if he had attacked her, the pain only physical. He could do more damage to her spirit than he could ever do to her body. He would destroy her if she stayed with him. He would never be free to make any promises or plans. His past nipped too closely at his heels.

No, he would take her to her brother. Caleb would keep her safe, and Nathan would . . .

He laughed out loud. Where could he possibly run?

Halfway back to the cabin, he spotted several boards jutting from the ground under a lonely spruce about fifty yards out. Dread tightening his chest, Nathan slogged the muddy distance to four raw mounds of beaten earth. He glanced over the simple writing, bravely etched into the wood: *Our Baby— February 21, 1870—Typhoid. Mary Alice—February 25, 1870— Aged 2—Typhoid. Andrew Jacob—March 1, 1870—Aged 5—Typhoid. Beloved Wife—Catherine Elizabeth—March 3, 1870—Aged 22—Typhoid.*

Anger and sorrow tore at Nathan. In little more than a week, an unknown man had watched his entire family die. The wife must have tended the children till their deaths then died quickly herself. The husband probably struck out soon after, leaving everything behind in grief. Nathan stared at the horizon and wondered when he would ever stop encountering death.

He turned away, cursing. How could a man abandon his family in the earth, the only witness to the passed lives? The writing would become indecipherable, grass would grow over the graves, and no one would remember the buried bodies.

Nathan lowered his head. His mother didn't have a proper tombstone. His father was probably buried in some unmarked grave. And he knew at least one other nameless, faceless man lying cold in soldier's sleep.

"Rest in peace," he muttered, stuffing his hands in his pockets. He shuffled back to the cabin and dragged himself up the porch steps. Why did he have to find those graves? He had enough worries about Samantha without learning the cabin's tragedy.

"There you are!"

Startled, Nathan glanced up. Fully dressed with every hair in place, Samantha laid aside a book where she sat at the table. Smiling radiantly, she sat in the path of a sunbeam that slanted across her shirt. She'd set out two plates, jerky, and a broken jar filled with storm-battered wildflowers. Nathan's melancholy evaporated like rain striking hot metal.

As he approached the table, she glanced away. Smiling, he put on a shirt from his saddlebags. She was truly an innocent.

"Reading Dickens again?" he said as he joined her. He lifted her hand to his lips for a kiss.

She flushed. "I just finished the book. 'It is a far, far better thing that I do, than I have ever done; it is a far, far better rest that I go to than I have ever known.'" Her eyes clouded, and she sniffled.

"I told you you'd cry. But hush now," he said softly, drawing her close for a tender kiss. He'd had all of death he could stomach for one day.

"It's a beautiful picture of Jesus," she said, wiping her eyes. "Just like Sydney Carton was willing to die for the woman he loved, Jesus was willing to die for us."

Nathan pulled back. "I wish I'd never given you that book, Samantha." He picked up the jerky and nodded at hers. "Now let's eat."

She bowed her head. Nathan watched while she moved her lips in silent prayer. Samantha raised her head and blushed when she caught his gaze.

"If praying gives you peace, don't be embarrassed," he said, annoyed.

"I'm not. I thought you might be."

"God gave up on me long ago. And I don't have much use for him either," he said bitterly.

"How can you say that? Especially after last night!"

"I had a bad dream." He shrugged. "If I frightened you, you should have left me in the rain."

"I wasn't frightened by you; I was frightened *for* you." She covered his hand with hers. "I want you to find peace, Nathan. I *pray* for you to find peace. That scar on your chest . . ." Her gaze drifted to his shirt then back up to his eyes. "It looks like a bullet hole."

Nathan clenched his teeth. "It was, and I don't want to talk about it."

"You haven't talked about much of anything since we've been together."

"And maybe you've talked about too much." He could see

the hurt in her eyes even as the words left his mouth, and he softened. "Look, Sam, don't get carried away. You didn't mean it last night when you said you loved me."

She raised her chin. "I've cared about you since I was a child. And you cared about me. Tell me you didn't."

"Stop talking nonsense."

"Tell me, Nathan!"

He looked straight into those deep blue eyes, and every lie fell apart on his tongue. Being with her these past weeks had reminded him of how much he'd once cared, how much he'd never stopped caring.

"If the war hadn't come, we would have gotten married," she said. "You would have become a doctor."

"Maybe we would have just farmed the Kansas soil alongside our families." He smiled bitterly. "Sometimes I wish that's what I was doing now."

"I often wish life had turned out that way," she said softly.

"Do you? Would you have been happy being a farmer's wife?"

"I would have lived anywhere to be with you."

His throat constricted, and for a moment he couldn't speak. "Sam, I can't tell you that I—"

"It's enough for now." She smiled gently. "When you're ready, you'll tell me everything."

Nathan bit down hard on the jerky. He would never be ready because to tell her everything would be to lose her.

Samantha wondered at his quietness for the next few days. He kept up his usual good-natured banter during the day and at night gave her a soft kiss before bedding down on the other side of the fire.

He seemed almost nervous as they rode, continually scanning the mountains as though he expected something or someone to suddenly appear. He had always been cautious for their safety, but he seemed doubly so now, ever since they'd left the cabin.

They rested by a stream, letting the horses graze nearby. Samantha lay on her elbows and watched Nathan splash water on his face and head. Then he walked back and sat beside her in the grass, leaning back.

"Tomorrow we should be there," he said after a moment. He gazed wistfully at the blue Wyoming sky. "I'm going to miss this."

"Don't you have a sky at the ranch?" she said playfully, rolling over on one elbow. "Or do you live in a cave?"

"The sky's even prettier in the mountains," he said, "and the cabin's big enough. Caleb and I got bored one summer and added two extra rooms. We also built a bunkhouse where our . . . workers . . . stay."

"Why didn't Caleb come with you? And don't tell me he had business."

"He didn't think I'd find you. He'll be surprised." Nathan looked away. "He'll assume the worst about you and me."

Samantha frowned. Nathan looked far too serious. "The worst?"

"Your brother and I grew to manhood together. He knows about my past."

Samantha's stomach flipped. "You mean women?"

"Yes, and don't give me that innocent look. It's different for men, Samantha. We have certain needs."

"The Bible doesn't say anything about *needs*. And it certainly doesn't give a special exemption to men."

"Believe what you want." Nathan shrugged. "But Caleb will automatically think that—"

"—you and I . . . ," Samantha trailed off, blushing.

"It wouldn't be difficult to believe," Nathan whispered, leaning closer for a kiss.

Samantha knew she should put distance between them, but his nearness unsettled her common sense, clouding her heart with confusion. Why shouldn't she share this love with him? Did it really matter if they were married?

Appalled by her thoughts, she rose and turned. She trembled, frightened by the power Nathan wielded over her. He had never even said he loved her.

She felt his hands on her shoulders. "This is between you and me, Samantha. Caleb doesn't have to know."

"God would."

He smiled sardonically. "Why would he care?"

Samantha blinked. *Oh, Lord, I'm not strong enough to fight him physically* and *spiritually!* "I don't know, Nathan. I don't know what the consequences could be, except perhaps a . . . a baby. But God's word doesn't just suggest I remain pure; it commands it. And he is our father, Nathan. He loves me—he loves you. Everything he tells us is for our good!"

"And that's what you believe in."

She turned and nodded, hoping that at last he understood. "Yes!"

Samantha held her breath, watching Nathan's face. She had waited for an opening to speak to him, and here God had given her one through her own weakness. If only Nathan had the ears to truly hear!

He frowned, then turned away. "It's just as well. You probably just saved me from losing a few teeth to Caleb's fist."

For the rest of the day, Nathan spoke little, even after they made camp for the night. They sat cross-legged by the fire and silently nibbled hard biscuits. Every other night they'd laughed and joked before heading off to bed.

Tonight Samantha felt as though Nathan weren't even beside her, as though he were somewhere else. So she said good night early and lay down on her blanket.

She felt a hand on her shoulder. "Sit with me awhile? The stars are lovely tonight."

Samantha rolled over. Nathan knelt beside her with his hand outstretched. She knew it wasn't wise, but her heart decided for her. She took his hand and rose.

He led her to a blanket spread beside a fallen log and leaned back. Showy and radiant, a multitude of stars lit the sky overhead. He put an arm around her, and she stiffened.

"My mother always said not to let the sun go down on your anger," he said softly. "You're a few hours late."

"Do you believe what she said?"

"I suppose."

"Then there *is* something in the Bible you believe."

He didn't say anything for a moment. Silent, he stared up at the sky.

Samantha covered his hand with hers, keeping her gaze focused alongside his. "Tell me about the war, Nathan," she whispered.

He turned his head sharply. "What have you heard?"

She thought for a moment. What answer could she give to a man who'd lived through it? "I heard it was . . . terrible," she offered.

"The soldiers had an expression for battle, Samantha.

'Seeing the elephant,' they called it. A lot of boys were anxious to fight, just like curious kids wanting to feed an elephant at the circus. But once there, they ran the risk of getting trampled."

"And some of the soldiers did."

Nathan laughed bitterly. "A *lot* of the soldiers did. I saw disease and death every day. No one who lived through it can ever be the same."

She heard him draw a deep breath. "There's so much you wouldn't understand," he said softly.

A shooting star blazed across the sky, its fiery pattern oddly reassuring. To Samantha the spectacular show of nature was a reminder from God that they weren't alone. The Lord had made the world for his children to enjoy. All that was needed were open eyes and an open heart. Samantha turned to tell Nathan, but his eyes were mournful, still focused on the sky.

"Life is so short," he murmured. He thrust out a finger. "Those stars have been in the sky from the beginning of time, but we aren't like that. Our lives flicker out in mere minutes compared to them."

"But we don't have to die, Nathan," she whispered, "The heavens declare the glory of the Lord, and the glory is that he wants us to live with him forever."

Nathan smiled cynically in the darkness. "I quit believing that when my father had me read the works of the great philosophers . . . Plato, Epicurus, Hume, Kant. They made so much sense, I couldn't see God anymore except as a puppet master who jerks us around by invisible strings. He makes our lives occasionally happy, occasionally sad, and then finally he cuts the strings altogether."

Nathan looked down at her with sad eyes, then lightly kissed her cheek. "Go to bed, Samantha."

She wanted to tell him he was wrong, to stay and argue until he saw the truth. But he turned away, gazing up at the sky, and she felt the brief opening God had given her close once again.

"Please soften his heart," she murmured as she lay down on her blanket. "Let there be fertile ground for your seeds of truth."

She lay awake for several hours in supplication to God, who was so much greater than the wide, twinkling sky he had made.

Near dusk the next day, Nathan reined in his horse and pointed to a cliff. "Just beyond there is where we're going. I guess it's too late to ask if you want to change your mind."

"I don't."

"All right then." Nathan straightened in the saddle. "They'll—"

"*They?*"

"Some of our workers. They help us guard the ranch. They'll see us long before we see them, so don't be surprised." He led the way up the trail, and Samantha followed at a distance, hesitant.

Just as they rounded the cliff's bend, a lone rider emerged in the road, planting his horse in the path between Samantha and Nathan. His hair was straight and black like Nathan's, but longer. His face and hands were deep brown, and he wore buckskins with a hunting knife sheathed to his belt.

Samantha reined in her horse sharply. *An Indian!* A gasp died in her throat as their eyes locked, Nathan's name dying as well on her lips. This wasn't a man but a boy. Probably no more than seventeen.

"Hamilton!"

The voice uptrail diverted her attention. A man with a long, droopy mustache had also emerged on the path. He extended a hand to Nathan, who clasped it briefly.

"You took ten years off my life, Broom!" Nathan laughed, turning downtrail. "And George! What are you doing lurking around? You must have scared Samantha half to death."

The boy continued to stare at her, but his face broke into a crooked smile. "Sorry. I act before I think," he said with a nasal accent. "You must be Caleb's sister."

"Yes." She nodded politely, urging her horse forward to be nearer to Nathan. As she passed the boy, she could see his eyes were a striking brown, but his skin wasn't as dark as she'd thought. He wasn't an Indian at all; he was white.

The man Nathan had called Broom smiled and touched the brim of his hat. "Ma'am." Adjusting the rifle resting in the crook of his left arm, he turned to Nathan. "Have a safe trip?"

"Safe as possible. Is Caleb around?"

"He's back at the cabin. He's mighty unhappy, though. Expected you weeks ago."

"I figured as much." Nathan headed up the trail. "You boys keep a close watch, hear?"

"Sure will!" Broom beamed. George nodded solemnly.

Samantha followed Nathan but glanced back. The man and the boy had disappeared. She had the eerie feeling the trail was still being watched. "Why does somebody stand guard?" she called out.

"Rustlers. Fortunately, this is the only trail into the area, so it's the only one we have to watch."

A ranch with only one trail seemed inconvenient, but maybe Nathan and Caleb had good reasons. "What about Indians?"

"The Shoshoni live on their reservation on the other side of this range. George was raised by them, so we've made friends with the Indians. Watch your step," Nathan said. "The trail gets narrow in places."

She wanted to ask about George, but her mare faltered on the rocks, quickly regaining her balance. Samantha leaned out of her saddle enough to watch the dun pick her way carefully around the rocks.

"How'd you find this place?" she called uptrail. Talking calmed her fears.

"A medic I worked with during the war gave it to me," he said over his shoulder.

"Gave? Why didn't he want it?"

"He got hit by a shell. As he was dying, he told me how to get here."

Samantha's heartbeat quickened. Nathan said it so matter-of-factly. How much death had he seen?

Her gaze had been so intent on the trail, she hadn't noticed they had leveled off into a small, fertile valley. Beside a small log cabin, one man tended his horse, another chopped wood, and still another idly threw a knife at the door.

She and Nathan rode past, and all activity stopped, all eyes turning to her. Especially the knife thrower's. He fingered the tip of the knife blade, flashing an insolent half-grin. "Ma'am," he said mockingly without removing his hat. Then he let out a low, wicked chuckle apparently meant for her ears only.

Shivering, Samantha followed Nathan straight to a larger cabin nestled among a cluster of firs. When they were ten yards from the porch, the door opened. A man emerged with an anxious look on his face.

Samantha caught her breath, turning to Nathan for confirmation. He slowed his horse until she pulled up beside him. "Yes, that's Caleb," he said.

She had been shocked by the years of change in Nathan, but she had had more than a month to adjust to the fact he was grown-up. This was her brother, who had been hardly more than a boy when she'd last seen him, whom she had lived with, played with, and quarreled with long ago.

Arms crossed, Caleb leaned against a post and watched her. His hair was still the same dark blond as hers, though he'd been blessed with their father's curls. Samantha noticed he also sported a respectable mustache. From where she sat, she could tell he stood a few inches taller, his shoulders slightly broader, than Nathan's. But the gun holstered securely at his right thigh was nearly identical.

"You all right?" Nathan murmured to Samantha as they reined in their horses.

She nodded, vaguely aware when he dismounted and put his hands on her waist to help her down. He knew she was perfectly capable of dismounting by herself, but she reasoned he was putting on a show for Caleb.

"Don't worry," he whispered, then said louder, smiling at Caleb, "Looks like we're here."

She smiled nervously and wiped her gloved palms against her riding skirt. Nathan tossed the reins to one of the men who had gathered nearby, then headed for the porch. Samantha followed closely.

Caleb broke into a smile. "Nathan. I was afraid something had happened to you." Caleb's voice was so much deeper than

Samantha remembered, and it seemed strange to see him and Nathan shaking hands.

"We ran into some bad luck and had to forego traveling by rail." Nathan grinned. He nudged Samantha forward. "Your sister has already mastered the art of jumping from a train."

"Really?" Caleb turned to her for the first time, and he smiled as his gaze swept over her. "It's good to see you, Samantha. You've certainly grown up quite a bit."

"You . . . you have too." Why did she feel so nervous? This was her *brother!*

Caleb laughed and drew her into his arms. "Is that all you can say?"

Samantha's throat tightened with emotion. He hadn't hugged her since they were little. "I missed you, Caleb! I worried about you so much! I didn't think I'd ever—" She broke off, weeping with joy that God had reunited them.

Caleb's arms tightened around her, and he pressed his cheek against her head. "Thank you, Nathan," she heard him say softly.

Nathan didn't reply, but Samantha heard him leave the porch and head in the direction of the other cabin.

NINE

"W"ell, look who's back."

Good-natured laughter followed as Nathan entered the bunkhouse. Three men rose from crudely hewn chairs, greeting him with rough handshakes.

Nathan warmed at their greeting. He and Caleb had made it a point to surround themselves with easygoing men. The last thing they wanted was to hook up with a mean temper prone to back-shooting.

"So you finally made it," a gravelly voice said.

Nathan turned to the one man whom he and Caleb disliked. The dark-eyed man caressed the side of his knife blade with his thumb, staring at Nathan with contempt and bitterness.

Nathan's smile faded. "Yes, Crawford. I made it."

He watched the large man settle himself away from the others. Nathan and Caleb avoided violence in their holdups; the threat of a gun was usually enough to ensure submission. But over the years, Justin Crawford had shown signs of becoming a cold-blooded killer, pistol-whipping victims who moved too slowly to suit him. Once he even shoved the barrel of his gun into the mouth of a terrified train conductor and laughingly pulled the trigger on what he knew to be an empty chamber.

He'd talked about moving on, though, and Nathan and Caleb agreed that after the next job, they'd pay him enough money to make sure he left. They regretted ever taking him in, but his imposing presence and skill with the occasionally necessary dynamite had won him a place in the gang.

Nathan dropped his saddlebags on the floor. "Any supper left? I've worked up a powerful appetite from riding."

"Here, Nathan." One man vacated a chair at the table.

"Thanks, Kelley." Nathan sat down gingerly, exaggerating his saddlesore expression for the benefit of their laughter. Someone handed him a bowl of stew and a spoon, and he dug in. While he ate, the three other men—all but Crawford—gave various accounts of the past weeks' activities, most of which seemed to involve a running card game.

Nathan basked in their company, warming to their humor and good-natured insults. When someone produced a deck of cards and a bottle of whiskey, Nathan eagerly pushed away his bowl and edged his chair closer to the table.

"You'll have Nathan's room, and he'll bunk with me," Caleb said. He led the way through the front room, a Spartan eating-and-sitting area with a rock fireplace, a dry sink and cupboard, and a rickety table with four chairs. A pair of snowshoes hung precariously from a nail on the wall, and another pair rested behind the door. Passing one bedroom, Caleb stepped inside the next. One wall was almost completely covered with shelves jammed with books.

Samantha grinned. "He wasn't joking when he said he always read. *Tom Sawyer* . . . *The Evolution of Man* . . . *The Republic* . . . *The Odyssey*."

"Like as not he's got his nose buried in a book. I keep

telling him it looks bad to the other men, but then Nathan pretty much does as he wants."

Caleb pitched her saddlebags and carpetbag on the floor. Samantha glanced at the bed and felt her face flush. It was just Nathan's room she'd be sleeping in, she reminded herself. It wasn't as if he would be sharing the quarters.

"There's stew," Caleb said, backing toward the front room. "We'll eat here, and the other men will eat in the bunkhouse."

"And Nathan?" she said casually.

"He'll probably eat with the others. He'd just as soon stay up all night playing cards."

"Oh." Had she managed to keep the disappointment from her voice? Maybe she would have a chance to talk to Caleb about her feelings for Nathan. She wanted her brother to know before he guessed it himself.

She hummed as she set the pine table. Caleb studied her thoughtfully and dished up the stew. They sat down, and she impulsively grabbed his hand as he reached for a spoon. "Thank you, Lord, that you have reunited Caleb and me. Thank you for this banquet."

She raised her head and saw that Caleb was frowning. "It's only stew, Samantha."

She smiled, joyful. "It doesn't matter what we eat. God's brought us back together."

Caleb shook his head and dipped his spoon in the stew. "Where'd Nathan find you, in a convent?"

"No, the orphanage."

Caleb studied his bowl. She saw him struggle with some inner conflict, and she waited patiently. He finally set down his spoon and trained his eyes—so like Pa's—on her. "Tell me what happened after we left you."

Nathan was in fine form. Warmed by the whiskey and male company, he easily won several expensive hands of poker. George and Broom, his best men, had joined the group, the former adding his wise silence and the latter his Texas humor to the gathering.

Cigar smoke drifted pleasantly, and Nathan tipped back his chair and blew three perfect Os. Life was at its best. Friends . . . money to be had for the picking . . . the nightmares had stopped coming every night . . . Samantha loved him.

He smiled to himself.

"So you found Martin's sister," a low voice said from the shadows.

The laughter subsided abruptly. "That's so, Crawford," Nathan said steadily. He rose from the table, yawning, and scooped his winnings into his pocket. "I'm out, fellows."

He made his way to the nearest bunk. George scrambled out from below and climbed to the upper bed. "Here, Nathan, you can have this one."

"Thanks, George." Nathan stretched the length of the bed and tipped his hat over his eyes. His mood sobered. He would rest for a while, then he had to tell Samantha the truth about their livelihood.

"Did you have a good time?" Crawford said.

The room tensed. Nathan raised his hat. The big man leaned casually against the foot of the wooden structure, stoic. George glared down from above.

"Did I have a good time doing what, Crawford?" Nathan said, irritated. He had more important things to do than banter with the drunken fool.

Crawford contemplated an unlit cigarette in his fingers. "Did you have a good time with Martin's sister?"

Nathan's blood rushed in his ears, nerves wound as tightly as a spring. Crawford studied the cigarette, rolling it between his fingers. He glanced up, baring yellow teeth. "Tell me, Hamilton. Is she as good as she looks?"

Fists raised, Nathan leaped from the bed and smashed Crawford in the face. The bigger man looked surprised as Nathan attacked with lightning-quick speed, his fists pummeling Crawford square in the face. Staggering from the blows, Crawford raised one hand to his bleeding mouth as his right hand fumbled at his holster. Nathan drew quicker, palming his own revolver in a flash. "Don't do it, or I'll blow your face backward!"

Nathan's head pounded with rage, but he was shocked by his own steadiness. Over the years, violence had gotten easier.

"Get out, Crawford, or I'll kill you," he said.

The other men were shocked into silence. They were accustomed to Caleb's temper and gunplay, but not Nathan's.

Glaring, Crawford holstered his gun. He pressed his bandanna to his mouth and fingered his jaw, then skulked past Nathan and flung open the door.

Nathan slipped his Colt back in its holster and gestured at George. The boy resheathed the knife he'd pulled. "Come with me," Nathan said. He grabbed a nearly full whiskey bottle and said to the others, "Not one word to Caleb about what happened, understand?"

They murmured their affirmations. Then, quiet as a cat,

George jumped from the upper bunk and followed Nathan. Once outside, Nathan uncorked the bottle and took a long swig. He offered the bottle to George, who declined with a head shake.

Nathan corked the bottle and stared up at the moon. "You're the best tracker, and you know how to move quietly so no one even knows they're being watched."

The boy shrugged. "The Shoshoni taught me well."

"Good. I have a job for you."

Samantha finished her narrative, then fell silent. Caleb stared at his plate, but when he finally looked up, his expression was more tender than she had ever seen it before. "I'm sorry we left you. And that it took us so long to look for you." He paused. "I assumed you'd been adopted long ago or gotten married. I owe Nathan a lot for going."

Her heart quickened, and she laid her hand over his. "Caleb, about Nathan . . ."

"He didn't force himself on you, did he? You and he didn't—"

Samantha blushed. "He was a perfect gentleman."

Caleb relaxed, leaning back in his chair. "You used to be in love with him," he said. His voice sounded accusing. "I remember that day at the river. I saw how you two looked at each other."

Samantha nodded. Caleb would understand that they were older now. He wouldn't be angry at all. "Nathan and I—"

"I don't care how you used to feel about him, just don't let him come near you. He'll break your heart. Someday he'll have to answer to that murder charge."

Samantha's heart slammed into her throat. *"Murder?"*

"He didn't tell you?"

"N-no!"

Caleb shifted uncomfortably. "About three years ago, I was in a card game in Cheyenne and winning heavily. Another player accused me of cheating. I calmed him down, but when I turned to leave, he aimed for my back. Nathan pushed me out of the way and shot him, but not in time to keep from getting shot himself. I dragged him out of there to a parlor house."

Heat flew to Samantha's cheeks. "Go on," she whispered, trembling.

"It took him several months to heal up. The doc said the bullet missed Nathan's heart by just a breath."

The scar, she thought dully. *The scar he didn't want to talk about.*

"The law charged him with murder because the man he shot turned out to be a financial officer for Union Pacific. The girls hid Nathan until he was strong enough to leave town."

"But he was just protecting you!"

Caleb laughed. "The law didn't see it that way once they figured out we were already wanted for robbery."

"Robbery?" she whispered.

"We'd already started robbing stages and banks. It's been even easier since we made this place our hideout. Nobody can find us." He frowned. "Didn't Nathan tell you any of this?"

She shook her head, speechless, but motioned for him to continue.

"Nathan'll probably hang if he's ever caught," Caleb said quietly. "I'll bet that was a sheriff on the train you jumped from."

A chill swept through Samantha as she remembered the

panic on Nathan's face. Her stomach lurched, and she thought she would be sick right there. Nathan a murderer! A robber! Dear God, how had he and her precious brother ever fallen into such a life?

"I was surprised when Nathan said we should try to find you. He said he'd been wondering ever since he got shot whether you were all right. That brush with death must have made him want to tie up some loose ends."

Loose ends. Samantha clenched her hands together under the table. "When did you first start stealing?" she said quietly.

A shadow of discomfort crossed his face. "You ought to ask Nathan. It was his idea."

"But—" She clamped her mouth shut. Caleb had already given her too much to digest. Her stomach knotted with grief. "I'll be back in a minute, Caleb. I . . . I have to go to the privy."

She fled from the safety of the cabin into the night. She shivered in the chilly air, but she wrapped her arms around herself and ran as fast as she could.

Holding his jaw, Justin Crawford dropped to a fallen tree trunk, wheezing from the exertion of running. His head and jaw ached, and he cursed out loud.

He would be glad to be free of this gang. Nathan Hamilton and Caleb Martin were too tame for his tastes. They didn't seem to understand that a little violence always provided more money in holdups. If you wanted to show a man who was boss, you struck hard at whatever you wanted, whatever hurt him most.

He heard something rustle through the bushes, and he whirled, drawing his gun. The Martin woman brushed past with her arms around herself, sobbing. She hadn't seen him in the dark.

Crawford got to his feet, and headed out in the direction she'd run. Smiling, he reholstered the gun—it wouldn't be needed. Before he left, he would have his revenge *and* a good time.

Nathan set the whiskey bottle in front of Caleb. "I thought I'd see how you two were getting on." He glanced around the room. "Where's Samantha?"

"Outside." Caleb jerked his thumb in the direction of the privy. He leaned back in his chair and crossed his arms.

Nathan casually uncorked the bottle and poured, feeling the heat of his friend's gaze. "Speak your piece before she gets back then."

Caleb leaned forward, frowning. "Her exact words were that you were a perfect gentleman during your little journey together. Now I want to hear what you have to say."

"Don't you believe her?"

"I believe you're heartless when it comes to women. And I believe my sister has feelings for you."

"She has feelings for a lot of things." Nathan gloomily tossed back his drink, then leveled his gaze with Caleb's. He grinned and swiped his forefinger twice across his chest. "Cross my heart . . . or rather the heart you claim I don't have. I didn't touch your sister."

"Then how did you manage to get her up here without letting on about what we do? About your murder charge?"

Nathan went cold. "You told her?"

Caleb nodded, crossing his arms. "And now you tell me

what I'm supposed to do. You've dragged her here, and now I'm responsible for her. Provided she decides to stay."

"She'll stay," Nathan said grimly, cursing inwardly for not telling her himself. "She doesn't have anywhere else to go. Besides, we can protect her here. She'll be safe."

Caleb poured himself a second drink, drank it, then set the glass down with a thud. He drew his gun, removed the bullets, and casually removed the cylinder. When the gun was in pieces on the table, he took out a cleaning rod and carefully scrubbed out the barrel and chambers. "I don't want to see her get hurt, Nathan," he said in a low voice. "Especially by you."

Nathan watched Caleb clean the gun, something he'd seen his friend do countless times over the last six years. "She won't," he promised.

Samantha staggered inside the privy and shut herself in. Weeping, she leaned against the door and pressed her cheek against the rough wood. *Oh, Father, not Nathan! Not Caleb! Why did you let them choose this path?*

The door jerked open, and she gasped as she fell into the arms of a hard, dark form. A man laughed, and his arms tightened around her. "Well, well, well."

Struggling, Samantha pulled back but couldn't free herself. She looked up and saw that the man's face oozed blood around a vicious smile. His eyes gleamed. "Hamilton's had you first, but I don't mind. I reckon he and your brother will think twice about crossing Justin Crawford again when they see what I can do."

Samantha tried to scream, but he clamped a hand over her mouth. She twisted in his grasp, but he easily lifted her off her feet and dragged her behind the privy. Laughing, he pressed her against the wood structure and wrenched at her dress, his breath hot and heavy against her neck.

She bit down hard on his hand, and he jerked it away, screaming. "You witch!" Dark with rage, he backhanded her. Samantha slid down the side of the privy, stunned from the blow.

His hands were on her then, and she squeezed her eyes shut. She heard his roar of laughter, but then suddenly, inexplicably, she heard a strangled sound, and he was jerked away.

A streak of silver flashed in the moonlight. The man Nathan had called George pulled Crawford's head back by the hair and raised his knife. "I'm going to cut your throat right now, Crawford. Or maybe I ought to scalp you first and let you die slow."

"Nnn!" The terrified man gagged. His legs kicked out uselessly, sending dirt flying.

Sickened, Samantha turned her head. "Let him go!"

"*What?*"

She trembled under George's blazing eyes. "Please . . . just let him go!"

Glaring, George pressed the knife point against Crawford's throat until a drop of blood appeared. Crawford struggled, but George shoved him to the ground and kicked him in the stomach. Crawford doubled up, wheezing.

George loomed over him, his face murderous. "Get out of here!" he said between clenched teeth. "Only because of her am I releasing you. But if I ever see you again, you'll have to answer to me."

"Sure, sure, Injun," Crawford gasped, raising his hands. He backed away, then whirled and ran.

George stared into the darkness, then knelt beside Samantha. His gaze fixed on her, and even in the dark she could feel the intensity of his young eyes. "Are you all right?"

She nodded, embarrassed, and clutched the torn edges of her skirt together. "Thank you for not . . . killing him."

George continued to stare at her. "Nathan asked me to watch out for you. You two are in love."

"How did you—?"

"You're in love," he said again, and this time it sounded like a question.

"I—"

"Good." He nodded as if in agreement. "I'll take you back so he can take care of you."

George gently helped her up and led her up the path. His moccasined steps fell noiselessly on the pine needles.

Samantha's face throbbed, and she fingered her jaw. Thankfully she hadn't lost any teeth, but she'd probably have a sizable bruise tomorrow. Her head was droning with pain.

By the time they reached the open area in front of the cabin, George had to support her. She felt so weak, she could barely hold her head up. Just a few more steps. A few more.

She heard rather than saw George slam open the door. Then they were inside, and she saw Nathan and Caleb's startled faces. George supported her as he rapidly related the story. The floor wavered and rose, and she was aware of Caleb's angry face moving toward her.

Nathan brushed him aside, and George handed her over silently and moved back to the doorway.

"Nathan," she murmured, leaning against him.

"It's all right now, Sam."

Caleb pushed forward. "I'll take her. She's my sister."

Nathan scooped her up in his arms and started down the hall. "But I'm in love with her," he said.

TEN

Nathan laid her on his bed as Caleb loomed over them, drawing his gun. Panicked, Samantha scrambled upright, but Caleb laid a hand on her shoulder. "Lie down before you pass out." He turned to Nathan and lowered his voice. "I'm going after him. You stay here and take care of her."

Nathan nodded, and Caleb stormed off. "George!"

Samantha sat up again. "Caleb can't—"

"Lie back." Nathan sat beside her and peered at her face, then cursed.

Flinching from his gaze, she quickly lowered her head. Her hands shook as she tucked strands of loose hair behind her ears.

Nathan gently cupped her chin. "Look at me, Samantha."

She kept her eyes focused on his shirt buttons, her heart beating so hard she could hear it in her ears.

"*Look* at me!"

She winced. "I . . . I can't," she whispered. "I'm too ashamed."

He drew a sharp breath. "Of yourself or me?" he said bitterly.

"Both."

The shutters of her heart had been thrown open, letting in

not light but darkness. The horror of the attack had driven home the ugliness of sin, the dark side she could expect with Nathan. He didn't even have a perfunctory interest in God and by his and Caleb's admissions had easily broken most of the Ten Commandments.

And then he'd told Caleb he loved her.

Shaking, Samantha stood and grabbed her carpetbag. He gripped her arm, his face dark. "What are you doing?"

"I'm leaving."

"Sit down, Sam. You're upset. You're not making sense."

"I'm making sense of everything," she said, trembling at his touch. This man she didn't know terrified her. She couldn't even look at him. "I don't want to talk to a . . . a criminal!"

Nathan released her, his voice cold. "It's dark outside. You don't know what's out there."

"I don't know what's in *here* either. I'll take my chances with the snakes and wild animals." She staggered through the front room and yanked the door open. In her haste, she nearly tripped down the steps.

Laughing, Nathan leaned against the doorjamb. "That's typical. The little saint is too good for the sinner."

She whirled around. "How *dare* you say that? All you've done is make fun of me and . . . and patronize me!"

"Patronize *you*?" He stomped down the stairs and didn't stop until he stood toe to toe with her. "Who's patronized who? You and your little prayers, your holding me in front of the fireplace like I was a child! I'm not a boy anymore, Samantha, I'm a man! I don't need you to look after me!"

Her head ached, swirling. "No, you're doing just fine on your own," she whispered. "You're a killer, a robber, and a . . . a . . . *fornicator*. You lied to me, bringing me here to your . . .

hideout . . . with other criminals. Including the one who tried to take the one thing I've been saving for my husband. I don't belong here, and I don't belong with you."

"Run, then!" He jerked his head at the road. "Run if you don't want to hear the truth."

"I'm not the one who's running, Nathan. You are." She turned and trudged down the road they had ridden together only hours before.

Dizzy, she struggled to keep her balance in the dark. Weaving, she stumbled on unseen rocks. Walking this unlit path seemed as useless as her life lately, every step leading into further darkness.

A pine branch smacked her in the face, and she tripped over a tree root. The carpetbag flew from her hands and she fell with a thud. When she got up, her shin smarted. Her probing fingers discovered a tear in her stocking and a warm, sticky trickle of blood.

Emotionally and physically defeated, she groped for the bag and crawled into the underbrush, taking refuge under a pine. Huddled on the needle-strewn ground, she drew her knees to her chest and sobbed out her fear and hurt.

"Oh, God, why couldn't you have sent me a decent Christian man? Or at least made Nathan a believer?" She dug her heels into the soft ground, resting her forehead on her knees.

You are a teacher.

Samantha raised her face. "But a children's teacher," she whispered.

Yes, a teacher of infants. But you who teach another, do you not teach yourself?

She bowed her head and held a hand to the burning in her heart. "I'm sorry, Father. I'm not perfect either."

In me the orphan finds mercy.

"Yes, Lord, you've always extended it to me." She smiled.

And are you the only orphan?

"Samantha!"

Nathan's voice sounded from up the road, preceded by a wavering light. As it drew closer, she could see she was well hidden; he would never find her. She could spend the night here and in the morning work her way down the mountains to the nearest town.

"Samantha, please answer!" His voice no longer sounded mocking but desperate, as though he were the lost one. Tucking the carpetbag under her arm, she rose and stepped from her hiding place.

The lantern light wavered, then lowered. She stood motionless as he came toward her, his face hidden by the dark.

"Samantha." His voice reflected relief. Joy. Love. Her heart wrenched in her chest, and she trembled.

How shall they believe in me whom they have not heard? And how shall they hear without a preacher?

The trembling intensified, flowing through her until her soul vibrated. It beat against her head, ribs, hips, and feet. God had spoken to her, reminding her that love was unconditional.

"I'm sorry, Nathan," she whispered, bowing her head.

He lifted her chin with one finger. "I was scared you might be hurt. And earlier tonight, Crawford might have—"

Samantha put her arms around him. "I was so frightened! He—if George hadn't—"

Nathan held her close. "It's over, Sam," he said softly. "Come home."

Taking up the bag and lantern, he wrapped an arm around

her as support. When they reached the cabin, he led her straight to his room, where he helped her take off her shoes, then tucked her into bed.

Nathan leaned forward in his chair, watching Samantha stir in her sleep. If he saw the least amount of anguish on her face, he'd wake her up. She hadn't done a single thing to deserve troubled sleep.

He rested his arm on the window sill and gazed out over the moonlit ground. What did she dream about? What were her secret desires?

Nathan smiled wistfully. She would never agree to his own secret desire.

Marriage was out of the question. He didn't have any security to speak of—not money, a real home, or even the assurance he would be alive tomorrow. All he could offer her was a cabin hideout shared with other men or a life on the run.

Nathan shivered. Even in the spring, nights in these mountains were cold. He pulled up the quilt from the foot of the bed and tucked it securely around her shoulders. Her face was peaceful and relaxed, and he lightly rubbed his cold fingers against her cheek.

What had he done to deserve a second chance with her? His inner scars were uglier than any mangled limb he'd seen on the battlefield. If she ever learned the whole truth, she would hate him.

Sighing, he turned and took up his station at the window.

Samantha bolted upright, pulled from the darkness of dreams by the daylight of reality. "Nathan?" She rolled over, confused by the strange bed. Her heart thudded. "Nathan!"

"Here, Sam."

She turned at the sound of his voice. He stood with his palms braced against the window sill, smiling. She wondered if he'd been there all night. Blushing, she pulled the quilt up to her shoulders even though she was fully dressed.

Nathan pushed away from the wall. "I'll take you down to the creek so you can clean up."

She nodded her assent, slowly lowering the quilt. Nathan stretched out his hand, and she took it, rising.

Nathan led Samantha through a meadow and into the woods where the creek ran. He sat on a fallen log and gestured upstream. "The creek bends up there a ways. I won't be able to see you from here."

She nodded and quickly retreated, still looking as scared as when she'd first awakened. He'd give anything if she'd relax; after all, they'd traveled together for the last few months. It wasn't as if he'd never waited for her to take care of her needs before.

When she returned, he could see her hair was damp and her face and hands glistened with water drops. The bruise on her jaw and cheek was more pronounced, and he cursed inwardly. He wished he'd gone after Crawford himself.

Nathan took her hands, and Samantha raised wounded blue eyes. "Why is Caleb hunting Crawford? Does the man deserve to be killed?"

Nathan clenched his teeth. "Weren't you scared? Didn't he hurt you?"

"Yes, of course, but—"

"And if George hadn't come along, you do know what would have happened?"

"Yes," she whispered.

"Then how can you ask if he deserves killing? Some people deserve death."

"Who? People unfit for polite society? People who don't live up to some man-made standard?"

"Some people deserve death."

"Does that include you?"

A gust of wind rustled pine and fir branches overhead. An elk poked its head through the trees, caught wind of them, then retreated. "Caleb had no right to tell you about what happened in Cheyenne," Nathan said bitterly.

"I guess he did, since you saved his life." She fell silent for a moment. "Has Caleb ever—"

"Killed anyone like I have?" Nathan snapped, then relented when he saw the shock on her face. "No, your brother has wounded a few men, but he doesn't shoot to kill. Until yesterday. Caleb loves you dearly, and he'd die protecting you."

"Or avenging me." She bowed her head. "What happened was terrible but not as much as taking another life."

"Even the Bible says 'an eye for an eye.'"

"The Bible also speaks of forgiveness. Caleb and I . . . and you . . . weren't raised to have so little conscience."

Nathan closed his eyes. Did she think he didn't have a conscience? *Did* he? He wasn't so sure anymore. He hadn't been sure for a long time.

He fought down guilt. "Why do you continue to remind me how we were raised? Those days are gone; our parents are gone. Now we decide for ourselves. If things had been different, maybe you and I would have been married, and you wouldn't be asking these questions. But we weren't dealt those cards."

"So you ignore God altogether and make up your own rules?"

He frowned, gently touching a bruise at her temple, muttering a foul curse. "You're not dizzy, are you? Feel sick?"

"No."

He turned her head, checking for further injury. "You have to be careful of swelling on the inside."

"Did you learn that from a book?"

"No. From the war." He paused. "There are some things books can't teach you. Head wounds are always the worst, especially when the brains spatter. Then there's the blood, and faces . . ."

He broke off, feeling Samantha's fingers lace through his. She pressed his knuckles against her lips, and he turned. Her eyes were gentle and questioning, but she kept her silence and he kept his. He inhaled a quiet breath, his heart thankful—she would never ask him what he didn't want to tell.

"For years I've lived with the memories, Sam," he said. "It's like a darkness that follows me. I don't want you to get hurt."

"All you've done is hurt yourself," she whispered. "You told Caleb you loved me. You must have known it a long time ago or you wouldn't have come for me."

"I had a strange feeling you needed help, but I shrugged it off for three years."

He couldn't bring himself to tell her he'd actually heard a voice. She wouldn't believe it, and he wasn't so sure he believed it himself.

"But you did come, and you do love me." Her eyes shone.

He cupped her sweet, innocent face, hating himself for his weakness. "Samantha," he said in frustration, "I'm as good as dead if I'm captured. If I have to leave you, I will. I won't put you in danger."

"You could give up this kind of life and settle down," she said, her eyes hopeful.

"You mean be a farmer or a rancher?"

"Yes."

Nathan laughed. "Farming's not for me, Sam. Trying to make a living of it almost killed my father. I had enough of that life growing up."

"What about going back East to study medicine? It's not too late to become the doctor you always wanted to be."

"I've seen too much, Sam, too many deaths. Besides, no decent school would admit a murderer as a student."

He turned and looked her straight in the eye. "I have no future to offer you."

"All I want is for you to give up this life you've chosen." She paused. "Tell me how you started stealing."

He felt the darkness rush through him, as overwhelming as that long-ago day. "I was punished for it long before I ever started," he said bitterly.

She moved closer. "Tell me, Nathan."

He closed his eyes, remembering. "During the battle of Nashville, I tended a dying man who begged me to take all his money. He'd stolen most of it, but he begged me to send it to his wife. I stuffed the money in my clothes and bag, intending to send it to her. The other men found it and accused me of being the thief."

Samantha touched his hand. "Oh, Nathan."

"Caleb tried to help me, but he hit a sergeant. For punishment, they put us both in the sweatbox."

"What's that?"

He suppressed a shudder. "A box eighteen inches square and only as tall as a man. You can't move your arms or legs, you can barely turn your head. And even though it was the dead of winter, the box grew incredibly hot."

"It sounds like a coffin."

He smiled faintly. "In many ways it was. I died that day to what I'd always believed was right. After the war, stealing from banks and stages didn't seem to matter. Right and wrong didn't seem so clear. Not after everything I'd been through. Not after everything I'd seen."

"While you were a medic, you must have saved a lot of men."

He shrugged. "I tried to help."

"And you saved Caleb's life in Cheyenne. You may have killed a man, but you're not a murderer."

She looked so earnest, so dead set on finding some redeeming trait in him. He suppressed a laugh, but he couldn't hide a cynical smile. "I'm afraid a jury wouldn't be quite as merciful, Sam."

"*God* is," she said quietly. "He can show you mercy and forgiveness and more, if you'll ask him."

His chest tightened defensively. Forgiveness. That was a joke. Some things just weren't forgivable. And besides, where had forgiveness gotten his mother and father? Nowhere but dead. God didn't look very merciful right now—what did he need that kind of a God for anyway?

ELEVEN

"I think we should put the carrots over here." Samantha pointed to the left edge of the furrowed field. "And there, the potatoes, then squash, then . . ."

George laughed, lacing his fingers over the handle of the hoe. "How much do you intend to plant?"

She turned, unaware her blue eyes sparkled like a reflection of the clear sky above. "Everything we can. I've wanted land to plant vegetables since I left my family's farm. We could have saved so much money at the orphanage if we'd only had more land to grow food. We had—" Aware of George's intent gaze, she broke off. He wouldn't be interested in her life story. "Well, we could have used more food. Just like we can use our own food up here. We need more than just meat and flapjacks to live on."

"We stock up on canned fruit from town."

Samantha laughed. "Canned fruit? That's your delicacy?"

"Yes, ma'am, I guess it is." The beginnings of a shy smile crossed his face. "But I sure enjoyed that johnnycake you made. And the wild berry preserves."

"Thank you. With Caleb and Nathan building that springhouse and promising to get a cow, we'll have butter and milk soon. And if we get chickens, we can have eggs. And that means fresh bread! And pies and—"

George flipped his hoe over. "You're making me hungry. I'd better finish these rows before you start preserving vegetables we haven't even grown."

Samantha laughed, taking up her hoe to dig alongside him. The summer sun beat on her neck in lazy waves. She'd been at the hideout for several months now, and she'd long ago abandoned the embarrassing split skirts she'd worn for horseback travel. Instead she wore the less practical but more feminine dress she'd brought from Kansas City. Working in the fields with her hem flapping around her legs reminded her of being back on the farm.

Caleb and George had returned a few days after they'd left, unable to catch Crawford. Nathan said George was the best tracker he'd known, and that if he couldn't find Crawford, the man couldn't be found. Though Caleb and Nathan were filled with anger, vowing eternal vengeance, Samantha breathed a sigh of relief. For her brother's sake, as well as George's, she was glad violence had been avoided.

Samantha glanced one row over at George, who attacked grass and hardened dirt as if they were lifelong enemies. He'd never said anything about his past. "I don't imagine you've done much farming before, have you?" she said.

George looked up, startled, then straightened. His face took on its usual stoic expression. "My family's farmed quite a bit since we've been on the reservation." He paused. "I wasn't much of a warrior, if you're interested in gory scalping stories."

Samantha felt herself blush. "No, I wasn't. I didn't think that of you—or your people."

"We've had our share of violence." He shrugged. "Like all men, no matter what their color."

Samantha turned, thinking of Nathan. She'd seen his violent streak in the restaurant in Kansas City when he'd pulled the gun on that ogling man, but ever since, it had been subdued. Yet she feared that, like a sleeping lion, it could reawaken.

She knew so little about men. The only men she'd known well were Christians—her father, Nathan's father, and the preacher, Frank Jordan. Now she coexisted with men whose lives centered around thievery. She had never received anything less than respect, but she never felt truly comfortable either.

She glanced at George, whose hoe still pounded the earth with purposeful fury. Funny, but she could talk to him without too much discomfort. Maybe because he was only a few years younger than she. "How did you meet Nathan and Caleb?" she said.

George kept digging. "I was separated from my parents when I was young, and the Shoshoni found and raised me. Two years ago, I was on a hunt by myself when a grizzly attacked me. He would have killed me if Nathan hadn't come along. He shot the bear and brought me back to the cabin to tend my wounds."

Samantha kept her eyes on her hoe, finding it easier to talk that way. "But you know English so well. Did you learn it on the reservation?"

"I remembered some of it from my childhood, but I didn't know my English name when Nathan found me. He said I looked like a George Addison and invited me to join the gang. Several times a year I go across the mountains to visit my tribe." He paused. "I'll go again in the fall. The other men here will leave then too."

"Why?"

"It'll be after the robbery."

The blade of her hoe thudded against the earth. "What robbery?" she whispered.

"Some bank." George straightened. "Nathan and Caleb usually like to do their robbing in the fall, then hole up back here in the winter. With all the snow, the law can't get through the pass. But most of the boys head back to their homes. Some of 'em have wives in other states and—"

"They can't rob a bank!"

George looked puzzled. "Why not?"

Samantha stared at him, then turned away. "Not even one righteous man," she whispered, bowing her head.

Oh, Lord, what should I do? Nathan isn't a believer, but it's still wrong! If I say something, will I turn him and Caleb away?

George touched her arm. "You're a believer in Jesus, aren't you?"

She turned, stunned. His gaze was intent, as though he was searching her soul. "Y-yes."

George stared at his hand and pulled it back sheepishly. "I've heard the priest on the reservation talk about your God. He talks about the Bible, too, but I . . . I can't . . ." George lowered his head.

"Can't what?"

"Read," he mumbled. "Nathan's such a smart man, but I couldn't ask him to teach me."

Samantha smiled gently. "Then I will, George."

The reserved smile appeared, then just as quickly vanished. George turned back to his hoeing. Samantha pushed her own hoe against the earth, hopeful. God had given her a chance to reach someone. Maybe one day it would be Nathan.

"What do you mean we can't do it?" Caleb crossed his arms and leaned back in his chair.

"I mean you can't do it." Samantha thumped the bowl of boiled potatoes on the table. "It's wrong."

Caleb laughed. "Samantha, we've been robbing for years!" He spooned out potatoes, chuckling.

She set her mouth in a firm line, glaring at her brother as she reached for the bowl. "All the more reason you should stop."

Caleb laughed again. "Where do you think we got the money to buy the food you're eating?"

Samantha stopped, then let the spoon full of potatoes fall back in the bowl. She lowered her eyes to her empty plate.

Caleb sighed. "Oh, for crying out loud. Nathan, talk some sense into her. If somebody doesn't, she may never eat again."

Samantha raised her face and met Nathan's empty green eyes. "Caleb's right," he said. "Didn't you think about that when you decided to stay?"

Did she? She couldn't remember. She thought she'd heard God giving her clear direction to be his light, but so far she'd been no more effective than an unused match. Every time she tried to talk to her brother about their parents' beliefs, Caleb shrugged her off as though she was still his pesky little sister.

And Nathan. When she first tried to talk to him, he usually laughed. Now he just ignored her. He'd even stopped making comments when she brought out her Bible to read before bedtime. She wasn't having any effect on either of them.

Nathan pushed back, and his chair scraped against the floor. "Come outside with me, Sam. We'll go for a walk to the creek."

"All right," she mumbled, her appetite gone.

Caleb's eyes twinkled, and he pointed his fork at her. "You'll come around yet, little sister."

She glanced at Nathan. "That's what I'm afraid of."

They walked in silence through the woods, the meadow, and along the creek, Nathan going first to help her over slippery rocks and a precarious path that rose along the water's edge. Trying not to look down, she kept her eyes fixed on him. She picked her way with caution, fear a constant companion to her heart, but Nathan was agile, his purchase sure. He was a confident mountain goat, and she but a directionless sheep.

Samantha glanced down at the rushing water, and her foot skidded on the muddy bank.

"Careful." Nathan grabbed her by the elbow. He smiled teasingly. "I don't want to jump from this height to rescue you if you fall in."

The path leveled off, then sloped downward. The roar of water intensified. Nathan led her to the end of the path and gestured at a waterfall. The rushing water pounded against her heart and exhilarated her soul. Cold, clear spray brushed her cheek. The fall seemed to have a life of its own, calling her, making her thirsty.

Nathan pulled off his boots and socks, then unbuttoned his shirt. He dropped it on the grass and held out a hand. The scar on his chest glistened. "Swim with me?"

She shook her head, shy. They weren't children at the swimming hole anymore.

He grinned at her, then dived into the waterfall. Samantha rushed to the edge, holding her breath until she saw him resurface. He flipped his hair back, then turned to the bank. He waved when he saw her, then dived underwater again.

Samantha dropped to the grass, letting out a long breath. If only Nathan could see that he had rejected the fountain of living water for a broken, empty cistern! "Make him thirsty," she whispered. "Give him a well of water springing up to eternal life."

She leaned back and covered her eyes with her arm. Dusk deepened around her, the sun dipping behind the mountains. Crickets chirped, lulling her troubled thoughts. She sighed, feeling peace enfold her like a soft blanket. "O Lord, how majestic is your name in all the earth. Nothing is too difficult for you, even reaching Nathan and Caleb."

She dozed until she heard a laugh and felt water drops on her face. "Fine thing. I leave you for two minutes, and you fall asleep."

She propped herself up on her elbows. Nathan knelt over her, water dripping from his hair, rolling off his shoulders and chest. Unnerved, she rose and turned away, pretending to study the waterfall in the darkness. She heard him dry himself with his shirt and button it up again.

From behind, he wrapped his arms around her and drew her close. Leaning against him, she felt warm and safe, but her heart was sorrowful. "You're going to rob the bank no matter what I say, aren't you?"

"Yes. Anyway, we'll be out of money and provisions by then."

She turned in his arms. "God can provide for us, Nathan. You and Caleb can get work. *I* can get work."

Solemn, he held her face in his hands, and his thumbs stroked her cheeks. "You already work hard enough. You take care of my home, you've planted my field, you cook for me . . ."

She smiled sadly. "Like a wife."

"Yes." He bent his head and kissed her slowly. Without hesitation she wrapped her arms around his neck. Her hands tested the dampness of his neck, fingers entwining his wet hair.

She turned away, ashamed. "But I'm not your wife," she whispered.

"You wouldn't marry me even if I could ask," he said quietly. "You would choose God over me."

Stunned, she touched his arm. "Nathan, I—"

"No." He held up a hand and smiled faintly. "I don't want to know. Let me have some hope."

Tears clouded her eyes. "He is the God of hope, Nathan. And I pray every day that he will fill you with joy and peace and hope." She drew a ragged breath. "Love hopes all things."

In the deepening gloom, she saw a shadow cross his face like a cloud across the moon. He lifted her hand to his face and laid it against his cheek. "I love you, Samantha," he murmured. "Is that what you want to hear? *You're* my hope."

"Nathan," she murmured, anguished. She should have left, should have fled down this mountain of isolation long ago. Truth was getting confused with her feelings for Nathan, endangering him and her as well.

She had replaced the Lord and become Nathan's stumbling block.

❧

"It's such a simple plan, it just might work," Caleb said. He, Nathan, George, Broom, and Kelley huddled around the table, deep in discussion. Samantha washed the dinner dishes, annoyance rising. Four months had gone by, and Nathan hadn't abandoned the idea of a robbery. He'd been right about one thing, she reflected as she scraped a plate. They were living strictly off the garden and hunted game.

"The simpler, the better, gentlemen," Nathan said. "Holdups are for the unimaginative. I'm willing to bet we could do this even without any guns."

Angered, Samantha slapped two dishes together as she put them away. Experience had taught her that displaying such emotion was futile, but every other method of voicing her displeasure with the robbery had fallen on deaf ears.

"I sure would hate to try it without a firearm," Broom put in mildly. "Just in case."

Samantha smacked the dishrag against a plate and rubbed vigorously. Why should she be meek? They were the sinners!

She snatched up a metal pot, clanging it with relish. Nathan turned to stare.

"Sorry," she said sweetly.

He turned back to the table. "Now, here's the arrangement, one more time."

Samantha towel-whisked the clean pot dry. Why should she curb her anger? She had good reason to be upset!

Samantha banged the pot on the bottom shelf, forgetting that the other end was unweighted. It flew up, hit the shelf above, and knocked down the overripe apples George had brought from town. They fell, one by one, and squashed on the floor.

Samantha bent down, her anger ebbing. She had looked forward to making a pie. Apple was Nathan's favorite. She picked up the gooey pieces and sadly dropped them into her apron.

Nathan knelt and handed her the remains of a core. "You're not hurt, are you?"

"N-no." She wiped her sleeve across her eyes.

Nathan chucked her under the chin. "It's just fruit, Samantha. It took a falling apple to teach Isaac Newton a lesson."

Samantha sighed and watched him return to the table.

Nathan rode alone in silence, the horse's steady clip-clop lulling, the sway of the carriage hypnotizing.

The autumn day was idyllic, cool but not cold, with little wind. His nerves stood on end, heightened, and he marveled at the beauty of the flat grassland of southern Wyoming. He wished he really were out for a pleasant business ride.

Scratching absently at his arm, Nathan groaned at the agony of wearing wool. But the gray suit, white shirt, and black string tie made him look like the respectable businessman he was supposed to be. He'd even trimmed his hair and splashed on some bay rum.

Nathan tried to concentrate on the Medicine Bow Mountains to the east. Their solid presence reminded him that they would still be standing long after he no longer lived.

His throat closed up, and he took a deep breath. He couldn't afford to lose his concentration; he needed a clear head for this job. Posing as a wealthy businessman, he would gain admittance to the bank president's office, where a special safe was kept. From the checking he'd done, Nathan knew it should contain several thousand dollars of profits from an eastern company with gold-mining interests. He would gain the president's confidence and demand to check the safe's security. Once the safe was open, Nathan would pull a hidden gun and demand the money. The president would be tied up and informed that others were outside the bank holding a gun on him through the window. Then, with nobody the wiser, Nathan would walk out. Heading out of town in the buggy, he would change into riding clothes and make a fast getaway with the rest of the gang.

"It's stealing!" Samantha told him before he'd left.

"It's a rich company," he countered. "They can afford the loss."

"You were raised on the Bible same as me. Don't you even feel the least bit uncomfortable?"

"No. I've been doing this for six years and haven't gotten caught. I must be doing something right. Everything will go fine."

"And even if it does, what about the next time? Or the time after that? What if you don't get caught for your whole life, rich beyond measure? You'll eventually have to stand before God and account for your actions!"

Since that conversation, Nathan had repeatedly gone over his doubts. Blast her for making him even question; she would wreck his concentration yet! As long as he came out with the money, the robbery didn't matter.

The day he'd left the hideout, Samantha had stood beside his horse and touched his boot in the stirrup. "I'll pray for your safety, but I won't pray for your success. In fact, I'll pray everything goes wrong!"

"You do that, Sam." He'd laughed, reaching down to pat her shoulder.

He laughed again, remembering, then sobered. The small town of Rockgate rolled into view, and he sat up straighter. The bustle of people going about their normal business seemed unreal, somehow out of place.

He drew a deep breath. It would be fine. Already he could

see Broom leaning casually against a post by the saloon, idly smoking a cigarette. The others had been in town for the last few days, their arrivals staggered to prevent suspicion. It would be fine.

He pulled up the team outside the bank and pushed Samantha's words to the back of his mind.

Nathan hitched the horses and confidently swept through the bank's door, taking off his hat as he entered. He scanned the room out of the corner of his eye to make certain no extra men had been hired to guard the money, then stepped up to the teller's cage.

"I need to speak to the president." Nathan kept his voice calm and clear, his smile engaging.

The teller's face was stoic as granite. "He's a very busy man. May I help you with something?"

Nathan feigned impatience. "It's about a substantial deposit, and I need to speak with him." He casually withdrew a bulging wallet from his suit coat. Nathan had earlier stuffed it with strips of newspaper cut to the size of greenbacks, surrounded on either side with a few real bills to enhance the illusion.

The teller's eyes flickered. "Just a moment. I'll see if Mr. Marsh is available." He scuttled to a door marked "President" in gold lettering and rapped quickly. A gruff voice sounded behind the door, and the teller scurried inside.

Nathan smiled, mentally ticking off seconds. Within a minute, the teller bustled back to his cage. "He'll be right out to help you, Mr.—"

"Williams," Nathan snapped. "Is there a problem?"

As if on cue, the door opened, and a stylish-looking man with muttonchops appeared. Nathan appraised the dark suit and vest with a gold watch fob prominently displayed. The man smiled and extended a hand. "Vernon Marsh, Mr.—?"

"Williams." Nathan briskly shook his hand. "I have some business to discuss with you, Mr. Marsh. In private."

"Of course!" Marsh ushered Nathan into his office and a leather chair. He closed the door, then settled himself on the other side of the desk, bobbing his head at the safe behind him. "I should have extra guards on hand. I'm awaiting a courier to pick up the profits of one of our eastern customers."

Nathan smiled politely. "Yes, I'm aware you have heavy dealings with some rather large companies."

"Which brings us to you, Mr. Williams. How can this bank be of service?"

Nathan steepled his fingers and frowned. "I'll have some money soon to deposit from a real-estate sale that I've come west from Pennsylvania to transact. I'm concerned that the bank I do business with be fiscally sound and physically safe."

"Let me assure you that our bank is indeed fiscally sound. And as I said, I can have extra guards on hand. There's no possibility that—"

"Talk is fine, Mr. Marsh, but I'd like to see where my money would be stored."

"Why, in our vault, of course." Marsh looked puzzled, but he rose. "If you'll just—"

Nathan nodded at the office safe behind the desk. "Is that where you keep the really important money? Or maybe you don't think my money deserves the same protection as that eastern company."

Marsh sat down with a huff. "We do keep money here, and I'll show you its safety." He swiveled around in his chair and reached for the combination lock.

Smiling, Nathan leaned forward, his fingers inching inside his jacket toward the hidden revolver.

⌒

Sighing, Samantha leaned back in her porch chair. The night seemed blacker than ever, the silence of the mountains more deafening. "Shouldn't they be home by now? It's been two weeks since they left."

Relaxed, George sat on the porch rail, his back propped against a post. He calmly continued to whittle on a willow stem. Since the night he'd nearly killed Crawford, nothing seemed to faze him. "Maybe they stopped to celebrate in South Pass City."

"What if—" She raised her eyes, and as though he sensed it, George raised his too.

He shrugged. "That's possible."

Samantha shivered, turning her face. "How will we know?"

"Nathan said to wait a month. If they aren't back, I'm supposed to take you to the reservation. The priest there will take care of you."

Samantha rose, wrapping her arms around her shoulders. The weather had turned decidedly colder, but the chill inside her heart numbed her more. She'd prayed constantly for Nathan and Caleb since they left, imploring God for their safety and begging for another opportunity to speak to them about trusting God to meet their needs.

"Please don't let them do this, Father. Bring them home safely," she whispered. In Kansas City, she'd once seen photographs of dead outlaws. Caught trying to rob a bank, the three men had been gunned down in the streets, their bullet-riddled bodies propped up proudly for all to see.

Every night for two weeks, she'd dreamed of Nathan and Caleb on display like that, their faces white with death, their bodies punctured by bullet holes. They would be mocked and jeered at as they had been in the army, thrown into a pauper's grave, and consigned to hell. All before she even knew about it.

"Would it make you feel better to help me with my reading?" George said. Together they had worked through some of Nathan's easier books and were now reading Psalms.

She was too edgy even to teach. "I think I'll just go to bed. When you get tired, you can sleep in Nathan and Caleb's room. You don't have to sleep on the porch like you have been."

"I can protect you better out here."

Samantha smiled. "Good night, then."

"Good night."

While she undressed for bed, prayers for Nathan and Caleb were still in her heart. What if they died, never knowing the truth? She crawled between cold covers, shivering.

You're so weak. Your prayers go unanswered. You can't even save those in your own household!

"Oh, hush," she mumbled, sleepy, drawing the covers over her head for warmth. "God is with me."

Is he? She thought she heard a laugh. *Can you feel him?*

Confused, she drifted into an uneasy sleep, images of Nathan and Caleb dead filling her imagination. She saw blood on her hands, the blood of her own guilt. She hadn't spoken enough to them, hadn't really been God's light in the darkness. Voices drew closer, pointing long-nailed fingers, laughing . . .

"Samantha . . . Samantha . . . Samantha . . ."

She opened her eyes, panting, expecting to see demons lurking in every corner.

"Samantha."

She gasped, then realized George was speaking softly at her closed door. "Wh-what, George?"

"Riders are coming. Get dressed."

"All right." Actions calmer than her emotions, she groped in the dark for her clothes and changed quietly. Her heart pounded. What if the riders were criminals bent on revenge? Or even the law? Maybe Nathan and Caleb had been caught and had told that she was here, an accessory to their crime.

She slipped on her shoes and hurried to the porch. The night was blacker than ever, clouds covering the stars, revealing that she couldn't have been asleep more than an hour or two.

Where was George?

Heart thumping, she eased down in the willow chair and clenched her fists around the arms. A thousand demons seemed to mock, a thousand doubts assailing her like arrows.

"The Lord is my light and my salvation. Whom shall I fear?" she whispered. "Though I walk through the valley of the shadow of—"

The sound of pounding hooves filled her ears. She rose but could move no farther. Riders approached. She watched, terrified, as five silent figures drew to a halt and dismounted in the darkness, then stepped into a tiny sliver of light.

Joy filled her heart and spread outward. "Nathan! Caleb!" She flew from the porch, not caring whose arms she flung herself into.

"Hey, little sis!" Caleb grabbed her up and swung her

around, then set her down. He smiled, but his eyes looked tired.

Nathan hung back, quiet, fingering the reins of his horse. Samantha stepped toward him and touched his sleeve. "What happened?"

Nathan sighed. He put his arms around her and held her close, then placed a quick kiss on her lips. "It didn't go well, Samantha," he muttered.

With sinking dread, she realized that she couldn't tell in the darkness if the other men were all there. What if they'd lost someone during the holdup? "Oh, Nathan, don't tell me—"

He sighed again, his shoulders drooping. "The president couldn't open the safe. I didn't get any money."

TWELVE

No money?" Samantha whispered, stunned. The hair on her arms prickled, followed by a rush of thankfulness. Happiness spread from her heart to her face. "You didn't get the money!"

"You don't have to look so cheerful," Nathan muttered. "All that way for nothing!" Cursing, he jerked the reins of his startled horse.

"I'll put him up for you." George stepped from the shadows, shrugging at Samantha's surprised expression. "I went through the woods to see who the riders were." He led Nathan's horse away.

Samantha took Nathan's arm. "Come inside, and I'll fix some coffee. You can tell me what happened."

He shook her off. "I'd rather not talk about it, and I'm dog-tired, Samantha."

"Oh, come on, Nathan." Caleb laughed. "It could be worse! You and I could both be dead."

"We could also be several thousand dollars richer!"

"Come inside," Samantha said softly. She took his arm again, and this time he didn't pull away. Inside, he slumped at the table. Caleb stoked the fire, and Samantha set the coffee to brew, then sat beside Nathan. "Tell me what happened."

He rubbed a gouged spot in the wood with his thumb,

eyebrows furrowed. "I got in the president's office just fine and had him convinced I was a wealthy, potential customer. He started to open the safe, but the lock wouldn't work. No matter how many times he tried the combination, it wouldn't work!"

"Couldn't anyone else unlock it?"

Nathan rolled his eyes. "He said the only other person who knew the combination and who he would trust to open the safe was the sheriff. I couldn't exactly wait around for him to open the safe then hold them both up. I also couldn't chance the sheriff recognizing me. I have 'wanted' posters in almost every sheriff's office in Wyoming, Colorado—"

"Nevada," Caleb put in cheerfully.

Nathan glared at him. "So I mumbled an excuse to get out of the office before he could actually get the sheriff. I managed to get Caleb and the other boys' attention, and we hightailed it out of town."

"Did they follow you?"

Nathan shook his head. "But when we went through South Pass City, we saw a Laramie newspaper that mentioned the near robbery and had my description. They figured out who I was."

Nathan turned, leveling serious eyes. "I was counting on that money for food. Now we'll have to rely on what we can hunt."

"That much money would have fed you for life!"

Nathan curved his palm around her nape, his fingers caressing. "I also wanted to take you somewhere special," he said softly. "Europe . . . a tropical island. Someplace we could enjoy together."

A thrill ran up her spine, and she shivered. Nathan's voice

did something strange to her stomach. His hand seemed to draw her closer to him, his fingers seductive like beckoning fire.

She drew a deep breath and leaned back. "We don't have to go anywhere, Nathan. I'm happy here. And as for the food, we have enough for the winter. Besides the game, we have vegetables George and I grew, plus the cow for butter and milk."

Nathan's face clouded.

Caleb reached into his coat pocket. "There was a letter for you in South Pass City, Samantha. It has the name Sally Jordan on the envelope."

"Sally!" She ripped the sealed flap, then paused. She would rather treasure the letter alone in her room. "I'm thankful you two are alive," she said softly. "I'll go back to bed and let you drink your coffee."

Caleb and Nathan rose with her. Caleb ambled to the fireplace, whistling, taking his time retrieving the coffeepot.

Nathan glanced at Caleb, then focused on Samantha. He bent his head for a slow kiss, then laid his hands under her jaw line. "If I could never see your face again, I wouldn't want to live," he whispered. "You're the only good thing in my life."

Samantha felt heat rise where he touched her. "Don't say that, Nathan. It sounds like you worship me."

"I do." He smiled. "Don't you know that, Samantha Martin? You've always owned my heart."

Samantha lowered her eyes. "You don't know what you're saying," she whispered. "One person can't own another's heart. God is the only one we should give our hearts to."

Nathan dropped his hands, and a frown crossed his face. "There's no room for anyone else in your heart, is there?"

Samantha felt the distance between them like a canyon. How could she explain that only Jesus could be their true bridge, that only he could complete the circle of their relationship? "Nathan, I do love you," she whispered. "If anything had happened to you . . ."

He laughed bitterly and stepped back. "Go read your letter, Sam. Nothing happened, as you can see. Nothing at all."

She started down the hall, then stopped. Nathan's back was turned, and he raked his fingers through his hair.

"I disagree, Nathan," she whispered to herself. "I'm not sure what, but I think something very important happened."

One week later, Jonathan Hamilton read a local Kansas newspaper article about the attempted robbery at Rockgate. Robberies in broad daylight were rare, and a robbery attempted by one man—right in the president's office—was unheard of. But the article noted that Nathan Hamilton's schemes were frequently daring and so far hadn't involved any gunplay or bloodshed, despite the fact that he was wanted for murder.

Jonathan leaned back in his chair, his heart aching with grief. He read the article twice to make sure he hadn't missed any details, then folded the paper and slapped it gently against his thigh. He let his feet thud to the floor and shook his head in resignation.

After the war, Jonathan had gone home expecting a happy reunion. What had greeted him was a ghost town of burned remains and the crude grave of his wife. He'd asked around about his son, only to discover that Nathan had joined the army. When the war ended and Nathan still didn't return home, Jonathan assumed he had died for the North. Until the newspaper articles began. He'd been reading about Nathan's exploits for several years now and had ignored the situation long enough. His son evidently had no intention of pursuing another line of work.

And why should he? The money was good; so far he'd been clever enough to elude capture; and his fame probably gave him his pick of the ladies. Rumor had it he was handsome, and women were often inexplicably drawn to unsavory types.

No doubt new rewards would be posted soon. Every lawman and bounty hunter west of the Mississippi would be on the chase.

Jonathan absent-mindedly fingered the tin star pinned to his shirt. The quiet town of Radleyville would have to do without its sheriff for a while. He had to find his son.

Struggling to forget their recent failure, Nathan and Caleb settled in to weather the cold months ahead. They knew from experience the heavy winter snowfalls would prevent anyone from reaching the cabin, and they, along with Samantha, prepared to wait for the spring thaw. Broom and Kelley headed out of the mountains just before the first snow fell. George left to spend the winter on the reservation with his family.

"If I eat one more pickled carrot, I swear I'll hop away," Caleb grumbled, pushing aside his plate.

Samantha smiled at her brother as she collected dirty dishes. "Well, it's not steak, but it is edible. And a 'Thank you for a great supper' wouldn't hurt either."

"It wasn't all that bad," he mumbled.

"It was good," Nathan said, smiling as Samantha lifted his plate. "Your garden came in handy."

Samantha hid a smile. It wasn't Nathan's way to admit he'd been wrong, but even he knew they hadn't really needed money to survive the winter. The vegetables alone had given them plenty to eat. He and Caleb even went hunting and occasionally brought back an elk or deer.

Nathan pulled out two cigars and handed one to Caleb, then reached in his pocket. "Cards?"

Caleb grinned, biting off the cigar's tip. "Long as you don't cheat."

"Who, me?" Nathan grinned innocently and started shuffling. "Sam, do you hear your brother? Do I cheat?"

"Probably," she tossed over her shoulder as she rinsed the last plate.

"You see?" Caleb laughed and struck a match against the bottom of his boot. He reached languidly for his cards and tipped his chair back on two legs.

Nathan blew a smoke ring at the ceiling. Samantha touched his shoulder as she passed, but he covered her hand to stop her. He smiled warmly, and her stomach danced. Shy, she retreated to the far side of the room. Even with her brother present, the close quarters already pressed against the walls of her morality.

Nathan turned back to deal cards, and Samantha settled herself in the big willow chair, brought indoors for the season. The winter wind whistled, and icy branches tapped against the glass. She shivered, tucking her feet under her. The gesture was more for security, for the front room radiated warmth from the late summer addition of a wood-burning stove.

Caleb slapped down a losing hand. "Are you sure you're not cheating?"

"Not me," Nathan said cheerfully, raking in the coins on the table. He smirked around the cigar clamped between his teeth.

Samantha smiled behind her hand then pulled her Bible from the end table. It felt so right to live with Caleb again, to trade good-natured teasing and insults as they had when they were children. She still looked up at him with younger-sister eyes, and she supposed she always would. Her heart filled with love for both Caleb and Nathan, grateful they had all at last been reunited.

That night Nathan read to them in the warmth of the front room, beginning a nightly winter ritual. His smooth, deep voice transported them beyond winter's icy grasp to Robinson Crusoe's island, the high seas in search of Moby Dick, and the creation of Frankenstein's monster. At Christmas he read *A Christmas Carol,* and as Samantha wiped away a tear at Scrooge's change of heart, she decided Mr. Dickens was her favorite author.

Some nights Samantha and Nathan would huddle together near the fire or stove, and he would read poetry exclusively for her. She often wished the poet would come right out and speak plainly instead of using big words, but Samantha loved to hear the gentle cadence of Nathan's voice.

One night she handed him the Bible.

"Read something, please?" If only he read the words for himself, maybe he would believe.

Nathan turned his head, obviously uninterested in the change in literature. "I haven't opened a Bible since my mother died."

Caleb sighed and rose. "I'm going to bed. Don't let the shouting get so loud that it wakes me up."

Samantha felt her cheeks flame, and she pulled the Bible back to her lap.

"Samantha," Nathan said quietly. "Why do you keep trying to convince me of something I know isn't true?"

"It *is* true. You know it is, Nathan. How could you grow up with parents who loved God the way yours did and not believe?"

"That's easy enough to answer." He laughed and rose, turning to the window. Snow swirled outside. "I've never seen any proof that Jesus is real."

"No proof?" Samantha laid a hand on his shoulder. "We're in the middle of winter, symbolic of his death. In the spring, everything will bloom again, just as he came back to life. As we have another life when we believe." She drew a deep breath. "No proof? Have you ever seen a newborn baby—"

"Don't use sentiment on me!" He whirled, his eyes so dark and foreboding she drew back. "I've seen the opposite of new life, Samantha. I've looked death in the face, with its bloody teeth and gnarled features, coming for men who didn't deserve to die. And I couldn't stop it. All the bandages and sutures in the world wouldn't help."

"But death doesn't matter if we believe. No matter how terrible a death, the joy we can expect afterward—and the joy we can have now—overshadows it all."

"Do you think God overshadows everything?" Laughing bitterly, he turned away. "Do you think he *forgives* everything?"

Samantha touched his arm. "You've been having bad dreams again, haven't you?"

"Not bad enough to wake me, but that's almost worse." He turned, his green eyes filled with sadness. "Someday I'll have to leave you because of what I've done. But I'll always love you."

She embraced him, wanting to embrace his pain as well. "You'll always have *God's* love too. No matter where you go, he'll always know where you are."

⌒

"Let me get this straight," Jonathan said, pouring another whiskey for the drunken man sitting across the green baize-covered table. "You say they're holed up in Wyoming?"

"That's right." Justin Crawford smiled viciously, reaching for the glass. "The Wind River Mountains."

Jonathan stared at the other man, sizing him up for the turncoat he was. It disgusted him to have to buy information, but no one from Kansas to Colorado had been doing any talking until he'd slipped enough money into the right hands. "Why'd you leave?" he bit out.

Crawford smiled coldly. "A little disagreement over a woman."

Jonathan pretended to take a swallow from his own glass, feigning nonchalance. "Women are usually more trouble than they're worth."

"You said it! I thought I'd have this one for mine, if that Injun-lovin' boy hadn't stepped in. That piece would've liked it fine. Pity she had to be Hamilton's woman. But for all I know, he's tired of her by now and shared her with the others. If Martin allowed it, of course, her bein' his sister and all."

Jonathan's head jerked up. "His sister is with them?"

"Sure 'nough. Hamilton fetched her from some orphanage and brought her to the hideout." Crawford's face twisted into a fiendish smile. He held out his glass for another drink, then gulped it down and belched. "He claimed she weren't his woman, but you and I know a man ain't gonna travel all that way with a purty woman and leave 'er alone." He squinted. "Why you want 'em, anyway? You a bounty hunter?"

"That's none of your business, Mr. Crawford," Jonathan said coldly. "I've got two hundred dollars if you'll tell me how to get to their hideout and where they have guards posted."

Crawford laughed amiably. "I'd like to see somebody haul 'em in. Hamilton's got a noose waiting for him, and it'd make me feel like things was squared if he got his neck stretched. In fact, if you don't turn 'em in, maybe I'll do it myself."

"Just tell me how to get there," Jonathan snapped. "And don't leave out any details."

THIRTEEN

The winter months passed slowly, and Samantha waited patiently until milder weather allowed Nathan to take her hiking to the high country. They climbed a switchback trail above the timberline, where bare ridges and outcrops of boulders jutted into the blue sky. Up high, the only trees that grew were dwarf pines, sheltered by snowdrifts and boulders.

In the woods they saw willow stems and fresh-cut lengths of aspen gnawed by beavers. Mule deer and bighorn sheep drank from cold, clear mountain creeks. Orange, green, and yellow lichen washed across boulders, and the earth smelled of sap, must, melting snow, and new growth. Closer to their cabin, they saw tiny aspen buds opened into shy green leaves. Mushy from the melting snow, the ground was covered with white marsh marigolds and yellow anemones. Life was reawakening under the Master's hand.

From her bed during the summer, Samantha could hear the creek rushing high along its granite bed and willow-lined banks, flooding the meadows. During the day she often slogged through the grass to the nearby woods, just to throw her head back and gaze up in wonder at the dizzying height of the pines and aspens.

She had never felt so isolated yet so filled with peace.

Nathan and Caleb considered the mountains a refuge from the law, but to her they were a sanctuary to God.

The other gang members returned, only to disappear for days, sometimes weeks, at a time. Then they would return with big smiles and burlap bags Samantha was certain were filled with money. Nathan and Caleb never went along, but she sensed they had helped planned the holdups.

Nathan brooded all summer as if restless. She often heard him pace the floor late at night. She figured he was either scheming or escaping the demons in his nightmares.

At the beginning of autumn, Nathan said he and Samantha couldn't hike the high country anymore, for snow had already begun to fall there. Indeed, she could feel the turn of seasons in the air, and the nights grew chilly once again.

Samantha hummed as she chopped the last remnants of tomato vines from the dead garden. She glanced at George working steadily beside her, knowing he was just as anxious to clear the field. The ground would lie fallow during the winter, but come spring, they would replant.

During the year, they'd harvested a variety of vegetables for summer consumption and preserved an abundance for the cold months ahead.

"The earth is the Lord's, and the fulness thereof," she murmured, grateful that this year, as last, God had provided.

Samantha placed her hand at the small of her back and stretched. Gardening gave her such peace. She thrilled to the budding sprouts in spring, the full bloom in summer, and even the care of the barren field for winter. She leaned against the hoe and sighed with contentment.

"Back hurt?" George asked anxiously, stopping his hoe in midswing.

"A little, but the work feels good. Besides, we need to finish before the ground gets too hard." She smiled at him, wondering if Nathan had once again asked him to watch out for her.

"Let me finish. You should rest. It's starting to get chilly now that it's late afternoon. You wouldn't want to get sick."

"I'm fine, George."

"Just the same, I'd—"

The sound of pounding hooves interrupted him, and they both turned. George stepped in front of Samantha, but as the rider drew closer, he backed away.

Broom reined up short, ignoring their salutations. His usually calm eyes were frantic, and his horse was lathered. "Where's Nathan?"

"I'll get him." George dropped his hoe and raced up the cabin steps. "Nathan! Broom's in from the lookout!"

Nathan strode from the cabin, his eyes flickering to Samantha before he turned to Broom. "What's wrong?" His voice was calm, but he frowned.

"A stranger came riding up the pass. Kelley and I stopped him, of course."

"He's alone?"

"Yeah, but it gets stranger. He handed over his gun without us asking for it. He said he had to speak to you. Says he knows you."

"Who is he?" Nathan's eyes narrowed.

"He wouldn't say. But he don't look like a bounty hunter, and he said he didn't want to hurt you. Just talk. He's an older fellow, probably forty-ish. Seems harmless, Nathan, but we weren't sure what you'd want. I left Kelley watching him while I came up here."

"Bring him here," Nathan said. "I'd feel better if he weren't out where somebody could rush in. Make sure you check for a concealed gun or knife. I don't want any surprises."

He turned to George. "Go with Broom and bring this man up here. Leave Kelley on watch. I'll take Caleb and have a look with the field glasses before he rides up here."

The men nodded at Nathan's command, and Nathan called out to the bunkhouse for Caleb, who was repairing a loose floorboard. Samantha laid a hand on Nathan's arm as her brother ambled toward them, and a sudden fear gripped her. What if this stranger was a bounty hunter come for Nathan and Caleb?

He glanced down at her and smiled. "Don't worry, Sam. I know what you're thinking, and I'll be careful. Go in the house and stay there."

She nodded, trying to quell the rising fear in her throat. "I'll start dinner. You'll be hungry . . . when you come back."

She turned at the cabin steps. Nathan and Caleb were saddling up, their expressions grim. Caleb checked his gun, then smoothly reholstered it. "Oh, Lord, please protect them," she murmured, watching fearfully as they rode away.

Nathan and Caleb galloped to the top of the ridge overlooking the path to the hideout. Neither spoke as they took their position flat on their stomachs behind low, heath-covered boulders. Nathan fiddled with the field glasses, impatient as he stared at the distant figure.

"Do you have any idea who it is?"

"None whatsoever." Nathan grimaced. He hated not knowing whether he should be properly scared. He'd never forgive himself if the presence of this stranger caused harm to Samantha.

Three riders finally moved slowly into view. Even from the distance Nathan could tell the man was older than Broom or George. His hair was flecked with gray, and he sat a horse with the dignified posture of a man comfortable in the saddle. Nathan adjusted the field glasses.

Shock and disbelief rippled through him. Surely he was seeing things. There wasn't a chance in the world the man down there was who Nathan thought he was. Nathan swallowed hard and lowered the field glasses, dumbstruck.

"Can you see him?" Caleb said. "Is it somebody we knew from the war?"

Nathan slowly levered himself to his elbows then got to his feet. Caleb followed, staring from Nathan to the three men below. They slowly passed from view behind the trees.

"Of all times for you to lose your glib tongue! Who is it, Nathan?"

Nathan gestured with the field glasses, then dropped his arm uselessly. "It's somebody we knew from the war, all right, Caleb," he finally managed to say. Feeling weak, he forced a thin smile. "It's my father."

"Your *what?*" Caleb strained to see down the path where the three had disappeared. "But your pa's—"

"Dead. At least that's what we were told."

"How'd he find us? I can understand him looking for you after all these years, but we aren't exactly the easiest people in the world to locate."

"Talking's not going to get us any answers, my friend." Saddle leather creaked as Nathan mounted. "And I'd rather get to the cabin before he does, so I can prepare Samantha."

Nathan led the way, riding at a fast gallop. He swung a leg over to dismount when he heard the clatter of hooves coming up the main trail.

Cursing, Nathan realized there wouldn't be time to talk to Samantha first. His body seemed paralyzed, his mouth dry. He could only manage to blink while he watched the approaching figure of his father astride his horse.

Nathan caught his gaze, as penetrating as it had always been, then his father rode past. Nathan tipped his hat back on his head and stepped out. His first impulse to run to his father was quickly squelched by guilt. He hadn't exactly been a sterling son these past years. Caleb stepped behind him.

Jonathan Hamilton dismounted and tethered his horse, his back to Nathan. George and Broom dismounted quickly, poised to head off trouble should it arise. Jonathan turned. His eyes widened at the sight of his son, and he moved toward Nathan.

Heartbroken at the sight of his father, Nathan rushed forward. He couldn't fathom that he was really alive when all these years they'd thought him dead. "Father!"

"Nathan."

Nathan felt his father's arms draw around him, warm and secure. He blinked back tears and straightened. Though older, his father's face was as familiar as ever.

Jonathan smiled. "Nathan," he said again, this time sadly. He glanced at the other men. "Can you and I speak in private somewhere?"

Nathan laughed, joyous. Turning, he raised his voice. "Boys, I'm sure my father hasn't come here to do me in, so you can all relax and get back to whatever you were doing. Father," he motioned with his arm, "let's step inside."

Caleb bounded up the stairs and burst through the door. "Samantha!"

She scurried up the hallway, then stopped short at her brother's grim expression. "Caleb, what's—?"

Jonathan entered just ahead of Nathan, and Samantha's hand flew to her mouth. She swayed, and Caleb put a hand on her elbow, helping her sit at the table. Nathan motioned for his father to sit also. "It's all right, Sam, you haven't seen a ghost after all. My father's alive!"

Samantha stared, dumbstruck.

Jonathan took a chair across from her. His eyes searched hers briefly, then he turned to her brother. "Caleb."

"Mr. Hamilton." Caleb shook hands.

Nathan moved behind Samantha and rested his hands on her shoulders. It felt so good to be together once again.

His father looked at all three in turn, finally letting his eyes rest on Samantha. Nathan curled his fingers protectively around her shoulders.

Jonathan shifted his gaze to Nathan, and his eyes misted. He cleared his throat. "I'm glad you're all here so I can talk to the three of you at once."

"About . . . ?" Nathan found it difficult to curb his impatience when a thousand questions rested on his tongue.

"About what you think you're doing."

"What's your meaning, Mr. Hamilton?" Caleb's eyes hardened.

The older man smiled faintly. "It's good to see you three grown, even if you are in more trouble than you seem to realize." He fixed his gaze on Nathan and Caleb. "There are some pretty serious 'wanted' posters circulating around with your descriptions on them."

Nathan's stomach clenched. "We've seen them, Father."

"Then why do you keep stealing?"

"It's how we make a living," Nathan snapped, bristling. "Did it take you seven years to come up with that question?"

Jonathan leaned back. Sighing, he reached in his coat pocket and withdrew a tin star. "I wanted to know because I'm a sheriff."

Nathan froze, shocked. Samantha gasped, and Caleb drew his gun. Jonathan glanced at it, obviously annoyed. "I haven't come to hurt anyone, Caleb. Or to turn you in."

Warily, Caleb reholstered the revolver. Nathan moved to the empty chair between Samantha and his father. "I made my way back to Kansas after the war," Jonathan said, "but you were gone. And so was the land. And your mother," he added softly. "I searched for you for years, Nathan, and finally gave you up for dead. I accepted a job as sheriff of Radleyville, and two years later I saw your 'wanted' poster."

Nathan's anger slowly boiled. "You and Mr. Martin were reported dead. After the farms were destroyed and Mother was killed, Caleb and I enlisted. We wanted revenge but didn't find any. All we saw was—" He choked back more words, fear churning in his stomach. Was he always going to have to question what he'd done? To hide the truth?

"I thanked God every day I was gone that I hadn't allowed you to join up, but when I came home, I learned it was too late," Jonathan said quietly.

"I wouldn't have left home, even when it was destroyed, if I thought there was a chance you were still alive!"

Jonathan's expression was pained. "I had a head wound and was unconscious for a long time in a Confederate prison hospital. It took me several months to even remember who I was. I suppose that's why I was presumed dead."

"Mr. Hamilton?" Samantha said, glancing at Caleb. "Do you think our father could still be alive?"

"No, Samantha," Jonathan said gently. "I saw your father fall in battle. He died instantly. I'm sorry."

Samantha bowed her head, and Caleb laid a hand on her shoulder. "We've always thought him dead, anyway," he said. "Nothing's changed."

"Nothing's changed," Nathan echoed sarcastically. He turned to his father, feeling bitterness rise within him like gathering steam. "Everything's changed since then! If you hadn't gone off to fight, none of this would have happened. I've wanted to ask you for a long time if your little act of heroism made you feel good."

"It wasn't heroism," Jonathan said firmly. "It was duty and honor and belief and—"

"Words! Just words, Father!" He knew he was shouting and making a fool of himself. The thought that his father had been wounded and alone in a hospital tore at his soul, yet he was still angry that his father had abandoned them.

Caleb moved to his side and laid a hand on his shoulder. "Let's go outside for a while and cool off."

Nathan glanced at Samantha. Her eyes were red from weeping, but she offered him a feeble smile. "I'll be fine."

He nodded and, not even glancing at his father, headed for the door.

Samantha closed her eyes and let out a long breath. She was devastated anew to learn of her father's death, but hope weaved its way in her heart like ivy in a patch of weeds. Maybe Jonathan Hamilton was the answer to her prayers for Nathan.

She smiled at him timidly, feeling shy after the years of separation. "Can I get you some water, Mr. Hamilton?"

His eyes met hers, and she straightened at the intensity of his gaze. "No, thank you, Samantha."

He glanced around the sparsely furnished room and nodded at the cast-iron cookstove. "Why do you have that way up here?"

"Nathan bought it for me so I wouldn't have to cook in the fireplace. In fact, I need to get back to making dinner."

"I'd be grateful to help you," Jonathan said. "It would give me something to do."

"You can help me peel potatoes."

He accepted the potatoes and knife and peeled quietly, standing, while she cubed a hunk of venison. The silence, if not companionable, was still soothing. She wondered how best to broach the subject of Nathan, when Mr. Hamilton cleared his throat. "So you've been here a long while?" he said.

"Over a year now." She drew a deep breath, taking courage. "Mr. Hamilton, Nathan—"

"Are you expecting a child?"

Samantha let her knife slip into the bowl. Jonathan's intense gaze met hers, and she flinched. "N-no! I . . . Nathan and I don't . . ."

"Don't what?"

"We don't . . . we're not involved . . . that way!"

He raised his eyebrows as if he didn't believe her.

Mortified, she backed away. "You don't understand. It's not like—"

"I can *see* what it's like, Samantha. My son is keeping you here as his mistress."

Samantha couldn't believe what she was hearing. How could Mr. Hamilton think such a thing about her? He'd known her since she was a small girl; surely he had known she would never do such a thing. But he continued to stare at her accusingly. She rushed for the door, flying down the steps and across the clearing into the woods. She stumbled over a fallen branch and fell among the pine needles.

She wrapped her arms tightly around her upraised knees and rocked back and forth, anguished. Mr. Hamilton couldn't know how hard she'd fought the urge to give in to Nathan. Or how hard it was for her to continue to pray in the spirit when her traitorous flesh screamed for the fulfillment of human desires.

A tear trickled down her cheek.

"Is it that bad?" She felt a gentle hand on her shoulder, and she looked up into a pair of concerned, deep brown eyes. George smiled faintly. "Your sorrow is wrapped as tight around you as your arms around your knees."

She relaxed and tucked her legs underneath herself. George sat beside her, waiting patiently. Funny how lately she forgot he was a boy. Or had he turned into a man without her knowing exactly when the process had taken place?

"Tell me what's wrong," he said quietly.

She drew a deep breath then told him everything that had happened with Nathan's father. The words spilled out in a rush of hurt and confusion, until she reached Jonathan's accusation. "He thinks Nathan and I . . ." She looked away, blushing, and her voice dropped to a whisper. "He thinks I'm Nathan's mistress."

"Maybe Mr. Hamilton isn't angry at you but at Nathan."

"It didn't sound that way!"

The corners of his mouth pulled up slowly. "You won't ever find out by hiding here in the woods. Come on, I'll walk you back." George grasped her hand and pulled her gently to her feet. "Nathan'll be worried about you anyway."

She hadn't thought of that. He was already angry enough at his father. She didn't want to add to his anxiety.

At the cabin, George touched the brim of his hat and headed off. Samantha stood with her hand on the doorknob, listening to Mr. Hamilton's and Nathan's heated voices. Their words overlapped before either man could complete a sentence, as though each one knew what the other's response would be.

"Father! Couldn't you—?"

"All the more reason why you—"

"You ever stop to think—?"

She rattled the doorknob to warn them of her presence. Both men turned as she entered. Nathan stood hunched over the chair she usually sat in, his knuckles white from gripping the back. His eyes radiated anger, and his jaw was clenched.

Mr. Hamilton stood at the stove frying venison and potatoes. Samantha expected to see a look of triumph in his eyes, but instead he smiled kindly and gestured at the table with a fork. "Sit down, my dear. The food will be ready shortly. Nathan, pull out a chair for your . . . for Samantha." He turned back to the food, flipping the meat and potatoes with smooth, experienced wrist work.

Nathan glared at his father's back, but he pulled out Samantha's chair and motioned for her to sit. When she was settled comfortably, he sat beside her at his customary place and reached for her hands. "He told me what he said to you, Sam. Are you all right?"

She managed a weak nod.

Mr. Hamilton set the food on the table and handed out the plates and silverware as though it were his house and he were the host. He took a chair on the other side of Samantha. "Nathan, this is your home. Would you please bless the food?" He bowed his head.

Nathan looked surprised. He glanced at Samantha, who quickly bowed her head. A long-forgotten litany seemed to return to him, and he intoned with his eyes open, chin held high, "For what we are about to receive, let us be truly grateful. Amen."

"Amen," Jonathan raised his head. He looked at Samantha and gestured at the food. "Please go ahead. It probably won't taste as good as if you had prepared it, but it will do."

"It looks fine," she said, begrudging him a smile. She ladled meat and potatoes onto her plate, surprised at her sudden hunger. The aroma made her mouth water. "We have lots of vegetables. I should have thought to set them out also."

"Vegetables? Good." Jonathan took the bowl from her and handed it to Nathan. "Do you have a cow? Can you get some fruit?"

Nathan thumped the bowl on the table. "Let's have it out now, Father. You have no right to come in here and call Samantha names, then lecture her on what to eat! For the last time, she's not expecting!"

Jonathan smiled sadly at Samantha. "You're hardly more than a girl. You've had the fewest choices of us all. I'm sorry if I offended you. I believed what I heard without checking for myself. Please accept my apology."

"What did you hear?" She glanced at Jonathan, then Nathan, and realized she was caught in a father-son struggle that had nothing to do with her. She pushed her plate away, her stomach churning with grief. If they were going to argue, she didn't want to stay in the room any longer. "If you'll excuse me, I'm going to find Caleb. Is he in the bunkhouse?"

Nathan nodded, but he made no move to stop her as she headed for the door. "Take a shawl," he said tersely. "It's getting cold outside."

She glanced at Nathan and his father, each pushed back from the table as though ready for a long, drawn-out fight. Then plucking the shawl from its peg, she wrapped it around her shoulders, praying silently that when she returned they would have found their peace.

FOURTEEN

Nathan watched the door close behind Samantha. He clenched his fists as a stab of pain tightened his stomach. How dare his father cause her unhappiness!

"She's grown into a lovely woman, Nathan. The kind of woman a man should be proud of."

"I *am* proud of her," he said fiercely. "That's why I don't appreciate you waltzing in here slinging unfounded accusations."

"You haven't married her, have you? Do you have any intention of marrying her?"

"No."

"Why?"

Defiance rushed through Nathan's veins. "Because one day they're going to come for me with a rope in their hands, and I'll swing from the nearest gallows. Samantha will be safer if they don't also find a *Mrs.* Nathan Hamilton. I don't want her to have my last name. *Our* last name," he added viciously.

"Do you think you can protect her by denying her your name?"

"She's not wanted. If I have to lead the law away from her, I will. I won't let anyone hurt her. She's a good woman."

Jonathan shook his head in disbelief, then gestured at the stove. "You bought her a stove, but you won't buy her a ring?

You're not treating her as though she's a good woman. You've set her up in this cabin with a life that's no more permanent than the play soddies you used to build on the farm. I remember you with your popgun, pretending to protect your family from the Indians, and Samantha with her favorite tea set and doll for a baby."

Jonathan leaned forward. "Just because she isn't carrying a child now doesn't mean she won't, Nathan. How much longer do you think the two of you can live in the same house without sharing the same bed?"

"I love Samantha," Nathan said evenly. "I have no intention of forcing her into something she's not ready for."

"What if she decides she is ready? It's written in her eyes that she adores you. How much resistance do you think she has?"

Before Nathan could answer, Jonathan slapped his palm against the table. "How can you ask her to perform the household duties of a wife and not be legally married to her? You say you love her, but you treat her like your maid!"

Nathan frowned. "She would never marry me even if I asked. She loves God too much."

"You don't think she can love you both?"

"I know she can't. She's never said so, but I know."

"But you would accept a physical relationship . . . without marriage . . . if that were her choice?" Jonathan said.

"That's all we lack from being married."

Jonathan leaned back, and his expression softened. "God intends physical intimacy as a seal, but it doesn't make a marriage. Our bodies are the only material possessions we truly own, and when a man and woman join together physically and spiritually, they give that unique part of themselves to each other. The two flesh literally become one in a physical seal between their souls. That's why the act was created for spouses . . . two people who would stay together, work together, *love* together until death. And ultimately, they would give of themselves only to each other as an unbroken bond."

Quiet, Nathan pondered his father's words. "I agree with that then. But it doesn't seem very important to go to a preacher or a judge just to get a piece of paper the law says we should have."

"If Samantha is a Christian, she won't agree to a marriage that isn't legal. Do you think it's for a piece of paper that a man and woman stand together before a preacher to unite themselves for life?"

"Isn't it?"

Jonathan shook his head. "It's to make a public profession of commitment. All sorts of promises can be spoken in the heat of passion. With no witnesses, the words can be refuted later by either the man or the woman. And in a Christian marriage, it's a profession before God—a request for his blessing."

Nathan pushed at his untouched food with his fork, guilt churning his stomach. He doubted he was eligible for anybody's blessing.

"Mother died, and I wasn't able to stop it," he said abruptly. "Then Caleb and I abandoned Samantha in an orphanage."

"I know." Nathan felt his father's hand on his arm. "Justin Crawford told me about her. He sold me the directions to your hideout."

Nathan uttered three curses strung together. "Did he also tell you he nearly raped her?"

"He intimated as much," Jonathan said. "I hated to pay him, but it was the only way to find out how to get here."

Nathan rose and turned, raking his hand through his hair. "If he told you how to get here, he'll tell anybody else who crosses his palm with enough money. This place isn't going to be safe much longer."

"Exactly. And do you want Samantha in the line of fire?"

Nathan turned back. He dropped his hands at his sides, deflated. How could he have ignored the truth for so long?

"Even if she's not your wife, Samantha is still your responsibility. Anyone can find you now, Nathan. Or her. And rest assured they'll come heavily armed, and some of them won't be long on compassion, even toward a woman."

"We've always been safe here, until now." Nathan sank wearily into his chair and dropped his head in his hands. "I suppose I could keep her with me on the run," he mumbled.

"You've been running long enough. Don't drag her any further." Jonathan paused. "Do you love her?"

Nathan raised his head. "I'd die for her."

Jonathan smiled faintly. "Your mother and I watched the two of you together, and we knew one day you would marry. But we'd hoped you wouldn't get married too young, before you had a chance to decide how you wanted to use the talents God gave you."

Nathan laughed. "I was a medic during the war, assisting the surgeons. It didn't take much talent to hold down screaming men while a doctor sawed off their legs and arms. Or to see that all the bodies were rounded up and buried. That war didn't require talent; it required guts. Only guts kept me going every day. Only guts let me help that poor man—"

Nathan squeezed his eyes closed and pressed his lips together, remembering.

"What man?" Jonathan said softly.

Nathan opened his eyes. "I started stealing because I was falsely accused of it during the war. I'm not proud that I lived up to the accusation, but it's a fact you should know."

Jonathan's face fell. "I'm sorry you chose that, son. How can you bear up under the burdens you carry without God?

"By loving Samantha."

"So you let her carry them for you?"

Nathan's heart fell. Was that what she had been doing? He bowed his head, chastened. "What should I do, Father?" he mumbled. "I don't seem to have a lot of choices."

"No, you don't." Jonathan straightened. "You're not going to like this, but it's the best advice I can give. Turn yourself in, and maybe the judge'll go easy on you."

"*Turn myself in?*" Nathan laughed. "They want me for murder!"

"Did you do it?"

"It was self-defense. I saved Caleb from getting shot by a Union Pacific mucketymuck who couldn't believe he wasn't cheated at cards."

"But you were already wanted, so you fled town?"

Nathan laughed again. "Eventually. I had a slug go clean through my chest—that held me up for a while."

Jonathan leaned forward. "We can get you the best lawyer there is for the trial, and Samantha can stay with me. You'd have to do time for robbery, but when you get out—"

"When, Father? In ten years? Twenty?" Nathan shook his head. "And what makes you think Samantha would wait for me, when she won't marry me now?"

"If she loves you she'll wait."

Nathan crossed his arms. "I can't see myself doing time. Even if I do manage to escape the hangman's noose."

"You asked for my advice, Nathan," Jonathan said. "It's not perfect, but it's what should be done. Your actions reap consequences. You're going to have to own up to your responsibilities sometime . . . to the law . . . Samantha . . . God. Or do you still believe, even now, that you don't need him?"

Nathan nodded firmly.

Jonathan's face fell, but he straightened his shoulders. "Do you have a better plan than turning yourself in?"

Nathan stared ahead. "Plans come so easily to me. I can figure out the best way to rob any bank in the country within a matter of minutes, but . . ." He was silent for a long time. "No, I don't have a better plan," he finally said.

"If you're worried about finding a place for Samantha to live, she can go back to Kansas with me. I can—"

"No."

"But she has experience teach—"

"*No!*"

Jonathan was quiet a moment. "There's going to be pain for both of you one way or another. Don't make Samantha a victim of your mistakes."

Nathan closed his eyes. "I need her, Father," he whispered. "She's all I have."

"Nathan." His father's voice sounded sorrowful. "If you love Samantha . . ."

Nathan whispered a curse. He turned his head, but he knew his father had seen the tears in his eyes. He felt a hand on his shoulder. Something buried in his soul cried out for him to turn into his father's arms.

"No!" He fought the urge by whirling around. *"I need her!"*

"You're going to destroy her," Jonathan said sadly. "She'll stay with you until one or possibly both of you are killed. Be honest with yourself, Nathan. You don't have to answer out loud, but do you understand that?"

Nathan shoved down anger and guilt like the lid of an overstuffed trunk. He shook his head then abruptly stood. "I'm going to the bunkhouse to get her. She didn't finish her meal."

Jonathan rose also. "I know my words are strong, but I had to come talk with you. If you won't turn to God, at least turn yourself in to accept the punishment you unfortunately deserve."

"It's too late for any of that, Father," Nathan mumbled. "This is the only life I know."

"Then I'll ride out in the morning." Jonathan started away, then glanced over his shoulder. "I will always remember a little boy who ran to jump in my arms every evening when I came home after a hard day in the fields. You're my son, my only child, Nathan . . . my last link to Hannah. It's almost impossible to give you up this time, knowing it might be forever. But I have to let you go once again and pray you find your way."

Nathan gave a short laugh. "You and Samantha. Always praying for me."

Jonathan's eyes were wet. "If you ever need me, I'm in Radleyville. It's near where we used to live."

"I know where it is."

"Don't worry about me or any trouble you think you might bring my way. Samantha too. Tell her to come to me if she needs help . . . in case you—" His voice faltered on the unspeakable. "In case anything happens."

Nathan raised his eyes and opened his mouth to thank his father. But suddenly the five-foot distance between them seemed wider than the seven years they'd been apart. His father lived in one world, he in another.

A mask settled over Nathan's heart like a black hood, and he jerked his head at Caleb's room. "You can sleep in there tonight." Then he turned and left the cabin.

Samantha was curious about Nathan and Jonathan's conversation. But after one look at Nathan's face, she knew he wouldn't talk about it that night. Or maybe ever. Jonathan was nowhere in sight when she returned to the cabin, and Nathan tersely explained that his father would stay in Caleb's room. He was leaving in the morning.

Nathan warmed up the food for her, insisting she eat. He didn't stay to talk but drifted out to the porch. Gazing through the window while she washed dishes, Samantha could see his red cigar tip glowing in the night.

She longed to sit beside him on the porch steps and have him point out the stars. But she knew from his rigid posture there would be no stargazing tonight. Her heart ached for Nathan and his father, but she realized she couldn't do anything except pray. When Nathan was ready to talk, he would.

FIFTEEN

Early the next morning, Samantha stepped onto the porch. She leaned against the doorjamb, sorrow filling her heart at the sight of Nathan. He sat on the top step, staring at the woods. She wondered if he'd even moved since last night.

"Is your father gone?" She sat down beside him.

Nathan tore his gaze from the woods. "Yes, he left well before dawn."

"You didn't resolve anything, did you?" she said softly.

Nathan's mouth quirked. "No, we didn't. If you were praying for a miracle, God chose not to answer this one."

"I did pray you two would settle your differences. Your father loves you very much, Nathan. His heart is breaking, and he wants you to come back to him."

Nathan laughed and rose from the steps. He stared at the woods again, clenching his hands behind his back. "How can I go back, Samantha? I would have to be a different man."

"You can be. A different man with a new heart—a clean heart."

He turned slowly, hurt and loneliness reflected in his eyes. "It's impossible for me to have a clean heart."

"With God *all* things are possible. He can make us new. Jesus can give us a new life."

Nathan held out his hands and helped her to her feet. She

let herself be enfolded in his arms and felt him tremble. "All you have to do is ask," she said softly. "Don't fight what you know is the truth."

"The only truth I know is loving you," he murmured, lowering his head. "Sam, if you—"

"Hush," she said, silencing his anguish with a kiss. She wanted to comfort him, to draw him close like a child, as she had done at the abandoned cabin. Surely God had called her to care for this man.

"Sam," he murmured, moving his hands down her back. His touch sent chills racing through her and made her heart thump with anticipation. He pulled her closer, and he moved his lips to her ear. "You said all I have to do is ask," he whispered. "Caleb's gone for the day. Please come inside with me. I need you!"

Her head swirled, and her stomach tingled. This was what the act was intended for. Comfort. And if anyone needed comfort, it was Nathan. He'd robbed, killed, dishonored his father, done any number of unspeakable things, but she could still hear a cry for help from deep in his heart. What he needed—

"Jesus," she murmured so softly she was certain Nathan couldn't hear. "Jesus."

Within her, power surged from head to toe at the name. The only name that could help her. The only name that could help Nathan.

She pulled away, smiling gently. "You're reaching for peace the only way you know how, Nathan. But you have to reach upward for God. Not outward to another person. If we were married, I would want to be with you. But it's not what you really want right now."

His face darkened. "You mean it's not what *you* really want. One more minute and you would have agreed." His eyes gleamed, brittle and cold. "And you know we'll never be married."

Even though temptation had passed, strength crashed around her like falling glass, piercing her heart. Hadn't he said this before? Hadn't she known all along he would never marry her? Why did she—

"Why are you even here?" he muttered.

Why *was* she here? Even as he spoke, the words rose in her heart and her doubts gave them wings. Had she really heard God's call or just the desires of her own unreliable heart? "I . . . I love you!"

She stepped toward him, but he stepped away, his face unreadable. "We need some time away, Samantha," he said quietly. "Someplace safe. Do you think your friend Sally would let us visit?"

"Sally!" A sudden joy stirred her heart at the mention of her dear friend. "I'd love to see her! She said in her letter I should come to visit. She even mentioned you and Caleb. If we go now, will we be able to come back before the cabin gets snowed in?"

Nathan tipped her chin up with his hand. "Don't worry, Samantha. Leave everything to me. We'll go tomorrow."

⁓

Just before bed, Samantha pulled out her old carpetbag, shaking out the dust accumulated from sitting under her bed for a year and a half. Then she stuffed her Bible and clothes into it.

Fingering the tapestry lovingly, she thought about Sally and Frank. How were Tommy and Maria? It would be so good to be around a Christian family, to hear someone else's prayers besides her own.

"Samantha?" Nathan rapped at her door, and she froze. He never came to her room.

She threw her shawl around her nightgown and opened the door a crack. Remembering their encounter that morning, she clutched the shawl at her throat. "What is it, Nathan?"

"Do you mind if I come in?"

Her heart beat faster. "I don't think that's a good idea."

"Caleb's in the front room. Just leave your door open," he said. "I want to get a few books."

Her shoulders sagged with relief. It *was* his room, after all, or it had been until she'd taken it over. She stepped back. "Come in."

Nathan ambled to the bookshelves and perused the titles. His gaze wandered to the open bag on her bed, and she blushed when she realized her undergarments lay on top.

He turned back to the books. "Yes, this one . . . and this one . . ." He carefully stacked three volumes under his arm, then moved toward the door. Stopping short, he glanced above her bed. Samantha's heart flipped at the object of his gaze—the charcoal of Jesus and the lamb. "You'd better take that with you," he said.

"But we'll be back before—"

"Sally might want to see it again. You said she loved the old lady as much as you did."

Samantha smiled, warmed that he would remember. "You're right. That's a good idea."

"Take the picture out and roll it up. It'll fit better, and the frame can stay here."

"All right. Thank you, Nathan," she said quietly.

185

When he didn't move but kept shifting his gaze from her to the picture, she frowned. "Is there something else you needed?"

He pulled his eyes from the drawing. "No, Samantha," he said softly. "I think that's all. Good night."

⌒

In the stable the next morning, George knotted the last string and tugged on Samantha's bedroll to make sure it was secured to the saddle. He turned with a sad smile and touched her hand. "Be careful. I'll be sure to practice my reading now and then."

"Of course you will, George. I'll be back in a few weeks, and we'll read together some more. That is, if you're still here. Nathan, don't you think we could talk George into staying with us all winter?"

Standing by his own saddled horse, Nathan nodded. He took both sets of reins and led the horses into the clearing where Caleb waited.

Nathan thought his heart would break a thousand times on the trip to South Pass City, but he ignored his emotions and forced himself to concentrate. His job right now was to ensure a safe journey. He couldn't dwell on the pain yet to come.

By the time they rode the train to Cheyenne, he couldn't shake the darkness covering him, threatening to drag him under. Yet the wall of silence he'd built stood firm. Excited about seeing her friends, Samantha never seemed to notice his depression, not even during the final leg of the journey, on horseback again, to the Jordans' farm in northern Colorado.

Caleb's presence soothed the long stretches of quiet. He

never offered his opinion on why they were making the trek—
though Nathan speculated he certainly had the right—but
kept them both smiling with his teasing and laughter. It was
as though he tried to cover Nathan's silence with extra talking
of his own.

The stars had just displayed their nocturnal twinkle when
the three rode up wearily to the Jordans' modest wood home.
The fragrant odor of burning wood promised warmth and
friendliness, but before they could dismount, the front door
opened slowly. Light spilled from behind, and a dark figure
stood in the door with a raised shotgun. "It's awfully late to be
traveling, friends!"

Nathan reined his horse in front of Samantha's, but she
called, "It's Samantha Martin, Frank! And my brother, Caleb,
and my friend Nathan."

The door opened wider, allowing a shaft of light to fall
across the yard. A woman ran out, crying, "Samantha!"

"Sally!" Samantha nearly jumped from the saddle, but
Nathan caught her around the waist and set her down gently.
"Be careful!"

Her eyes met his in the dim light, and he could see joy filling her face before she scampered off. Sally met her halfway
up the walk, embracing her warmly. "I can't believe you're
here! Why didn't you tell me you were coming?"

"There wasn't time!" Samantha laughed. "Nathan decided
we should leave right away."

"Come inside, Samantha. Gentlemen. You'll catch your
death out here," Frank said. He extended his hand to Caleb,
then Nathan. "Sorry about the shotgun, fellows."

"It's all right," Caleb said. Nathan nodded in mute

agreement. Out West a man either lived with a gun or died without one.

Frank smiled. "I'll put up your horses. Sally's still got some coffee on, and I'll bet if you ask nice, she might let you have some of her famous dried-apple pie."

Leading the way inside, Sally laughed. "Oh, Frank!"

Nathan curled his fists. Did every Christian have to be so happy?

Sally ushered them to a trestle table. "You may not feel like sitting after that long ride, but I do have a pie, and there's just enough for everyone. But first let me see if I can guess who's who. You must be Samantha's brother, Caleb. Your face looks like hers."

"Yes, ma'am," Caleb said, removing his hat.

"And you," Sally turned, and her eyes twinkled, "are Nathan. Samantha talked about you nearly every day we were at the orphanage."

"She's talked about you quite a bit too," he mumbled, embarrassed.

"Me? Oh, Samantha, how could you? Some of the stories you must have told!"

"Actually, Sally, I haven't told all that many," Samantha said, her face flushed. "Nathan's not too interested in those orphanage days."

Nathan laughed, and cold resentment rose within him. Who were these people to be so joyful? He'd better set them straight before they dragged out their hymnals and prayer books! "I'm not a believer, Sally," he said, smiling. "Samantha knows I don't like to hear any God-talk."

Samantha stared at him, then turned away. Sally cast a

worried glance at Samantha, then at Nathan. Her face light-ened, and she motioned Caleb to a chair. "As I said, you may not feel like sitting, but—"

"With all due respect, ma'am, I'm really not hungry," Caleb said. "I'd just as soon call it a day. If you'll just tell me where I can bed down . . ."

"Oh dear." Sally's face wrinkled with worry. "We only have one extra room. "I can move Maria in with Tommy, but—"

"The barn will do me and Nathan just fine, ma'am," Caleb said. "I'll help your husband with the horses, then make myself a bed in the hay."

"Frank can give you some blankets, and he assures me the barn is warm." Sally blushed, as though they might assume he had actually been forced to sleep out there. "Well, he says the stock don't complain."

"Thank you, ma'am." Caleb smiled, then nodded at Nathan and Samantha as he opened the door.

Resuming her chatter, Sally hastened Nathan and Saman-tha into chairs and served pie and coffee. They were down to the last forkful when Frank entered.

He was a large man—well over six feet tall but made of muscle obviously developed from hard farm work. He had curly, sandy-brown hair and laughing blue eyes. Other than the smile that always seemed to light his face, Nathan never would have guessed he was a preacher.

"Well! I see Sally didn't waste any time showing off her pie!" He laughed as he sat next to Sally. "Is it too late to ask a blessing? Ow! Sally!" Frank rubbed his shin, bewildered. "Did I say something wrong?"

"No, Frank." Sally sighed. "And I'm sorry I kicked you. But I think you should know Nathan isn't a believer."

Frank held Nathan's gaze, friendly but firm. "We always thank the Lord for our blessings, and having Samantha and you here is surely a sign of his work."

"Is it?" Nathan smirked. "Samantha hasn't had a chance to tell you about me."

"Nathan," Samantha warned in a low voice.

"No, Sam. Your friends should know the truth before we go any further." He turned to Frank and Sally. "Samantha's brother and I are not only unbelievers, we're sinners of the worst kind. We're wanted by the law."

He sat back and crossed his arms. There. That ought to take the wind out of their sails. Them and their holier-than-thou attitude.

"Robbery, right?" Frank said. "Sally, are you going to pass me the pie or not?"

Nathan straightened. Didn't they understand? "Yes, robbery. Guns, money, all that. Banks, railroads . . ."

Frank and Sally nodded, their faces cheerful. "We've seen your name in the newspapers," Frank said. "Samantha had mentioned your name so often, we knew it was you." He scooped a piece of pie onto his plate. "So how long can you stay?"

Stunned, Nathan faltered. "I . . . I don't know."

Samantha stared at her lap, her shoulders hunched. Frank and Sally might not be affected by his honesty, but Nathan knew Samantha was. She knew he was baiting her friends, and her hurt was palpable. He had destroyed the reunion with a cold reminder that he could never truly be a part of it.

Sally glanced up, a concerned expression on her face. "Are you all right, Samantha?"

Samantha brushed at her eyes and smiled weakly. She glanced at Nathan, and her smile fell. "I'm just tired."

Sally rose, smiling. "You've had a long trip. I'll show you to your room."

"That's a good idea. Good night, Samantha," Nathan said. Trying to keep his emotions in check, he watched as Sally led Samantha behind a closed door. He wanted to be the one to take care of her, to hold her close and reassure her, but he couldn't. If he were close to her right now, he would melt. He couldn't let that happen. He had to be strong.

Nathan turned to find Frank's gentle eyes fixed on him, full of sympathy and sorrow. His gaze made Nathan uncomfortable, and he looked down.

He could understand anger and violence in a man—he had plenty of both in himself—but this compassion was unnerving. It made him feel guilty for acting so cold. Frank and Sally obviously loved Samantha; they helped her when she'd been left at the orphanage, and they were helping her now. If it made them feel better to have God as a crutch, who was he to criticize?

Nathan shifted uncomfortably. "Look, ah, about how I—"

"Forget it. Sally and I understand."

Again Nathan met Frank's gaze. An indescribable wave swept through him—he felt as though Frank really did understand. Even better than he did himself.

Frank turned to the stove. "More coffee?" he said, then refilled Nathan's cup in response to a silent, bewildered nod.

Sixteen

Smiling, Sally gestured at the high double bed in the corner of the room. She scooped up a sleeping bundle so quickly Samantha never saw a face. The child slept on, and Sally left.

Groping in the darkness, Samantha lit a lamp. The room was comfortably furnished with yellow muslin curtains, a large braided rag rug, and a cushioned rocker. Several scattered dolls indicated this was Maria's room.

Samantha slumped on the bed, drained of emotion and energy. Nathan had deflated all of the evening's joy for her.

Sally slipped back into the room and wrapped an arm around Samantha's shoulder. "You love him, don't you?"

A warm tear trickled down Samantha's cheek, and she swiped it with the back of her hand. "I've known Nathan for so long. He's changed from when he was a boy. He's so unhappy, so bitter."

"And it's difficult for you because he's not a Christian."

She nodded. "No matter what I do or say, it doesn't make any difference. His heart is just as hard today as it was the day he came for me at the orphanage."

"It's probably softer than you think," Sally said. "He put up that defense for me and Frank because he's scared."

"He knows the truth, but he won't admit it!"

"Maybe he's ashamed of himself."

"Nathan ashamed?" Samantha laughed. "Even if that were true, he must know God forgives anything."

Sally's hazel eyes were luminous. "No, Samantha, maybe he doesn't. You may have told him that, but he has to find out for himself. Leave the work of God to the Holy Spirit." She patted Samantha's hands and rose, smiling. "The best thing for you right now is a long sleep."

Sally brought a pitcher of water and said good night. Samantha undressed for bed, then leaned back against the pillow and closed her eyes. Maybe Sally was right. "I'm sorry for my pride, Lord," she murmured. "It is your work, not mine. But please draw Nathan to you, please—"

She tried to finish the prayer, but her mind and heart felt clouded, her spirit muddled. Through the mist, all she could see was Nathan's face.

She awoke refreshed, even humming as she washed her face and hands and got dressed. God's mercy was new every morning, and hope rose as she made her way to the front room. Maybe away from the hideout, Nathan would relax and be more open. Maybe Frank could talk to him; another man might make more of an impression than she had.

"Good morning, sleepyhead!" Sally lifted a pan of risen bread dough to the table to knead. "I knew you were tired, so I didn't disturb you. But you missed breakfast." She wiped her floury hands together. "You didn't tell me your brother had such a healthy appetite."

Samantha grinned. Maybe Frank could talk to Caleb too.

"Mama! Mama!" Two small bodies, one towheaded and the other dark, flung themselves through the front door. They raced to Sally and wound around her knees like hungry house cats.

"Tommy! Maria!" Sally laughed, bending down to embrace them both before they bumped into the wooden table. "You'll knock Miss Samantha's cup over!"

Samantha smiled, her arms aching. It had been so long since she had held a child. Not since Aaron had she felt such a strong pull.

"Miss Samantha!"

As one, the children turned from their mother. Soft arms tugged on her skirt, and she lifted both children with ease to settle them in her lap. "Tommy! How you've grown! You must be four now!"

"I'm four and a half," he announced proudly, nodding his blond head.

"Me! Me!" Maria tugged at Samantha's sleeve. The dark-haired girl had rich brown eyes and skin, evidence of her Mexican heritage.

Samantha hugged her and kissed her cheek. "You don't remember me, do you? You were only one when you left. So now you're—"

"We think somewhere between two and three," Sally said. "We set her birthday six months after Christmas."

The children bounced on Samantha's lap, happy, loved, loving in return. More than once Tommy put his arm around Maria as well as Samantha, apparently not too old to display brotherly affection for his little sister. Samantha cuddled them closer, kissed the tops of their soft heads, and murmured childish nonsense to detain them on her lap.

She heard the front door open, but she continued to laugh with the children, playfully tickling their sides and making faces. At last she realized Sally had grown still, and she glanced up. Sally's gaze was fixed on the door, and Samantha turned.

Nathan stood in the doorway, motionless, watching Samantha entertain the children. His eyes met hers over the blond and black heads.

Samantha's mouth went dry, and she turned her face into Maria's long hair to hide her expression. What would it be like if she and Nathan had children of their own? What would it be like to have a child with dark hair like Nathan's, a child who wasn't afraid of secrets in the night?

Nathan cleared his throat. "Frank sent me in for some twine, Sally."

Sally's laugh sounded more shrill than usual. "I borrowed it from him and neglected to give it back. He likes to keep it out in the barn." She moved to a shelf, glancing at Samantha and the children. "Did you meet Tommy and Maria, Nathan?"

"Yes. They're good kids."

"Here's the twine. Children, why don't you go outside for a while? You can help your father."

"Aww," Tommy moped, turning blue eyes up to Samantha.

"Go ahead." She forced a smile. "I'll come out later, and you can introduce me to the animals."

"Me too?" Maria beamed.

"You too." Samantha gave her a pat on the back, then set them both down. She glanced up at Nathan, who waited quietly by the door.

"Bye!" The children raced under Nathan's outstretched arm as he held the door open. He smiled crookedly at Samantha as they passed, then followed.

Samantha stared at the closed door, desolate.

Somehow she made it through the day without screaming in frustration at the slowly moving hands of the Jordans' anniversary clock. She felt an inexplicable urgency to see Nathan. His demeanor had been so strange this morning.

Sally sensed her anxiety and kept up the conversation as they rolled out bread dough. "When we moved out here, I fell in love with the land at first sight. I was afraid I would be lonely since we're miles from other women. But the children keep me pretty busy."

She laughed softly. "You should have seen my first attempts at housekeeping! You know how terrible I always was at cooking and cleaning. Poor Frank suffered some of the worst-burned meals in the Rockies!"

"But you learned," Samantha said. She glanced around the room, admiring its neatness and cheerfulness—its permanence. The Jordan home was not only tidy but filled with love. A child's stool waited in a corner; the family Bible lay on a table; the scent of warm pie wafted through the air . . .

Sally smiled. "I had to learn or Frank would have starved! You really can't live on love, after all."

Samantha frowned. Had she and Nathan been trying to do that? She had taken care of the hideout cabin, but compared to Sally's life, she was just pretending. She and Nathan weren't even married.

"And let me tell you about the time I tried to dye a shirt for Frank!"

Sally told one hilarious tale after another. They were still laughing an hour later when a steady pounding startled them. Samantha nearly dropped a china dinner plate.

Sally smoothed her hair as she bustled to the door. "It's probably just Noah. He's our closest neighbor, if you can call five miles away being close. He's a bachelor, and he gets lonely." Sally winked. "But I think he really comes over for my cooking. Now that I *can* cook."

She opened the door. "Why, Noah Cameron! Isn't it just like you to show up at suppertime!"

Noah grinned, his eyes twinkling beneath a mop of dark hair. "Hello, Sally. I couldn't find Frank outside."

Samantha adjusted a plate from where she sat at the table, and Noah turned. He straightened and removed his hat. Sally took his arm and drew him forward. "Noah, this is my good friend, Samantha Martin."

Samantha nodded politely. "How do you do, Mr.—?"

Noah raised brilliant gray eyes, and she could feel their power in a shiver to her marrow. "Noah Cameron, ma'am." He nodded.

Sally ushered Noah to the easy chair by the fire. "Here, Noah, warm up a bit. Samantha, you sit down too. You've been a great help all day."

Uneasy at the stranger's presence, Samantha perched on the rocking chair opposite Noah's. She felt his piercing eyes on her as she adjusted her skirt and folded her hands in her lap.

Why was she so nervous? Her gaze flickered to his gun belt. Maybe it was because he wore the holster tied down. Caleb said only men who were serious about their firearms did that. It made it easier to draw.

She tensed, holding her breath. Noah smiled, his eyes shining. "You can relax. This is just a social visit." The crinkles around his eyes indicated he was only teasing.

Samantha exhaled with relief. "I know that, Mr. Cameron."

"Then I beg your pardon for my impertinence, Miss . . .

Mrs. . . ."—his gaze drifted to her left hand and back to her eyes—"ah . . . Martin."

"*Miss* Martin," she said quietly.

Noah cleared his throat. "Did you come here all by yourself?"

"No." Samantha tried to relax. She didn't need to be rude, even if the man did make her nervous. "I came with my brother and my, ah, his friend for a visit."

Noah nodded. "That was wise of you. It's not safe for a woman to travel alone."

Sally glanced at Samantha, then Noah. She smiled broadly. "If you two are acquainted now, I'll get back to my food." She bustled to the kitchen.

Silence filled the room. "I, ah, live in Wyoming," Samantha offered tentatively.

"Oh?" Noah fingered the brim of his hat, then cleared his throat and set the hat down. "Wyoming's beautiful country. Whereabouts?"

"The Wind River Range," she answered automatically. One glance at Noah's puzzled expression, and she froze. What if she'd given away Nathan and Caleb's hideout? "My brother has a . . . a farm." Well, that wasn't a lie. They *did* grow vegetables.

"Not a whole lot of people in those mountains except trappers and Indians." Noah stared in puzzlement at her for a moment, then his face cleared. "But it is beautiful country. I've been to the Shoshoni reservation a time or two myself."

"Really?" Samantha leaned forward. George had promised to take her there, but so far he hadn't made good on it. "I have a friend—"

She closed her mouth. George was probably wanted just as much as Nathan and Caleb. She certainly didn't want to bring trouble to him or his family by leading someone to arrest him.

"You have a friend . . . ?"

"I, ah, have a friend who t-told me about the reservation. It sounded interesting." She sat back and gripped the arms of the chair. Why didn't Sally return? The anniversary clock on the mantel ticked louder and louder.

"How do you know Sally?"

Samantha started. "Wh-what?"

Noah's smile was slow and genuine, not mischievous like Nathan's. Samantha realized she was probably acting as jumpy as a cat and smiled back. She loosed her grip on the chair.

"That's better," he said gently. "Now tell me how you met Sally."

Glad for safer waters, Samantha told him about Mrs. Matlock and the Good Shepherd's Home. Noah seemed sincerely interested, but he offered no information about his own past. Eventually the conversation turned more general: his farm, the amount of expected snowfall this winter, and the wonderful smell of the dinner Sally was preparing.

Samantha admired the stranger's quiet confidence, which seemed grounded not in vanity but in honest self-assurance. Maybe it was her own confusion lately or the impasse in her relationship with Nathan, but she sensed a kindred, friendly spirit in Noah Cameron.

He told her anecdotes about ranching, which she gathered was a new profession for him. He made her smile, made her forget her aching heart. She forgot all about the gun he was wearing and laughed out loud after his observations on the ornery nature of Colorado cattle.

"I'm glad to see you smile." Noah's voice was soft, and he patted her hand.

Panicked, Samantha drew back, and Noah quickly withdrew his hand. "I beg your pardon. I didn't mean to be so forward." His horrified expression told her that he truly had nothing but the best of intentions.

"It's all right," she murmured.

The door opened, and Samantha straightened, her heart pounding.

Nathan entered slowly, his eyes dark as he took off his gloves. Without a word to Samantha, he walked straight to Noah and extended a hand. "I'm Jack McAllister," he said, his voice cool and restrained.

"Noah Cameron. I'm Frank and Sally's neighbor."

Confused, Samantha drew back. Nathan cast her a sidelong glance but said nothing. Sally came in from the kitchen and stood to the side, quiet.

Caleb stepped up behind Nathan, and Samantha hurried to his side. "And this is my brother—"

"Robert Martin," Caleb said.

"Noah Cameron."

Jack McAllister? Robert Martin? Of course! "Robert Martin" was Pa's name. She'd never thought about Nathan and Caleb using aliases. If Frank and Sally recognized their real names, others might also.

Nathan crossed his arms. "So where do you live, Cameron?"

"Five miles south of here."

"Come over here a lot?"

Noah shrugged. "I don't often get home-cooked meals. I'm a bachelor."

"Oh, really?"

Sally stepped between Nathan and Noah. "Noah's a good friend of ours . . . Jack. He knows he's welcome in our home anytime."

Nathan clenched his fists at his side and moved toward Samantha. He opened his mouth to say something, but Frank entered with all the bluster of a large, playful bear. "Noah!" His voice boomed across the room.

Sally closed her eyes briefly as though in prayer, then hurried to her husband's side. "No need for introductions, Frank. Noah's met Samantha and her brother *Robert Martin* and *Jack McAllister.*"

"Well, sure, Sally," Frank said. "I knew you'd introduce everybody." His eyes looked bewildered, but his smile never faltered.

"Uncle Noah!" The children rushed in and hurled themselves at his legs.

"Hey, cowpokes!" Noah scooped up and hugged each giggling child. "How would you like some more company for dinner?"

"Yes! Yes!" They clapped their hands.

Sally shooed Tommy and Maria toward the table and smiled. "Now that that's settled, let's eat."

She hastily added an extra plate, and they sat down to enjoy her chicken and biscuits. Samantha found herself seated next to Noah and across from Nathan.

Frank, Sally, Noah, and the children bowed their heads.

Samantha lowered her own, thanking God for the presence of fellow believers. Caleb looked away with annoyance, but Nathan stared directly at Noah with unabashed disgust.

"Noah, would you please return thanks?" Frank quietly said.

A moment's silence followed, as though Noah was waiting to be told what to say. "Father, thank you that we are all here together. Not by accident but, like everything else, by your design. Thank you for this good food and for allowing me to share it with these friends and strangers. Help us all to know your peace that passes all our human understanding and to know your will for our lives. We ask these things in Jesus' name. Amen."

Samantha's face warmed as she raised her head. Noah was a believer! She should have known by his eyes.

Reaching for the biscuits, Noah's hand brushed Samantha's. Noah graciously withdrew his. Samantha was so flustered, her fingers trembled as she picked up the plate. *We are all here together . . . not by accident . . . but by your design.*

Samantha felt Nathan's gaze, and a chill ran through her. Had God's design truly worked its way through her life or had she just followed her own whim?

"So, you're a *Christian*, Cameron," Nathan said coldly.

Samantha felt her face flush again with embarrassment for Noah, but he didn't seem to mind the question. He smiled broadly. "Yes, thanks to Frank."

"You were the stubbornest man I ever met." Frank chuckled as he accepted the chicken from Sally. "Noah used to argue from the edge of the crowd when I was an itinerant preacher."

Noah laughed too. "Well, I usually had a half-empty bottle in my hands, Frank. That gave me a little extra courage."

"So what happened?" Samantha glanced from one man to the other. Having started the conversation, Nathan was completely silent. Samantha didn't dare look at him.

Noah shifted in his chair, and his gaze locked with Samantha's. He studied her for a moment, then smiled. He had obviously read the condition of her soul through her eyes. "Frank had a way of talking about the Lord that made me mad. Who was this man to act like he was God's best buddy? Where did that leave the rest of us? So I kept arguing with him every chance I got."

Noah chuckled. "One day Frank turned the tables and started following me around. He'd show up in the saloon and sit with me while I drank myself into a stupor or gambled away my money. I think he would have even followed me upstairs when I . . . Beg your pardon, ladies," he said, dropping his gaze.

"Go on," Sally said softly, spooning food for the children.

Noah cleared his throat. "Well, I'm not quite sure how it happened, but my resentment of Frank turned to admiration. No preacher I'd ever known actually met the people where they lived. When I finally told him that—grudgingly, I might add—he laughed and said the greatest preacher of all scorned the religious people of his day in favor of common folks like me and him."

"Jesus," Samantha said, smiling. Noah's gentle gray eyes met hers, and she inhaled softly.

"And then one day . . ." Frank prompted.

"And then one day I took a good, hard look at myself and didn't at all like what I saw. I realized I couldn't possibly save myself from the life I was living, so I gave it all to the only one who could."

"Noah gave up whiskey and the . . . well, the other things he was entangled in," Frank said, his face reddening.

"Must have been hard to give up the alcohol and . . . the other things," Nathan put in mildly, his smile crooked.

Noah shook his head. "Not hard at all. Once I admitted my need for him, Jesus took away all my other so-called needs."

Samantha turned her head to hide a broad smile. Not since Mrs. Matlock had she heard anyone speak so openly, so lovingly, about Jesus. It had been so long since she'd had true fellowship, she had almost forgotten its power. She should have recognized the strength surrounding Noah. She'd seen it often enough during her own childhood, in her father and Nathan's father.

She glanced at Nathan across the table. His eyes were fixed on Noah, his face unreadable. She tried to catch his attention, but his gaze dropped to his plate. The longer she stared, the more he seemed to avoid her gaze.

Nervousness crept from her stomach to her heart. The conversation hummed around her, changing from religion to farming. She was aware of Caleb chiming in with some regularity, along with Noah, Frank, and Sally. But she couldn't get her mind off Noah's words about coming to Jesus. She was certain, by Nathan's glaring silence, that he was thinking about it too. Maybe after dinner they could have a few words together. Alone.

The talk dragged on until well past the last slice of Sally's apple pie. Samantha stood to collect empty plates, dejected. She and Nathan wouldn't get a chance to talk tonight after all.

Nathan pushed his chair back from the table and rose. He turned to her and extended his arm. "I hope Sally will excuse you while we take a walk."

Samantha clutched Noah's plate. So he did want to talk!

"Go ahead," Sally said cheerfully, setting Maria alongside Tommy on the floor. "The men can keep these two entertained, and I'll take care of the dishes."

Samantha nodded, mute, and set the stack of plates on the table. Nathan tucked her hand into the crook of his arm, close to his heart. Through a daze, she saw the others' expressions—especially Sally's encouraging smile and Noah's puzzled frown—as she and Nathan pushed through the door and into the night.

SEVENTEEN

The full moon lit the landscape like a balloon of white sugar ready to explode. Clear and black, the sky twinkled with innumerable stars.

Nathan tilted his head back and breathed the mountain air deeply, inhaling the distinct scent of fir, pine, and soil. If he closed his eyes, he could imagine himself as a boy again in Kansas . . . could almost hear the corn stalks whispering to each other . . . could sense Samantha, fourteen again, beside him. And he could feel the newness of love in his heart.

Samantha looked at the ground, seeming almost bashful, as though they had never been alone together. Had Cameron's presence made her wonder what it would be like to be in love with a decent man?

He drew a deep breath, steeling himself. He'd told his father he'd give his life for Samantha, and that was the truth. But giving her back her own life would be even more difficult.

"It's lovely out tonight, isn't it?" she ventured, rubbing her arms against the chill.

"Yes." He forced a hardness to his voice.

"I hope all that talk at the table didn't upset you," she said quietly.

Nathan stopped short and laughed. "Do you think a few religious fanatics can upset me?"

She stared at him a moment, then lowered her gaze. "No, Nathan. Sometimes I don't think anything upsets you except the ghosts of your own past. Whatever they are."

Nathan felt a stab in his heart and watched as she moved forward, her form silhouetted in the moonlight. A lump rose in his throat. How could he let her go? *Why* should he let her go?

If you love Samantha, his father had said.

Did he? How much?

Samantha turned and stretched out her hand. Nathan accepted it reluctantly, wanting to flinch from her intense gaze. But that ever-present peace in her eyes beckoned. When he looked closely, he could almost see a light, like a candle glowing in the window of a distant house on a snowy night.

Nathan felt as if he'd been stumbling in the snow all his life. He'd weathered heavy blizzards, but even during clear weather he'd slogged through gigantic drifts toward no true destination, no home with a candle in the window for him.

She put her arms around him and pressed her face against his chest, tangling her hands in his hair. He returned the embrace, swallowing hard. To his surprise, he heard soft weeping.

"I don't want anybody to hurt you," she murmured. "I want you to believe, but I don't want—"

She clutched the back of his shirt. "It's my fault, Nathan. I haven't said the right words, haven't done the right things. If I had—" She lifted her face, and her voice dropped to a whisper. "—you would know God."

His love for her swelled like a wave, then abruptly crested and dashed against his foolish heart, crushing all emotion with the sheer force of reason. He smiled cynically. "Is my salvation still your greatest dream?"

"Haven't we been through enough for you to realize that?"

"I've been through more than you'll ever know."

"Then *tell* me, Nathan. Please let me help you! All this time, you've kept your secrets, and I've never asked. But I'm asking now, begging! Something happened during the war, didn't it? Tell me! Let me help!"

Ashamed, he lowered his head. The heaviness welled in his soul and heart like a boulder pressing the life from him. "I can't tell you," he whispered. "I can't trust you."

Immediately he straightened and stepped back. Cold self-loathing knifed through him, and he dropped a mask of in-difference into place. If she knew the things he had done, how wicked he was, she would never be able to look him in the eyes again. If he waited much longer, the whole awful truth would spill out of him, and then she would truly loathe him.

"Come on, let's get out of the wind," he said gruffly, jerk-ing her toward the barn. Before she could protest, he pushed her through the door.

"What's wrong, Nathan? What's—?"

He slammed the door shut and grabbed her from behind, wrapping his arms around her in a fierce embrace. "I almost kissed you once before in a barn. Remember that day Caleb was sick and we played in the hay?" He kissed the tender flesh below her ear, smiling bitterly when he felt her tremble.

"That was . . . long ago," she murmured. "We were just . . . kids."

Nathan turned her around and cupped the underside of her jaw, searching her eyes for the truth. She couldn't hide anything from him in those blue eyes. And right now they were watching him. Wanting him. And oh, how he wanted her. Ached for her. Ached for the hole in his heart to be filled.

"I'm going to kiss you now," he said softly, his lips so close his words were soft breaths across her mouth. "But it won't be as a kid, but as a man."

She nodded. Her eyes closed just as his lips gently touched hers. He lost himself to her, remembering their first kiss on the train. What would he remember about this final kiss?

The first time, the last time. *It was the best of times, it was the worst of times.* Where had he read that? And why had he thought of it now?

His need for her love, her security, fueled his veins. If only he could make her understand that he didn't need God. He needed her. Letting her go was more frightening than all the years of blood and destruction in the war. Without her, he had nothing, was nothing.

Nathan raised his face. Her eyes were still closed, her expression full of love and trust. Just like a lamb. "I'm leaving tomorrow," he said.

Her eyes flew open. "But we can't leave! We just got here!"

"I didn't say you were going."

"But—"

"You've been nothing but trouble since I brought you from Kansas City," he said, forcing a grimace. "First Crawford, then the bungled robbery, even turning George into a farmer."

"But I—"

"Your prayers . . . Oh, let's not forget your prayers! You think you caused that safe to remain shut, don't you?"

Samantha looked anguished. "No, but—"

"I'll tell you what it was. It wasn't the prayers; it was you! You're a . . . a jinx! You've been nothing but a jinx since I found you, and you're messing up my life!"

209

Samantha lowered her head. "Then why did you want me to stay?"

He tilted her chin up with his hand until their eyes met. "Because you were a challenge."

Her eyes misted with tears, and her lips quivered. "You're just saying that."

"No." Nathan stepped forward, his eyes hard. A frightened expression on her face, she backed away, but he grabbed her in his arms and pressed her back against the barn. "But the truth is, I still want you for my own, Samantha."

"I . . . I can't marry you," she whispered.

He smiled cynically, though his heart was crying. "Who said anything about marriage?" He bent his head and pressed his lips to the pulse of her throat. "You know I don't want marriage. But you do know what I want. Here. Now. Prove that you love me."

Her pulse raced against his lips. "God doesn't—"

"You always use him as an excuse! Choose who it'll be, Samantha, right now! Because tomorrow I'll be gone."

Her face froze, anguished, but she lifted a trembling chin. "I have to serve the Lord," she said quietly.

"Fine." He pulled away, smiling coldly. "There are other women."

She cringed, bowing her head.

The barn door creaked open. Nathan stepped back and drew his gun.

"Nathan!" Caleb hissed. "I know you're in here!"

Nathan relaxed. "What do you want, Caleb?"

"Cameron's acting suspicious. You better get back to the house. Nobody takes a walk as long as you two have been gone. Especially as cold as it's getting."

Nathan glanced at Samantha, whose head was still lowered. "Take your sister back, Caleb," he said. "Tell them I've gone to bed or something. Tell them anything."

"Sure. I'll be outside."

The barn door creaked closed, and Nathan jammed his revolver back in its holster. "Caleb's leaving with me in the morning, so you'd better say good-bye to him too," he said bitterly.

"Not Caleb!" she whispered with a catch in her voice. "So you're both running away again, leaving me?"

Nathan swallowed hard, blinking. "Go on," he said brusquely. "Get out of here. Get out of my life. I don't need you!"

He stepped away before he could take back the words. Better for him to shoulder the guilt. He deserved it. He deserved worse.

Shoulders slumped, Samantha put her hand on the door, then turned. "Don't let yourself get arrested, Nathan. I couldn't . . ." Her voice caught in her throat. "I couldn't stand that." She yanked open the door, and she was gone.

Nathan stared at the closed door, a wave of longing and regret sweeping over him. He stared at the spot where she had stood so close to him, and his fists opened and closed helplessly. He was alone in the dark.

Weak with grief, Samantha leaned against the barn. Her legs buckled, and she slid down until she hit her knees. She wrapped her arms around her middle, pressing against the burning sensation that surged from her stomach to her throat.

"Why, Lord, why? Didn't I stay with him? Didn't I love him unconditionally? I thought you gave him to me! I thought I heard you!"

"It's all right, Samantha." Caleb eased her into his arms

and held her. "Shh." He rocked her so gently, so tenderly, the sobs she'd held back spilled out. When her shoulders stopped shaking, he untucked the front end of his shirt and wiped away her tears.

"He's leaving me, Caleb. Why? What did I do?"

Caleb pressed his cheek against the top of her head. "You need a husband who's just as good for you as you would be for him."

"But, N-Nathan—"

"Nathan's a man with only one thing on his mind," Caleb said fiercely. "You're better off without him."

"And better off without you as well? You're leaving too!"

Caleb took her hands and helped her rise. "I'll send you some money as soon as I get some. But until then, the Jordans are good people. They'll take care of you."

Her stomach clenched. "Caleb, please don't leave. You're the last family I have!"

He touched her cheek. "You're better off without me too. Now let's go back. We'll have to come up with a good story about your lengthy absence. I'm supposed to be out smoking a cigar."

Drained, Samantha allowed Caleb to lead her toward the house. She glanced back at the barn, hoping to catch a final glimpse of Nathan, but all she saw were shadows.

"More coffee, Noah?"

Noah shifted his gaze from the door and held out his cup. "Sure, Sally." He smiled. She had refilled his cup repeatedly during the past thirty minutes, as though she didn't want him to leave.

He grinned into his coffee. He didn't need encouragement

to stick around. Samantha Martin had the loveliest face he'd seen in a long time, and the softest-looking blond hair. When he'd asked God that morning—as he had almost every morning for a year—to send him a wife, he certainly hadn't expected to find a prospect that very day.

She was hiding something though. Even her eyes had given her away. She might be a believer, but she was somehow tangled up with Jack McAllister. When they had been talking earlier, Noah had finally gotten her to relax, but she'd turned downright nervous when McAllister appeared. And now the two of them had been outside far too long together.

"More coffee?"

He plunked his empty cup in its saucer, disheartened. "No, I'd better head out. I've got stock to look after."

Sally held up the coffeepot. "Can't you stay for just one more—"

Samantha stumbled through the door. If her brother hadn't been holding her arm, Noah felt certain she would have fallen. Her face was wet with tears, her hair loose about her shoulders, and dirt clung to her skirt.

Noah drew a deep, angry breath.

With a multitude of questions in her eyes, Sally stared at Robert Martin. He clenched his jaw, his hand firm on his sister's shoulder. "She's all right. She and Jack just saw a bear. That's all. Samantha fell trying to get away."

"Bears have usually begun to hibernate by now," Noah said.

Martin turned with a hard look of disapproval. Samantha stood motionless, but her lips trembled.

Sally touched her arm, worried. "You're safe now, Samantha. You're all right."

"No," Samantha whispered. She wrapped her arms around herself as though she were in pain. "You don't know what's happened."

Noah cleared his throat, embarrassed. He'd hoped to talk to her again, to figure out what Jack McAllister meant to her, but he knew now he'd better take his leave. Everyone seemed so agitated all of a sudden. He'd certainly never seen Sally so jumpy. He had a sneaking suspicion Sally and Frank knew more than they were letting on.

"I'll be leaving now." Noah made for the door, then paused. "I hope you feel better soon, ma'am. If you're staying with the Jordans for a while, I imagine I'll see you again. God be with you."

Samantha turned toward him. "Thank you, Mr. Cameron." She smiled sadly. "You've been most kind." He was moved by the pain he saw in her eyes, and he wondered again if this was the wife God had chosen for him.

Glaring, Martin blocked his way. "Here's your hat."

Noah held his gaze. "Much obliged. Sally, Frank, thanks for dinner."

"Good-bye, Noah." Frank saw him to the door, then shut it firmly behind him.

As he silently saddled his horse in the dim light of the barn, Noah wondered again what was going on. If Jack McAllister had something to do with the hurt on Miss Martin's face—

"She'll be staying with the Jordans a long time."

Noah spun around, his hand automatically reaching for the gun he now wore only for absolute protection. A dark form separated from the shadows, and Jack stood before him.

"Why?" Noah dropped his right hand, relieved. "She has a home in Wyoming."

"It's not really her home. It belongs to her brother and me. She's a single woman, alone in the world." His eyes narrowed. "Of course, having a husband would make her life easier."

Noah shifted to widen his stance. "Why would you think I'm interested in her problems?"

Jack laughed. "You are. In the first place, you claim to be a Christian. So I guess it's your duty to be concerned about people. In the second place"—he stepped forward until he was two feet from Noah—"I can tell you're interested in her. I saw how you made her smile. How she let you hold her hand."

"I wasn't holding her hand. I touched it by accident," Noah said, "and I apologized for being forward."

"Good. Then if you are indeed the upstanding, decent man you make yourself out to be, I'd expect your intentions to be nothing but honest. Nothing short of marriage."

Jack drew his gun and aimed it at Noah's heart. "Do you understand?" he said in a low voice. *Nothing short of marriage.*"

Even though his instincts told him Jack wasn't a cold-blooded killer, Noah stood stock-still. He had seen countless men draw a gun as a threat, with no intention of firing. Jack had the same lost look in his eyes he himself once had. He relaxed, resentment turning to pity. "I wouldn't take advantage of any woman," Noah said.

Jack reholstered the gun. "Remember what I said, Cameron. I'm trusting my gut feelings about you, and I hate to be wrong. If your intentions are honest, take care of her.

But if your piousness is just an act, if you hurt her in any way, I'll come back here and break your fool neck."

"She's already hurt," Noah said.

Jack laughed bitterly. "She'll get over it."

Noah turned back to his horse and tightened a cinch. *Lord, your hand must be in this. Your will be done.*

He straightened and led the horse forward. At the door, he paused and looked back at the shadows. Jack had disappeared from sight. "I'll watch out for her, McAllister," Noah said. Then he mounted and rode toward his farm.

⁓

Before the first pale light of dawn, Nathan awoke with a start, wondering in a sleepy fog why he'd slept in the hayloft. Then he remembered. He and Caleb were heading back to Wyoming.

He had to leave now. He couldn't risk seeing Samantha before he left. If he told her good-bye again or even saw her sweet face, he'd do something foolish like drag her back with him. No, he had to get up and get moving.

Quietly he pulled on his boots and gun belt, then rolled up his blanket. On his way to the ladder, he gave Caleb a gentle kick. Caleb jerked awake, and Nathan nodded at the ladder. Caleb sat up quickly and rubbed his eyes. The sooner they left, the better. Nathan sure didn't want to see Noah Cameron again either.

He'd called on every ounce of selflessness he possessed to suggest Cameron marry Samantha. He'd sized the farmer up as a decent man. At least he and Samantha had their religious beliefs in common. Once married, she'd never come looking for Nathan. She'd be a faithful wife, and more important, she'd be safe. Truly and forever safe.

Still, the thought of Noah Cameron actually making Sam his bride made Nathan see red. He had to leave and *now*.

At last Caleb joined him outside. Without a word between them, they mounted up and rode away.

Samantha dropped her hold on the curtain as she listened to the fading sound of galloping hooves. She'd known it was foolish, but she wanted one last look.

She smiled bitterly. She hadn't even seen their faces. She could only discern Caleb and Nathan as trees moving in the darkness. Apparently Jesus hadn't seen fit to give her full sight yet.

Taking a deep breath, she knelt on the floor and leaned over the bed. She couldn't see faith either, but she called on it for strength.

"Lord, forgive my unbelief," she whispered. "I can't see your work in this, but I know it is. Please forgive me for being weak. I don't know why you let the people I love leave my life—Ma, Pa, little Aaron, Mrs. Matlock . . ." She brushed away a tear then whispered hoarsely, "Nathan and Caleb."

She drew a deep breath. "Thank you for letting me sow seeds with them both while I had the chance. If I didn't do enough, I'm sorry. Let what little I did take root and find water and sun and good soil for nourishment. Watch over them both, Father, and keep them from harm. Show them the evil of their ways."

She laid her forehead against the bed, and the sob in her chest rose as a cry of anguish. "And forgive them."

EIGHTEEN

January 1872

I t's mine!"

"No! I saw it first!"

"Tommy! Maria!" Sally stepped between the bickering children and whisked the wooden soldier from Tommy's fist. "We don't fight in this house, remember?" She put an arm around each child and glanced sternly at one abashed face then the other.

"Y-yes, Ma." Blond head bowed, Tommy plopped down on his stool by the fireplace. He sniffled once and wiped a flannel sleeve across his nose.

Sally sighed, glancing up for moral support. Samantha grinned and laid a hand on Maria's head. "Come on, sweetheart. Let's lie down on your bed together, and I'll read you a book."

"Thank you, Samantha." Sally wiped the back of her wrist against her forehead. She wrinkled her nose at the smoked elk she was preparing for dinner and put a hand against her stomach. Her face contorted. She looked white and clammy.

"Are you all right?"

Sally drew a long breath and grinned. "I will be in about seven months. I'm pretty sure now I'm in a family way."

Samantha clapped her hands. "A baby!" She hugged Sally, then pulled back quickly. "I'm sorry! I don't want to make you sick."

Sally waved a hand. "It's actually getting better. Frank hasn't even noticed, so I'm sure it will come as quite a shock to him when I tell him tonight."

"He doesn't know? You have to tell him! Now!"

Sally ducked her head. "I wanted to tell him in private."

"Oh." Samantha's smile fell, and her face flushed with warmth.

"'Mantha! 'Mantha!" Maria tugged at her skirts. "I want a book!"

"Of course, darling." Samantha scooped up the little girl. "Sally, sit down before you keel over. I'll take care of supper after I put Maria down for a nap."

Sally looked relieved. "Thank you. I believe I will lie down for just a minute."

Samantha carried Maria into the room the little girl shared with Tommy, and together they read over several books until Maria dozed off. Samantha lay still beside her, tucking a folded arm under her head.

She prayed joyfully for the new life in the household and asked God to keep Sally and the baby healthy. But with her prayers came an increased awareness that had bothered her for the past few weeks. She was taking up room in the Jordan household. She didn't feel right about imposing on them.

Maria stirred in her sleep, murmuring. She didn't seem to mind sharing this small room with Tommy, but with a new brother or sister, the room she'd given up to Samantha would be needed.

Samantha sighed and rose. In Sally's room she found not

only Sally but Tommy asleep under the wedding-ring-patterned quilt. Samantha smiled and closed the door softly.

With Frank out in the barn, the house was quiet. She glanced at the half-cut meat Sally had left and decided it could wait for a moment. She sat by the fire and rubbed her tired eyes.

An ache rose in her heart. Three months, and still the pain wouldn't go away. If she tried hard, she could almost believe this was last January, when she and Nathan and Caleb had been snug and happy in their cabin in Wyoming. Nathan had read to them every night.

She blinked back a tear. Did Nathan miss her, as she still missed him? He probably didn't even think about her anymore.

The tear rolled down her cheek, but she dashed it away. She didn't want anyone to know she'd been crying.

Noah reined up just outside the Jordans' barn. The dun gelding's breath whooshed out in a visible snort, and the animal pawed the trampled snow. Noah led the horse to the barn, where he saw Frank inside, mending a harness. He was grateful for the chance to talk to him alone.

The preacher raised a hand in greeting, but his smile died. "What's wrong, Noah? You lose some stock during that last snowstorm?"

"No." Noah led the gelding to a stall for a rubdown and feed while Frank went back to his harness mending. They worked in companionable silence.

Noah owed Frank Jordan his spiritual life. Then when he'd run into the Jordans on their way to Colorado, Noah had decided to come along and buy adjoining land. Whatever

God had called Frank Jordan to do, Noah wanted to be a part of it. So Noah left his job and itinerant life, deciding to become a farmer as well.

Once he'd sown and harvested his first crop, he realized his life was still incomplete. He felt a restless yearning to share his life, to start a family. The lack of women in the region had been a serious handicap, until, like a gift from God, Samantha Martin appeared at his neighbors' home.

"Must be woman trouble," Frank said cheerfully, leaning against the stall.

Noah kept brushing the horse, never cracking a smile. "You've known Samantha a long time, haven't you, Frank?"

"Since she and Sally were fourteen."

Noah hesitated. "I'm in love with her," he finally said, "but I know she doesn't love me. Yet every day I feel like God's telling me to ask for her hand." His voice lowered. "It's all I think about, no matter how hard I try to put her out of my mind."

"If God's telling you something, you'd better listen carefully. I had the same doubts with Sally, but she was just too bashful to let on she cared about me."

Noah glanced up, hopeful. "Do you think Samantha loves me?"

"Only the Lord knows the condition of her heart," Frank said gently. "But many great marriages have begun on a love that's less than romantic."

Noah resumed brushing. "Besides the orphanage, she hasn't told me much about her past. This Jack McAllister . . ." Noah looked his friend straight in the eyes. "If there's something I should know about her, Frank, I wish you'd say so now."

Frank looked away, his guilty expression already betraying some secret knowledge. He fiddled with the mended harness, running it between his fingers. "Only Samantha can tell you about her past," he said. "But she's a strong Christian woman. She'll never hide any secrets if she agrees to marry you."

"Samantha."

Sally's voice stirred Samantha from her concentration on slicing the smoked elk. Samantha hesitantly looked up, unwilling for Sally to see the lingering tears in her eyes. "You didn't rest very long."

"We have to talk."

Sighing, Samantha laid the knife aside. Dinner was still hours away, but the work took her mind off her troubles.

"We have to talk about Noah."

Samantha reached for the knife, but Sally stopped her. "He's been courting you. There's no other word for it."

Samantha laced her fingers together on the table for lack of better occupation. "Yes, I suppose that's true."

"And would you marry him if he asked you?"

Samantha felt heat rush to her cheeks. "Did he put you up to that?"

"No. I'm asking on my own. Noah's like a brother to me."

Samantha smiled. Noah had become like a brother to her too. A gentle, loving brother. A strong, godly man.

But he wasn't Nathan.

Sally sighed. "I hoped I was wrong, but I can see by your eyes I wasn't. You still love Nathan, don't you?"

"I've prayed about it over and over," Samantha whispered. "I've even begged God to take this desire from me. But never in my life has the Lord been so silent. Sometimes I feel like he isn't with me at all."

"But he is," Sally said quietly. "He's seen us both through some horrible times." She drew away, thoughtful. "Nathan fought in the war, didn't he?"

"Yes." Samantha shuddered. "He helped the doctors with the wounded."

"You can't understand what war's like, Samantha, unless you've been there." Sally drew a deep breath. "I never told you about my mother, did I?"

"No."

Sally smiled bleakly. "I never knew my father. But my mother always had a lot of what she called 'gentlemen friends.' About the time the war started, we ran short of money, so she signed up as a camp laundress for the Union Army. She hid me in her tent."

"You traveled with the troops?"

Sally nodded, her eyes misty. "You know what laundresses were mainly hired for, don't you?"

"I . . . think so."

She drew a deep breath. "One night a man got mad at her and said she'd cheated him. I was hiding in the other end of the tent, and I watched as he killed her. An officer found me and took me to his church in St. Louis. They sent me on to the Good Shepherd's Home in Kansas City."

"Oh, Sally, I—" Samantha stepped forward.

Sally held up a hand. "That was a long time ago and before I came to know Jesus. But the point is that sometimes we have to travel some rocky roads before God brings us to a beautiful mountaintop. We just have to hold on to his hand, even when we can't feel it."

Samantha smiled tenderly. "And he has brought you to a beautiful place, hasn't he? Now you're a mother yourself and expecting your own child."

A knock sounded at the front door. Sally smiled at Samantha. "That's bound to be Noah. Now, no more crying."

Samantha smiled, but her stomach knotted. Her problem still wasn't solved.

Sally let Noah in, and he glanced around the room until he saw Samantha. A smile lit his face. "Hello!"

Sally laughed. "Take off your coat and sit down, Noah. You, too, Samantha. Have a good talk while the children are still napping. I have to get back to dinner." She winked, then headed for the kitchen.

"Hello, Noah," Samantha murmured, moving to sit by the fire.

Noah took off his coat and hat and hung them on a wooden peg. He moved next to her and rubbed his hands in front of the flames.

Samantha caught him studying her. She blushed and looked away.

"What's wrong, Samantha?" Noah knelt beside her. He looked concerned, his rugged, handsome face puzzled but not demanding. He never demanded. Not her heart, her friendship, or even any answers. Yet she knew he had questions and emotions he wanted to share if she'd only indicate her willingness to do the same.

"I was thinking about . . . my brother. I wonder what he's doing."

"You don't hear from him or Jack?"

"No," she said flatly, "and I don't expect to."

Noah touched her hand. "You don't talk about them

much, Samantha," he said softly. "Did you have a falling out before they left?"

His eyes were so sincere, so understanding. She felt she could tell him almost anything. "Yes," she whispered.

The warmth of his hand was like a balm on her broken heart. The longing for Nathan had been so strong the past three months, the loneliness so great. Even though he was the love of her heart, she knew he would never claim her as his wife.

Yet here was another man, one she could honestly call friend. Noah's thoughtfulness, humor, and unspoken protectiveness had helped her throughout her sorrow. Hadn't he come to call almost every week since she'd been here? She could never love him the way she loved Nathan, but she knew instinctively that Noah wanted to take care of her. He loved her, but would that love be enough?

Peace filled his tender gray eyes. Peace and strength. "It's not good to be alone in the world," he said gently. His thumb rubbed her wrist slowly, lovingly, over her rapid pulse. "God planned for man and woman to be together. And well, Samantha, I've been thinking about it for a while now . . ." He paused as if uncertain about what to say next. "I'm not a fancy man with big words, so I'm just gonna say this outright. Will you marry me, Samantha?"

Her heart leaped, then fell. She would have treasured those words from Nathan, but he could never say them, and she could never accept.

Noah smiled sadly, as if he saw right through her, right to the sorrow of her soul. "You're still in love with Jack."

Samantha rose to run, but Noah gently drew her into his arms. His embrace felt so warm and secure. She buried her face against his shoulder and cried.

Noah smoothed her hair. "He didn't hurt you, did he? I'd chase him to the ends of the earth if he did."

"N-No. He just didn't want marriage. And he wasn't a b-believer."

Noah's arms tightened. "Let me take care of you. We're both believers; we both love God. We can have a good life together . . . the farm . . . children."

She closed her eyes. He was offering her everything she wanted—God, security, and family. Maybe the time she'd spent with Nathan was actually meant to prepare her for a life with Noah.

"I can't give you an answer today," she whispered.

Noah tenderly kissed her forehead. "Take as long as you need. If you say yes, Frank can marry us whenever you like."

Whenever you like. She wasn't sure there would ever be a day she liked, when she couldn't forget the man she truly loved.

That night she lay in bed, listening to the murmurs of Frank and Sally in the next bedroom. Sally must have told Frank about the baby, for Samantha heard his whoop, followed by gentle shushing from Sally. Then there was silence.

Samantha rolled over and studied the moon through the window. Before she went to bed, she'd read Paul's chapter on marriage in Corinthians. Ma had told her long ago that all life's problems were answered in the Bible. But tonight Samantha hadn't come any closer to learning whether she should accept Noah's offer.

If only she could have married Nathan! A verse in that chapter said an unbelieving spouse was set apart by marriage to a believer. Perhaps if she'd managed to marry Nathan, it would have brought him closer to the Lord.

But she hadn't. If she became Noah's wife, they would have a strong foundation and family. Noah would never speak against the Lord, would never make her cringe with words of unbelief. Like Nathan did.

Samantha pounded her pillow then lay back down with a sigh. So why couldn't she go to sleep?

"Hamilton!"

Gunfire cracked, and whizzing Minié balls exploded on impact. Men drowned in rivers of blood, their screams unholy.

"Over there!" McGregor pointed to a creek. "There's some down!"

Nathan's legs felt like butter, but he loped to the creek. He ducked instinctively, panting as he stumbled down the bank to the water.

It was quiet down here, like being at the bottom of a well. He could hear the sound of battle above him, but here it was peaceful. The creek gurgled pleasantly, and he took off his boots and waded in. The water was cool and soothing. He raised his face and felt warm sunlight. Smiling, he removed his coat. He had died, and this was heaven.

He lay back on the bank, drowsy and satisfied.

"Please . . . kill . . . me."

Nathan lifted his head. He'd thought he was alone.

"Please . . . God . . . kill . . . me."

The voice came from under the body, which was lying face-down. The sounds of battle rushed down the bank.

"Please . . . kill."

Horrified, Nathan rolled the body over, and his heart stopped. The bank shifted under a sea of skulls, sucking him under.

"Nathan! Nathan, help me!"

"Samantha!" He screamed and tried to claw to the surface. The faceless body was on his back, moving with him, hampering his progress. "Please . . . kill . . . me."

"Nathan, help me!"

He screamed and lost his balance. He fell end over end. The body fell with him.

"Please . . . kill . . ."

"No-o-o!"

Nathan jerked upright, panting. His hand shook as he dragged it across his face. Three pairs of eyes were trained on him as though he were a lunatic.

Maybe he was.

"Nathan?" Caleb stepped away from the table.

"Is a'right." Nathan's words came out slurred, and the outline of a bottle wavered beside him. Of course. The whiskey. The whiskey had brought on the nightmare.

He grabbed the nearly empty bottle and staggered to the window. Kelley and George turned back to their card game.

Nathan grimaced and took a long pull on the bottle as he peered into the darkness. He couldn't see outside any better than he could see beyond the depravity of his own heart.

"You're going to drink yourself into an early grave, my friend," Caleb said behind him.

Nathan wiped his mouth on the back of his sleeve. "I got nothin' t'live for."

"I thought we were going to talk tonight about our next bank robbery. You said you had a plan."

Nathan shook his head. He rubbed his face, scratching his hand on a three-day-old beard. "M'father's right. All 'm good for's a hangman's noose." He squeezed his eyes shut. "Ya don't know, Caleb. Ya don't know ev'rthin' I done."

Caleb grabbed Nathan by the arm. "I know you're ready to sleep this one off."

"No!" Nathan shrugged away, glaring. "I won't go back t'that room! She used t'be there!"

He pressed the bottle against his thigh and leaned against the window sill for support. His chin dropped to his chest. "The railroad man shoulda killed me back in Cheyenne. Somebody shoulda killed me a long time ago."

He hurled the bottle to the floor and watched it shatter. He dragged his gun from its holster and pressed the cold metal against his temple. "Oh, God, jus' take the pain," he mumbled. His finger quivered against the trigger.

"No!" Caleb grabbed for Nathan's wrist.

Nathan closed his eyes, just before he felt a tremendous burst of pressure in his head and saw an explosion of light.

⁓

Grinning, Justin Crawford passed the nearly empty bottle back across the table. Lady Luck was hanging on his shoulder, that was for sure.

He couldn't believe he'd seen Broom stroll into this back-water Denver saloon. He'd been hoping to get a free drink or two off the friendly Texan, but once Broom had gotten liquored up, he'd given Crawford more than he had hoped for.

The two hundred dollars Crawford had made by selling the gang's location had long been spent. He'd lived it up with the best liquor, the prettiest women, and the fanciest digs. When the money ran out, so had his friends. Since then, he'd hooked up with one gang, then another, always looking for the one big strike that would let him settle down for good. Then he'd cross the border into Mexico, find a pretty señorita to take care of him, and spend the rest of his days doing whatever he pleased.

Now Broom had given him all the information Crawford needed to make his dreams come true.

"So the old man was Hamilton's father," he said casually.

"Yep." Broom reached for another drink. "He never planned on turning Nathan in, though he might as well. When I left the mountains a few months ago, Nathan was pining away for Samantha. I think he wishes he'd never left her in Colorado."

At the mention of Samantha, Crawford smiled. He remembered how she'd felt in his arms, how she'd struggled. The first time he'd seen her, she'd been all prim and reserved, but she'd fought him like a she-cat. She'd probably fight him again when he took her out of Colorado, but by the time they reached Wyoming, she'd do whatever he said. All he had to do was keep her alive long enough to get past the guards at the hideout entrance.

And then he'd get Nathan Hamilton. Union Pacific had just raised the bounty on his head to four thousand dollars. Dead or alive, no questions asked.

NINETEEN

Nathan awoke, aching from the top of his head to his toe-nails, but that was nothing new. He'd awakened that way a lot lately. He would live with the pain until early evening, then start drinking again before the emotional pain of reality attacked full force.

Groaning, he sat up in bed, the usual headache intensified by a peculiar facial pain. He gingerly tested his jaw, probing tender, bloodied flesh. What had happened? He couldn't even remember going to bed.

Nathan stumbled to his feet and yanked his suspenders up over his shoulders. He swayed, his hands trembling as they thrust out for support. His head felt like the inside of Notre Dame's bell, the hunchback ringing for dear life in Nathan's pounding temples. His stomach lurched, and the room spun. Nathan groaned.

Steadying himself, he glanced above the bed to the empty frame. He wished he'd told Samantha to take it along with that stupid sheep picture. He didn't need any reminders of her.

Holding his head, Nathan wobbled to the front room. His stomach lurched again, and his parched throat screamed for water. Using the dipper from the barrel, he drank noisily then poured cold water over his head. He studied himself in the shaving mirror, turning his jaw to examine a colorful bruise and cut.

His hands shook as he poured a cup of coffee from the pot simmering on the stove. Turning, he started, nearly spilling the hot liquid. George lounged at the table.

"How long you been here?" Resting the cup on the wooden surface, he pulled out a chair. The effort of sitting down made Nathan drop his head in his hands.

"Long enough. I've been waiting for you to wake up. I'm not stupid enough to try to talk to a hungover man before he's had his first cup of coffee."

Nathan sipped the warm brew and glanced at the window. The muslin curtains Samantha had made were pulled closed. "What time of day is it?"

"Early afternoon."

The hot liquid warmed his gut, but the pressure of the cup on his bruised lip made his mouth ache. He frowned and fingered his face. "You got any idea what happened to my jaw?"

"You tried to shoot yourself last night. Caleb punched you."

Nathan thumped the cup to the table. "I wouldn't do a stupid thing like that!"

"You were drunk," George said calmly. "Nobody figured you knew what you were doing. Least of all Caleb, but he was still hopping mad. He said he didn't want to have to clean up the mess if you'd actually pulled the trigger."

Nathan felt a reluctant smile cross his sore face. It was just like Caleb to save his life, then crack a joke about it.

George shifted in his chair. "But that's not why I'm here. I've been holding off for a few days before coming to you, but after last night I figured you ought to know. A few days ago I had a dream about Samantha. A vision, if you want to call it that."

Nathan raised his eyebrows. "Are you trying to tell me you're a shaman? A medicine man? Is that what the Shoshoni have been telling you?"

"All I know is a few days ago I had a vision of her, and she was in trouble."

"She's probably getting married," Nathan said through clenched teeth. "If you saw anything at all, that's what it was."

"No, you don't understand. Someone was trying to hurt her."

Nathan sat up straight. What about his own dream? Nathan had heard her voice calling him, pleading for help. He shook his head. "I can't go riding all the way back to Colorado! She'd just tell me off but good." He stared blankly at George. "Then again, she's probably already married Cameron and is happy being his wife."

George leaned back and crossed his arms.

"Still . . ." Nathan's heart raced at the thought of seeing her again. "You and Samantha always did have a special friendship, some kind of strange bond. And I *have* always valued your opinion." He locked eyes with George. "Even if it's true, do you think I can help her?"

George shrugged. "I'm willing to go with you to find out."

"You can't be serious!" Caleb's protest echoed loudly as he followed after Nathan. "First of all, it's the dead of winter. You and George could get stuck in a blizzard. Then there's the fact you very clearly left my sister. You're only going to break her heart if she sees you again—or break your own if she's married that farmer by now."

Nathan tightened the cinch on his horse. "I know all that, Caleb. But I trust George."

"*Trust George?* What does he know? He's not even a full-blood Indian or even a half-breed! What makes you think he has this great gift anyway? Or that those crazy savages actually can predict the future at all?"

Nathan whirled around. "Caleb, shut up for once! I owe you for saving my life last night, but that doesn't give you the right to run off at the mouth. Maybe it's a second chance for me and Samantha. All I know is I have to take it. Nothing could be any worse than the condition I'm in now."

Caleb stepped back and held up his hands. "All right then, go! I've seen that dead-set expression before, and it always spells trouble. I can't stop you, you stubborn fool."

Nathan smiled sadly. "We've been friends a long time, Caleb. Under other circumstances, we might be brothers by marriage."

He held out his hand. Caleb stared at it a moment, then clasped it strongly, pulling Nathan forward for a momentary embrace. Embarrassed, he released him quickly. "You always were a sorry piece of work, Nathan," he mumbled.

Nathan grinned. "Yeah? Just remember who's older."

"By only two months!" Caleb returned hotly but smiled at the familiar taunt. He sobered. "You and George be careful."

"We plan on it."

Late one afternoon a knock sounded at the Jordans' door, and Sally smiled at Samantha. "It's probably just Noah. You two have been very friendly lately."

Samantha blushed, attacking the pie dough she and Maria

had been rolling out. She'd put off giving Noah an answer. Though he visited frequently, he hadn't pressed the issue; in fact, he hadn't even brought it up again. But she could tell by the way he looked at her that he hoped she would decide in his favor. Soon. "Noah didn't say anything about coming over today, Sally."

"Uncle Noah!" Tommy raced ahead of Sally, stretching for the door. Before he could reach the knob, the door crashed inward. Sally yanked Tommy back and gasped as Justin Crawford sauntered in.

Smiling evilly, he scanned the room until his gaze landed on Samantha. His smile widened at her stunned silence. "Can't you at least give a man a greetin' after all this time?"

Samantha pushed Maria behind her, her heart pounding with fear. Sally stepped between her and Crawford. "I don't know who you are, but you—"

Crawford's face darkened. "Shut up! I ain't interested in you or your family, but it'll go easier for you if you stay out of what don't concern you. All I want is this piece of blond baggage."

Sally's gaze flew to Samantha, then to the rifle by the door. She lunged for it, but Crawford drew his gun before she could even touch the stock. He laughed as she straightened with fear. "That's right, lady. Just back away. You might as well tell me where your man is."

Sally raised her chin. "H-he's in the fields."

Crawford's smile fell, and he lowered the pistol and aimed at Maria. Sally screamed. "For the love of—"

"Mama!"

"Where is he?" Crawford said evenly, cocking the pistol.

Samantha tried to shield the trembling little girl, but

Crawford moved lightning quick and aimed the gun at Maria. "Now tell me the truth, lady. *Where is he?*"

"H-he went to town for the day! Now, please let my daughter—"

Crawford pushed Maria away, and Sally rushed forward to scoop the little girl into her arms. Tommy trailed after them, sobbing. "Come on," Crawford said, waving the gun. "Outside. I'm going to lock you and your brats up where you won't be in the way. I'm taking your friend here on a little trip back to her lover's hideout." He grinned. "Just as soon as we settle some unfinished business."

Grabbing Samantha, he marched them all outside, where he pushed Sally and a sobbing Tommy and Maria into the barn. With a laugh, he slammed the door and pulled down the bar. "There. That ought to keep them." He turned to Samantha, waving the gun for her to head back to the house. "I like it better in there."

She shuddered as they walked, his hand like a vise around her arm, the gun against her head. She wanted to scream and run and hide, but she had not only herself to think about but Sally and the children. Sally's unborn baby. They might be in the barn, but they wouldn't be safe until Crawford was gone.

Inside, Crawford banged the door shut. Trying to stay calm, Samantha gripped the back of a chair for support. "Why don't you sit down and let me finish this pie?" she said evenly. "You can eat and leave before Frank comes home. He won't get back until dark."

Pushing his hat back on his head with the gun barrel, Crawford laughed. "Lady, I've got other ideas for you instead of pie making. I figure Hamilton'll give himself up real fast when he sees I got you. Then I can take him in for the reward." He whistled. "All four thousand dollars. And the railroad don't care if he's dead or alive, neither."

"H-how did you find me?" she said, stalling.

"Broom. I ran into him in Denver."

She forced herself to laugh, the sound shrill to her own ears. "Nathan won't care about me. Didn't Broom tell you Nathan left me here? Or didn't you pay him enough to find that out?"

"Broom told me all I needed for just a few shots of whiskey. He said Hamilton was moping about you, so I figure he'll do what I say, for once. And I'll get all that money."

Samantha's heart pounded cold. He'd said Nathan was wanted dead or alive. Crawford would never let him walk into a jail cell; he'd kill Nathan just for the pleasure of seeing him dead.

Crawford smiled viciously, reaching into his pocket for a strip of leather. "Now step forward and let me tie your hands. We'll get acquainted first, then be on our way."

Panicked, she backed up. Crawford followed her, grinning. She threw a chair at him, but he ducked and kept coming. He moved slowly, like a cat with a cornered mouse. She looked around wildly, searching for some route of escape, knowing that if he tied her hands, she'd narrow her chances of getting free.

She tripped over Maria's stool, then threw it in panic. This time her aim was sure, clipping Crawford on the side of the head. He cursed, rubbing the red mark it had left. "That's enough," he said, the smile gone. "Face facts and save yourself a lot of extra pain."

"No!" Samantha tried to dash around the table for the door, but he caught her in his arms, laughing.

"I like feisty women," he murmured in her ear, his breath hot against her face. "I'll bet Hamilton liked you too."

The mention of Nathan pumped fury in her veins. Screaming as loudly as she could, she stomped down hard on Crawford's instep, then kneed him squarely, the way Caleb had shown her years ago.

Crawford howled with pain, and she grabbed his gun from the holster and ran for the door. Flinging herself outside, sobbing, she saw a figure riding up on a familiar dun gelding. Noah!

He dismounted quickly, catching her as she fell into his arms. "Samantha, what—"

"He's a criminal! He wants to take me to get Nathan!"

"Drop the gun, mister! And let me see your hands!" Crawford shouted from the doorway, the Jordans' rifle in hand.

Noah dropped his gun and held up his hands. He moved in front of Samantha. Trembling, she stepped around him and leveled the gun at Crawford's gut. *Oh, Lord, I don't know if I can do this! Was this how Nathan felt when he shot that railroad man? Sick to his stomach that he had no choice?*

"Samantha," Noah said quietly. "Toss me the gun and hit the ground behind me. I've got a better chance of hitting him."

Her hand trembled.

Crawford laughed and leaned lazily against the doorjamb. "Well, well. I think we got us a standoff. Let me just tell you a few things, missy, while you're deciding whether you've got enough gumption to kill me. The first is that I'm a much better aim, and this rifle's more accurate at this distance than that revolver there. I ought to know because it's mine. Second of all, you might shoot me, but I'll get a shot off first. And I'll be shooting to kill."

"I don't care if you kill me," she shouted, quivering with fear. "At least you won't get Nathan!"

He laughed again. "Oh, I'd just wing you. The first killing will be your friend there."

"Don't listen to him," Noah said fiercely. "Toss me the gun, Samantha. It's our only chance!"

Crawford's face darkened, and he straightened. "Come on, woman. You're going with me one way or another. Do you want me to kill this man first? If not, toss that gun over here real easy-like."

Samantha glanced at Noah. He stood tall and determined, unafraid. She couldn't risk his death over something that had nothing to do with him.

Defeated, she pitched the gun in the dirt toward Crawford.

He leaped on it, and Noah moved in front of her. "Samantha," he said sadly.

Crawford was instantly on them, hitting Noah on the back of the head with the butt of the rifle. With a moan, he crumpled to the ground.

Samantha cried out, but Crawford grabbed her wrists and savagely knotted the leather around them. "I told you to do what I said! Now *get in the house!*"

Trembling with fear, Samantha moved forward. Her legs buckled, and Crawford pushed her onto the porch with the butt of the rifle. She cried out, sobbing. *Oh, Lord. Please deliver me! Deliver us all!*

"Hold it, Crawford!" a voice rang out from the barn.

At the doorway, Crawford stopped in his tracks, clutching Samantha closer for protection. "What the—?"

Samantha heard the distinct click of a gun hammer and saw a barrel appear from around the doorway and press against Crawford's temple. "You make one move and I'll blow your head off. Now drop the guns."

Crawford complied and slowly held up his hands. Samantha stepped away, gasping as a familiar form rounded the doorway. "Nathan!"

"Stay back, Samantha!" Nathan stepped outside, keeping the barrel of his revolver pressed against Crawford's temple.

"Samantha!" Sally and the children raced across the front yard from the barn. "Someone named George let us out of the barn. He said he was a friend of yours. He's helping Noah—" Her hand flew to her throat. "Nathan!"

Relaxing, he smiled mischievously. "Good to see you again, Sally."

Samantha moved to Nathan's side. "Crawford was going to use me to get to you and the reward on your head."

Nathan sucked in his breath, glaring at Crawford. Shifting the gun, he poked Crawford in the shoulder. "Get inside! And keep your hands where I can see them!"

Sally shooed the children through the door first then scurried after them. Nathan herded Crawford to the table and motioned him to sit down. He kept his gun trained but glanced at Samantha. "Are you all right?" he said sharply.

She nodded, mute.

Holding the back of his head, Noah staggered inside. Sally helped him to a chair, bustling around him, but he brushed her away. "I'll be all right, Sally."

"Want me to take over, Nathan?"

Samantha turned, smiling. "George!" He grinned at her and replaced his knife in his waistband.

"Sure, George," Nathan said, handing over his gun.

"Take all the time you want."

"I didn't do nothin'!" Crawford said, then glared at George. "Injun," he muttered under his breath.

Sally laid a wet cloth on the back of Noah's head. He winced but didn't say anything. He stared at Nathan, then Samantha, his gray eyes piercingly sad.

Nathan put his arm around her and drew her away from the others. He unknotted the leather binding her wrists, and she shook her hands to get the blood flowing. Nathan cupped her cheek, then jerked his head in Noah's direction. "You didn't marry him, did you?"

She shook her head. "I thought I'd never see you again," she whispered. Her mouth curved into a smile, her joy child-like. It was like a fairy tale, with him coming back for her, sweeping her off to . . .

She frowned. Where could he take her? And should she even go?

Nathan's arms closed around her. "We need each other no matter what the risks or differences," he whispered. "Will you go back with me?"

Her heart battled her head. "I . . . I don't—"

"I'll marry you. You're not safer without me, and I'm not safer without you. One night when I was drunk, I almost killed myself thinking about all the trouble I've caused, and—"

Horrified, she covered his mouth with her hand. "Please don't say such things!" She glanced at the others. "We can talk later."

He nodded and straightened. His expression hardening

again, he moved back toward the table. "Get up, Crawford. You and I can go outside now."

Samantha grabbed his arm. "What are you doing?"

"I'm going to shoot him."

"No!"

Nathan took the gun from George's hand and waved Crawford toward the door. "Let's go."

"Nathan, no!" She clutched his arm, but he shook her off.

"This isn't your concern, Samantha. He has to be punished."

"Then let a court do it!"

"She's right." Noah rose. "It's Nathan Hamilton, isn't it?" Noah had obviously put two and two together and figured out Nathan's true identity. "You don't want to shoot him."

Nathan laughed. "I wouldn't have figured you to be the soft-hearted kind, Cameron. Surely you understand."

"I understand how you feel, but I also understand the law. You want to add one more murder to your charges?"

Nathan narrowed his eyes. "What do you know about that? You interested in the reward like Crawford?"

"No, but I know you're a wanted man. I'm just interested in justice."

"And why is that?" Nathan smirked.

Noah paused. "Because I'm a United States marshal. I've taken a leave of absence, but I'm still duly authorized."

TWENTY

Samantha's jaw dropped.

"You're a *what?*" Nathan roared.

"You still want to shoot him, Hamilton? You'd not only have *two* murders on your head but a lawman as a witness."

Anguished, Samantha stepped toward Noah, whispering so that Nathan wouldn't hear. "I'm sorry I couldn't tell you about Nathan before."

Noah grimaced. "How did you hook up with a criminal like him?"

"We grew up together. He and my brother left me in an orphanage and went to fight in the war. He came back for me two years ago, and I've been living with them since."

Noah drew a sharp breath. "As his lover?"

"No!"

Noah relaxed. "Now that I know who he is, I understand why he left you here. He wanted to protect you." He rubbed the back of his neck and stared at Nathan as if he didn't know what to do with him.

Samantha struggled to regain control of her tumbling emotions. "Noah, I'm s-sorry. You're such a good man. But I could never marry you."

"I know, Samantha," he said. "Better for us to know now."

Nathan moved toward Crawford at the table and waved the gun at the door. "Enough talk. Outside."

Glaring, Crawford rose.

Samantha's stomach twisted. "Nathan!"

Noah turned to her. "Is this the man you want? A man who would kill?"

"You're no choirboy!" Nathan said, lowering the gun. "You—"

Crawford suddenly lunged across the table and grabbed Samantha. Nathan spun around with his gun raised, but Crawford elbowed him in the face, sending Nathan sprawling. Crawford grabbed the revolver.

Noah and George backed off as he jammed the barrel of the gun under her chin. "You and me, missy, are gettin' out of here."

"Leave her out of this." Nathan rose slowly. "You don't want her. She'll just slow you down."

Crawford laughed. "I don't plan on keepin' her long, Hamilton. I guess you won't mind if I borrow her. You won't be around to know the difference."

"He won't hurt you, Sam," Nathan said, keeping his gaze trained on Crawford. "You're not the one he wants. Unless he's a coward who shoots women."

"Coward?" Crawford's face mottled red. He tightened his arm, and Samantha cried out.

"Samantha!" Sally cried. Noah pulled her and the children back.

Crawford grinned, stroking Samantha's hair. He hooked both arms around her and, laughing, aimed the gun at Nathan's heart.

"Listen to me, Crawford," Nathan said calmly. "You can turn me in for the reward. But give the woman to Cameron. That way you won't have to deal with her slowing you down."

"I ain't gonna turn you in alive, Hamilton," Crawford said coldly. "I wasn't figurin' on draggin' you along too."

"I know. I'm worth just as much dead. But she's not worth anything at all."

"He's right." George stepped one foot closer to Samantha. "You don't want to mess with the woman. She'll just bring you trouble. Leave her and take him."

"Let go!" Samantha twisted in Crawford's steely grasp and looked desperately at Nathan. He stood stock-still, and his determined eyes met hers.

Her heart pounded with fear. "No! Don't shoot him!"

"I'll think about your kind offer, Hamilton." Crawford sneered and pushed her away. He raised the gun to Nathan's heart again, an evil smile on his face.

"No-o-o!" Samantha leaped in front of the barrel, stretching out her arms.

The door burst open. "Sally!" Frank yelled. "What's—"

Crawford cursed. "You fool—"

Nathan pulled Samantha to the ground. A knife flew from George's hand, and the gun discharged at the ceiling as Crawford fell. He stared down at his red, sticky chest then looked up in surprise. "Why you Injun—"

Samantha buried her face against Nathan's chest and heard Crawford's head thud back against the floor.

Ashen-faced, Nathan leaned over Samantha. "Sweetheart . . . Sam . . . You little fool! What were you doing?"

Samantha's hands trembled as she held his face. "I love you," she whispered. *"I love you!"*

Shaking, he pushed her hands away. "You should have married Cameron!"

Holding the gun, Noah knelt beside them. "Are you all right, Samantha?"

She nodded, shivering, clutching her arms around her middle as she and Nathan sat up. He drew her in an embrace, and she pressed her face against his shoulder.

"I have all the guns now, Hamilton," Noah said quietly. "You know you're under arrest."

"Yes." His arms tightened around Samantha, and she heard him draw a deep breath. "I'll go with you."

"No!" Panicked, she pulled away. "No, you can't!"

Nathan turned weary eyes to her, his expression sad. "I can't run anymore, Samantha. I've put you in too much danger."

"But you, you—" She couldn't let him go! They needed more time! She drew a deep breath. "You said you'd marry me!"

"Marry you!" Nathan echoed. His eyes lit up for a moment, then died. "No."

"Yes!" She insisted, rising to her feet, pulling him with her. "Please, Noah! I know you have to take Nathan, but let us be married first. You know he's . . . he's going to hang."

Noah's expression was sorrowful. "Samantha, you—"

Looking defeated, Nathan nodded. "She's right, Cameron. Let me give her a legal married name. It's easier for a married woman, even a widow, to make her way in the world."

Samantha smiled up at Nathan, then looked to Noah. "You see?"

Noah looked helplessly from her to Nathan, then back again at Samantha. "You need to talk to Frank," he said quietly. "You seem to be forgetting a few things."

"Fine." She raised her chin and strode to the Jordans. George and Frank had lifted Crawford's blanket-covered body and were carrying it through the open door.

"Samantha!" Sally clutched her sniffling children. "Are you all right?"

She nodded, and Sally's eyes filled with tears. She crushed Tommy against her. "I was so . . . so . . ." She trailed off, weeping.

"Mama, is the bad man gone?" Tommy sniffled again.

"Yes, darling." She hugged him and Maria closely. "He's gone."

Frank knelt beside his family. He hugged each one, then Samantha. "Thank God all of you are all right."

"He was good to us all," Samantha said, then drew a deep breath. "Noah seems to think I need to talk to you."

"Why?"

"Noah's going to arrest Nathan, and I want to marry him before he goes."

Frank glanced up, puzzled. "You want to marry Noah?"

"No!" Samantha blushed at her outburst and glanced sideways to the other end of the room. Noah and Nathan stood silently, watching her. "I . . . I want to marry Nathan."

Frank followed the direction of her gaze, then sighed. He handed Maria back to Sally, then held out a hand to Samantha. "Noah's right. We need to talk."

"Reverend Jordan." George stood at the door. The blanketed form of Crawford lay just beyond the porch. "I found a shovel. If you'll just tell me where—"

Frank grimaced. "I suppose I ought to go with you to say a few words."

Nathan let out a curt laugh, and Samantha felt her face warm with embarrassment. "Go on, Frank," she said quietly. "I'll wait."

"Please help Sally with the children," he said. "Noah, don't do anything until I've talked to Samantha."

"I'm not going anywhere with this fellow. Yet." He turned to Nathan. "But it is time for a bit of business. Hold out your wrists and let me tie them together."

"I promise not to escape, Cameron," Nathan said with a cynical smile.

"Humor me then."

Nathan laughed and held out his wrists.

Samantha couldn't bear to see his hands tied, and she pushed past Frank for the door. "Excuse me. I'm going for some air."

"Do you want me to come with you?"

Noah shot Nathan a hard look. "You just stay right here. Let's let the preacher have a word with her first, then we'll see what he says."

Outside, Samantha dropped into the willow porch swing. Turning her face to the setting winter sun, she rubbed her arms against the chill and bowed her head. She could hear Sally preparing dinner inside, but she didn't move.

At last the swing dipped as Frank sat beside her. He brushed the dirt from his hands and sighed. "Tell me why you want to marry Nathan."

Samantha raised her face. "I want to be his wife before he goes off to die. I've tried to share the Lord with him for years now and met with resistance at every turn—I've given up. Now I just want to love him!"

Frank's expression softened. "You know what Paul wrote about believers not being yoked to unbelievers."

"Does it matter, when Nathan's going to die? Paul also wrote that an unbeliever is set apart by a believing spouse. If I marry him, wouldn't that grant him some grace?"

"It certainly wouldn't give him salvation. He has to find that on his own. And I can't believe God will honor a marriage if you deliberately disobey his word."

"How can I send Nathan off to die alone? He once said I would never marry him even if he asked because I loved God more than him. It's true, Frank. I do love God with all my heart and soul, but I love Nathan too! As much as I'm sure Sally loves you. As much as any C-Christian woman . . . loves her husband." She blinked back tears.

Frank put his arm around her. "Samantha, a marriage is an expression of love. A lifetime commitment," he pleaded softly as he drew back, searching her eyes.

"Nathan only has a short lifetime left," she whispered. She clutched his arm, choking down the catch in her throat. "P-please marry us, Frank. *Please!*"

Frank swallowed, his eyes tormented. Samantha tried to stop the tears, but she didn't have the energy. If Frank denied her request, she felt her heart would literally break in two and fall to the porch.

If she'd left Nathan when she first found out about the stealing, it would have hurt, but she would have survived and started a new life somewhere else. But she had been so certain

God wanted her to stay, to be his example. Now she wasn't certain what God wanted anymore. He felt so far away.

Frank kissed her cheek. When he pulled back, his eyes and smile were weary. "I'll marry you two, Samantha."

"Thank you!" Samantha hugged him quickly, then bounded up from the swing. She hesitated, then turned back, smiling sadly as she whispered again, "Thank you."

TWENTY-ONE

"Dearly beloved, we are gathered here today in the sight of God..."

Nathan clutched Samantha's hand, hardly daring to breathe, hardly daring even to look at her. When she'd emerged from Sally's bedroom wearing her friend's fancy black dress and hat, Nathan's heart leaped to his throat. She walked calmly toward him, eyes fixed on his, a loving smile lighting her pale face. Common sense told him to bolt out the door and head straight for Cheyenne, but his heart overruled. He extended his arm, and she trustfully placed her hand in his.

"Marriage is an outward symbol..."

Nathan briefly closed his eyes, his father's voice echoing in his head. *A public profession... a request for God's blessing... the two flesh literally become one...*

He opened his eyes, turning slightly. Samantha smiled shyly, then soberly turned her attention to Frank. Had the preacher smiled even once since they began? Nathan was aware of George standing quietly at his left and Sally at Samantha's right, the two children looking on solemnly at their mother's side. But where was—?

"Who gives this woman to be wed?"

Noah stepped forward from behind Nathan and

Samantha. "I do," he said evenly. He bent his head and brushed his lips against Samantha's cheek.

She smiled, her eyes shining. "Thank you, Noah," she whispered. "I know God will bless you with a spouse who loves the Lord as you do."

Noah's face hardened for a moment. "I wish God was blessing you the same way." He glanced at Nathan, then stepped back.

Frank cleared his throat. "Do you, Nathan, er—"

"Adam," he supplied.

Samantha glanced at him with surprise, and Frank smiled gratefully. "Nathan Adam, take this woman to be your lawfully wedded wife? To have and to hold, from this day forward, for better or worse, for richer or poorer, in sickness and health, till death do you part?"

Nathan lifted his chin. "I do."

"And do you, Samantha Alice, take this man to be your lawfully wedded husband? To have and to hold, from this day forward, for better or worse, for richer or poorer, in sickness and health, till death do you part?"

Nathan stared straight ahead. He felt her shift closer to him, felt her love radiate even before the words were spoken. "I do."

"May I have the—" Frank's voice trailed off, and he glanced up.

What kind of groom neglected to give his bride a ring? "I don't have one," Nathan said bitterly.

"Here." Sally stepped forward, working a band off her right hand. She handed the ring to Nathan, smiling apologetically. "It was my mother's."

Nathan glanced at it briefly, grimacing. Silver, not even gold. Probably not even pure silver, at that.

"Place it on her finger."

Nathan and Samantha turned to each other, and he lifted her trembling left hand. Silent tears washed her face, but instead of a smile, her lips quivered.

"Sam?" he said softly.

She wiped both cheeks with the back of her hand. "G-go ahead, Nathan." She gave a weak smile, but her lips wouldn't stop trembling.

Nathan glanced helplessly at Frank, the ring still poised at the tip of Samantha's finger.

"With this ring . . ."

"With this ring."

"I thee wed."

Nathan gently pushed the ring past her knuckle. "I thee wed," he whispered.

Frank smiled, no doubt a forced concession to the event. He raised his hands. "And now what God has joined together, let no man put asunder."

"Amen," Sally murmured, lowering her head.

"You may kiss the bride."

Nathan pulled Samantha gently into his embrace. She raised her face, and his heart broke at the innocent expression, the pure trust, he saw there. His lips crashed down on hers, but the kiss was surprisingly soft and gentle. She smiled when they pulled apart, a genuine smile now.

"Samantha," Sally murmured, drawing her friend close. Nathan numbly shook hands with Frank, George, and a silent Noah. He watched helplessly as Sally and the children pulled

Samantha away to a food-laden table. Samantha bent down, her lips curving into a sweet smile, and spoke a few words to Maria. The little girl's face glowed with wonder, her dreamy eyes fixed on the bride.

Nathan's heart twisted. What kind of wedding had Samantha dreamed of as a girl? Surely she'd imagined lots of white—not just a dress but ribbons, a veil, and cake to match. And what of her dream groom?

Nathan frowned. Was he the only one who noticed that Frank hadn't asked if there were any objections to their marriage?

Samantha raised her hand to adjust the stiff lace collar of her dress, the movement crying out to Nathan. What kind of groom let his bride wear funeral colors at her wedding?

Samantha barely tasted Sally's smoked ham and mashed potatoes. The silence of the others didn't help her roiling emotions either. No matter how many sips of water she drank, her mouth felt as dry as a Kansas drought. Her stomach churned and rolled like the time she'd had the wind knocked out of her from falling out of the hay wagon.

She looked at Nathan and felt better. Frank had loaned him a suit and string tie. Nathan had never appeared more handsome—more like the Nathan she'd always wanted to marry.

She smiled to herself. His middle name was Adam? How appropriate. The first man—the only man—she'd ever loved.

"More ham?" Nathan held out the platter. He glanced at her picked-over food, his eyes concerned. "Please eat," he murmured. "If you don't, you'll get sick."

She nodded mutely, lifting a fork. She felt everyone's gaze on her and Nathan.

Samantha laughed out loud. "This is supposed to be a wedding supper! Can't you at least be happy for me? For Nathan?"

Sally lowered her head under the pretense of spooning more food onto the children's plates. Frank soberly laid aside his fork. "It's difficult, Samantha," he said. "You and Nathan won't have much of a married life together."

"No, but who ever knows how much time they have? Any one of us at this table could be dead just as—"

"Sweetheart." Nathan squeezed her hand, his eyes gentle. "They know that. Let's enjoy the time we have together."

Tears welled in her eyes. "You accept these short hours with gratefulness when it's nothing compared to the eternity God offers."

Nathan glanced around the table. "Samantha," he said in a low voice.

Why didn't everyone just go away? She didn't care who heard her, but she didn't want any more intrusions on her time with Nathan.

Noah cleared his throat and rose. "Hamilton, I'll spend the night in the barn and be in for you at first light. I'm hoping you won't decide to try to escape."

"I won't," Nathan said. "You have my word on that, Cameron. For whatever you feel it's worth."

A look of compassion flickered across Noah's face, then he smiled. "It's worth more than you think."

George pushed his chair back and rose beside Noah. "If Nathan says he won't leave, he won't. You can tie me up in his place, marshal."

Noah smiled faintly. "That won't be necessary." He glanced at the window, yawning. "Guess I'll call it a night."

Samantha rose and embraced Noah quickly. "Thank you for giving me away."

Noah pulled back, his face taut with discomfort. "I hate having to take him in, Samantha."

She lowered her eyes. "I know you do."

Noah looked relieved. "Thank you, Frank . . . Sally." He glanced around the room once more, avoiding looking at Samantha or Nathan. Frank brought his hat and coat, and Noah left.

George took Samantha's hands and kissed her on the cheek. "You're a beautiful bride, Samantha."

Samantha smiled. George. He would always have a special place in her heart. "Thank you."

"Thanks for standing up with me, George," Nathan said. "It means a lot."

Solemn, George shook Nathan's hand and nodded.

"You're welcome to stay with us as long as Samantha does," Sally said.

He nodded again, then was gone.

Silence filled the room. Even the children were unusually quiet, their hands toying with the tablecloth. Samantha lifted a plate and prepared to help Sally clean up.

"For goodness' sakes, Samantha." Sally bustled over and pulled the plate from her hand. "It's your wedding night. You don't need to worry about the dishes! Don't you want to be alone with your husband?"

Samantha glanced at Nathan, who stood motionless, watching her with curious green eyes. Her heart beat faster. *Her husband.* She swallowed hard, curling her fingers around the back of a chair.

"We'll clean up," Frank said, linking his arm around Sally's waist. "Good night."

"G-good night," Samantha stammered. "Tommy . . . Maria. Can I have a hug?"

The children soberly complied, Tommy even adding a grown-up handshake. At the gesture, Samantha pulled them both closely against her, remembering other baby arms wrapped around her neck, another baby head snuggled against her breast. Trembling, she could almost feel her womb leap within her, crying for fulfillment that she was sure would never come.

"Good night, darlings," she whispered. When she rose, the children scampered to their mother.

Samantha raised her head and found Nathan once again gazing at her. Slowly he extended his hand, his angular face solemn. She moved forward, guided by her heart.

Nathan ushered Samantha into the bedroom, closing the door softly behind them. He leaned against it, watching her, studying her nervous movements.

Hands trembling, she removed the little black hat and carefully set each pin on the dresser. She pushed back the tendrils of hair framing her face, then patted the thick, coiled braid on the back of her head. Her hands lowered to the black silk dress, smoothing the skirt, adjusting the basque, fingering the sleeves.

Touched by her innocence, Nathan moved away from the door. She glanced up with a look of surprise and a faint sense of panic when he placed his hands on her wrists. "You look fine," he whispered. "You make a lovely bride."

"I . . . I'm sorry the dress was black. I didn't have the heart to turn down Sally's offer to let me wear it. It's her nicest dress and better than anything I have."

He shook his head, smiling. "It wouldn't have mattered what you wore. You were beautiful. You *are* beautiful."

She glanced away shyly. "You look very nice too."

Her hands lifted, fluttering, and he stilled them with his own before she could start adjusting her clothing again. "Samantha," he said softly, "there's no reason for you to be nervous. Just because we're married, we don't have to—"

"Will you please brush my hair?" she said abruptly, raising hopeful eyes.

He stepped back, puzzled. "Brush your hair?"

She nodded, shy again. "I've always dreamed of my husband taking the pins out of my hair and brushing it at night."

Nathan grinned, pleased she had shared this childhood secret. He himself had always harbored a secret desire to brush her hair, to have an excuse to let it fall against his hands as it had that day by the bunnies' nest long ago.

He lifted her brush from the dresser and gestured at the chair standing sentinel by the bed. "Have a seat, m'lady."

Samantha sat sideways so he could brush unhindered by the chair's back. Her spine was as straight as a rod, but when his hands touched the first pins, he felt her shudder. Slowly he removed each pin, loosening the braid by degrees. When at last it swung free, he set aside the pins and slipped off the bit of ribbon. He loosened the blond tail and carefully finger-combed its silkiness.

It was softer than he'd ever imagined. Nathan's mouth went dry. "Tell me more about when you were a girl," he said gently.

Samantha shifted in the chair. "There was always Caleb and you."

Nathan slowly moved the brush from the crown of her head to the end of her hair, near her waist, and she drew a deep breath. "You were . . . you were always my hero."

The brush stilled in his hand. "I'm nobody's hero, Samantha," he said bitterly. "And especially not yours. What I've done—"

She turned, surprising him with her anguished eyes. "Nathan, you've fed yourself ashes for many years, and your own deceived heart has turned you from God. You can't save yourself—you've admitted that to me before."

The brush clattered to the floor, and he turned away. "Don't you know how I've longed for this ache to go away? To go back to being the hero you looked up to when you were a girl?"

She rose beside him, tears in her eyes. "You can, Nathan," she whispered. "Through Jesus. God loves you. No matter what you've done or what you think you've done. Jesus himself suffered so you could—"

"No." Nathan covered his face with his hands. He drew a steadying breath, collecting himself. He had to get out of here, had to get away from her. Why had he married her? Just to make her a widow? "I'll tell Cameron I'm ready to leave now," he mumbled into his hands. "I don't care if we ride all night in the dark. I don't care if he shoots me now and saves time for a judge and jury. I don't care if—"

"Don't you care about me?"

Nathan heard her whispered voice, felt the soft brush of her hair against his bowed head, inhaled the clean scent of her. He felt the security of her arm around his shoulders, and he lifted his head in wonder. He drew a shattered breath. "You love me in spite of everything, don't you? You would still love me even if I told you what I've done."

She nodded. "Of course I would love you. Just as God loves you. No matter what."

Nathan's mouth went dry again, and his body went limp. He was so tired of carrying the secret alone, but he couldn't afford to tell her the truth. Not even now. "I can't tell you," he said.

She nodded, her eyes wet. "God already knows everything about you. You can't hide from his spirit, Nathan. Or flee from his presence. If we go to heaven, he's there. If we go down to hell, he's there too."

Nathan pushed down a sob in his throat, reaching out wordlessly. When Samantha talked like this, he could feel hope unfurl like a rosebud among the weeds of his soul. But as much as he wanted the peace she had, the peace written all over her face and in her eyes, he couldn't let go, couldn't give her the one thing she wanted. Not even with death waiting for him, visible as a black specter at the end of a straight road.

"Please, Nathan," she said softly, clutching him closer. "Please accept God before it's too late."

"Oh, Sam . . ." He kissed her face, cradling it gently between his hands. "I have nothing to give you, and you've given everything!"

Samantha pulled back. "You're wrong, Nathan," she said quietly. "About both things. I've given you everything as a friend but nothing as your wife."

He watched as she lifted his right hand and gently pressed

it over her heart. "And you . . . you'll have to teach me," she whispered, covering his hand with hers.

Nathan's heart shattered, and he cupped her chin to raise her face. His green eyes met her blue ones, solemn, trusting, and full of love. "No, Sam," he murmured as his lips met hers. "You'll have to teach me."

TWENTY-TWO

Leaning back in the chair, Nathan sighed. The pen slipped from his fingers. He must have held it motionless for half an hour, readied to be dipped in ink once the proper words presented themselves. He'd never found it difficult to express his thoughts before, but right now he couldn't possibly string together any cogent words. If he didn't come up with something soon, Samantha would awaken and he'd have to tell her in person.

He flipped open his pocket watch and glanced at the still-dark window. Not much longer till dawn.

Sheets and quilt rustled, and he jerked his head toward the bed. Samantha still slept. He relaxed, smiling faintly, remembering how hard she'd tried to stay awake all night, promising to greet the sunrise with him.

"Go to sleep," he'd murmured.

"No," she said, groggy. She touched his face as if to make sure he was still there. "I want . . . every minute with you. I won't get to . . . see you again . . . until I come to Cheyenne."

"Don't come for my trial. I don't want you there."

"Yes, you do," she murmured, smiling sleepily. "I'm your . . . wife."

But in the end, he'd held her close, murmuring soft words until, despite her best efforts, she'd fallen asleep. When he was sure she was slumbering soundly, he resisted the urge to stay and watch her until dawn and instead got out of bed to say good-bye in a letter. He felt like the worst of cowards, but he couldn't face her again.

Nathan picked up the pen once more, sighing deeply. His gaze wandered above the dresser where he sat, and he smiled faintly. He hadn't noticed it last night, but there was the picture of Jesus and the sheep nailed to the wall. He started to rip the picture free, then remembered how much Samantha loved it. He carefully worked the nail loose, and the picture slid into his hands. Curious, he laid it out in front of him and absentmindedly scratched the top corner with the nail.

What was it about the picture she loved? It was just a charcoal sketch of Jesus. Even Nathan remembered the story of Jesus as the Good Shepherd. That was the problem with God: He wanted his followers to be sheep, not living, breathing people who could think or look out for themselves. Did Samantha think of herself as just one of the flock?

Ashamed, Nathan glanced at the bed. Last night he'd certainly led her like a lamb to the slaughter, accepting her guilt offering without hesitation, knowing she somehow hoped to cleanse him. And when, despite his tenderness, tears rose in her eyes, he knew instinctively their source lay not in her physical pain or impending widowhood but in her concern for him. Only for him. Always for him.

He scratched the nail deeper against the paper, wearing a groove. Nathan stared at the image of Jesus, and he felt envy swell his chest. *What was it about this picture?*

"You'd know what to write to Samantha, wouldn't you?" he whispered fiercely to the charcoal-drawn man. Shoving the paper aside, he exhaled an anguished sigh and slumped forward until his head dropped into his hands.

One thing is needful.

He raised his head, his heart thudding. He'd heard those words long ago, when he'd sensed something calling him to find Samantha. A chill coursed down his spine.

He shuddered again. A need? Samantha had no needs. Not where he was concerned anyway. Why had he ever thought otherwise?

Anguish pierced his heart, filling his body, ascending to his throat. He clenched and unclenched his fists against the truth. Samantha had never been afflicted with poverty of circumstance or the soul. Like a daughter of royal birth, she had been cared for at every turn, in every way. And he had foolishly imagined himself some sort of gallant knight—her hero—out to vanquish dragons that didn't even exist!

In reality, he was nothing more than a beggar standing barefoot in the snow, gazing through the palace window at a life he could never hope to have. Certain the door knocker's weight alone would drive his starving body to its knees in death, he couldn't even bring himself to beseech the master inside for so much as a crumb.

And now he, a child of the flesh, had wed a child of the spirit and made her his.

Nathan blinked, and his tears fell on the charcoal drawing, smearing the image. Cursing at his carelessness, he pushed the picture aside and plucked a book from his saddlebags. He set it before him, dipped the pen in ink, and scribbled furiously.

Gathering his saddlebags, he paused at the side of the bed. So still and relaxed, she even slept like a lamb. Nathan gently brushed her cheek with the back of his fingers. "Good-bye,

Samantha," he whispered, laying the book beside her. "I'll always love you. I hope you can forgive me."

～

Without opening her eyes, Samantha knew she awoke as a different woman. With the utmost compassion, Nathan had tenderly shown and explained to her the mysteries of marital love she had only blushingly read about in the Song of Solomon. They had forged a permanent bond, and Nathan had placed his seal over her heart.

"My beloved is mine, and I am his," she whispered, smiling. She cautiously opened her eyes, then shut them against the sunlight of a new day.

A new day?

"Nathan!" She jerked upright.

Birds chirped outside in reply, but the room was still and empty. If he wasn't here, she knew instinctively, he wasn't anywhere else in the house. He had made her his wife, and now he was gone.

Shutting her eyes in despair, Samantha slumped to the bed. Her hand brushed a leather volume, and she closed her fingers around the spine. Trembling, she drew the book into her lap and opened to the title page. Just below "A Tale of Two Cities" was an inscription in a clear, precise hand: *Samantha— May you find a worthy hero. Love, Nathan*

Broken, Samantha wept.

She rose, clutching the book against her breast. She lifted the picture of Jesus and the lamb from the desk, and a nail clattered to the floor.

She had carried the drawing from Kansas City to Wyoming to Colorado, in a frame, in a carpetbag, then rolled up, and not once had it incurred a single blemish. But now it was altered forever, indelibly displaying the condition of Nathan's mind and heart. In the upper corner was a deep scratch where he'd dug the nail against the paper, trying to understand.

In the center of the picture, where the lamb's face once turned up to look at Jesus, the charcoal had smeared, damp with what she could only guess to be Nathan's tears.

Weak with grief, she sank to her knees. "Oh, God, how could you let him go without saying good-bye? He still doesn't understand, does he? How could I fall asleep and not spend more time talking to him?"

Mortified, she lowered her head. "I promised him we'd watch for dawn together."

What had she done? Had she married him just to satisfy her own curiosity? Her own lust? Even the ring she wore was a prostitute's. Nathan himself had said they didn't have to consummate the marriage. He would have slept on the floor without complaint, whereas she had enticed his body instead of his soul.

"I'm so sorry, God. I let him down. I let you down. I promise I'll talk to him in Cheyenne."

She straightened, drawing a deep breath to steady herself. That was it. Cheyenne. Surely she would be able to talk to him then. They couldn't refuse a condemned man a visit with his wife.

Samantha touched the picture, shivering. "Oh, Jesus, stay with me. I can't feel your arms around me, and I need them!"

Hands bound, Nathan accepted the cup and stared into the flickering campfire. What was she doing? What was she thinking? Would she come to Cheyenne, or were her religious sensibilities so appalled by what they'd done together that she wouldn't even want to see him again?

"You all right, Hamilton?" Noah Cameron hunkered down beside him, his gray eyes intent. "You've been quiet all day. I'll admit I'm not the company most men would want on the second day of married life, but it can't be helped."

"I told you I'd go without any trouble. Do you expect me to be a sterling conversationalist too?"

Grinning, Noah poured himself another cup from the coffeepot. "Even without talking, you're a lot better at conversation than most of the criminals I've had the misfortune to escort. Better educated, too, I'll bet."

Nathan smiled faintly. "Sometimes book learning doesn't do much good."

"No, sometimes you just have to follow your heart."

Nathan studied Cameron's profile, wondering why the marshal seemed intent on whitewashing the whole situation. Maybe because he knew Nathan was as good as dead, and his religion demanded pity.

"Was that really true, what you said about Frank talking to you about God?" Nathan said abruptly.

A smile broke slowly across Noah's face. "Every word. Frank told me later God had sent him to witness to me."

"And did God send you to witness to *me*?"

Noah sobered. "Not me, Hamilton. He sent Samantha."

Find her.

Nathan swallowed hard and set the cup in the dirt. "How do you know?"

Noah turned, his eyes searching. "Tell me why you traipsed all the way from Wyoming to Kansas City just to pick up a girl you once knew."

Nathan felt something stir in his heart, as though Noah had reached straight down into his soul. He shifted uncomfortably. "I . . . Caleb and I were . . . concerned about her. As it turned out, she didn't have a place to live."

Noah's gaze remained steady. "You could have been arrested anywhere from Wyoming to Missouri, yet you risked your life. Why?"

The lie that sprang to Nathan's lips died, and a peculiar sensation spread throughout his body. He took a deep breath. "I came for her because I heard a voice."

"A voice?" If Cameron was surprised, he didn't show it.

Nathan nodded. "After we left Samantha in the orphanage, Caleb and I joined the army. I saw a lot of death, a lot of pain. I helped the doctors in the field hospital. Then, later in Cheyenne, I killed a man who tried to kill Caleb."

"You're saying it was self-defense?"

"Yes, but who would believe two outlaws? By now, there's no telling where the other witnesses are. They weren't too eager to speak up for us right after it happened."

Noah looked thoughtful. "What about the voice?"

Nathan hesitated. "I've never told anyone about this, Cameron. Not even Samantha. But sometimes I heard a voice saying 'Find her.' At first I thought for sure I'd lost my mind, but one day I heard something else. As clearly as I hear you now, though with my heart and not my ears, if that makes sense."

Noah smiled faintly. "It does. What did the voice say this time?"

"One thing is needful." He laughed, but the sound rang hollow in his ears. "The mystery voice was certainly wrong, wasn't it? God has a funny way of working if he sent me to meet Samantha's needs."

"You don't believe that," Noah said in a low voice. "You're smart enough to understand the real need."

Nathan stared. His heart felt pierced. All of a sudden, he couldn't wait to get to Cheyenne and away from Noah Cameron.

The hiss and crackle of the fire filled the silence, and the surrounding darkness reminded Nathan of his own heart. By Noah's own admission, he, too, had once had darkness in his heart. But now he was a lawman, not a criminal. Surely that would count for something in God's eyes.

Weary, Nathan rubbed a hand against his face. He'd known his life would come to this eventually. If only he hadn't gone back to the Jordans' and messed up Samantha's life too.

"I guess you'll be heading back to your farm once you deliver me," Nathan finally said.

"No. I plan to stick around for your trial. I'll be called as a witness. But beyond that, well, consider me an interested friend." Noah turned. "Something tells me God hasn't finished his good work in you, Hamilton."

Nathan laughed. "How can he finish something he hasn't even started?"

Noah just smiled, a smug, lazy grin. Samantha would have seen that smile every day if she'd married him.

Nathan cleared his throat. "Cameron, for all you did for Samantha, thank you. I almost wish she had married you, so I wouldn't have to worry about her."

"She'd never have been happy. You're the only one she loves, Hamilton."

The quiet words burrowed straight into Nathan's anguished heart. He turned away before Noah could read the sorrow in his eyes.

George glanced around the barn, pausing to wipe his brow with his wrist. Even though the last snowfall lay unmelted, he'd worked up a good sweat cleaning out the stalls. He leaned against the pitchfork and sighed.

Samantha had pestered him for two days now to take her to Cheyenne. He'd put her off as long as possible, hoping she'd give up the crazy notion of watching Nathan die.

She'd do it too. She'd stand right at the foot of the scaffold, probably praying or singing some hymn, worrying more about Nathan's soul than the condition of her own breaking heart. George had seen hangings before, and the sight was gruesome enough for a man, let alone a lady.

He knew Nathan wanted Samantha to be shielded from such ugliness. Nathan was so smart, he'd normally have figured out some way to keep her from going to his trial. But since he hadn't had the time to make the arrangements himself, George knew he'd want him to protect her.

Discouraged, George jabbed the pitchfork into the hay. He still had to write Caleb. Maybe he could come up with some ideas. But whatever the case, George needed a plan— something to ensure that Samantha's last memories of Nathan weren't of him gasping and twitching at the end of a rope.

He lifted the pitchfork and scattered hay in the air.

"Samantha, will you come away from that window?" Sally called, teasing. "George may not even come back today."

Samantha turned. "How many days does it take to go to town and back for supplies? George knows I'm anxious to leave. I haven't even been able to eat since he left!"

The door flung open. Tommy and Maria raced in with the

cold to the warmth of the kitchen. "Mama!" Tommy said, breathless. "There's a—"

"Hold on." Sally rapidly unbuttoned her son's coat. "You're going to faint, running inside like that."

"That man's . . . putting up his horse!"

Samantha's heart raced. "George?"

"Yes'm!"

Samantha rushed to the door, but it opened before she could turn the knob. Frank entered soberly, followed by a silent George. Samantha grabbed his arm, dispensing with any greeting. "Did you get what we need? Can we leave today?"

"Hello, Samantha." George smiled faintly, his eyes magnetic. He took her hand and gently ushered her to the table.

"Sally," Frank murmured, drawing his wife close. "Sit down."

"What's wrong?" she said, but Frank gently shushed her.

George stood beside Samantha and cleared his throat, then glanced away. "Samantha."

A shiver raced down her spine, and she instinctively braced her hands against the table.

"Samantha . . . I don't know how to tell you other than to just say it."

Her heart froze. "No, George," she whispered. "Don't say it! Please don't—"

"Nathan's dead."

Grief washed over her, the words clanging in her head like a silver dollar in a glass bowl. Her hands whitened around the tabletop. "No."

"There was a telegram waiting in town for the Jordans," George said. "Nathan tried to escape, and Noah had to shoot him."

"No!" Samantha reeled, growing suddenly dizzy. George pulled her to her feet to keep her from falling, but the darkness of despair had already engulfed her, as though she'd fallen headfirst into a black pit.

"How could Noah shoot him?" Dry-eyed, she pounded a fist against George's shoulder. *"How?"*

George awkwardly patted her back. "Please don't be angry. I'd rather see you cry."

She gulped. She wanted to cry—big, hot, soul-cleansing tears until she drowned. Anything to escape the pain hammering inside her chest.

White-faced, Sally placed a hand on Samantha's shoulder. "Frank and I will do whatever we can to help. You'll always have a home here."

"I'll help too," George said quietly.

Samantha pulled away. "I . . . I can't think right now. I have to . . . to go outside."

"Please let me go with you," he said.

"No, George." She touched his arm, not wanting him to be offended. "I need to be alone."

Wrapping her arms around her middle, she stumbled to the door. "At least take a . . ." Sally's worried voice trailed off as Samantha closed the door.

Outside, she staggered to the barn. Cold, sharp wind stung her cheeks and plastered her hair against her head, penetrating her clothing. Snow fell in thick flakes around her and blanketed the ground. Maybe she could stand outside long enough to let them cover her from head to toe, blotting out her existence.

Was that what Nathan's life had come to?

For years he had had such bitterness in his heart. She had

prayed over and over that it would be rooted out, like a weed, and replaced with fertile seeds. She had promised she would talk to Nathan again, but God hadn't listened.

Gasping from the cold, she flung the door open and fell to her knees in the darkness of the barn. "You said in your word that you are not willing that any should perish but that all should come to repentance! Why did you exclude Nathan? I don't understand! I even married him so that—"

Shocked, she stopped praying. Why *had* she married Nathan? Since he left, she'd pushed the thought down, but now the truth loomed large and ugly.

She covered her face and sobbed until the barn door opened, and George gently drew her into his arms.

TWENTY-THREE

Judge C. R. Taylor leaned back in his overstuffed leather chair and propped his chin on steepled fingers. His gaze rested on Noah Cameron, who sat on the other side of the mahogany desk.

"So you've delivered Nathan Hamilton, eh?" he finally said, frowning. "Your request is highly unusual, Marshal Cameron. If I thought you were trying to sway my opinion on this trial before it's even started . . ."

"I assure you that's not the case," Noah said. "Hamilton's committed the crime of robbery—and more than once, but I understand there's a witness to disprove the murder charge. Assuming—and I realize it's a huge assumption, your honor—he's found innocent of murder, I recommend he be given a lenient sentence regarding the robbery charges. He's never harmed anyone during his holdups. I've also spent some time with him, and I believe he can be rehabilitated."

Judge Taylor drummed his fingers on the desk. The ticking wall clock seemed unusually loud to Noah's ears. He counted the seconds until the judge finally spoke. "I'll reserve judgment until after all the evidence is presented," he said. "Who's the witness to the alleged murder?"

Noah suppressed a grin. "Caleb Martin turned himself in today so he can testify on Hamilton's behalf. He claims

Hamilton saved his life. I can't believe Martin would lie, seeing as how he's given up his own freedom."

Noah quickly decided to press his advantage before the shocked judge had time to recover. "Your honor, before I go, may I have a few further words with you? This time regarding Caleb Martin."

Nathan heard the outer door open, and he cursed under his breath. After weeks of incarceration in the Cheyenne jail, he wasn't much interested anymore when someone came to see him. It was usually either his lawyer or Noah Cameron anyway.

He fixed his gaze on the book they'd allowed him, determined not to even look up. Two sets of feet shuffled past, then a key squealed its protest in a rusty lock two cells down. The guard shoved somebody in, banged the slatted iron door shut, and relocked it. His footsteps retreated, and the outer door banged shut.

Nathan's fingers tightened around the book. He knew the other prisoner was staring. Fine. Let him stare. He was tired of being gawked at. Another infamous outlaw brought to his knees at last.

The other man harrumphed.

Nathan slammed the book closed and rose. "Look—"

Caleb leaned against the bars. "Figured you needed some company."

Nathan grinned for the first time in weeks. Somehow he'd known Caleb would come. Had Samantha told him about everything that had happened? "How'd you find out I was here?"

"George wrote me. He explained what happened with

Crawford and that Cameron arrested you." Caleb brightened. "Is Samantha in town?"

So he hadn't heard from her. "No." Nathan laughed bitterly. "I guess she decided she didn't want to acknowledge a murderer for a husband."

"You two got married?"

Nathan nodded, uncomfortable. He couldn't talk about her, not even to Caleb. Blinking, he cleared his throat. "I guess that makes us brothers, of sorts."

"We've always been brothers," Caleb said. "You saved my life; now it's my turn. Don't fold on me."

Nathan looked at Caleb's outstretched hand. With the distance of a cell between them, it would be impossible to shake. He held out his hand anyway. "All right, Caleb. I won't."

"The defendant will rise."

Nathan stood. Wrists shackled together, he flattened his hands against the table and stared straight ahead.

"Nathan Hamilton, you have been found not guilty of murder."

A buzz of excitement raced through the courtroom. Nathan exhaled loudly, slumping. The judge banged his gavel several times, restoring silence, and Nathan straightened.

"But to the charge of grand larceny, you have been found guilty." Another din rose, and this time the judge banged the gavel only once. "You are hereby sentenced to four years in the Wyoming Territorial Penitentiary. May I add, young man, that you have received an extremely light sentence, although a fair one. The testimony of your accomplice Caleb Martin saved your neck from hanging, and Marshal Cameron's character recommendation prompted the lighter sentence. You'll be transferred to the penitentiary within the week."

He banged the gavel one final time and shouted above the crowd, "Court is adjourned!"

Nathan sagged, his knees threatening to give way. If only Samantha had been here.

The guard tugged on his arm to return him to his cell. Nathan looked back at the crowd, and pushing his way through the sea of strange faces was Noah Cameron.

"Good luck, Hamilton," he said quietly. "I'm sorry Samantha didn't come to your trial. I could send a telegram—"

"Don't bother. When you go back to your farm, tell her . . ." Nathan paused, blinking. "Never mind."

The guard yanked his arm. "Come on!"

Cameron nodded. "God go with you, Hamilton."

The guard hauled Nathan back to his cell, but the memory of the curious light in Noah's eyes lingered. *Why had the marshal spoken up for him?*

Back in the cell, Caleb was ecstatic. "Congratulations!"

Nathan sat on his bunk as the guard slammed and locked the door. Nathan waited until the jailer left, then he slumped down.

Caleb laughed. "It isn't every day that a man cheats death. Don't you have anything to say?"

"I'm relieved . . . grateful . . . scared."

"I'd have killed you myself if they'd found you guilty of murder," Caleb said. "After all, I risked my own hide for you."

"And I appreciate it," Nathan said. It still hadn't quite sunk in that he wouldn't have to live with a hangman's noose hovering over him.

But what about the other man—the one he *had* murdered?

He curled his hands into fists. "I won't think about that!" he muttered.

"You say something?"

Nathan relaxed. Nobody knew, not even Caleb. He could keep the pain inside himself, and in four years, he would be a free man.

"You and Samantha have a chance now," Caleb said. "You'll be separated for a while, but—"

"She's better off without me."

"Something happened to keep her from coming to Cheyenne. I know she loves you!"

Nathan's gaze rose to meet Caleb's. He still didn't want to talk about her, so he cleared his throat. "They'll be sending me over to the new prison in Laramie this week. If I don't get another chance to tell you—"

"You'd have done the same for me. I'm sure I'll be joining you soon enough."

Nathan nodded. "If you don't . . . well, we'll see each other sometime."

"Sure. Besides, you owe me fifty dollars."

"I owe *you* fifty dollars?"

"Sure do! Don't you remember when—"

The heavy door creaked open, and the guard clumped toward them, keys jangling. He unlocked Caleb's cell. "Marshal Cameron wants to see you for some reason, Martin."

Shrugging, Caleb followed him from the cellblock. Nathan waited the rest of the day and two more besides, but Caleb never returned.

Samantha eased the window up with both hands, hoping the sash wouldn't squeak. She groaned under the weight and braced her legs. The snow had melted, leaving behind a strong April warmth. Good traveling weather, she decided, although the roads were still muddy enough to leave plenty of hoof-prints.

Samantha glanced around the room, fighting a wave of dizziness. What had begun as nervous excitement to go to Cheyenne turned into a downright inability to eat since news of Nathan's death. Sally had fussed over her, fixing tempting dishes, but nothing appealed to Samantha's appetite. Nearly three months had passed, and her dress hung slack against her gaunt form.

It was time for her to get on with her life elsewhere. Sally's baby was due in a few months, and Samantha refused to be the Jordans' charity case. But where should she go? Certainly not to Caleb at the hideout. That's the first place anyone would look. And he didn't want her anyway. One look at her pitiful condition, and he'd send her back to the Jordans like some sort of runaway child.

Sally and Frank had insisted they wanted her to stay. "You can help me with the baby! With Tommy and Maria!" Sally had said by way of encouragement. Samantha had only smiled bleakly, tired, her head dull, heart sick, stomach rolling.

How could she stay with the Jordans? She felt so ashamed. She might as well have committed adultery with Nathan for all their marriage had meant. And the last thing Frank and Sally needed was a moping widow taking up a much-needed bedroom and eating their food. She had imposed on them long enough as it was.

And George. He had some crazy idea about bringing her

to live with his family. His concern for her grew more evident every day, his knowing eyes scrutinizing her as though he could read her mind, as though he could tell she was hiding something.

Samantha worked her wedding ring loose and tossed it and a note on the bed. Praying for forgiveness even as she committed her sin, she snatched up her carpetbag, stuffed with her clothes, Bible, wedding license, and ten dollars from the Jordans' household savings. She wouldn't have taken any money, but she had to eat. She had to stay healthy, even though she could barely keep her food down.

Samantha's eyes drew back to the picture of Jesus, and she rolled it up and shoved it in the bag. She should probably leave it behind, but she couldn't.

Just as she couldn't leave the other possession she'd grown to cherish. The book. Nathan's book. She laid it tenderly on top of the picture, smiling sadly. The book was the only thing she had left of him.

She pressed a hand against her stomach, closing her eyes against a fresh wave of nausea. The only thing left except for the child she was now certain grew within her.

Drawing a deep breath, she threw one leg over the sill. A guiding voice whispered in her head, and she felt a tiny measure of peace. Kansas. That's where she'd go. Home.

⌒

"George! Frank!" Sally flagged them down as they rode up the lane. Breathless, she clutched her rounded abdomen as she ran up to where they stopped. Eyes red and hair loosened from its usual fastidious bun, she thrust a piece of paper in George's hands as he dismounted.

"I had no idea. Why didn't she . . . ? She might . . ."

George held up a hand. "Quiet, Sally. I don't read so fast. Samantha promised we'd practice." His fingers gripped the paper.

"She's gone!" Sally turned to Frank. "She said she didn't want to be a burden to us anymore. She took money from us, although she apologized, and she gave back my mother's ring." She covered her face with her hands. "Oh, dear God, why didn't I see it coming?"

"Don't blame yourself," Frank said. "We all knew it would take time for her to get over Nathan's death."

George handed back the paper. Grim-faced, he turned to remount. "Nathan's not dead."

Sally grabbed his arm. "But—"

"Noah never sent a telegram. I made it up to keep Samantha from going to Cheyenne to watch Nathan die."

"Oh, George, there's no telling what she'll do. Where she'll go. You have to find her!" Sally said.

"When did she leave?" He put a foot into the stirrup and threw a leg over.

"Sometime this morning. She told me she was going to lie down for a while. But when I went in to wake her, she was gone."

"I'll go with you, George," Frank said, turning to mount also.

"I can go faster on my own. But I'll find her. And I'll tell her the truth."

"God go with you then," Frank murmured. He drew Sally closer.

George nodded absentmindedly and spun his horse around, fixing his gaze on what had to be the last set of hoofprints to leave the farm.

Samantha stood on the boardwalk, clutching the carpetbag against her. The raucous laughter and music from inside the saloon was almost as annoying as the passersby who jostled her without a thought.

A month was gone, and so was the money. She'd spent the last of it last night for the cheap room, hoping an answer would come to her today.

But inspiration had been silent, as it had been ever since the train had crossed the border from Colorado into Kansas. She'd gotten off at the first stop, convinced that somehow just being in Kansas would give her direction. She'd slept and eaten as cheaply as possible, but now she hadn't eaten for two days.

The door swung open, and Samantha timidly stepped toward the inebriated man who exited. "Excuse me," she murmured, "but I'm looking for the sheriff. He wasn't in his office next door."

"Down th' street and one over," the man muttered, reeling. "White pick't fence."

"Thank you." Sighing, Samantha trudged down the street, her heart as heavy as her feet. Thankfully the nausea had vanished weeks ago, but the agony of her heart was far from healed. "Oh, Lord, I hope this is the right thing to do. Help me accept whatever I find here," she whispered.

She cut to the cross street the man had indicated, and Samantha heard a pounding hammer. The noise grew stronger as she neared the end of the street and the white picket fence. She stood outside the gate and tilted her head back, blocking her eyes from the sun.

Up on the roof, Jonathan Hamilton removed a nail from

between his lips and pounded it against a shingle. Samantha noticed the newly constructed addition to his house.

The hammer rang out once more. "There!" he announced, smiling. He turned to the street and caught sight of her. His smile fell. "Samantha!"

Samantha clutched her bag. "Hello, Mr. Hamilton."

"Go through the gate, and I'll meet you in the yard," he said, disappearing beyond the roof.

Samantha did as he'd said, waiting nervously. The small yard was clean but bare, save for one lone apple tree. Wouldn't it look pretty to have some roses here, black-eyed Susans there, perhaps—

"I certainly wasn't expecting you."

She forced herself to meet his gaze. "I wasn't expecting to come here."

He studied her for a moment, then his face softened. "Come inside." He gently took her arm. "First something for you to eat. You don't look like you've eaten much lately."

"I haven't," she admitted, devoid of pride.

"I'm afraid I don't have much more than bread and cheese right now. I've been busy working on the house."

Like the yard, the home's interior was Spartan but clean, with a rock fireplace, a heavy rocker, and two comfortable chairs. He led her through the front room to the kitchen, and she noticed fresh pine shelves, a large round table and matching chairs, and a shiny new cookstove. Beyond the kitchen was the new addition, evidently a small bedroom. The room was empty, but she could smell the odor of freshly cut lumber.

Jonathan gestured her to the kitchen table and moved to the shelves for bread. Samantha sat down gratefully, her feet hot and swollen. She'd walked the last ten miles to Radleyville.

"Did you recently move to this house?" she said to make conversation.

"No. I've lived here for quite a while now."

"Then, the new addition, the new shelves . . ."

Jonathan set a slice of bread with jam and a glass of milk in front of her. He sat down, and his eyes filled with tenderness. "About January, I felt God telling me to add on to my house and to spruce things up. I've spent all these months wondering what his purpose was." He paused, and his hand covered hers. "Did Nathan send you away?"

Samantha's eyes misted. "Nathan's dead, Mr. Hamilton."

He drew a sharp breath and leaned back. His eyes watered. "Dead!"

Samantha nodded, and her chin quivered. "He was under arrest, but he was shot . . . for escaping." She paused, gathering courage. How could she admit to this man that his assumptions about her were correct? "We were married the night before he left . . ." She drew a deep breath, blushing. "And now I'm expecting a baby."

Jonathan rose, his face concerned, and held out his hands. "You're my daughter, Samantha," he said firmly. "I waited for my son to come home, and now I know he won't. But I would like it very much if you and your baby would live with me."

Samantha tried to straighten, but her body slumped instead. Jonathan Hamilton had every right to call her whatever he wanted, whatever he'd called her in the past. It was true. All of it was true.

His eyes pierced hers as though he could read her thoughts. "You married my son, Samantha," he said softly. "And soon you will have a child who needs a strong mother. And you *are* strong."

Samantha felt whatever energy she had left crumple to the floor. "No, I'm not, Mr. Hamilton," she said. She swayed, weeping softly. "I thought I was strong, but I'm weaker than anyone."

Jonathan's arms encircled her in a fatherly embrace. He stroked her hair and let her sob against his shoulder. "Just remember, my dear," he whispered tenderly. "God's grace is sufficient. And his strength is made perfect in all our weaknesses."

TWENTY-FOUR

Samantha stooped over the bucket of soapy water and rubbed a knotted fist against the small of her back. She hardly remembered a time when walking, sitting, and standing were simple activities. Surely her stomach couldn't get any bigger in this final month.

Since she'd moved into her father-in-law's house, she'd sent countless letters to Caleb in care of the South Pass City post office, all to no avail. She hadn't heard a word in return. For all she knew, her brother was dead too.

She'd returned the ten dollars—plus ten more—to the Jordans. Embarrassed about her condition, she wrote that she was all right and they shouldn't worry, but she didn't tell them where she was living. She didn't want any surprise reunions; she was certain she'd fall apart if she saw their kind, pitying expressions.

Samantha knelt and plunged a rag into the bucket, sloshing water onto the floor. Keeping the house clean was almost an obsession lately. At least it kept her busy.

The baby shifted, and she smiled. She never failed to be amazed when she could distinguish an arm from a foot or an elbow. Samantha laughed softly. "That was a hand, little one. You can't fool me."

Two months ago the child jerked rhythmically for several

minutes, and a scared Samantha sought Jonathan's advice. "Do you think I should see the doctor?" she whispered, near tears.

Jonathan frowned with mock seriousness. "Every few seconds, you say?"

She nodded, solemn.

Jonathan eyed her stomach, and she turned her head, embarrassed. When she felt another round of undulations, she dared to meet his eyes. "There! You see?"

Jonathan smiled patiently, and the corners of his eyes crinkled with obvious amusement. "The baby has the hiccups, Samantha. Nathan used to do that to Hannah all the time."

Nathan. The rag stilled in Samantha's hand, and she sat on the floor, deflated. Just one month until she would hold his child in her hands. A living reminder of the man she loved but had not been able to save from himself. All the talks, all the tears, all the prayers, had been for nothing. And in the end, she had only compromised her own faith.

"You shouldn't be cleaning the floor." Jonathan stood in the doorway.

Samantha hastily wiped away a tear and rose awkwardly to her knees. She dipped the rag back in the bucket then washed with renewed vigor. "It looked dirty, Mr. Hamilton."

"Samantha, you've been living with me for several months now. Can't you call me Jonathan?"

The rag stilled again, and Samantha felt heat rise to her face. Nathan's father had shown her nothing but kindness by taking her into his home and caring for her. He even bought her a simple gold band to replace Sally's substitute wedding ring, explaining quietly that Nathan would have done so himself. Jonathan proudly introduced her to everyone in town, especially the young mothers. He referred to her as the widow of his long-lost son, never mentioning Nathan's name.

"Samantha." Jonathan knelt beside her and gently took the rag from her hands. "It's time we had a good talk. Why won't you ever tell me what you're feeling or at least talk about Nathan?" His face softened, and his voice lowered. "I'd like to talk about him too."

The baby kicked several times in a row, as though seeking a comfortable position. Blinking back tears, Samantha laid a hand over her stomach. Would the child look so much like his father she would never be able to forget? Never be able to stop wondering if there was something else she should have done? Never be able to forgive herself?

Jonathan helped her to her feet. "Let's have a cup of tea. I'll finish cleaning the floor later."

He seated her at the table, then bustled to the stove to heat water. He pulled tea and two cups from the shelf, then leaned against the wall, studying her. "You've tried so hard to stay aloof from me since you've been here. I see the gratefulness in your eyes, but there's so much you keep to yourself. Don't you trust me?"

Samantha shied from his penetrating gaze. "I do appreciate your help. I just don't feel worthy."

"Do you think you have to earn my love?"

"No, of course not. But you don't know . . . about Nathan and me."

"You only slept with him once? The night you were married?"

Her face warmed. "Yes."

"Then why are you ashamed?"

"Because I married him at all. I somehow convinced myself that if I did, he would get some sort of immunity from God for not being a believer."

Jonathan furrowed his brow, trying to understand her logic. "And now you regret what you did?"

"Yes! I mean, no!" She glanced away. "I don't know what I believe. All I know is that since the marriage, I haven't felt God's presence or been able to hear his voice. I'm afraid that what I did was terribly wrong."

Jonathan brought the tea to the table. "It sounds to me as though you're repentant, whether or not you've actually sinned."

"I am sorry. Sorry I didn't stop to pray or even think about what I was doing. I was desperate to have more time with Nathan, but in the end I think I just wanted to please him." She lowered her head. "To give him something special before he died. The one thing he wanted."

"You."

She blinked back tears and nodded. "Me."

Jonathan sipped his tea thoughtfully. "You realize Nathan never thought of you as a prostitute, don't you?"

"I know he loved me."

"Did you offer yourself before you were married?"

"No. After the wedding, he even said we didn't have to."

"So he married you of his own free will, not even expecting intimacy?"

"Yes."

Jonathan set down his cup. "I think if there was any sin, it was the marriage itself. Not what came after. Paul does say that believers shouldn't be yoked to unbelievers, and I'm sure he meant that for ten years, a year, a week, or a day."

"Yes," Samantha murmured. "Frank and Noah tried to tell me."

"And you didn't listen," he said without any condemnation in his voice, then continued with a sparkle in his eyes, "But Paul also says that for those who love God, and that includes you, all things work together for good."

Samantha nodded, feeling hope rise. "Trusting God is so easy when things are going well. Why do I always forget when the going is hard?"

"Because you're human. Sometimes we try to take matters into our own hands and can't understand when God gently tells us to give them back to him. But he is always faithful to forgive us, to wipe the slate clean, and tell us to go on."

His eyes shone warmly, and for the first time in many months, Samantha felt the burden of her heart lighten. Just as God had led her to Mrs. Matlock long ago, he had undoubtedly led her to Nathan's father.

"Thank you . . . Jonathan," she said softly, leaning forward to kiss him on the cheek. "You're such a smart man, yet you have such a humble love for God. I wish Nathan had been like that."

Jonathan smiled faintly. "The guilt you feel for not being able to save him was once double in my own soul. God finally convinced me that I had done my duty as a parent by raising Nathan with the Word, just as you talked to him and tried to be a living example. But the final choice was Nathan's, not ours."

"I still have trouble understanding why God allowed him to die unsaved."

"I don't understand why God allowed it either. But I trust

him enough to accept that he knows what's best—that he has a future for each of his children.

Samantha sighed. "I wish I could understand his plan. Or the good to come from all this."

Jonathan smiled tenderly, his eyes warm and gentle. "You will, Samantha. Rest in his promise."

Wyoming Territorial Penitentiary
October 1872

"Frank Jordan!" Nathan stared as the guard opened the narrow-slotted iron door. "They told me I had a visitor, but I didn't dream it'd be you."

"It's good to see you, Nathan," Frank said warmly, stretching out his hand.

Nathan shook it cautiously, confused by his presence. "Have a seat on the cot. It's either that or the floor."

Why was the preacher here? In the several months he'd been here, Nathan hadn't heard from Samantha or anyone else. Several times he'd nearly broken down and written her a letter, but he couldn't bring himself to remind her of the unhappiness he'd caused.

Impatient, Nathan sat on the edge of the cot beside Frank. "How is Sally?"

Frank smiled. "Our little boy David was born in August. Tommy and Maria are beside themselves over their little brother."

"Congratulations," Nathan mumbled. Samantha probably would have liked to have children. She *had* been a teacher before he'd come back into her life.

Frank laid a hand on Nathan's arm. "I'll get right to the point, Nathan. Samantha—"

Nathan froze. "She's dead?" he whispered.

"No! At least, well, we don't know for certain. We haven't seen her since April. George made up a story about Noah sending a telegram that said you were dead. He didn't want Samantha to come to your trial and watch you hang."

"She *didn't* hate me!"

Frank shook his head. "She was so upset by your death that she ran away. Her note said she didn't want to be a burden anymore. George tried to follow her, but he lost her tracks near Denver. He figured she hopped a train there. He spent the last six months looking for her from San Francisco to Kansas City, but he couldn't find her."

Nathan clenched his jaw. "*George* did this."

"He looked everywhere, Nathan." Brightening, Frank reached in his pocket and withdrew a folded piece of paper. "The good news is that two weeks ago, we got a letter from Samantha. She says—"

Nathan snatched the paper from Frank's hand. He read rapidly then tenderly touched her signature. "She doesn't say where she is," he said, dejected.

"No, but she's all right. George finally came back to tell us he was leaving for the reservation. I don't know what he'll do to himself. He feels he's let you down."

"He has! How could he do this to me? To Samantha!"

"He was just trying to help, Nathan, to spare her from a broken heart. Do you have any idea where she might have gone?"

Nathan shook his head.

"If your father's still a sheriff, maybe he can help you find her."

"No!" Nathan stormed the six feet to the opposite wall of his cell. The door was left open for visiting day, and he had the sudden urge to run through the cellblock and out of the prison. He didn't even care if they shot him. "I won't ask for his help!"

"You'd let pride keep you from making sure Samantha's safe?"

"My father warned me I'd come to this. I'm not going to give him the satisfaction of saying he told me so!"

The guard appeared in the doorway. "Time's up, reverend."

"Just one more minute, please," Frank said. The guard shrugged and stepped away.

Frank drew a small book from his pocket. "I know you're not a believer, Nathan, but maybe this Bible will help you pass the time."

"You sound just like my father, finding comfort between the pages of a book! What kind of God would let Samantha, one of his followers, run off by herself?"

"A God who is protecting her. A God who loves us and wants us all to come home."

Nathan stared bitterly through the open door to the solid wall less than six feet away. "What kind of fool believes such nonsense? I was foolish to marry Samantha. All I did was cause her more heartache. I should have left her alone with her God!"

"The Lord has plans for you, Nathan." Frank pressed the book into his hand. "Keep this. I'm sure you get bored, and maybe the Psalms will give you comfort. Look at them as good literature, if nothing else. Samantha always said you liked to read."

Nathan opened his mouth for a sharp retort, but the feel and smell of leather in his hands drew him like a drunk to liquor. He hadn't read one book since he'd been incarcerated.

Frank laid a hand on Nathan's shoulder. "I left some cookies for you with the guards. Sally sent them. Is there anything I can get you?"

Nathan's fingers dug into the leather volume, and he cursed softly. "Nothing, Frank. Just give my best to Sally. If you hear from Samantha again—" His voice broke, and he turned away.

"We'll let you know. In the meantime, we'll keep you both in our prayers." Frank stepped outside, and Nathan heard his fading footsteps.

"Prayers," he echoed scornfully. He sank to the cot, shoulders slumped. He lifted the book to hurl it across the cell, then changed his mind and laid it carefully beside him.

Bowing his head, he covered his face with his hands. In the ensuing silence, he listened to his heartbeat and dug his fingers into his face.

Samantha was gone. Vanished. And she thought he was dead? What if she got hurt or died? What if she remarried?

He couldn't do a single thing for her. He hadn't felt so helpless since the war, since he'd encountered the mangled soldier. Nathan had thought he was helping him, just as he'd always thought he was helping Samantha.

He cried out in anguish and leaned back as grief overwhelmed him.

"Jonathan," Samantha whispered at his bedroom door, tightening the sash of her wrapper as she leaned against the wall. A fresh pain assaulted her, and she pressed her hands against her stomach, wincing.

Jonathan appeared, fully dressed. "I wasn't asleep, Samantha, just read—" He grabbed her arm as she crumpled. "The baby?"

She nodded, teary-eyed. The pain was worsening. "I felt him moving a lot . . . just before I went to bed, but I didn't . . . think anything about it. Then it got worse, and . . . oh!"

Jonathan wrapped a steadying arm around her. "Is there time between the pains?"

She nodded, feeling the pain crest and break. "About ten minutes, I think."

"Good. I'll get Mrs. Barnett to help you. Then when it's time, I'll get the doctor."

Samantha clutched at his arm. "You mean you're leaving me?"

Jonathan smiled sympathetically. "She's just next door, Samantha. I promise I'll be back before the ten minutes are up. The best thing to do is to walk. That'll speed things up."

"Please hurry," she whispered.

"God's watching out for you, Samantha. Don't worry."

The door closed behind him.

Samantha shuffled through the house, picking up objects and studying them as if she'd never seen them before. She tried to pray, but she couldn't concentrate. The fear of pain ran up and down her spine, fear for her baby, fear for herself. It seemed only a moment had passed when the door creaked open again and Jonathan and Mrs. Barnett were at her side.

She wrapped an arm around her middle, doubling over.

Jonathan's hand steadied her elbow. "The Lord is my shepherd . . ."

"I . . . shall not want. He . . . he maketh me to . . . to . . . oh!"

"You're doing fine," Mrs. Barnett said from behind her. "I had seven children myself, and I know your pain. Do you want me to walk with you, dear?"

Samantha raised her face to meet Jonathan's. What would she have done without him? He loved her as though she were truly his daughter and had accepted her and the baby without question. "Will you stay with me?" she whispered. "Until it's time? It may not seem fitting—"

"It's very fitting," he interrupted softly. His gentle gray eyes shone peacefully. "I would be most honored. Mrs. Barnett can help you when it's time for you to be in bed." Jonathan lowered his head. "Father, please protect Samantha and her baby. Please ease her pain as she gives birth to this precious child."

Samantha smiled, her heart full. *Oh, Nathan, how fortunate you were; how fortunate I am!*

Jonathan smiled and helped her step forward. "We'll say the easiest words to remember."

Samantha drew a deep breath. "He maketh me to lie down in green pastures. . . ."

They walked for several hours, Samantha sagging against the wall or in Jonathan's arms during the intensifying contractions. Jonathan whispered gentle words of encouragement or prayed, holding her up with an arm around her back until the pain passed. Mrs. Barnett brought Samantha sips of water and encouraging words of her own.

After a particularly strong contraction, Samantha was

barely aware of Mrs. Barnett taking her from Jonathan's arms and guiding her to the bedroom. The kindly woman pulled back the covers and encouraged Samantha into bed. "It won't be much longer. Jonathan's gone for the doctor."

Samantha could only nod, the pains breaking one on top of the other. Then she wasn't cognizant of anything except the wild animal of hurt that crushed her bones and tore into her with sharp teeth.

" . . . very close," she heard Mrs. Barnett say as the doctor entered the room.

"I want Jonathan," Samantha moaned, desperate. "Please!"

Then he was there beside her, bending down. "I'm here, Samantha."

She groaned, doubling up, then recoiled in pain at the effort. Why was the doctor torturing her like this? Wasn't there something he could do to ease the pain?

"You're going to have to help me," Dr. Hanson said from somewhere near the foot of the bed. "Don't fight the pain when it comes. Hold on to Jonathan. When I tell you to push, push as hard as you can. Squeeze Jonathan's hand if you need to."

Samantha could barely squeeze his fingers, the pain was so intense. She heard Jonathan pray softly. "Oh, heavenly Father, please send your healing spirit to Samantha and her baby. Guide Dr. Hanson's hands as they bring this child into your world."

The contraction passed, and Samantha raised her head. "Please . . . the picture," she said softly from between parched lips.

Jonathan smiled, following the direction of her eyes. He removed the picture of the shepherd and lamb from the side wall and placed it on the dresser where she could turn her head to look at it.

"It's almost time, Samantha," Dr. Hanson said. "You'll be holding that baby soon!"

Samantha glanced at the drawing. *Oh, Jesus, please hold me . . . hold me . . . hold me . . .*

"I can see the head, Samantha. Push now! Push as hard as you can!"

"You can do it," she heard Jonathan murmur.

She tried to rise, then fell back. "No! I'm too . . . weak."

Jonathan eased an arm under her shoulders and gently raised her up. "You can do it. This is Nathan's baby."

Galvanized by his words, she gathered all her energy and will. When the pain returned, she held her breath and pushed with a fierceness that surprised her until she slumped back, exhausted.

A lusty cry filled the air. Startled, Samantha opened her eyes and saw the smiling doctor hold up a baby, wiping the flailing body clean with a white cloth. "Your daughter, Samantha. You have a girl!"

"A . . . girl!" Samantha stared at the tiny dark-haired stranger she had dreamed about for nearly nine months. All smiles, Mrs. Barnett accepted the child from the doctor and tenderly washed the baby's tiny face, an incredibly perfect face that was emitting a nonstop, indignant wail. "Is she . . . is she all right?" Samantha said.

Everyone laughed. "She's just fine," Jonathan said, squeezing Samantha's hand. "She has wonderful lungs!"

Mrs. Barnett wrapped the shivering, wailing child in a clean white blanket and moved to the bed. Hands trembling,

Samantha reached out wordlessly. "Meet your girl," Mrs. Barnett said with tears in her eyes.

"A . . . a girl!" Samantha repeated, stunned. She touched the downy head in wonder, and amazingly, the cries quieted to whimpers. Samantha cradled the baby against her, unable to take her eyes from the precious, beautiful face. "You're a miracle, little girl. An absolute miracle," she whispered.

"Why don't you try nursing her?"

Startled, Samantha glanced up. "Do you think she's hungry already?"

"Probably not." Mrs. Barnett smiled. "But it'll help the two of you get acquainted."

Jonathan cleared his throat. "I'll leave you alone." He bent to kiss Samantha's damp forehead, then straightened. Samantha saw tears in his eyes as he stroked the baby's smooth cheek with his fingers. "Here's the good you've been waiting for, Samantha. This is the Lord's handiwork. Life renewing itself. It's all part of his perfect plan." He drew a deep breath. "I see Nathan in her face. And you. And my own . . . Hannah."

"I'd like to name her Hannah," Samantha said shyly.

"Thank you, my dear," he whispered, then straightened and turned away.

After Jonathan and the doctor left, Mrs. Barnett unbuttoned Samantha's gown and placed Hannah at her breast. The little girl quieted at the warm contact. Her wrinkled, red hands flailed, and her tiny mouth opened and closed, searching. Mrs. Barnett chuckled, stroking the soft little cheek until the baby's tiny lips clamped down and suckled contentedly. Mrs. Barnett adjusted the blankets over mother and child, then withdrew to give them privacy.

Samantha leaned back and closed her eyes. An indescribable joy filled her, buoying her tired body and spirit. This truly was God's work, the answer to her prayers. "Thank you, Father," she murmured. "Thank you for giving her to me."

She smiled with wonder at her daughter, hesitantly touching her soft, dark hair and marveling at the precious closed eyelids. "You never even knew about this child, Nathan," she said sadly.

Blinking, Samantha glanced at the picture. Her tears blurred her vision. Though it was still smeared, the lamb in the shepherd's arms took on the appearance of her own newborn daughter.

TWENTY-FIVE

C ome on, Hamilton, you're the only one smart enough to figger a way outta here!" Berris whispered.

Nathan gritted his teeth and stacked another brick. If the guard caught him talking, he and Berris would both be punished. The only talking allowed in the brickyard—or anywhere else for that matter—had to be work-related. Prisoners weren't even allowed to talk in their cells or while marching to the kitchen for their food.

The Code of Silence, they called it, was designed to break a prisoner's spirit and keep him from making plans for escape. Which Berris had begged Nathan to do for days. The inmates managed to whisper a few words now and then, exchanging names and tidbits. Nathan's reputation preceded any introduction, and the other prisoners looked up to him with jail-yard awe.

The guard turned away, and Berris pleaded, "Don't you wanna see your wife? You could get out and look for her!"

Nathan banged two bricks together so loudly, the guard shot him a menacing look. Nathan shrugged and resumed the stacking, glaring at Berris. The other man had been here only

301

two months out of a mere year's sentence, less than that if he behaved himself. The prisoners got a day off their sentence for every month they behaved.

Berris had struck a nerve with Nathan. He knew the man couldn't begin to guess how badly he wanted to escape. He'd spent the last two and a half years waiting for a letter or a visit—anything or anyone from the outside to tell him about Samantha. Once a month he faithfully received a letter from Frank and Sally, but they hadn't heard anything either.

It was as if everyone he knew had dropped off the face of the earth and left him to rot in his six-by-six-by-eight-foot cell. He was fed decently enough, but he could feel his strength ebbing away a little more every day, his will to live dissolving.

The guard looked away, and Nathan said between clenched teeth, "I don't know where my wife is. She's dead for all I know."

"No, she ain't!" Berris's eyes blazed. "We gotta get outta here, Hamilton! You hafta figger out a way!"

A brick crashed into Nathan's stack, jarring the top two rows lose. Frowning, Nathan looked up into the twisted face of Owen Halloran. He was in for murdering a railroad agent, and he fancied himself the king of the inmates.

"I know where your wife is." Halloran smirked. "She's gone back to Colorado."

Nathan's throat tightened. "What do you mean?"

"I heard how Marshal Cameron was sweet on her. I used to know him, too, back when he worked the Indian Territory. His appetite for the ladies wasn't cheap." He whistled low. "How much do you suppose your wife charges?"

Nathan drew back and threw his weight into a right

uppercut, following with a quick left. Halloran roared and answered with a knuckled blow of his own. Nathan could hear the guard yelling, but two years of leashed frustration snapped and ran wild. Blood spurted—from his own face or Halloran's he couldn't say.

The last thing he remembered was hearing Berris say mournfully, "You've done it now!" and then he felt a blow to the back of his head.

When he struggled back to consciousness, he was lying on his side. His cheek pressed against canvas, and he knew he was on a cot. Glancing through narrowed, puffy eyes, he saw that he wasn't in his cell. Groaning, he stretched but discovered that iron shackles limited the movement of his wrists and ankles. He coughed and nearly choked on a heavy cloth gag.

Solitary confinement. He'd heard of it, heard the only thing worse was the dark cell. There, disruptive prisoners were chained to the door or ceiling for days, sometimes weeks on end, and given only bread and water. He'd seen it break even the hardiest and most belligerent of men.

He struggled to sit up, and every muscle in his body strained. Weakly rattling the irons, he groaned, the sound muffled against the gag. Along with the outside world, now even the prison officials didn't know he existed.

Nathan fell back. He might as well be dead. Samantha probably was. She shouldn't have bothered to jump in front of Crawford's gun; the last eleven years of his life had been wasted. He might as well just give up and—

No! His heart thumped against his ribs. He wouldn't give up. Not until he knew for certain Samantha was dead! He'd retrace George's steps and start looking for her again in Denver.

He'd stop in every town if he had to, asking every person he met if they'd seen a sad-eyed blond woman at the train station.

He would find her or die trying!

Two weeks later, even more gaunt, but with the fire of determination burning in his heart, Nathan quietly informed Berris in the brickyard that he would think of a way for them to escape.

⁓

"Mama! Mama! Another worm!"

Samantha leaned on the handle of her hoe and smiled at her two-and-a-half-year-old daughter. The girl considered gardening a great adventure, burrowing small fingers into the freshly turned earth to search out earthworms. "That's good, Hannah! How many does that make?"

"Five!" came the reply, and Samantha knew with a mother's love that the number was probably more on the order of three or four. Hannah had a tendency to disregard the numbers two and three when she counted, no matter how patiently Samantha struggled to teach her.

"Put the worms back in the ground, sweetheart. They're good for the soil." Samantha bent over to chop more dirt clods into the smooth soil that would be their vegetable garden for the summer.

"Wanna keep 'em!"

Samantha smiled at her black-haired daughter. Her sweet little Hannah. Seeing her there, drinking in the warmth of a summer day, reminded Samantha of her own childhood when Caleb and Nathan would race off in pursuit of boyish pranks and Hannah Hamilton would chase away Samantha's tears of rejection by serving cookies and tea from china cups and saucers in the parlor.

"They're just silly boys, Samantha," the older woman would say cheerfully, pouring tea. "We women can have a wonderful time by ourselves, can't we? Why, in London, the finest ladies take tea every afternoon in what they call drawing rooms! Let's pretend we're in England right now."

Samantha dashed away a tear before it passed her cheek. If only Nathan's mother—and Samantha's parents—had lived to see this precious grandbaby.

The little girl raced by Samantha, who paused in mid-hoe. With long, thick black hair and brilliant green eyes, Hannah had a mischievous smile that gave Samantha an odd twist of pain in her heart. She looked so much like her father. "Mama, look! Oh, look!"

Samantha shook her head to chase away her reverie. She'd never stop loving Nathan, would probably never love anyone else, but that didn't change the fact he would never come back to her.

"Hannah!" she called as the girl wandered from the vegetable patch, distracted by a colorful butterfly. "It's time we went inside to make those ginger cookies your grandpa's so fond of."

"Good!" The girl clapped her hands, and the worms that were cradled in her palm fell. She made a beeline for the house, her hair streaming behind her. Samantha's heart lurched at the beautiful fluid motion of youth. *Oh, Nathan! If only . . .*

"Stop thinking about him!" Samantha told herself sternly. "I'm grateful to have Hannah." She rubbed her soil-covered hands together briskly, wishing she could shake Nathan from her mind as easily.

That night Jonathan opened the Bible and turned to

where they'd left off reading the night before in the book of 2 Samuel. Hannah scrambled to the floor with her rag doll, and Samantha straightened to listen. As Jonathan read, she squirmed in her chair. David slept with another man's wife and had her husband killed. The prophet warned David that his sin had not gone unnoticed by God. David's son, the product of his adultery with Bathsheba, became ill and died after seven days.

Jonathan closed the book and shut his eyes, praying out loud as he did every night. Samantha bowed her head but tilted her face so she could watch Hannah playing quietly on the rug. The little girl was her greatest joy. She could well understand David's grief but not his obedient submission. Samantha shuddered and tried to concentrate on Jonathan's prayer.

By the time Jonathan returned from his office late the next day, Samantha had tucked Hannah into bed. She could hear him call for her, but didn't have the heart to answer. She and Hannah had played in the garden all afternoon, but by suppertime, the girl stopped laughing and complained of a sore throat.

"What's the matter?" Jonathan knelt beside the bed and pressed the back of his hand to Hannah's flushed cheek. "Aren't you feeling well, Button?"

She whimpered in reply, turning her face. Jonathan glanced at Samantha, and she motioned him to the hall. "We'll be right back, sweetheart. Grandpa and I will get you a cool cloth for your head."

Hannah moaned in reply. Samantha tiptoed from the room. "I'm scared, Jonathan." She reached out instinctively, and he embraced her.

"How long has she been like this?"

"The last few hours. I was afraid to leave her alone. I think she has a fever, and the rash on her chest—"

"Rash?" Jonathan broke away. "I'll go get Doc Hanson. Just keep her cool."

Samantha laid a hand on his arm, and her chin quivered. "What do you think it is?"

Jonathan's face was grim. "It might be scarlet fever," he said, then yanked the door open.

⁓

Nathan held the Bible close to the flickering candle stub. His eyes squinted not only against the faint light but in concentration.

He hated to admit it, but Frank had been right. Out of all sixty-six books in the Bible, the Psalms brought him the most comfort. It was to them he returned night after night, fascinated by the emotional writing.

He'd read the Bible straight through many times over, even memorizing verses when boredom weighed too heavily on him. Some Proverbs, a little Job, verses from Luke and John, Ephesians. Whatever struck his fancy.

"Against thee, thee only, have I sinned, and done this evil in thy sight," he whispered so the guards couldn't hear. He'd long ago begun reading aloud just to exercise his voice. After a time, he found he understood passages better if he argued vocally as he once had argued with his father. Sometimes he could almost feel his father's presence answering back in love.

He frowned over the psalm he'd been studying for a good hour and skipped down a few verses. "Behold, thou desirest truth in the inward parts: and in the hidden part thou shalt make me to know wisdom."

He thumped his fist quietly against the book, his voice a hoarse whisper. "What truth? And what's this mean about the sacrifice of a broken spirit and a broken heart?"

He shut the book with a sigh. "What David did with Bathsheba, murdering her husband, even! What kind of a man would do that? He deserved to die! And what kind of God would listen to his simpering?"

He set the Bible on the floor and kicked it under his bed. Lying back on the cot, he placed his palms under his head. No answers came to him tonight, no flashes of intuition.

Nathan stretched, his nerves thrumming with life. It was just as well. He was escaping tomorrow. He had more important things to worry about than the condition of a man's heart.

Samantha wrung out the cloth in the basin and laid it against Hannah's forehead. The girl's face burned with fever, and the water evaporated almost as soon as it touched her skin.

Samantha dipped the cloth again, then squeezed water between her daughter's lips. Her tongue had lost the strange red-spotted white coating and had turned bright red. Hannah refused the sips of water the doctor advised Samantha to give her and would only accept it in dribbles.

On that first frightening visit, Dr. Hanson had been almost cheerful. "She's a strong girl, Mrs. Hamilton. She'll pull through!"

But five days later, he had drawn Samantha and Jonathan into the hallway, a sober expression dominating his craggy features. "Best just to make her comfortable. I think the fever may have affected her heart and—"

"No!" Grief-stricken, Samantha all but lunged at the doctor. "Don't lie to me! She has to live! She has to!"

Samantha's vision blurred with tears. That was yesterday, and today she could see the intense labor of her daughter's every breath. Every childish wheeze pounded against her own heart as though driving a nail into its core.

Even a broken Jonathan had left an hour ago to beseech God at the church altar.

Samantha squeezed her eyes shut and covered Hannah's small, folded hands with her own. She bowed her head against the sheets, kept wet to ease Hannah's fever.

"Dear Father, please watch over my little girl. She's so small and so young. Please give her the strength to fight this. Give me the strength. I'm so tired of fighting. She's lain here for seven days now, not even—"

Her hands felt suddenly cold against her daughter's fevered ones. *Seven days . . . adultery.* David and Bathsheba's son had died after seven days because of their sin.

Had God really forgiven her? Was this her punishment for Nathan?

Samantha lifted up her eyes and raised trembling hands. "Oh, God, why? Not this little girl! *Please*, not my little girl! Don't punish her for my sin!"

Warm tears bathed her face, and her heart shattered like glass. "You've always wanted everything, haven't you? My parents, my home, my brother, little Aaron, Nathan . . . Oh, Lord, do you want Hannah too? Do I have to give everything to you?"

Would you withhold your daughter, your only child, from me?

Samantha's hands fell, and she slumped to her knees. A

storm raged around her, blowing and whistling, cold and wet. "Lord, you've asked everything of me," she murmured, defeated. "Everyone I love. Even when they don't love you, I've had to give them to you. To trust you. I didn't, with Nathan, Father. I didn't trust your Holy Spirit to do the work alone."

She covered her face with her hands and wept. "I'm so sorry. Forgive me. I know I can't fight you. I don't want to fight you. Take Hannah, Jesus. If it's your will, take her."

Warmth spread outward from the middle of her body, sweeping over and in her with a slow, wavelike force. She was cradled in strong arms, comforted and cherished. The storm stilled, and love covered her from head to foot, filling her, renewing her. Just as the Shepherd once had found her, so now he held her, as he always held her, close to his heart.

"Oh, Jesus. Thank you. Thank you," Samantha whispered. The room seemed to drift away, but she didn't care. She and Hannah were both safe in wide, loving arms.

TWENTY-SIX

Wyoming Territorial Penitentiary

Nathan's head jerked up, and his eyes flew open. Why did he even try to sleep? He tried to move his wrists and cried out in frustration. His numb arms refused to work.

"What . . . time is it?" he rasped. A scratchy sound issued from his throat, the best he could manage instead of a laugh. "What *day* is it?"

Here in the dark cell he could talk and make all the noise he wanted. Nobody cared. But after days of being handcuffed to the ceiling, he barely had the strength to whisper.

He hung his head, finding it nearly impossible to stay on his feet. He tried to shake his wrists but again found himself unable. His stomach burned, and his shoulders, sides, and legs ached. Every time weariness overcame him, his body relaxed in sleep only to be jerked upright by the merciless ceiling irons.

On the first day, after he'd accepted the physical pain, he'd spent hours trying to cope with the darkness. He thought surely once his eyes adjusted he would at least detect various degrees of black. But no gradations resided in this dungeon. Light entered—blinding and overpowering—only when the guard brought bread and water and allowed him to relieve himself.

For the first three days, Nathan had refused to beg for release from this black place when they unhooked the manacles for him to take care of his needs. By the fourth, he fell to his hands and knees at the guard's feet, crying and pleading for mercy.

"Sorry, Hamilton." The guard seemed sympathetic, helping Nathan back to his feet. "You shouldn't have tried to escape."

No, he shouldn't have. He and Berris had overpowered the brickyard guard, then stolen his wagon and team. They actually made it to the Laramie Mountains and hightailed it on foot before the law surrounded them. Confused and wide-eyed with terror, Berris had screamed, "You ain't takin' me back! You ain't takin' me!"

They hadn't. They gave him every opportunity to surrender, but he refused to throw down his stolen gun. Nathan gave in without a word, raising his hands high as he rose behind the boulder and stepped over Berris's lifeless body.

It seemed like a week since the solid steel door had last opened. The guard wouldn't tell him how long they intended to punish him. Maybe they would leave him as a skeleton for the next poor fool who earned the same fate to find.

He closed his eyes. "All things . . . come alike . . . to all," he murmured. He held his breath, his tired mind straining to recall where he'd heard those words.

"Ecclesiastes. Then . . . Father said . . . said . . ."

What had he said?

"Your father said, 'God will bring everyone into judgment for every secret thing we've done, whether it's good or evil. It's not a matter of what's right in our eyes, but what's right in his.'" The weary voice spoke from the left.

Nathan's head snapped up. Now he was talking to himself. Dementia, that's all it was.

"What did your father mean?"

Nathan's dry lips curved up and cracked at the ends. He tasted a trickle of blood and pressed his thickened tongue against the roof of his mouth. "God knows . . . everything . . . we do. The . . . good and . . . the bad."

"Do you believe in God?"

"Not . . . especially." Nathan paused. He might as well enjoy this diversion while it lasted. "Do you?"

No answer.

"Do you . . . believe . . . in God?"

Silence.

Disappointed, Nathan lowered his head. Insane. That's what he was. Even if his body healed, his mind never would.

Did he want it to? Did he have anything left to live for?

He closed his eyes and drifted off until his knees sagged. The weight of his body pulled his wrists against the cuffs, and he cried aloud. He could feel fresh blood run down the already caked paths marking his arms. A few drops spattered his face. He tilted his head back and forced his mouth open. Could he catch the drops on his swollen tongue? He couldn't even remember what water tasted like.

Every secret thing. Every secret thing.

The words hummed in his ears, and his body flushed hot with anger at his rambling mind. Secret things? What secret things did he have to be judged for?

The hum intensified, reverberating against the brick walls. Nathan ground his teeth, wishing he could cover his ears. The noise drove straight to his heart and made him tremble. The chant accelerated, tumbling like clear, swift water over smooth stones. Nathan felt his soul quiver and his heart pick up speed. He was about to die. That explained it. He'd made it through that hellish war, through the shooting in Cheyenne, through every robbery, through Crawford's attack. But death would find him in a cold, dark basement, trussed up like a Thanksgiving turkey.

Eyelids shuttered hot, puffy eyes. Let death come. Samantha had to be dead. He could see her again. If there was an afterlife.

"What secrets are in your heart?" The voice spoke again, tired but kind.

Nathan's throat had nearly swollen closed, but he felt curiously compelled to answer. "No more . . . than any man," he croaked.

"Tell me."

Nathan's body sagged, and his knees gave way. "The Bible . . . would say . . . I haven't . . . honored my father."

"No, you haven't. What else?"

"Robbery . . . lying . . . women . . ."

"Samantha."

"No! I . . . loved her!"

"Lust. Love of the flesh."

"And . . . her!"

"You would have turned her against her own beliefs. You would have lain with her—"

"No!"

"—even without being married."

Nathan's body crumpled, and his head drooped. "I . . . married . . . her," he said wearily.

"A man shall leave his father and mother and cling faithfully to his wife. They will be one flesh. It has been the plan from the beginning. When did you marry her?"

"When I had . . . no other . . . choice," he mumbled, defeated.

He'd ignored his father's teachings and broken his own marriage covenant even before it existed by joining with other women. And if Samantha herself had yielded to him, he would have turned her against her beliefs for his own selfish purposes.

Chastened, he closed his eyes. "Lust," he whispered. "But she . . . was strong. She stood firm."

Nathan heard rising voices, indistinct words from an angry mob. He lifted his head. "What—?"

"What other secrets . . . are in your heart?" The voice was distinctly more weary.

Nathan drew a deep breath. So it was another man after all. They must have hung somebody else up in here when Nathan had passed out.

"What . . . else?"

Nathan's feet slipped, but he righted himself. Why couldn't this be over faster?

"Is death in your heart?"

Nathan felt his chest would explode. "I . . . I was a medic . . . in the war. I've seen death many times."

"Yes, you have. So have I. Many men . . . gave their lives . . . and many had it taken away."

Nathan's inflamed chest tightened, and his breathing quickened. This man wanted Nathan to tell him the truth. Only Samantha had ever asked. Just that once. "I killed the man . . . in Cheyenne," he said, hoping to distract from the truth. "It was . . . him or Caleb!"

"Not Cheyenne," the voice said quietly. "Oof!" He drew a deep breath as though he had sustained a blow. "The war," he gasped. "The soldier. Tell me what . . . happened with the soldier."

"Lots of . . . soldiers," Nathan mumbled.

"Unnhh." Another groan. The sound of iron striking iron. "The soldier . . . at the creek. What did you do?"

The nerves in Nathan's body screamed with pain. Fear welled inside him, and revulsion spread up from his gut like black bile. The words tumbled out as though in escape. "I thought . . . he was dead."

"And then?"

"And . . . I heard him say . . . 'Please kill me.'" The bile lodged in his chest. Nathan drew a deep, wheezing breath, then couldn't draw another. He was suffocating! He gasped, drawing a measure of air into his lungs. "And I . . . rolled him over . . ." Blood pounded in his head, behind his eyes. "And he didn't . . . have a face! His nose and his eyes . . . had been blown off!"

Nathan felt his heart expand, and his soul tear in two. "He was alive! I might . . . have been . . . able to save him. I . . . should have *tried*. But with no ears . . . or face . . ."

"So you—"

Nathan's dry body amazingly produced tears. They flowed down his cheeks and swollen lips onto his chest. "I . . . picked up . . . a rock . . . and . . ." His voice faltered. "And held it . . . over . . . his head. Then I . . . I . . ."

"You can say it," the voice weakly encouraged, then groaned.

A scream gathered in the pit of Nathan's soul and welled past the constriction in his chest. "I bashed the rock . . .

against his head! I thought I was helping . . . but I killed him! I *murdered* him!"

Nathan sobbed, pulling against the iron chains. "Oh, God, forgive me! It wasn't my decision to make . . . but yours. Please . . . forgive me!"

The roar grew, and the mob closed in.

"Ha! You aren't who you said you were!"

"Let him die!"

"Liar!" Someone spat on the cold stone floor. "You said you could help us! You can't even help yourself!"

Nathan twisted his head toward the darkness where the voice had been. His heart hammered against his ribs. Where was the man who had heard Nathan's secret and not condemned him? What had these people done to him?

"If you are . . . who you said, save us!" From the far side of the cell, an agonized voice rose above the din of the mob.

The mysterious man groaned, and Nathan's heart constricted. "I don't know . . . what you've done, mister," he addressed the far voice in the mob, "but I deserve to be here. You probably . . . deserve to be here too. But this man . . . hasn't done anything wrong!"

"Remember the psalm you read in your cell." The man in the middle spoke as though he had just raised his head. His voice sounded stronger, directed at Nathan. "Remember that one thing is needful."

Nathan's soul stilled, listening. *Who was this man?* "What do you want from me?" he whispered.

The man's groan sounded as though it came from the depths of hell. "For you to know the truth."

"'Thou desirest . . . truth in the inward parts,'" Nathan whispered. He arched his entire body toward the voice and

317

drew a deep breath, his soul poised and quivering. "What is truth?"

Light broke through the ceiling, bathing the mysterious man in a warm, white beam. Arms open wide, his hands and feet were nailed to a battered wooden cross. He lifted his head toward Nathan, his eyes fixed, unmoving.

"I am the way, and the truth, and the life," he said. "No one comes to the Father, but through me."

Nathan bowed his head, feeling every evil thought and action flow from his body and into the man of white light. "'Against thee, thee only . . . have I sinned, and done . . . this evil in thy sight,'" he murmured.

Nathan lifted his head, emboldened. He looked the man straight in the eyes, seeing peace even in his agonized glaze. "Remember me . . . when you come into your kingdom, Lord," he gasped.

Warmth radiated and filled Nathan with peace. "I promise you will be with me in paradise," the man said.

The mob's chant rose. The man's lips moved, his words a tune that swelled and swirled, gentle yet powerful. Nathan strained to hear, his entire being alive, vibrating. A foreign language! Many foreign languages! Some sounded like . . . names.

He froze. The music passed the man's lips. He could hear English now: "John . . . Mary . . . Peter . . . Matthew . . . Paul . . . Hannah . . . Jonathan . . . Nathan . . ."

A sorrowful thrill coursed through Nathan's body. Even at the point of death, the Lord remembered him.

Beautiful, staring eyes lifted, and a ragged voice groaned with the shudder of the body. "It is finished!"

As suddenly as it appeared, the light vanished, plunging

Nathan into total darkness. An echo resounded against the walls, against Nathan's heart.

"You shall know the truth, and the truth shall make you free.

"You shall know the truth, and the truth shall make you free.

"You shall know the truth . . ."

TWENTY-SEVEN

Samantha felt her chest rise and fall, and her fingers curled and uncurled around the blanket draped over her. Her breathing deepened, and she opened her eyes. Weak from her vigil, she pushed herself up from the floor and struggled to her feet. Hannah lay still, her raspy breathing now silent.

"Oh, baby," Samantha whispered, moving forward. A lump formed in her throat, but her heart was peaceful. "Let me hold you one last time." Knees giving way, she sagged.

"Samantha!" Jonathan wrapped an arm around her.

"I'm all right." She turned, and he touched her cheek, brushing away a tear she didn't even realize had fallen.

"Hannah—?"

Samantha smiled. "She's all right, too, Jonathan. She's gone to be with the Lord."

"Oh, Samantha." He studied her face, then a sad smile broke across his own. He squeezed her hand. "God's called our little one home," he whispered. He bent over Hannah's face, and his trembling lips brushed her forehead. "Good-bye, my sweet—"

He pressed his fingers gently against her throat. His expression shifted, and Samantha leaned forward, puzzled.

"Mama?" Hannah murmured. Her eyes fluttered open.

Samantha's heart lurched, and she placed her hands over

Hannah's. "Hannah? Sweetheart?" She pressed her hands firmly against her daughter's warm ones. "Jonathan! She's not—"

Jonathan's face shone, and he rested his hand against the little girl's forehead. "Praise God, Samantha. The fever's broken!"

"But . . . but . . . her breathing! She couldn't breathe!"

"She's breathing all right now." Jonathan laughed, lifting his face heavenward. "Thank you, Father, for your healing. Thank you, Jesus, for your love!"

Samantha sank to her knees. Hannah had closed her eyes again, but Samantha could see she indeed breathed easily. "You truly are an awesome God," she whispered. "Thank you!"

Jonathan knelt beside her and embraced her, shaking. She felt his infectious laughter to the soles of her feet. Joy filled her, overflowing, and she wrapped her arms around him. "Oh, Jonathan, can you believe it?"

"Yes, I do!" He laughed again, pulling back, and he cupped her face with his strong hands. "God promises to give us the desires of our heart, Samantha, and Hannah's life has been my constant prayer for the past seven days. As I know it's been yours."

Samantha bowed her head. "I was afraid God wanted to take her because of my sin. Like David and Bathsheba."

Jonathan's hand lifted her chin, his gaze warm on her face. "I thought you'd settled that, Samantha. God punished David, but that doesn't mean he would punish you. Because of what Jesus did for us, the bad things that happen aren't punishments for wrongdoing. We have a loving, forgiving father. We have to trust him."

"Trust him," she echoed. She embraced Jonathan again. "God's been with me all along, even when I couldn't feel him."

"Yes, he has been. Think of how he took care of you, even though your parents died and you lost your home. He led you to the orphanage, then to Nathan, then to me." Jonathan drew a deep breath. "I told you years ago you were my daughter, Samantha, and I meant it. I'll do everything I can to help you and Hannah. I love you both."

"I love you too," she whispered.

I love you. How many times had she seen green eyes dance when she spoke those words?

Nathan.

Her heart crumbled like broken bricks, but the foundation beneath was rock-solid.

⌒

"You're looking better today, Hamilton."

Nathan laid his book down and looked up at the warden. "I feel better, sir. Can I go back to my cell soon?"

Smiling, the warden sat down on a chair by the bed. "Don't you like our hospital ward? You've only been here a few days."

"A few days is long enough to lie in bed." Nathan grinned in return. He brushed a lock of hair from his face. His wrists were swathed with gauze. "I'm ready to get up and moving again."

"Dehydration's a serious thing. So were the lacerations on your wrists. The dark cell is for punishment, not for death."

"I realize that, sir," Nathan said. "But I'm all right now."

"So I see." The warden nodded at the Bible on Nathan's chest. "The chaplain told me you've been reading constantly since you regained consciousness. Are you trying to memorize the book?"

Nathan's mouth curved up in the old impudent grin. "I'm getting reacquainted with a friend."

The warden looked puzzled. "Well, anyway, I have some good news. We've decided to release you."

Nathan's mouth went dry. "Release me?" he whispered.

"It costs a lot to keep a prisoner here each day, and since your term is almost up and you did, er, suffer from your punishment . . ."

"You're letting me go." Nathan closed his eyes and sank back against the pillow. Energy drained from his body, and he pressed a hand over his heart. "Thank you, Jesus," he murmured. "Even though I don't deserve it."

The warden cleared his throat. "I understand you don't know your wife's whereabouts."

Nathan opened his eyes, his joy momentarily overshadowed. "No. I don't."

"Where will you start looking for her?"

Nathan thought for a moment, listening quietly. He smiled, then looked up at the once-again puzzled warden. "I don't know where I'll start looking for her," he said softly, "but I know where I have to go first."

⁓

Samantha heard the gate slam, followed by the front door. "Hannah?" Her heart quickened, and she wiped her hands on her apron as she rushed to the bedroom they shared. Was Hannah ill again? *Oh, please, Lord. It's only been a few months!*

Muffled sobs emanated from the bed. Hannah had flung herself onto her stomach, her face buried in the pillow.

Relieved, Samantha smoothed her daughter's straight black hair. "What happened, sweetheart?"

"Daisy s-said I don't have a d-daddy!"

Samantha's hand stilled against Hannah's hair. *Oh, Father, how am I going to tell her? What am I going to tell her?*

Hannah rolled over, her spiky black lashes wet against her cheeks. "But everybody has a daddy, don't they?"

"Of course they do."

"Then my daddy'll come back?"

Heavy footfalls sounded in the doorway. Samantha looked up and saw Jonathan, his patient eyes puzzled. "What's wrong? I saw Hannah run past my office without stopping to say hello."

Hannah sat up, her green eyes snapping. "Where's my daddy? Why don't I have one?"

Jonathan sat beside Samantha and took Hannah's hand. "Button, you—"

"No, Jonathan. I should tell her." Samantha smiled, smoothing her daughter's hair again. The upturned baby face was so anxious, her eyes so full of hope. How could she dash the little girl's dreams? "Sweetheart, your father isn't alive."

"He's gone to heaven? To be with Jesus?"

Samantha's smile crumbled. How many nights had she agonized over that very thought? "He . . . isn't alive."

"What happened to him, Mama?"

Samantha felt Jonathan's eyes on her. "Your father died . . . in an accident," she said.

Hannah's eyes filled with tears. "Oh, Mama! I want my daddy!" She threw out her small arms and buried her face against her mother's breast. Her body jerked with sobs.

Samantha wrapped her arms around her daughter, and

they rocked back and forth. Samantha tried to soothe her daughter with motherly murmurs but had to blink back her own tears. Nathan would have loved this little girl so much.

Samantha felt Jonathan's hand on her shoulder, and she hastily wiped her eyes. "Sweetheart," she said softly, gently disentangling Hannah's arms, "wash your face, then go back out to play. We'll talk about your father some more later."

Hannah nodded mutely, sliding away from her mother's embrace. She barely glanced at her grandfather as she trudged outside.

Jonathan hugged Samantha and kissed her on the cheek. "You're a good mother."

"I'll have to tell her one day about her father being a criminal. And her uncle." She paused. "I wish I knew where Caleb was. Or if he's even still alive."

"Maybe it's time you write Sally and tell her where you are. And tell her about Hannah."

"I feel guilty about running out on them. And Noah's their neighbor. I . . . I don't think I want to know what he's doing." She bowed her head. "I don't blame him anymore for Nathan's death, but I should write and ask his forgiveness."

"Don't do it because you think you should, Samantha. Do it because God tells you to. Listen to him, and your actions will come from a pure heart." Jonathan rose. "Now it's time to get back to work. Don't worry about that little granddaughter of mine. Someday she'll be ready to learn the truth about her father."

"I know she will," Samantha said. "But I'm not sure I'll ever be ready to tell her."

Nathan's boots kicked up dust as he trudged down the street. Frustrated, he rubbed a hand across the beard he'd grown since prison. Just his luck the sheriff's office had been empty. At least the man lived in town.

The saloon proprietor gave directions, then leaned across the bar. "You look like a young buck who could use some female company. The sheriff don't allow no working girls in this town, but I know a gal who . . ."

"No, thanks." Nathan tipped his hat, smiling at the row of liquor bottles behind the bar. Even the urge to drink had vanished. "Appreciate the information about the sheriff though."

He left his horse outside the saloon and decided to walk. He'd ridden all the way from Wyoming, and every mile had grown increasingly more difficult. Not from the physical strain but from the thought of what he must do—apologizing had never been one of his strengths. Nathan touched the small Bible tucked in his vest pocket and felt better.

Ah, the white picket fence. It enclosed a bountiful flower garden at the front of the well-maintained house. He swallowed hard, memories stirring of Samantha smiling and gardening at the hideout. Those vegetables had kept them alive all winter, just as her love and prayers had kept his spirit alive.

He squinted against the sunlight and saw a small dark head moving among a clump of yellow chrysanthemums. His heart sank. He must have the wrong house. Maybe one of the child's parents could show him the right one.

Wiping his palms against his thighs, Nathan leaned against the gate and cleared his throat. He knew he still looked gaunt and ragged, but hopefully they'd see he was friendly and meant no harm. He sure didn't want to scare the kid.

"Hello."

The voice startled him, and he glanced down. The small girl knelt in the dirt with a spoon, smiling up at him.

"Hello, yourself," he said. He couldn't resist smiling back at the picture she made, dress trailing in the dirt, her face smudged, hands buried in the soil. "What are you doing there?"

"Digging for worms," she said solemnly, turning to her work.

"I didn't think girls liked worms." Nathan opened the gate and entered the yard. He knelt beside her. He could see she had dug many holes, and he remembered again how Samantha had loved to work the soil.

"I like worms," the girl said. "Mama said I'm 'most big enough to go fishing with Grandpa, but I don't wanna put a worm on a hook. That's mean!"

Nathan smiled. "Not if you want to catch a fish."

"I s'pose."

She stopped digging and raised her face, assailing Nathan with the deepest green eyes he'd ever seen. Dark hair framed a clear, innocent face. He frowned, absently brushing away a dirt smudge from her cheek. She reminded him of someone. Something about the eyes in that face, the set of the mouth . . .

"What's your name?"

"Nathan." He solemnly held out his hand, and she laid her small grubby one in his palm for a grown-up handshake. "What's yours, sweetheart?"

She beamed. "Mama calls me sweetheart too." She looked thoughtful and poked at the dirt. "My daddy's in heaven."

"I'm sorry."

"It's all right. He's with Jesus."

Nathan gazed at her sweet, hopeful face. She obviously had a love for God already. *Father, please don't let her go astray like I did. May her mother love and train her as faithfully as mine did!*

Samantha had taken down all the books in her bedroom for dusting. Stacking them carefully on top of each other, she smiled at the top volume—*A Tale of Two Cities*—and opened to the flyleaf. Her heart twisted, and she sighed, replacing the volume on the stack.

Realizing she hadn't heard Hannah's voice for a while, Samantha stepped to the front window and pushed aside the curtains. She'd warned her about wandering off, but the girl's adventurous spirit sometimes led her astray.

Two figures knelt in the garden, her daughter beside a strange man with his back to the house. Samantha watched as the man reached out to touch Hannah's cheek, and panic gripped her maternal heart. Jonathan hadn't returned yet. What if this man was a criminal out to do the sheriff or his family harm?

Her mind raced. Jonathan kept a shotgun for protection in the house, but where was it? She pressed a palm to her temple, sighing with disgust. What difference did it make? She couldn't shoot another human being. The man didn't even appear to be wearing a gun.

Samantha jerked the door open. But she'd fight to the death before she'd let this man harm one hair on Hannah's head.

Her heart beat so wildly she thought it would burst as she

tromped down the steps. "What do you want, mister?" she said in her loudest voice.

The man turned slowly, then rose. He squinted into the sunlight behind her and cocked his head. She stared at the bearded stranger, noticing immediately that he seemed awfully thin for his height. But his stance was familiar, and the hair . . .

Her chest tightened, explosive, as recognition slowly dawned. She clutched her throat. *No, oh no! It's not possible! Dear God in heaven!*

"Mama!" Hannah took the man's hand in hers, apparently unaware that the two adults were frozen with shock. She smiled up at the man and then at her mother. "This is my new friend. His name is Nathan."

"Nathan," Samantha repeated stupidly. With her hand still at her throat, she sank to her knees in the dirt as he covered the distance between them, crying her name.

TWENTY-EIGHT

amantha!" He swept her into his embrace and buried his face against the curve of her neck. *Oh, God, it can't be!* His heart leaped into his throat at her familiar scent, and his arms tightened around her as though afraid she might take flight. "Sam! Where . . . ? What . . . ?"

"Nathan!" Tears coursed down her face and onto his shoulder. She shook with sobs, clutching his shirt in both fists. Her soft form pressed against him, and he felt the love and security he'd been missing for three years wash over him like a spring rain.

He reluctantly released her and cupped her face in his hands. Her tears turned to the most beautiful laugh he had ever heard. She placed her hands on his face also, giggling at the unfamiliar scratch of his beard. Nathan felt like a drowning man drawn to shore by the lunar pull of her love and warmed by the solar power of the God who'd answered his deepest desire.

He touched her tentatively—face, shoulders, arms—to be certain she was really there and not a vapor that would vanish once he blinked his eyes. He smoothed her left arm with his hand and drew a deep breath when he brushed across her knuckles. A gold ring. Not the cheap silver one from their wedding. He dropped her hand and glanced away, blinking. He was too late.

She smiled tenderly. "I gave Sally back her ring. Your father bought this one for me, Nathan . . . for you."

"Is my father here?" Nathan glanced around anxiously. "I have to tell him something."

"He's down at the—" She broke off and peered into his eyes. Her mouth formed a perfect O. "You . . . you know the Lord!"

A wide grin broke across his face. "Is it that obvious?"

She gripped his arms. "I thought you had died without knowing. I told Hannah—" She broke off again and stared behind him.

"I've been in prison, Sam. For the past three years. Frank told me you thought I was dead and ran off. Why didn't you tell the Jordans where you were? They could have told you the truth."

"I was too ashamed about running away," she whispered, distracted. "Nathan, I need to—"

"No more shame," he said softly. "I'm just glad you're safe."

"Mama?"

Nathan heard the small voice behind him, and he caught his breath. Slow comprehension spread, and he turned by degrees. Three years ago . . .

The girl stood quietly, and the wind gently billowed her dark hair. Nathan's heart pounded. The little girl's eyes, the hair, the mouth . . .

"Hannah." Samantha held out her hand. The girl obediently moved to her mother's side. Her eyes never left Nathan's face. Samantha turned, tears filling her eyes. "Nathan, this is your daughter."

Daughter! He stared at her, then Samantha, then back at the girl. Samantha smiled. "Hannah, I thought your father was dead . . . that he was in heaven. But he's come back to us, sweetheart."

Hannah continued to stare at Nathan. His heart dropped with disappointment. He was nothing more than a stranger to his own daughter, and a sudden fear overtook him. Would she reject him as he'd rejected his own father?

Hannah laid her palm against his cheek. "Daddy," she whispered. "I'm so glad you came back. I prayed every night you would."

Her hand was the sweetest, gentlest touch he had ever felt, her words the most heartfelt. Nathan closed his eyes and drew her into his arms. She felt small but right at home there, and he wept. "Hannah."

Tears spilled down Samantha's face. Nathan drew her into the embrace and, choking back a sob, bowed his head. "Heavenly Father, thank you. I didn't come here expecting Samantha. You've not only given her back to me but a precious child I knew nothing about. Thank you . . . *Thank you!*"

"Thank you," Samantha echoed. She bent her head to kiss Hannah on the cheek, then turned to Nathan. Her gaze fixed on his face and swept over him, lingering on his hands. She lifted them and turned them over. He winced, but let her gently touch his thickly scabbed, swollen wrists.

"Oh, Nathan, what happened?" she whispered.

"It doesn't matter, sweetheart. It's a small price to pay for salvation."

Hannah squirmed from their grasp. "Grandpa!" she squealed. "Grandpa! Daddy's come home!"

Nathan's heart leaped and hung, suspended in midair. He swiveled his head toward the gate. His father stood on the other side, his hand on the latch as though for support. Hannah flung open the gate and threw herself at his knees. Jonathan bent for a hug and kiss, then straightened as she ran back to her mother.

Nathan swallowed and got slowly to his feet. "Father."

"Nathan."

They stared at each other, motionless. Nathan curled his fingers into loose fists. Why didn't the man say something? Why didn't he move?

You must go to him, my child. Have you come all this way to let the distance of a yard separate you from your father's love?

Nathan choked down a sob and took a shaky step forward. Then another. And another. Until he stood in front of him, face to face, and lost himself in his father's wise, gray eyes.

Nathan stretched out his hand to his father's right one. He intended to start with a handshake, but when he actually touched his father's hand, he felt the last brick from the wall of pride crumble. "Father, I—" He let out a sob and, clutching his father's hand, dropped to his knees. He bowed his head. "I'm . . . so sorry! All these . . . years!"

He braced himself. He deserved a sharp reprimand. A harsh rebuke. What good had he ever done his father? What respect had he shown? He'd ignored nearly everything the man had taught him and scorned his advice and intervention. His love.

Nathan lowered his head further. "I . . . I don't deserve to be called your son," he whispered.

Jonathan knelt in the dirt and placed his hands on Nathan's shoulders. Slowly, cautiously, Nathan raised his head. Joy and love emanated from his father's face, spreading into Nathan's own foolish heart.

"My son," Jonathan said quietly, "you were lost but now are found. I thought you were dead, but you've come back to life." His hands tightened, and his voice broke. "You are . . . indeed deserving!"

Nathan buried his face against his father's shoulder, feeling forgiveness embrace and wash over him with all the warmth of the man's strong arms.

By dinnertime, Samantha and Nathan had shared both sides of their three-year separation. She listened with awe as he glossed over the details of his physical punishment but retold every vivid word and memory from his encounter with Jesus.

"I had so much hate inside me," he said. "Toward you, Father, and George, for lying to Samantha. And ultimately toward myself."

Nathan glanced down at Hannah, who sat in his lap and beamed up at him with complete adoration. He turned his gaze back to Samantha and Jonathan. "Later, I have to tell you about what I did during the war."

Samantha laid her hand over his. "It doesn't matter, Nathan. If you want to tell me, I'll listen. But God's forgiven you."

He turned his hand over so that their palms touched. "To you, I owe the greatest apology," he whispered. "I never should have let you marry me. I didn't intend for us to—"

She withdrew her hand. Heat flushed her face, and she glanced at Hannah. "We can talk later." She lifted her face, a new smile present. "Frank told you George went back to the reservation, but what about Noah and Caleb?"

"I don't know. Noah called for Caleb just after my trial, but I never saw either of them again."

"I suppose Caleb's still wanted . . . or in prison." Samantha glanced at Hannah again. The little girl played with Nathan's beard, fascinated.

Nathan grinned over Hannah's head. "Noah got me a reduced prison sentence. Maybe he helped Caleb too." His expression sobered. "Noah cared about you, Samantha. He stood by us when we got married and arranged for us to be together again now. In freedom."

"Yes, he did," she whispered. "Maybe someday we'll be able to thank him for all he did."

"I'd like that, too, sweetheart." Nathan covered her hand with his. "He gave us the time to be married instead of arresting me on the spot."

"Married," Samantha echoed, nervous. Nathan's gaze was all too intense again.

Jonathan cleared his throat and rose. "I'm going to the hotel tonight," he said. "Hannah can sleep in my room. Tomorrow we'll make up a bed for her in the parlor."

"You don't have to—"

"Son." Jonathan settled his hat on his head and laid a hand on Nathan's shoulder. "Proverbs says to rejoice with the wife of your youth." His eyes twinkled. "You're not sixteen years old anymore. I'm not going to reprimand you."

Samantha suppressed a smile, and Nathan chuckled. "No sir."

Jonathan tipped his hat. "Good night."

They sat motionless, then heard the front door close.

Samantha caught Nathan's gaze and blushed. Looking embarrassed, Nathan cleared his throat and hastily kissed the top of Hannah's head. She held a small fist against her mouth and yawned. "Wanna go to bed," she said sleepily.

"Yes, it's time," Samantha said. "Nathan, will you carry her down the hall?"

He smiled and rose. Hannah whimpered but was silent by the time he pulled back the covers. Samantha gently removed her shoes and dress.

Together she and Nathan tucked the covers around her and kissed her forehead. Samantha's love swelled at the peaceful sight of their sleeping child.

They paused outside Samantha and Hannah's room, then Nathan walked in. He studied the room and caught sight of the picture of Jesus and the lamb. He smiled to himself.

Samantha squeezed his hand, and he turned. "I thought I ruined it," he said. "I thought I'd smeared the lamb's face."

Samantha smiled tenderly. "It *is* smeared, Nathan. But it's even better because of your tears. Now when I look at the lamb, I don't see its face but the face of each person who loves the Lord." Her voice lowered. "And now especially the man I love."

Nathan drew a quick breath, his eyes bright. "Why don't you get ready for bed? I'll be back in a minute. I want to get Father's Bible so we can read together."

Samantha nodded, but nervousness returned. After he closed the door, she hastily washed with water from the pitcher and put on her nightgown. She perched on the edge of the bed and pulled the pins from her hair. She had just started brushing when the door opened. Freshly shaven, Nathan stood in the doorway, Bible tucked under his arm, his green eyes dancing.

"Nathan!" She padded to him, smiling as she laid her palm against his bared jaw line. "Why?" she said softly, though secretly pleased. This was the Nathan who had filled her waking days and sleepless nights for three years.

He shrugged, rewarding her for the first time that day with his rakish smile. "I felt like a stranger. With my wife."

Wife.

He took the brush from her hands and turned her around. She felt the strength of his hand, of him, as he gently ran the bristles through her hair, and she shivered. "I want to do this for you every night for the rest of our lives," he whispered. "When I was in prison, I dreamed about your hair . . . about you."

"Oh, Nathan." She turned, her throat aching with emotion. His eyes were tender and full of the peace she had so long prayed for. He was once again the gentle boy she'd known, yet so much more as a man who had chosen the Lord.

He smiled and drew her to sit on the bed. "I also dreamed about reading the Bible with you. Every night."

Samantha nodded, her stomach tingling. It didn't matter what he read, whether it was all the rules in Leviticus or the begats in Matthew. Nathan's deep tone had always made her body feel boneless while setting her spirit to soar. And now . . . to hear him read Scripture! What a joy!

He found his place, then never looked down again. "Rise up, my love, my fair one, and come away. For, lo, the winter is past, the rain is over and gone."

The warmth in Samantha's stomach increased. "By night

on my bed I sought him whom my soul loveth," she whispered. "I sought him, but I found him not."

Nathan lifted her hands to his lips. "Thou hast ravished my heart, my sister, my spouse; thou hast ravished my heart with one of thine eyes."

He gazed intently at her, his eyes passionately embracing her. He gently closed the Bible.

Samantha's senses heightened with fullness, the completion of the circle of their union. She had loved him as long as she could remember, and at last he had come home.

"You are my beloved, Nathan," she whispered as his lips met hers, "and you are my friend."

Many hours later, while it was still dark, Nathan slipped quietly out of bed. He raised his eyes to the promising dawn beyond the open window and filled his lungs with fresh morning air. Love filled his heart. God had richly blessed him with his father, Samantha, and Hannah.

His hand brushed a dust rag and a stack of books. Lifting the top volume, he smiled. *A Tale of Two Cities.* Was it . . . yes, there was the inscription he'd written for her when he'd thought he was going to his death. She'd kept the book all these years.

With a smile, he replaced it on the stack. He *had* gone to his death, but he'd been born anew. God had shown him the only worthy man to walk the earth.

"Nathan?"

He turned to see Samantha struggle to a sitting position, her eyes still half-closed with sleep. Blond hair tumbled in soft waves, and he remembered the braids she'd worn as a girl. His tagalong little tomboy had grown into a beautiful woman, spiritually and physically.

"Go back to sleep, Sam," he whispered. He slid under the sheet and held her against him. He kissed her temple gently and heard her sigh as she settled in his embrace.

Somewhere in the distance a rooster crowed, and Nathan smiled.

ACKNOWLEDGMENTS

The Wyoming Territorial Penitentiary accepted its first prisoner in January 1873. For purposes of this novel, the date was moved up a year.

Thank you to Brad Potter and Mike Harris for historical information about firearms.